NOT THE ▮

"I know what you see ▮▮▮ ▮▮▮ ▮▮ ▮▮▮ next door, nice and swee▮ ▮▮▮ ▮▮▮▮▮▮▮. Ethan's voice lowered to a deadly pitch. "You see me and you think I'm the guy who'll make love to you in a room full of flowers and candlelight. You picture sweet, sweet kisses and oh so tender caresses—isn't that right, Juliet?"

Her heart began to pound, a sharp staccato that pulsed in her blood and drowned out her thoughts. The look on Ethan's face was terrifying. Thrilling. His hazel eyes gleamed with raw heat. Unadulterated *danger*.

PRAISE FOR ELLE KENNEDY'S KILLER INSTINCTS SERIES

Midnight Games

"When it comes to dark and gritty romantic suspense, it has not taken Kennedy long to carve out her own niche! Readers looking for nail-biting danger, thrilling spy action, and sizzling passion should look no further: They can get megadoses with this terrific tale!"
—*RT Book Reviews* (4½ stars, top pick)

"Kennedy's delicious third Killer Instincts romantic thriller (after *Midnight Alias*) takes readers on a terrific emotional roller-coaster ride full of relentless action, heated sexual tension, and nail-biting plot twists. . . . Fantastic recurring characters, a deftly drawn plot, and breathless passion will leave the reader begging for more."
—*Publishers Weekly* (starred review)

continued . . .

"All in all I adored this installment of the Killer Instincts series. The books and characters keep getting better and better with each book. The romance and relationships are flushed out to perfection, and the plots continue to be intense and engaging. I am so excited to see what Kennedy has in store for us next, and hope that she continues to write in this series for a long, long time"

—The Book Pushers

"In *Midnight Games* the risks and stakes are higher. . . . I was kept on my toes the whole time." —Under the Covers

"The beginning of *Midnight Games* completely sucked me in with the action and the way Elle Kennedy doesn't hold back during the fight scenes. People die, characters grieve, and the action keeps coming"—Happily Ever After-Reads

"*Midnight Games* is as sexy as it is exciting. Elle Kennedy hits all the right notes in this faced-paced, adrenaline-filled third installment to her outstanding Killer Instincts series." —Joyfully Reviewed

"I can see this series lasting a long time and that is a good thing. So far each book has been suspenseful, heartbreaking, and full of sexy times, with *Midnight Games* being the best yet." —Fiction Vixen Book Reviews

Midnight Alias

"Balances the gritty side of humanity with sizzling passion." —*Publishers Weekly*

Also Available in the Killer Instincts Series

Midnight Rescue
Midnight Alias
Midnight Games

MIDNIGHT PURSUITS

A KILLER INSTINCTS NOVEL

ELLE KENNEDY

A SIGNET ECLIPSE BOOK

SIGNET ECLIPSE
Published by the Penguin Group
Penguin Group (USA) LLC, 375 Hudson Street,
New York, New York 10014

USA | Canada | UK | Ireland | Australia | New Zealand | India | South Africa | China
penguin.com
A Penguin Random House Company

First published by Signet Eclipse, an imprint of New American Library,
a division of Penguin Group (USA) LLC

First Printing, April 2014

ISBN 978-0-451-46569-6

Printed in the United States of America
10 9 8 7 6 5 4 3 2 1

To my family

ACKNOWLEDGMENTS

I couldn't have written this book without the research expertise of Sean Sipus and the plotting assistance from Travis White. You two really helped me make the characters and settings come alive!

Early readers Jane Litte and Sharon Muha—your feedback was invaluable, as always.

And finally, my amazing editor, Jesse Feldman, who believed in this series from day one and supported me through the process of creating the dark and dangerous world of Killer Instincts. I'm going to miss working with you, J!

Chapter 1

Nothing beat a cup of steaming-hot coffee in the dead of winter, at least in Ethan Hayes's humble opinion. As he stepped onto the enormous cedar deck of the chalet-style house, Ethan was unbelievably grateful for the heat of the ceramic mug seeping into his cold fingers. February in Vermont meant biting-cold temperatures, buckets of snow, and frigid wind, but he wasn't complaining about his surroundings. The isolated house and surrounding area were so idyllic, he'd be a total moron to find fault in them.

He approached the wooden railing and gazed at the snowcapped peaks of the mountains in the distance. White mist shrouded the jagged tips, giving off a ghostly vibe, and dozens of feet below the deck, a sheet of pure white snow covered the hills and valleys that made up the landscape. Tall pines jutted proudly from the land, branches swaying in the early-morning breeze.

A postcard. That's what it looked like, and Ethan found it hard to believe that a woman with the cold and deadly nickname Queen of Assassins had ever lived in such a beautiful slice of heaven. Then again, Noelle had given the house away without batting an eye, so clearly the blond assassin hadn't been too attached to the place. He just hoped she didn't spring a surprise visit on him while he was here—Noelle made him damn nervous, and he had no desire to spend any quality time with the woman.

He'd just taken a sip of coffee when his cell phone rang. He wasn't surprised to find Trevor's number flashing on the screen—he'd been expecting the call ever since Trevor and Isabel had rushed out the door in a mad race to make their private charter.

"I already arranged for a new one," Ethan said in lieu of greeting.

An amused male chuckle sounded in his ear. "What are you, a mind reader?"

"Nope, I just know how attached women are to their phones."

Trevor laughed again. "Yeah, Isabel's incredibly annoyed she left it behind. She didn't realize until we got here that it wasn't in her bag."

"You guys are at the airport?"

"About to board the plane. She wanted to drive back and get the phone, but I managed to talk her out of it. She claims she needs it in case of an emergency—aka any minor crisis that requires us to abandon our honeymoon so she can offer her assistance to some poor soul."

Now Ethan laughed. He'd liked Isabel Roma from the moment he'd met her nearly two years ago, and her endless compassion was one of his favorite things about her. It was refreshing when you spent most of your time with hardened mercenaries. But the downside to all that compassion was that Isabel would drop everything to help out a friend, even cut her honeymoon short.

"Don't worry," he assured his teammate. "Her phone is safe and sound, and I already called the provider to have a replacement ready when you two land in Maui. Tell her to text me the new number, and I'll forward her entire contact list to the new phone."

"Thanks, rookie. You're a lifesaver." There was a snort. "Remember, don't throw any wild parties while we're gone. I'm kind of in love with the house, and I don't want you trashing it."

"Damn, but I was planning a kegger."

"Funny."

"Make a stupid remark and get a stupid answer." Ethan grinned to himself. "Trust me, I'm looking forward to the solitude. Sometimes it's nice to be away from the others."

"Enjoy it while it lasts. I hear Sully and Liam are moving to the compound this week." Trevor suddenly sounded distracted. "Shit, gotta go, rookie. The pilot's waving us over."

"Cool. Say hi to Isabel and have fun in Hawaii."

"Will do."

Ethan disconnected the call and tucked his phone into the back pocket of his cargo pants. He took another long swig of coffee, returning his attention to the picturesque mountain scene before him. The chalet was located in the middle of nowhere, directly on the top of a rocky hill surrounded by dense trees and a creek that hadn't frozen over despite the below-zero temperature.

As he stood there on the massive deck, he couldn't help but feel like the last man on earth. It was so damn quiet here, a huge change from the noisy jungle he'd been living in for the past ten months. The mercenary team he worked for had previously been based in Mexico, but after the team's compound had been destroyed by a private hit squad last year, Jim Morgan had relocated his men to a sprawling estate in Costa Rica, where the air was forever humid and the wildlife couldn't seem to shut up. Thanks to the jungle that bordered one side of the new compound, Ethan spent his days listening to birds squawking and monkeys screeching, and his nights listening to the constant drone of insects. Needless to say, the silence was blessedly welcome.

He was actually looking forward to these next two weeks. He couldn't remember the last time he'd been truly alone. For the past three years, he'd lived with his fellow mercenaries, which meant someone was always underfoot—D in the shooting range, Kane and Abby hanging out in the game room, Morgan brooding on the terrace. No matter where he went, he was bound to run into someone.

Normally he didn't mind the company—he welcomed it, in fact—but every now and then, it was nice to have some quiet time to collect his thoughts. He was off rotation for a few more weeks, thanks to the mandatory vacation time Morgan regularly inflicted on members of the team, which gave him the perfect opportunity to . . . to what?

He faltered for a moment, his hand freezing before he could raise the mug to his lips. What exactly was he hoping to accomplish during this time off? He didn't quite have an answer for that, but what he did know was that he'd been feeling out of sorts these past few months. Restless, edgy . . . unfulfilled.

But why? What reason did he have to feel unfulfilled? He worked for Jim Morgan, a deadly supersoldier and one of the most honorable men Ethan had ever met. He had friends he'd lay down his life for, a shit ton of money in the bank, a roof over his head, and food on the table. No serious girlfriend, sure, but he'd been casually seeing someone in Costa Rica, a cute tour guide who worked at one of the many resorts dotting the coast. But it wasn't serious, and he wasn't sure he wanted to keep that going anymore.

He wasn't sure what he wanted, period.

A wife?

A house of his own?

A family?

One day, of course, but, hell, he was only twenty-five. He had plenty of time to do the whole home-and-hearth thing.

So then why couldn't he stop feeling like there was something missing in his life?

Philosophical this morning, aren't we?

Sighing, he moved away from the railing and strode into the house through the glass doors that spilled into the living room. Isabel had given him a quick tour before she and Trevor had sped off in Trevor's Range Rover, but Ethan doubted he'd spend much time anywhere but this room.

With its high ceilings, wood-paneled walls, and big leather couches, the living room was the very definition of cozy. He was looking forward to lazing around in here, maybe grabbing a few books from the tall oak shelves lining the walls and spending the next couple of weeks doing nothing but reading, eating, and sleeping. And maybe hot-tubbing, he had to amend. Considering this place offered a rooftop eight-person hot tub, he'd be a fool *not* to make good use of it.

He'd just plopped down on the couch and set his mug on the rustic pine coffee table when an unfamiliar ringtone broke the silence.

Shit. Isabel's phone. He'd forgotten to ask Trevor for the password so he could forward Isabel's calls to Trevor's cell in the meantime. He'd have to get it after the couple landed.

He leaned forward and swiped the phone off the table to check the caller ID, intending to let the call go to voice mail, but he reconsidered when he glimpsed the name on the screen.

Juliet Mason.

Almost immediately, his body reacted, groin stirring and stiffening.

Well, this was a first. He couldn't remember ever getting hard from the sight of a woman's *name*.

But he knew it was less about those eleven little letters and more about the images her name triggered. Long, dark hair and chocolate brown eyes. A tall, willowy body. High, perky breasts. Sassy little smile, great ass, endless legs . . .

What man in his right mind *didn't* get hard at the thought of such a gorgeous woman?

At the same time, his reaction annoyed the shit out of him. Same way Juliet had annoyed him when they'd crossed paths last year. As hot as she was, the woman had rubbed him the wrong way, driving him crazy with her sarcastic barbs and her relentless teasing about his age.

He shifted awkwardly on the couch and willed away his erection, still debating whether to take the call. Isabel's phone didn't require a password to answer, so in the end he pressed the TALK button before he could second-guess himself.

"Isabel's phone," he said in greeting.

There was a beat.

Then another one. And another.

But the shallow breaths tickling his eardrum told him she was still on the line.

"Juliet? It's Ethan," he said gruffly. "Ethan Hayes . . . We met last year. I work for Jim Morgan."

Silence.

He suppressed a sigh. "I know you're there. I can hear you breathing."

"I . . . need Isabel."

The moment she spoke, his guard shot up a good thirty feet. Weak. Her voice sounded weak and shaky, not the confident, throaty tone of the woman he'd worked with after his team's compound had been targeted.

"Isabel and Trevor are on their way to Hawaii." His wariness escalated, rivaled only by the concern tugging at his gut. "They won't land for several more hours, but I can tell her to call you when she picks up her new phone. She left this one behind."

"No . . . time . . . Need her now . . . Can't reach Noelle . . . Need help."

Every muscle in his body went tighter than a drum. "What's going on?" he demanded. "Are you hurt?"

"Big . . . fucking . . . mess . . ." To his surprise, a wobbly sob echoed over the line. "He's dead . . ."

Ethan's back went ramrod straight. "Who's dead?"

Another pause. "Nobody . . . Never mind . . . Please get Iz. Tell her to come."

"Come where?" When she didn't respond, a tremor of concern rippled through him. "Juliet," he said sternly, "tell me where you are."

"Belarus. Grenadier Hotel in Minsk . . . room . . . room two-six-four . . . no, two-four . . ." Her voice grew strained. "Two-four-six. Med kit . . . Tell her to bring a med kit. Antibiotics and . . . um . . ."

If he didn't know any better, he would have suspected she was high as a kite on something, but Juliet hadn't struck him as a user. Besides, the pain in her voice was unmistakable. She was wounded. Fuck, she was wounded and alone on a whole other continent.

"Stay where you are," he finally ordered. "Someone will be there soon."

No response. And no more breathing sounds.

As the phone beeped in his ear, he realized Juliet had hung up.

Shit.

Shooting to his feet, Ethan raked a hand through his hair and quickly went over his options.

Option one: Stay put and pass Juliet's message along to Trevor and Isabel when they checked in hours from now.

But that would mean ruining the couple's honeymoon, because Isabel would hop right back on the plane to help her injured colleague. And who knew what kind of shape Juliet would be in by the time Isabel got there? Not only would Juliet have to wait for Isabel to land in Hawaii, but also for the twelve or so hours it would take Isabel to get to Europe.

His second option was to contact Noelle, but clearly Juliet had already tried that without any success.

Option three: Get someone else to answer the SOS. He'd call up a few contacts, arrange for a trusted medical professional to tend to Juliet, and while the doc took care of her, one of Ethan's teammates would make his way to the wounded operative. Abby might be able to . . . No, Abby and Kane were heading up an extraction in Bolivia, he remembered.

D was off rotation, though. Maybe . . . No, there was no point in involving the surly mercenary, especially when Ethan could easily do the job himself.

You don't even know the woman.

No, he didn't know her. In fact, he wasn't sure he even liked her, which was damn ironic, seeing as he was about to come to her rescue.

"For Isabel's sake," he muttered to himself.

Right, he would do this for Isabel. And for Trevor. The couple had gone through so much to be together. They'd earned this quality time, and he'd be damned if he interrupted their newlywed bliss.

With a heavy breath, he glanced around the cozy living room, his gaze resting on the gorgeous stone fireplace he'd yet to make use of.

So much for his quiet mini vacation.

Looked like he was going to Belarus. In the dead of winter.

Jeez.

It didn't sound at all appealing, but what other choice did he have? Juliet had stepped up and helped the team when they'd needed her last year.

The least he could do was repay the favor.

Chapter 2

Forty-eight hours earlier

The phone rang at three in the morning, but Juliet wasn't sleeping. Her companion, on the other hand, was snoring softly beside her, so she was careful not to jostle him as she slid out from between the black silk sheets and tip-toed across the dark hotel suite to the armchair on which she'd left her purse. Her cell phone's generic ringtone sped up, indicating it would bump over to voice mail soon, but she fished it out of her bag in the nick of time.

She almost didn't pick up when she glimpsed the unfamiliar number, until she noticed the country code. Her spine went rigid. 375. That was Belarus. And she knew only one person in Belarus.

It had to be Henry, but why wasn't he calling from any of his usual numbers? The late hour didn't raise her guard; for a man with a genius IQ, Henry clearly hadn't grasped the concept of time zones, because he always seemed to call her in the wee hours of the morning. But the number . . . that's what made her uneasy.

"Hello?" she murmured as she lifted the phone to her ear.

A quick glance at the bed told her that Joe was still sleeping soundly. Or wait—maybe his name was John. Definitely started with a J, but she hadn't paid much attention to the introduction portion of their flirtatious encounter at the hotel bar. She'd invited the man up to her room for his rock-solid physique and handsome face, not his name. It was sex, pure and simple. That's all she'd wanted from Joe/John, though, in all honesty, the hour they'd spent in the sack had been the furthest thing from mind-blowing. If she had to pick an adjective to describe it, she'd probably go with *adequate*.

"Is this Juliet Mason?" a female voice inquired in heavily accented English.

Juliet's eyes narrowed. "Who's this?"

"My name is Sasha Petrova. I'm a surgical nurse at St. Anne's Hospital in Minsk and I'm calling on behalf of Henry Jonathan Albright—this number was listed under his emergency contact information. Are you Juliet Mason, Mr. Albright's sister?"

Juliet felt all the blood drain from her face as cold fear seeped into her bones. Frowning, she hurried out of the bedroom, closed the door behind her, and stepped into the living area of the suite. Across the room, the floor-to-ceiling windows revealed the bright neon lights of Las Vegas, shining bright despite the late hour. She approached the windows in nothing but a pair of skimpy panties, uneasiness trickling through her.

"What's wrong?" she asked sharply. "What happened to Henry?"

"Are you Ms. Mason?"

"Yes, goddamn it! Now tell me what happened to my brother."

"Mr. Albright was brought in several hours ago with four gunshot wounds to the abdomen," the nurse said gravely.

Juliet gasped. "What?"

"There was extensive damage to multiple organs, as well as internal bleeding, and he was just taken to surgery. The surgeons are hoping to repair the damage and control the bleeding . . ."

Juliet saw a *but* coming, and, sure enough, the nurse continued after a long pause. "But I'm afraid the prognosis isn't good, Ms. Mason. Dr. Vlacic asked me to contact Mr. Albright's next of kin."

"How long will he be in surgery?" Juliet asked briskly, already moving away from the window.

"Several more hours, I believe, but I'm afraid his chances of survival are—"

"I'll be on the next plane out. Tell those surgeons they'd better do everything in their power to keep my brother alive until I get there."

She found it hard to breathe as she hung up the phone and crept back into the bedroom, where a sleeping Joe/John was completely ignorant to the turbulent emotions swirling inside her.

Four gunshot wounds to the abdomen.

Shit, what the hell had happened? How had Henry gotten himself shot?

She swallowed her panic as she searched for her clothes, dressing soundlessly while her companion continued to snore on the queen-size bed.

Henry couldn't die.

He *couldn't.*

He'd been Juliet's rock when they were growing up, her only friend, her one confidante. He was two years younger than her, yet he'd always felt decades older, even when they were two kids sleeping on a ratty old couch because their foster mother had been too much of a bitch to give up the spare room she'd used as an office.

They'd protected each other back then—though, if she were being honest, *she'd* done most of the protecting. Henry was too damn sweet and kindhearted, and if it weren't for Juliet, he probably wouldn't have survived a day in that foster home. Those protective instincts had stuck with her even when their lives had gone in drastically different directions. They might not be related by blood, but Juliet considered Henry her brother, and if her brother needed her, then she would damn well go to him.

For a second it occurred to her this might be a trap, but she refused to dwell on the unsettling notion. A woman in her line of work made a lot of enemies, but the good thing about being an invisible assassin was that the people connected to those she killed had no idea she even existed.

But . . . what if someone had tracked her down? And what if that same someone had shot Henry and was now using him as a pawn to lure Juliet into the open?

Then you'll deal with it when you get there.

She slipped a thin black sweater over her head, then buttoned up her jeans and bent down in search of her leather boots. She zipped them up without making a peep, having perfected the art of silence. She possessed the ability to move like a ghost, and the man on the bed remained oblivious to the fact that he was about to be ditched in a Vegas hotel room.

She didn't feel any remorse. Joe/John had known the score when he'd approached her in the bar.

What he *hadn't* known was that he'd just picked up a wanted thief–turned–contract killer who could murder him in his sleep if she chose to.

As she gathered up the meager items of clothing she'd packed for her weekend getaway and shoved them into her carry-on, she couldn't help wondering what she might encounter in Minsk. She hadn't spoken to Henry in six months, but the last time they'd touched base his life had sounded great. He was still working for the Red Cross, still volunteering as a medic in rural hospitals, still madly in love with his longtime girlfriend.

Had the shooting been a random occurrence? A robbery gone awry? Or were there more sinister undertones to the whole thing?

She chewed on the inside of her cheek, wishing like hell she wasn't walking into the situation blind. Her colleagues teased her about being reckless and impulsive, but the truth was, she was more cautious than they gave her credit for. Every move she made was a calculated one, even those that seemed spontaneous. Hopping a plane to Belarus and strolling into a public hospital without vetting it ahead of time wasn't just impulsive, but potentially dangerous.

But she had no choice. There were only a handful of people she cared about in this world, and Henry happened to be one of them.

She conducted a quick sweep of the room, making sure to wipe down all the surfaces she'd touched. She wasn't particularly worried about anyone lifting her prints, but, hey, better safe than sorry. She had no intention of winding up in the authorities' clutches again.

Been there, done that.

After she'd erased all traces of her presence from the suite, she zipped her leather jacket, picked up her suitcase, and slid out the door. All without sparing another glance at the sleeping man in her bed.

Fourteen hours later, an exhausted Juliet was being led to Henry's private hospital room.

"You got here just in time," the nurse said quietly. The petite brunette had introduced herself as Sasha Petrova, the same woman who'd called more than half a day ago. She was younger than Juliet had expected, with a gentle demeanor and big blue eyes that swam with compassion.

"He's alive?" Speaking in fluent Russian, Juliet managed to voice the question despite the enormous lump constricting her throat.

Sasha nodded. "But barely," she warned. "The surgeon wasn't able to stop the bleeding. Ms. Mason . . . Your brother isn't going to—"

When the woman halted abruptly, Juliet glowered at her. "Isn't going to what?"

Sasha quickly backpedaled. "I'm not qualified to discuss his condition, I'm afraid. Dr. Vlacic will be in shortly to explain the situation to you."

"He's going to die," Juliet said flatly. "Just say it."

The nurse didn't budge. "The doctor will speak to you shortly. Why don't you sit with your brother until then?"

Juliet nodded tersely. If Sasha didn't want to be the bearer of bad news, fine. It was probably in the woman's best interest anyway. The phrase *don't shoot the messenger* hadn't sprung out of nowhere, after all, and Juliet couldn't promise she wouldn't be doing some shooting if she lost Henry.

As she reached for the door handle, Sasha's voice stopped her. "You really don't resemble your brother at all."

"We were both adopted."

"I see." The nurse stepped away. "I'll let Dr. Vlacic know you've arrived."

Juliet offered a nod of gratitude, then opened the door.

Uncharacteristic tears filled her eyes the moment she walked into her brother's hospital room. The figure lying prone on the bed looked nothing like the man she'd seen only a year ago. His normally thick brown hair was oily and stringy, plastered to a forehead that was as pale as the rest of his face. His wire-rimmed glasses were gone— it was so strange to see her nerdy little brother without those glasses.

The ominous beeping of a heart monitor punctuated each step she took. She stood over her brother, sweeping her gaze over the white sheet covering his slender body. On the lower part of his torso, she noticed the unmistakable outlines of heavy bandages beneath the sheet.

"Jesus Christ," she mumbled.

At the sound of her voice, Henry's eyelids fluttered. He blinked rapidly, panic entering his brown eyes and causing him to thrash on the bed. The oxygen tube fell out of his nose, the IV line in his arm stretching taut as he struck out.

"Hey, lie still. Try not to move." Her sharp tone contrasted with the gentleness of her hand as she touched Henry's arm.

"J-J-Juliet?" The croaky voice cut through the sound of the beeping machine.

She smiled. "It's me."

"You . . ." He relaxed, blinked again. "You look different."

Each word came out wheezy and hoarse. It was obvious the simple act of speaking was a huge strain for him.

"I just came from a costume party," she said lightly.

Henry didn't question the flippant response. She knew he suspected what she did for a living, but she'd always appreciated that he never demanded details. He was definitely aware of her former life as a professional thief, but she'd made sure to keep the rest from him. She knew he wouldn't approve, nor would he ever understand how she could take a human life without remorse.

That was the problem with Henry. He was too good, too naive. So damn ignorant to the evil that pervaded the world, the sick men and women who committed acts so atrocious that even death wasn't a suitable enough punishment for them. Juliet had encountered these people, she'd studied them, followed them, and ultimately rid the earth of them, but no matter how many evil fucks she eliminated, five more cropped up to take their place.

But Henry wasn't like her. In spite of their childhood, he believed everyone possessed some shred of good, making it his mission in life to help others. And even though she found his bleeding heart incredibly annoying and oftentimes inconvenient, Henry's compassionate nature was her favorite quality of his. How ironic was that?

"I don't like it," he mumbled. "You're not a blonde."

She couldn't argue. Thanks to her olive skin tone, she didn't pull off blond hair as well as some of her colleagues, but since she was still wanted in Europe and couldn't very well advertise her presence, she'd had to disguise herself in a hurry, which meant making do with what she'd found in the gift shop of her Vegas hotel. The wig, tortoiseshell glasses, and preppy outfit did a sufficient enough job, and the makeup she'd used had succeeded in giving her a fair, washed-out look.

She shrugged out of her brown suede jacket and headed for the metal chair next to Henry's bed, lowering her weary body onto it and arching her sore back in a long stretch. With her boss on assignment, the "company" jet had been available, but Juliet hadn't been able to enjoy Noelle's luxurious aircraft. Rather than curl up in one of the plush cabin chairs and sleep, she'd spent the long flight fretting about her brother and making use of her colleague Paige's tech skills to figure out what happened to Henry.

Paige had hacked into the Minsk police department and e-mailed Juliet the preliminary report she'd found on the lead detective's computer. Unfortunately, all they knew so far was that Henry and his fiancée, Zoya, had been shot by an unknown intruder. According to the report, Henry had arrived home to find Zoya's lifeless body crumpled on the floor. The gunman then opened fire on Henry, who'd miraculously survived the four shots and was able to call the police and even give a brief statement before losing consciousness.

There had been no other details in the detective's notes, which meant Juliet would need to rely on Henry's recollection to piece everything together.

Now she raked a tired hand through her shoulder-length blond wig and met his slightly glazed eyes.

"What happened?" she asked quietly.

Henry's English and Scottish heritage had given him a lily-white complexion that burned crimson in the summer, but tonight his skin was so ashen, he looked like a character from a vampire movie. His Adam's apple bobbed as he drew a labored breath, and then he gazed at her with such anguish that her heart constricted with pain.

"He killed her," Henry whispered. "He killed Zoya."

Juliet forced herself to suppress all emotion. If she wanted to find the person who'd done this to Henry, she needed to keep a clear head and treat him not like a brother, but a man she needed answers from.

"The police report said you came home and found her body. Did you recognize the man who shot her?"

Confusion filled his eyes. "Yes. I mean, no. I don't know." He started to wheeze again, his heart monitor speeding up. "I don't . . . know . . . She was just lying there . . . and he . . . he looked annoyed with me. I left the hospital . . . I left early. And he . . ."

Juliet held up her hand to silence him. "Stop. Take a breath, little brother. You need to relax."

He did as ordered, sucking in deep gulps of air.

"Okay, let's start again." She leaned forward and rested her elbows on her knees. "You were working at the hospital. This hospital?"

He shook his head. "A little town . . . two hours north. Only three doctors on staff, a couple of nurses . . . Small, it's really small."

"All right. So you were doing your Red Cross thing, changing bedpans or whatnot, but you left early. Why?"

"Zoya . . ." A moan of distress slipped out of his throat. "She didn't go to work. She was sick. Went home to take care of her."

Juliet reached out and took his hand, stunned by how cold it was. She wrapped her fingers around his icy knuckles and squeezed gently. "And when you got home, she was already dead?"

Another moan, this one laced with hot agony that made Juliet vaguely uncomfortable. She knew Henry worshipped the ground Zoya walked on, but that kind of devotion was completely foreign to her. She'd shut off her emotions so long ago she didn't remember what it felt like to love someone that deeply.

But she had. Loved deeply, that was. Just once.

And never again.

Pushing aside her thoughts, she waited for her brother to continue, which he finally did after a long silence and several ragged breaths.

"She was dead. Shot. Shot in the head."

Juliet frowned. "In the head?"

"Three times. *Three.* Goddamn. Times."

The frown deepened. "You saw three distinct bullet wounds? Are you sure?"

His breathing grew shallow. "Three holes, Jules. One at each temple. One between her eyes."

Every muscle in her body stretched tight. Something niggled at the back of her brain, a crazy thought. A really, really crazy thought. But she shoved that away too, deciding to return to it later.

"You're telling me the intruder shot Zoya in both temples and between the eyes," she said slowly.

Henry nodded.

"What did he do when you walked through the door?"

"He swore."

"In what language?"

"Russian. And then . . . he raised his gun and pointed it at me. I . . . heard a hiss. Or a pop. Or both. And then my stomach was on fire . . ." Henry's brown eyes were becoming more and more unfocused. "The gun didn't make a sound."

"He must have been using a suppressor." Juliet paused, unease gathering in her belly like a snowball rolling downhill.

Why would the gunman use a suppressor?

He had to be a pro, then. A skilled professional who knew that even the slightest noise could screw up a job.

And the way he'd shot Zoya . . .

She swallowed. "Tell me what happened next."

"I'm not sure," Henry said, his expression displaying pure defeat. "I think I blacked out. I was out of it, slipping in and out. And when I woke up again, I was here."

"What did he look like? What do you remember about him?"

"Tall . . . he was tall. Not skinny, but not bulky." Henry took another weak breath. "He was wearing all black."

"Hair color? Eye color? Any distinctive features? Tattoos, moles, scars?"

"Black hair. Slicked back. Dark eyes . . . scary eyes. Very pale. That's . . . that's all I can remember."

Juliet studied Henry's familiar features, looking for any sign that she was being played, but there was nothing disingenuous in his expression. Besides, he'd never been a very good actor. As kids, she'd been the one to take the lead whenever their foster mother caught them doing something bad. Lying had come naturally to a young Juliet, while Henry blushed like a tomato when faced with evidence of his guilt.

She believed he was telling her the truth. She believed that a man had broken into Henry and Zoya's house, killed Zoya, and mortally wounded Henry. But unlike the lead detective on the case, she didn't need to investigate further in order to determine what happened. Because she already knew.

This had been a straight-up assassination.

And Henry's fiancée had been the target.

"I'm going to die."

Her head jerked up. "Don't say that," she snapped at her brother.

"But I am."

He sounded so very tired, and although there was no denying he looked like a man on his deathbed, Juliet refused to let him go that easily.

"Don't you dare give up," she said fiercely. "I mean it, Henry. You're going to live, you hear me? You're—"

"I'm sorry to interrupt," a male voice said in Russian, and then a short, stocky man in green scrubs entered the room. "You must be Ms. Mason."

Juliet rose from her chair. "Dr. Vlacic?"

The man nodded. "May I speak to you out in the hall?"

She didn't want to leave Henry, but the surgeon's stern expression brooked no argument, so she reluctantly followed him out the door. When they were alone in the hallway, she crossed her arms and met his eyes. "How is he?" she demanded.

Vlacic had harsh features that no one could ever

deem attractive, but his voice was much gentler than she'd expected. "Would you prefer I speak English or Russian?"

"Doesn't matter. Just tell me how my brother is."

Vlacic chose the latter language, proceeding to describe Henry's injuries and surgery using a lot of technical mumbo jumbo that made her head spin.

"Stop," Juliet cut in, her patience beginning to wear thin. "Tell me one thing: is he going to make it?"

His brief pause was not at all encouraging. "I'm afraid the damage to his organs was too extensive. They are failing, one by one. He's also lost a substantial amount of blood and continues to bleed internally. He's weak. He's in great risk of going into shock. And signs of renal failure are already being exhibited." Another beat. "He won't make it through the night."

Juliet almost keeled over. Her chest suddenly felt bruised, ravaged. She'd asked Vlacic to be blunt, but his brusque admission that her brother was going to die cut her right to the core.

She took a breath, her throat tightening to the point of pain. "There's nothing you can do for him? Nothing at all?"

Vlacic slowly shook his head.

"Goddamn it."

"I'm sorry, Ms. Mason. I wish I had better news for you, but your brother suffered major trauma. Frankly, I'm surprised he made it through surgery."

"He's stronger than he looks." Her voice cracked mid-sentence.

"Is there any other family you'd like to call?"

"No." She swallowed. "I'm the only family he has."

After offering a few more words of condolence, the doctor stalked off, leaving Juliet alone outside Henry's door. Her heart hurt. It literally hurt, throbbing and pulsing as cold reality seeped into it. Henry was dying. The only person who'd ever truly cared about her was dying.

She blinked through the sting of tears and tried to collect her composure, then walked back into Henry's room. She pasted on a smile, prepared to say something optimistic, but he spoke before she could.

"Let me guess. I'll be dead by morning."

Her pulse sped up. "Don't you fucking say that."

"Why not? It's true. I know that's what he told you. I . . . can feel my body . . . giving out on me." His breathing quickened, frustration flashing across his ashen face. "We're . . . wasting time. The longer you're here . . . less likely you'll find him."

"Find who?" she said sharply.

"The motherfucker who killed Zoya."

She stared at him in shock, and not just because this was the first time she'd ever heard Henry curse. Was he seriously asking her to track down the man who'd shot him?

Her silence triggered a knowing glimmer in his eyes. "You can find him. I *know* you can."

"Henry—"

"You think . . . I don't know . . . what you do?" His heart monitor beeped faster. "The secrets? The traveling? You're . . . filthy rich . . . You wear a different . . ." He was panting now. "Disguise every time you come to see me. You keep me in the dark."

Guilt trickled through her. "I never wanted to endanger you. I didn't want my work to harm you in any—"

"I don't want the details," he interjected. "Don't need the details. The choices you've made . . . I don't know if I approve of a lot of them, but . . . you're a good person, Jules. You care, no matter how much you pretend not to. And I know you can do this. You can find him."

"Possibly," she admitted.

"Not possibly. Definitely. You *can*," he insisted, revealing that tenacious streak he'd first exhibited as a child.

Even back then, Henry had been stubborn to the core. Each time Juliet tried convincing him to run away with her, he'd stuck to his guns, arguing that living as street urchins was not a smart alternative to the abusive foster home they'd been forced to endure. Juliet had disagreed, but the younger boy had been too damn pigheaded, and she'd refused to go without him.

"I loved her," Henry choked out. "Zoya is . . . She's the only person I've ever loved. Other than you. Love you too, Jules. But Zoya . . . she's a good woman. She has . . . such a big heart. She didn't deserve to die." He gasped for a few seconds before lifting his chin and fixing her with a look of determination. "You're going to kill him for me."

Juliet found herself unusually flustered. "Henry—"

"Don't you . . . goddamn fight . . . with me. You will kill him. I will go to my grave . . . knowing . . . knowing that bastard is dead. I can't avenge Zoya, but I know you . . . you will avenge me."

Agony flooded her gut, burning her insides and making her feel sick.

"Don't pretend you won't." He jerked a thumb at the machine next to his bed. "When it stops beeping . . .

when you see . . . the solid line showing my heart stopped . . . you'll go out and kill the man who took me away from you. We both know it. So don't put up a fight . . . Don't waste time . . . Don't wait for me to die to get your vengeance."

He was right. It didn't matter whether Henry lived or died. Whatever the outcome, she would still find the man who'd done this to him. Only the method of execution was subject to change. If Henry survived, she would probably show some mercy and use a rifle. If Henry died . . . well, she'd use every weapon in her vast arsenal to make sure his killer suffered before she took the son of a bitch's life.

"Kill him for me," Henry begged softly. "Leave . . . leave this room right now, Jules, and kill him for me."

"I can't leave you." Tears burned her eyes. "I want to be here with you. I'm staying with you until the very end, little brother."

"You've always been there for me." His voice was getting weaker and weaker. "You . . . never left my side . . . when Deke burned my arm with the cigarette . . . didn't leave me when they locked me in the closet . . . You sat outside the door . . . for hours. But you're going to leave me now. You have somewhere more important to be."

The tears spilled over and streamed down her cheeks. She was crying in earnest now, gulping for air.

Jesus Christ. She never cried. She never, ever cried. She was thirty-one years old, but she felt like a child again. A lost little orphan who hadn't known a shred of kindness until she'd met the equally young and equally lost Henry Albright.

Gulping hard, she returned to his side and bent over

his weakened body. She didn't want to aggravate his injuries by hugging him, so she simply stroked his cheek before brushing a tender kiss over his freezing-cold skin.

"I love you, Henry."

"I love you, Jules." There were tears in his eyes too, and his features strained with effort as he lifted one hand to her cheek.

His icy fingertips on her skin felt like a caress from death. She fought another wave of tears, then took a couple of shaky steps back. She wanted to say something more, but words eluded her. Finally, she just smiled through her tears and murmured, "Good-bye, little brother."

She was two feet from the door when he spoke again.

"You have an idea, don't you? About who he is?"

She glanced at him over her shoulder. "Yes."

"Good." A satisfied gleam, and then his brown eyes closed and he whispered that ominous phrase once more. "Kill him for me."

Juliet checked into a small suite at the Grenadier Hotel, a modest downtown establishment with the kind of sloppy security she looked for in a hotel. She took the stairs up to her second-floor room and went straight to the bathroom, slightly startled when she glimpsed her reflection in the mirror. Her cheeks were splotchy, her eyes red and swollen beneath the fake glasses, which she removed and set down on the laminate counter.

After she'd washed the tears and makeup off her face, she left the bathroom and settled on the queen-size bed with her cell phone. She pulled up the number she needed, but didn't press SEND yet. She had to make sense of a few things first.

Like the fact that Zoya had died from three neat bullet holes to the head.

Alone, that could be nothing more than a random detail, but the precise positioning of the shots was too familiar to ignore. One temple, *bang*. Second temple, *bang*. Right between the eyes, *bang*. It screamed execution, but, more than that, it was a signature.

And Juliet knew of only one contract killer who possessed that macabre signature.

But why would he want to kill Zoya? That was the million-dollar question.

Zoya Harkova didn't have any enemies—Juliet knew that for a fact, because she'd had the woman investigated once Henry began dating her. Zoya was a schoolteacher. She was a tad timid, way too sweet, but she'd been perfect for the kindhearted Henry. The only noteworthy detail about Zoya's life was that she happened to be the daughter of a lower-level official in the Ministry of Justice. Her father was hardly a political powerhouse, Juliet recalled, just an insignificant cog in the government machine, but maybe his position in the ministry was the reason the man's daughter had been targeted. Or at least it was the only one Juliet could think of, and she made a mental note to get Paige to dig into his background ASAP.

Chewing on her lower lip, she finally raised her phone to her ear. Three rings later, a deep Irish brogue danced over the line.

"Why, hello there, luv. Long time no speak."

Sean Reilly sounded thrilled to hear from her, which came as no surprise. Juliet knew Sean would jump into bed with her in a nanosecond if she gave him the okay, but although she liked him well enough, she didn't mix business with pleasure. And she valued Sean's talent for producing information from thin air far too much to risk losing such a crucial contact.

"How've you been, Sean? How's Ollie?"

"We're both peachy. Though my brother is probably peachier—he's in the Bahamas at the moment, lying in the sun and drinking piña coladas, while his poor twin is shivering his ass off in bloody Michigan."

"You're in the States? Why?"

"Meeting a few folks," he said vaguely.

"Sounds exciting. Anyway, listen, I need a favor."

"Let me guess—you require some intel."

"Yep."

"Then it's not a favor. It's a job," he said smugly. "I'll decide on the fee after you tell me what you need."

"Asshole." With a sigh, she leaned against the headboard and stretched out her legs. "What do you know about the Siberian Wolf?"

"The Siberian wolf . . . a majestic breed, usually gray, weighing anywhere from sixty to a hundred and forty pounds—"

"Very funny, smart-ass. But you know I'm not talking about a goddamn dog."

"Someone's feeling cranky today." She could practically hear him smirking. "Fine, I won't ruffle your feathers, little bird. The Siberian Wolf—I assume you mean the Russian assassin who's eluded Russian law enforcement, Interpol, and multiple federal agencies for the past five years?"

"That's the one."

"What do you want to know?"

"All I need is a name and address."

A low whistle sounded in her ear. "You planning on paying the Wolf a visit, luv?"

"Maybe. Maybe not. Can you handle that for me?"

"Maybe. Maybe not," he mimicked before his tone turned serious. "Look. I'll be honest, Jules. I rather like you."

She arched a brow. "Where are you going with this, Sean?"

"I like you so much that I don't want to see you dead," he clarified. "And messing with a Russian psychopath will get you dead. The man is a mass murderer."

"As flattered as I am to hear how much you care, I don't need you to protect me," she retorted through clenched teeth. "Can you help me or not?"

There was a long pause. "What do you want with him?"

An atypical feeling of helplessness crawled up her spine.

"He shot my fucking brother." She swallowed. "The doctor said Henry won't make it through the night."

"I'm sorry, luv." The Irishman's sympathy seeped through the extension. "I don't know what I'd do if someone killed Ollie."

"Bullshit. You know *exactly* what you'd do." Determination hardened her tone. "Get me his name and address. I don't care how much it costs."

Sean released a heavy sigh. "It won't cost you a dime. I already know the identity of the Siberian Wolf."

"Since when?"

"Since he first became active. Ollie and I make it our business to know anyone who might be of interest to us or to our clients." Sean sounded smug again. "We maintain a database of all the active and inactive contract killers operating on the globe."

Wariness rippled through her. "Do you have a file on me?"

"Of course." He chuckled. "You've led an exciting life. We should have a pint one day and exchange stories."

"What's the point?" she said dryly. "Clearly you already know everything about me."

"Yup, but it'll be more fun hearing it from you."

"Don't count on it. Now, quit stalling and give me his name."

"I wasn't stalling. And his name is Victor Grechko."

She leaned forward and scribbled the name on the complimentary notepad she found on the bedside table. "Address?"

"Give me a sec. Just need to get my laptop."

As she waited for Sean to return, she tried not to think about Henry lying there in his hospital bed. Pale. Weak. Alone.

He didn't want you there.

She bit the inside of her cheek, knowing the gentle voice in her head was right, but at the same time wishing she'd stayed with her brother. Nobody should die alone.

We all die alone.

Now that voice was scornful, and she forced herself not to dwell on the depressing point it raised. She considered calling the hospital for an update on Henry's condition, but Sasha Petrova had promised to contact her if there was any change. Besides, Henry had been adamant about what he wanted her to do, and sitting vigil at his bedside was not it.

He wanted vengeance.

Luckily, Juliet knew all about vengeance. And revenge. The two concepts tended to get so tangled up that sometimes she wasn't sure which one motivated her.

"All right, luv," Sean said a minute later, "we've got three known addresses for the Siberian Wolf. One is in Russia, way up north and a bitch to get to, according to our files. The second is in Belarus, about three hours east of the capital, close to the Russian border. The third is in Budapest, an apartment in the west end of the city."

The news didn't please her in the slightest. Three known residences? She wasn't in the mood to traipse around checking out three different sites. She wanted him *now*, damn it.

"I'd try the Belarus one first," Sean said helpfully. "Your brother was hit, what, twenty-four hours ago?"

"About that."

"Then chances are Grechko would want to lie low for a couple of days. He won't want to hop a plane to Hungary or make the trek to Buttfuck, Russia. Not until he knows it's safe."

"Thanks. I'll get right on it."

She was about to hang up when he spoke again. "Jules . . ."

"What?" she said irritably.

"Be careful."

"I always am."

She disconnected the call and rose from the bed, already making plans in her head. She'd need a new disguise. A car. Better weapons than the shit she carried in her go bag.

With Noelle out of touch it would be harder to procure the necessary supplies, but her boss possessed a vast network of contacts that Juliet could tap into.

Deep in thought, she changed out of her preppy outfit and into her own clothes, then spent the next hour and a half on the phone, making arrangements.

She was just leaving the suite when the nurse from St. Anne's called to inform her that her brother had died.

Chapter 3

Present day

Her body was on fire. Hot, relentless flames licked at every square inch of skin, and as she lay there in a pile of fiery flesh, her head pounded and the room spun before her eyes. Her lower abdomen throbbed with dull, pulsing pain that seemed to vibrate in time to the erratic beating of her heart.

Even in her feverish state, Juliet was capable of chastising herself for not packing more than a basic first-aid kit in her go bag. She'd gotten cocky. Hadn't thought she'd need more than the essentials.

Antibiotics. She needed antibiotics, damn it. But she was too weak and too dizzy to move.

How much time had passed since she'd returned to the hotel?

Hours?

Days?

She couldn't remember. Couldn't seem to make her brain function.

She remembered the drive east. She remembered the six hours she'd spent staked out in the snowy woods behind Victor Grechko's remote farmhouse. She remembered making her move, disabling the alarms, breaking into the house.

She remembered getting shot.

She remembered shooting back.

And she remembered every grisly moment that followed once she'd gained the upper hand on Grechko.

Everything after that was a blur.

An anguished moan escaped her dry lips. God, she was thirsty, but the water bottle on the nightstand was so far away. Miles and miles away. She shifted on the bed, attempted to sit up, but that only resulted in another wave of crippling agony, followed by a round of shivers that made no sense because her body was on *fire*.

She gave up and sank back on the firm mattress. Images from the past forty-eight hours circled her tired brain like a school of sharks. Henry in the hospital. Henry pale and dying. That bastard Grechko and his empty black eyes as he'd sat there tied to the chair, refusing to talk.

But she'd made him talk.

She'd broken the Siberian Wolf. Broken him. He might've taken the first shot, but she'd had the last laugh. The final victory.

No, not final. Because it wasn't over. It wasn't goddamn over.

"Orlov," she mumbled. Just saying the name out loud took a physical toll on her, made her abdomen throb with pain.

She hated this. Hated feeling weak. Hated being powerless.

God, where was Isabel?

Had she even called Isabel?

She had no idea what was real anymore.

Tired. So fucking tired.

And hot. She'd been stuck in this sauna for hours and hours and hours.

Juliet whimpered and began clawing at her clothes, but her hands felt like two lead pipes and she couldn't seem to lift up her shirt. Eventually she stopped trying and lay there, soaked in a pool of sweat, her eyes unable to focus and her body devoured by flames.

She must have passed out, because the room was dark when her eyes opened again. No light seeped through the crack in the drawn burgundy drapes. Her mouth was so parched, she felt like someone had stuffed a bag of sand inside it. Water. She needed water.

It took every ounce of strength she possessed to grab the bottle on the night table. Her fingers trembled as she twisted off the cap. She managed to bring the plastic bottle to her lips, managed to take one sip, two, before her lead-pipe hands failed her and the bottle slipped from her grasp.

The cold sensation that washed over her chest was welcome. She nearly moaned in delight, but before she could appreciate the respite from the flames, the shivers came in full force.

When she blacked out the second time, it was not because of the fire, but the ice.

Minutes, hours, or years later, a voice lured her back from the darkness.

". . . uliet . . ."

Had she turned on the television? She didn't know where the voices were coming from.

"Juliet."

Panic spiraled through her, briefly overshadowing the blistering agony. The voice knew her name.

And big warm hands were grabbing at her.

Her instincts kicked in, years of training taking over and giving her a burst of strength she hadn't thought possible. Her fist shot out, connecting with something hard.

A muttered expletive filled the air.

"Settle down . . . It's . . . here to help . . . name is Val . . . Ethan sent me . . ."

The voice kept fading in and out. Her head hurt so bad, she wanted to tell her attacker to shut up. Just kill her and get it over with.

". . . let's take a look at . . ."

He was muttering in Russian now, but she couldn't make out the words, and suddenly she was being rolled over, an action that brought a streak of excruciating pain to her side.

". . . infection . . . giving you a shot of . . ."

Something pricked her arm, but she was too tired to strike out again.

". . . really got yourself in a bind, didn't you? That's it. Lie still . . . All right . . . just going to take out these stitches and clean you up . . . Then I'll stitch you up agai—"

When those male hands touched her wound, she passed out like a light.

"What do you mean, you left her?" Ethan demanded as he slid into the backseat of the airport taxi.

"It's past midnight, Hayes, and I have a wife and kid at home. I had no choice." Val Markin didn't sound the least bit contrite. If anything, he seemed annoyed as he continued in a slight Russian accent. "It will be hard enough to explain the black eye to my wife, let alone why I had to drive to Minsk in the middle of the night."

"What black eye?"

"Your lovely friend is a wildcat. The second I got near her, she unleashed a right hook."

Ethan had to grin. Yeah, it figured that even an injured Juliet would start a fight. It was actually rather impressive that she'd managed to gain the upper hand on Val. Not many people did. Markin was as deadly as they came, a former soldier and medic in the army who'd been discharged the prior year due to a shoulder injury. But Val wasn't out of the game completely. He still took on the occasional contract job for Morgan, and he was the only person Ethan knew in Belarus, which was why he'd dispatched the soldier to tend to Juliet until he arrived.

"Other than a solid right hook, how is she?" Ethan asked.

"She's in bad shape, brother. Single gunshot to her left side, but it's the infection that did a number on her. She must have stitched herself up in the field—did a decent job, all things considered."

He couldn't help but feel a spark of admiration. The woman was a true warrior. He'd known from the moment they'd met that Juliet Mason was tough as nails, so it didn't surprise him in the slightest that she hadn't let a measly bullet wound keep her down. Unfortunately, not even warriors were immune to infection.

Ethan didn't even want to think about what would've happened if he'd decided not to answer Isabel's phone.

"I was with her for six hours," Val went on. "I gave her

two rounds of antibiotics, but the fever was still high when I left. The bullet itself didn't do much damage, and the wound will heal fast. Once you contain the infection, she should be fine. Give her another shot when you get there and change the dressing every few hours."

"Got it. Thanks for taking care of her, Val."

"No problemo, rookie. Tell your boss to give me a call one of these days. I'm itching for some adventure."

"Will do."

As Ethan hung up, he felt the cabbie's eyes on him in the rearview mirror. "You here visiting your girlfriend?" the older man asked. "Is she sick?"

It figured that he'd get the one cabdriver in Belarus who spoke perfect English.

"Yeah, she has pneumonia," he said absently, before shifting his gaze out the window.

The city was covered with a blanket of light snow, but the roads had been plowed and the driving conditions weren't bad. Only a few brave souls roamed the streets, most likely heading home from a pub or a party, their breath coming out in visible white puffs. The temperature hovered just below zero degrees Celsius, and Ethan suddenly noted the irony of him sitting in this cab wearing a parka, wool hat, and gloves, while Juliet was burning up in some hotel room.

It took only ten minutes to reach the Grenadier Hotel from the airport. It was a low-rise brick building with frost-covered ivy strands clinging to its walls and an arched entrance featuring a pair of enormous oak doors.

Ethan didn't enter from the front. Instead, he waited for the cabbie to speed off, then ducked around the side of the building.

Getting in through the service entrance was no trouble at all. He didn't encounter a single employee or locked door, which made him want to find the manager and tell the dude how shoddy his security protocol was. Then again, that's probably why Juliet had chosen the place. Easy access, easy escape.

Her room was on the second floor, another strategic move on Juliet's part—a former thief like her would have no problem scaling the second-floor balcony—and the suite she'd booked happened to be situated next to the stairwell door, serving as yet another escape route.

He climbed the stairs with energy he certainly didn't feel, not after enduring an eleven-hour flight sandwiched between two loudmouthed businessmen. He hated flying commercial, but he'd had no choice. Morgan's jet was in Bolivia with the team, and he would've had to wait too long for a charter at the airfield in Denver, which meant sucking it up and hopping on a regular flight like a normal person. He'd become spoiled these past five years, what with the private charters and endless network of contacts that allowed Morgan's team to go undetected anywhere they wanted.

Val had left Juliet's door unlocked, but it didn't really matter because the lock was so cheap, a third-grader could've picked it. Ethan strode inside, doing a cursory sweep of his surroundings before heading for the queen-size bed in the center of the room.

His breath caught when he laid eyes on the unconscious woman on the bed. Shit, she didn't look good at all. Her dark hair was pulled back in a low ponytail, but several loose strands were matted to her sweaty forehead. Black leggings and a long-sleeved shirt were damp and plastered to her willowy body, and her face was flushed a deep crimson from the fever.

She didn't stir at his approach, which was a bad sign. Any operative worth her salt possessed highly honed instincts, and the fact that she hadn't sensed his presence told him she was out cold.

Ethan couldn't control the worry swimming inside him as he leaned down to examine Juliet's injury. Judging by the reddish brown puddle soaking the sheets, she'd bled quite a bit, but at least she hadn't bled out, thank God. According to Val's initial update, the bullet had missed any vital organs. It was through and through, and if you were going to survive a shot in the gut, the bullet had connected with the absolute best place for it.

He carefully lifted the corner of the bandage covering the entry wound and found the puckered hole in her side oozing blood, the area around it red and swollen. Same went for the exit wound. And her skin felt like molten lava.

"Son of a bitch," he mumbled.

Without delay, he grabbed the med kit Val had left on the bedside table and fished out a syringe and a vial of clear liquid. It took a second to administer the dose of antibiotics, but the waves of heat radiating from Juliet's body concerned him. Christ, he needed to lower her core temperature before she self-combusted on the bed.

Exhaling slowly, he swept his gaze over Juliet's features. With her eyes closed and her skin flushed, she looked young and vulnerable, a drastic contradiction to the smirking, sassy smart-ass he'd met last year.

Okay, now was definitely not the time to notice the tiny mole above her lush top lip. He marched purposefully toward the small bathroom across the room and filled the tub with lukewarm water—anything colder could potentially shock her system—and then he hurried back to the bed.

She'd probably murder him if she knew what he was doing, but Ethan didn't dwell on the fact that she could probably pull it off. As he peeled off her leggings and averted his eyes, it occurred to him that this was not the way he'd envisioned this ever going down. He'd figured that if for some miraculous reason he was ever lucky enough to see Juliet Mason naked, it would be in an entirely different context.

Like maybe they'd cross paths on another job and fall into bed.

Or maybe she'd infiltrate Morgan's compound late one night and seduce him.

Or maybe he'd be the one doing the seducing. Maybe *he'd* track *her* down and rock her ever-loving world, proving to the infuriating woman once and for all that he was not the kid she believed him to be.

All right, fine. So clearly he'd put *way* too much thought into all the tantalizing possibilities, but truth was, Juliet had been on his mind ever since they'd parted ways last year. He hated to admit it, but she'd affected him way more than he'd expected.

A throaty moan jerked him back to the present, to the woman who was now moving restlessly on the blood-and-sweat-soaked mattress, batting at his hands as he tried to remove her shirt.

"Hey," he said gruffly, "hey, it's me. It's Ethan."

She didn't respond. Just kept fighting him, even as her eyes stayed closed and her fists were too weak to connect with anything solid.

Pinning her arms down took no effort at all, but made it difficult to get her out of the shirt. A minute later, he finally succeeded in ridding her of the garment, only to discover that she wasn't wearing a bra.

His stint in the Marines made it easy to act like a soldier rather than a red-blooded man. Ignoring her nude state, Ethan effortlessly lifted Juliet into his arms. She'd stopped struggling, her slender body limp and motionless as he carried her to the bathroom and lowered her into the tub. Once her body was submerged, he soaked a hand towel in the water and ran it over her forehead to cool her face.

He kept her in the bathtub for almost a half hour, his knees digging into the uncomfortable linoleum floor as he stayed at her side, running the cloth over her face. The water and antibiotics must have done the trick, because he could see the flush leaving her olive-colored cheeks, feel her skin getting cooler beneath his touch.

When he was satisfied that the fever had lowered, albeit slightly, he left her in the tub and went to the closet by the door, where he grabbed a fresh set of linens and proceeded to strip the bed of the bloody sheets and bedspread.

A few minutes later, he deposited Juliet between the clean sheets and covered her with the thin blanket he found in the bottom drawer of the pine dresser.

She didn't rouse the entire time, but he wasn't worried about her state of unconsciousness. She needed rest, first and foremost, while her immune system battled the infection.

Fuck, he needed rest too, he realized when he felt his eyelids drooping. Sighing, he unzipped his parka and tossed it on one of the two armchairs by the curtained window. He removed the shoulder holster that housed his twin Sig Sauer pistols, but held on to the Glock that had been tucked in the waistband of his cargo pants. As he sank into the second armchair, he caught sight of a black duffel bag sticking out from beneath the bed. Juliet's gear. Val had already checked it out, commenting that the woman traveled with a shit ton of firepower.

As an afterthought, Ethan quickly got up and dragged the bag over to his feet. Just in case Juliet came to, forgot who he was, and decided to surprise him with a bullet to the chest. He made a mental note to peek at the contents of the bag later, but first, he had to get some sleep.

He needed to be firing on all cylinders when Juliet woke up. He got the feeling men underestimated her, too dazzled by her gorgeous face and delectable figure, but Ethan knew that even injured, Juliet Mason posed a serious threat. He had no intention of letting her weakened condition lull him into a false state of security.

Which was why he kept a tight grip on his Glock even as he drifted into much-needed slumber.

Juliet opened her eyes to find a very familiar man sleeping in the chair across the room. She squinted, blinked, tried to orient herself. Tried to make sense of why Jim Morgan's man was in her hotel suite.

Where the hell was Isabel? Now that the fog was slowly lifting from her brain, she remembered the SOS call she'd made to her colleague, but she couldn't recall whether she'd actually spoken to the blond chameleon. No. No, she hadn't. She'd spoken to . . . Ethan Hayes.

Goddamn it.

Why had he come?

And why was he pointing a gun at her?

Okay, it wasn't pointed *at* her. The sleek gray weapon was resting on his thigh, with his right hand casually draped over it. But he was armed nonetheless, which kind of irked her.

She swallowed repeatedly, hoping to bring moisture to her arid mouth, then allowed her gaze to settle on Ethan's face. He was too damn good-looking, an observation she'd first made back in Monte Carlo when she'd joined forces with him and his team to track down his missing boss.

Ethan had those classically handsome features that rubbed her the wrong way—straight nose, defined cheekbones, perfectly shaped mouth. His hair was light brown and cut short, and though his eyes were closed at the moment, she knew they were hazel and deeply intelligent.

Men as handsome as him tended to be manipulative scoundrels, at least in her experience. And just because she hadn't gotten a slimebag vibe from him last year didn't mean he wasn't one.

Although it pained her to admit it, she remembered a lot about this man. Like the fact that he was young— twenty-five, if she recalled correctly. He was also a rookie on Morgan's mercenary team, a former Marine, and way too polite for his own good.

Well, not *always* polite. He'd definitely gotten snippy with her more than once when they'd last met. Granted, her needling him about his age had probably contributed to that. It sure had been fun teasing him, though.

But finding him here? Now?

Not fun. Not in the slightest.

She shifted on the mattress, noticing that the blood-stained sheets had been replaced with crisp, clean white ones. And her side wasn't throbbing anymore. How long had she been out?

The second she slid into a sitting position, Ethan's eyes snapped open and homed in on her.

"Good. You're awake." His voice was deeper than she remembered. Huskier.

Sexier.

She ignored the inane thought and met his concerned gaze. "What are you doing here?"

"Saving your ass." He rose from the chair in one fluid motion and, still holding his gun, strode toward her.

"And why the fuck are you armed?" she added irritably.

He glanced down at his hand as if he hadn't realized the weapon was in it. "Ah, sorry. I wasn't sure you'd remember me."

"What, you thought I'd wake up and kill you?"

"The thought crossed my mind," he said dryly.

"Aww, kiddo, are you scared of me? I'm flattered."

Those hazel eyes darkened. "I'm not scared of you. I just happen to have a healthy respect for your skills."

He set the gun on the dresser, then walked back to the bed. When he reached for the sheet covering her body, she scowled and pushed his hand away. "What do you think you're doing?"

"Checking your dressing." Without missing a beat, he shoved *her* hand away and pulled down the sheet.

It took her a second to realize she was wearing nothing but a pair of skimpy black panties.

Her jaw dropped with incredulity. "Did you *undress* me?"

"Yep. Your fever was out of control, so I had to give you a bath."

"You gave me a *bath*?"

"Yep."

Juliet had to smirk. "So, how was the show? Did you like what you saw?"

"I didn't look. I was too busy keeping you alive. Now, quit moving around so I can peek under the bandage."

She was oddly annoyed by that breezy "I didn't look" remark of his but, at the same time, impressed by his professionalism. Most men would have totally ogled the naked woman in their arms, unconscious or not.

"You still haven't answered my question, by the way," she told him.

"Which question was that?" He bent his dark head to check her dressing, and his woodsy, masculine scent surrounded her. The fragrance was familiar, one of those classic manly aftershaves that smelled like citrus and leather and a hint of spice.

Lord, his scent was addictive. So good she had trouble focusing.

"What you're doing here," she said through gritted teeth. "Where's Isabel?"

"On her honeymoon. She forgot her phone, and I happened to be in possession of it when you called."

Pain streaked through her when Ethan peeled away the tape holding the bandage in place, but the confusion swimming in her head overshadowed the discomfort. "So you came all the way to Eastern Europe yourself instead of giving Isabel the message?"

"She's on her honeymoon," he repeated. "You're telling me you would've wanted her to abandon her new husband and race to your side?"

Juliet's indignation faltered. He had a point. Isabel was happy for the first time in her life, married to a man who adored her, a man who'd been able to look past her shitty background and fucked-up issues, a man who saw her for who she truly was.

Juliet had no doubt that her friend and colleague would have dropped everything to come to her aid, and she suddenly felt like a total ass for putting Isabel in that position. Sheesh. Maybe it was a good thing Ethan had intercepted her SOS.

And yet . . .

"Why didn't you send Abby?" she asked suspiciously. "Or ask Abby to get in touch with someone? Why did you travel halfway across the world to help a chick you don't even know?"

Rather than answer, he made a satisfied noise with his tongue. "The wound isn't oozing anymore. Those antibiotics must be working. How do you feel? Hot?"

Before she could respond, he placed his palm on her forehead, then pressed it to her cheek.

For some absurd reason, her heart actually skipped a beat. Oh, for Pete's sake. Why was she reacting to this man's touch? Scratch that—this *kid's* touch. Because that's what he was. A kid. A young, handsome, sweet kid that a woman like her would eat alive.

"Fever's definitely gone down," he said with a pleased nod. "And to answer your question, I came because I owed you one. You helped us out last year. I'm just returning the favor."

He swiftly covered her with the sheet, then straightened up and took a step back.

It occurred to her that he hadn't glanced at her chest the entire time he'd tended to her bullet wound. Not even once.

What kind of man didn't react when presented with a pair of bare tits?

A gentleman.

Jeez, maybe she was still feverish. That would explain why she couldn't seem to take her eyes off Ethan Hayes. He looked bulkier than before, but that could also be due to his black cable-knit sweater. The thick material hugged his broad chest, and though his dark green cargo pants were by no means tight, they couldn't hide the muscular legs and taut ass beneath them.

The kid had a spectacular body—that was for sure.

"So, are you going to tell me what happened?" he asked, one eyebrow arched.

She tucked the sheet around her torso and slowly swung her legs over the side of the bed. The mere act sent another shooting pain to her gut, but it was a bearable pain, not the excruciating agony she'd experienced when the infection had been ravaging her body.

"Hey, easy," Ethan warned, as she stumbled to her feet.

He was at her side in a flash, one large hand landing on her waist to steady her.

"I'm fine," she insisted. "Seriously, I can walk."

Rather than go all alpha male on her, he released her with a dubious look. "If you say so."

She ended up proving him wrong, walking toward the

bathroom with steady steps while clutching the sheet around her naked body. "I heal fast," she informed him. "Nothing keeps me down for long."

"I can see that." He sounded amused. "By the way, don't think I haven't noticed you're avoiding the question."

"What question?" She tossed him a look of pure innocence, then ducked into the bathroom and shut the door.

She took her time washing up and using the toilet, a part of her hoping that Ethan would simply leave if she stalled long enough. An examination of her wound revealed that someone had torn out the stitches she'd given herself in the car after she'd left Grechko's farmhouse. She wondered if it had been Ethan, but she had a vague recollection of a fair-haired man leaning over her, his large, graceful hand moving like a maestro's wand as he threaded her flesh with a row of neat stitches.

"Hey, did you arrange for a doctor to come here?" she called out, her stalling attempt trumped by her need for answers.

"Not exactly," he replied from behind the door. "I contacted a colleague of mine before I left Colorado, told him to fix you up. He was with you until I got here." There was a beat. "And you're still avoiding the question . . ."

An unwitting smile sprang to her lips. The kid was persistent; she'd give him that.

"How about grabbing me some clothes, kiddo?"

She heard footsteps, rustling noises, and then a sharp knock sounded on the door. She opened it a crack and accepted the pile of clothing he handed her. As she got dressed, her side started to throb again, a reminder that she still wasn't even close to recovered. She'd need to take it easy for a few days if she wanted to be in prime condition to take down Orlov.

Goddamn Orlov.

For a moment there, she'd actually forgotten about the son of a bitch. And her brother.

Now it wasn't just her side that ached.

Chapter 4

Eight hours. The infuriating man had stuck around for eight hours already, and seemed to be in no hurry to leave, in spite of the numerous and not so subtle hints Juliet had dropped about his services no longer being required.

She couldn't believe how stubborn Ethan was about needing to know who hurt her. He hadn't left her side for an instant, except to let her use the bathroom, and there was no getting rid of him. She'd tried to achieve that result by suggesting he go and grab them some food. In response, he'd promptly called up the mercenary who'd stitched her up and had the man deliver food, coffee, and supplies right to their door.

Now Juliet eyed her rescuer-turned-intruder over the rim of her coffee mug, feeling more than a little resentful. "I can't believe Markin just showed up here like a deliveryman. What—if you work for Morgan, you just snap your fingers and people drop their lives for you?"

Ethan sipped his coffee. "Val technically works for Morgan too. And even if he didn't, the merc community looks out for its members. Now, quit deflecting and tell me how you wound up shot and bleeding in a Minsk hotel room."

She decided to throw him a small bone.

"I had a run-in with a competitor, okay? Some bullets were exchanged, I got hit, and that's all she wrote."

His lips twitched as if he were holding back laughter. "You really think I'm going to be satisfied with that half-assed explanation?"

"Frankly, I don't care if you're satisfied or not, baby." She emphasized the word *satisfied* and threw in the *baby* just to see if she could make him blush, but he didn't give her the desired reaction. If anything, he looked annoyed, and, to her dismay, even more determined.

"You can deflect all day long, *baby*," he said mockingly, "but I'll get some answers, one way or another."

She smirked. "What are you gonna do, beat the story out of me? Or are you planning a different approach? Fucking it out of me, perhaps?"

Annnnnd there it was—the blush. Except his flushed face was accompanied by a gleam of heat that turned his eyes from hazel to smoky, sensual green.

The idea turned him on.

Jesus. It turned her on too. Her nipples were now harder than icicles and her core had clenched involuntarily, making her regret ever opening this can of worms.

"As appealing as either of those options sound," Ethan said, his voice coming out raspy, "I'm choosing option number three."

Her mouth had gone dry, so she had to clear her throat before speaking. "And what's that?"

"The shadow method." Now he was the one smirking.

"I'm not leaving your side until you tell me what happened. I'll stick to you like glue. Wherever you go, I'll go, until you're so sick of me you'll be begging me to *let* you tell me the whole story."

Fighting her annoyance, Juliet stared longingly at the cell phone on the bedside table. It was practically screaming for her to use it.

"Go ahead," Ethan cajoled. "Make your calls. I promise to stay quiet as a mouse."

She scowled at him. Goddamn it. She didn't want to bring him into the loop, but at this point, what other choice did she have? The guy clearly wasn't going anywhere. To make matters worse, he'd asked his colleague to procure a startling amount of supplies—enough for them to hunker down in this room for weeks without ever having to step foot out of it.

Except now it was a matter of principle. She wasn't going to spill her guts just because he demanded it. Maybe that made her petty, but she hated taking orders from anyone. She followed Noelle's commands only because she trusted the woman implicitly and liked the arrangement they had, but there'd been times when even Noelle couldn't push her around.

"Nah, the calls can wait." Setting down her cup, she picked up the remote control and turned on the small flat-screen that was mounted to the wall over the dresser.

The TV screen came to life, turned to a local news channel, but the lead story was of no interest to her. Something about a piece of legislature a senator was lobbying to pass, and it sounded so boring she promptly pressed the MUTE button.

"You're ridiculously stubborn. You know that?"

She glanced over at him. "Funny, I was just thinking the same thing about you."

"Hey, I don't think it's unreasonable of me to ask how you ended up with a bullet in your gut. You're the one who's being difficult."

She shot him a sugary sweet smile. "You know, if you hadn't given me the whole shadow speech, I probably would have told you."

"That's bullshit and you know it."

Ignoring the accusation, she reached for her coffee and took another sip. "So, how's the new compound working out for you?"

"We're making small talk now?"

"Why not? It's better than sitting in silence."

"Fair enough."

He leaned back in the armchair, drawing her attention to the defined muscles beneath his navy blue polo shirt. He'd removed that heavy sweater a while ago, and, she had to admit, she was thoroughly enjoying the view provided by this tighter shirt. His chest was rock hard and rippling with power, a clear reminder of what he did for a living. He was a soldier. A warrior.

Jeez, why was she always attracted to dangerous men?

Wrong on both counts, she had to remind herself.

Yup, because Ethan was neither dangerous nor a man. He was a twenty-five-year-old kid, and, sure, he had the skills necessary to excel as a mercenary, but he certainly didn't throw off any danger waves. At least none that she could see.

"The new place is pretty nice," he said. "It's a damn fortress, totally impenetrable. And Costa Rica is hot. Humid as hell down there."

She arched a brow. "Can't handle the heat?"

"Oh, I can handle it. Doesn't mean I like it, though. I've always been more of a winter person." He offered an adorable shrug. "I like the snow."

She jerked her thumb at the window. "Well, there's plenty of snow out there. Why don't you step outside and enjoy it?"

He rolled his eyes. "Nice try."

She sighed. "Why do you live on the compound, then? Why don't you just pick somewhere cooler to live?"

"My place is with the team."

"Do you have any family?" she asked, then kicked herself for it. Hadn't she decided she didn't want to get to know him?

"Nope. You?"

"Nope," she mimicked.

They eyed each other for a moment, sipping their coffee in silence.

Until finally Juliet couldn't take it anymore. "Seriously, kiddo, I don't need a babysitter. I'll be back on my feet in a day or two, and then I'm outta here. Wouldn't you rather head to Izzy's house in Vermont and go skiing or something?"

"You'll be outta here, huh?" He tilted his head thoughtfully. "And where will you be going?"

"Nice try."

This time *he* sighed. "You can trust me, you know. Whatever trouble you've gotten yourself into, I might be able to help."

"What makes you think I'm in trouble?"

"Says the woman with the hole in her side."

She waved a dismissive hand. "Hazard of the job. Believe me, I'm not in any trouble."

"You said something about a run-in with a competitor? What exactly does that mean? Were you working a job for Noelle and someone else interfered?"

"Why do you care so much? Can't you just trust me when I say it's nothing for you to worry about?"

"Can't you just trust me enough to offer a few measly details?" he countered.

Argh. The frustration returned, lodging in her throat like a piece of gum. She didn't understand Morgan's men and their need to throw themselves into matters that didn't concern them. Kane Woodland had done it with Juliet's colleague Abby a couple of years ago, inserting himself into Abby's mission, and Morgan seemed to call on Isabel whenever he needed someone to do undercover work for him.

And whenever those dudes found themselves in a jam, they had no qualms about reaching out to anyone they could.

Juliet *never* asked for help. She was even loath to contact Noelle when shit went south, only doing so as a last resort. And truth be told, "favors" aside, she'd helped Morgan's team last year because her boss had instructed her to, not out of the goodness of her heart. In Juliet's world, people looked out only for themselves, and when they came to your aid, it was only because they wanted something in return.

Well, she didn't want to owe any favors, and she certainly didn't trust anyone to look out for her. She'd been taking care of herself since she was five years old. Whatever obstacles she encountered, she was perfectly capable of facing them alone. She would be the one to avenge her brother. She owed him that.

"Look, if you're worried I'm going to interfere or pass judgment, don't be." Ethan's quiet voice broke through her thoughts. "I just want to know what happened." He paused. "I won't even offer to help with whatever it is you're planning, not unless you ask me to."

She heaved out another sigh. "You really won't leave unless I tell you, huh?"

He just grinned.

Damn it, he looked cute when he grinned. Boyish. Which only cemented the fact that he was, essentially, a *boy*. In theory, the six-year age difference between them wasn't that huge, but Juliet had always felt older than her years. At six years old, she was already preparing meals for herself and her foster siblings. At ten, she was shopping for groceries. At twelve, she was working illegally at a dry-cleaning place to pay for her foster dad's booze.

And at thirty-one, she felt ancient. Far too hardened and embittered for someone as bright-eyed and bushytailed as Ethan Hayes.

Not that she was interested in the guy or anything.

"Fine, I'll tell you," she grumbled. "But only if you promise to get lost afterward."

He chuckled. "So eager to get rid of me, aren't you? My feelings are hurt."

"Too bad. Now, pay attention, because I'm only saying this once."

"Yes, ma'am."

She ignored the mock salute he gave her. "My brother and his fiancée were gunned down a few days ago."

Surprise flickered in Ethan's eyes. "Oh. All right. I wasn't expecting that." He paused again. "I'm sorry to hear it."

At the thought of Henry, her chest clenched with despair, but she forced herself to move past it. "When I visited my brother in the hospital, he described—"

"Wait. Your brother survived?"

"For a day. And then he died." Her heart squeezed. "Anyway, Henry described the gunman to me, and when he told me about the way his fiancée had died, I knew immediately that it had been a hit. Two bullets to her temples, one between the eyes. There's only one contract killer I know of with that signature. So I tracked him down."

Ethan's eyebrows shot up. "You tracked him down just like that? Who is he?"

"A man named Victor Grechko. Aka, the Siberian Wolf. He was well-known in assassin circles," she said ironically.

"Was?"

"Let's just say Grechko is no longer a card-carrying member of the killer club."

"You eliminated him." There was no judgment in Ethan's voice.

"Yes, but not before I persuaded him to reveal who hired him."

Suspicion crossed Ethan's expression. "And how'd you do that?"

She kept her answer vague. "A lady never tells."

"Okay, so what you *are* telling me is that someone put out a hit on your brother and his fiancée—"

"Just the fiancée," she cut in. "Zoya Harkova was the

target. Henry was a casualty. He wasn't supposed to be home that evening. When he showed up unexpectedly, the Wolf pumped him full of lead and got the hell out of there."

The pain returned like a flash flood, filling every inch of her body. Henry was dead. God, a part of her wished she was still feverish and unaware. At least then she could remain oblivious to the fact that the only person who'd ever truly cared about her was dead.

"Who was the fiancée?" Ethan asked briskly. "Why was she targeted?"

"I think it has something to do with her father. He works for the Ministry of Justice, but he's not a major political player, so I can't figure out why anyone would want to kill his daughter."

"Did Grechko shed any light on it?"

"Nope. Most assassins don't question a client's motives. They just take the money." She frowned. "Grechko said he was given Zoya's name and ordered to kill her. And she wasn't the only one he bumped off—apparently he'd already completed several jobs for the client, starting about eight months ago."

Ethan's eyes narrowed. "How long did it take you to break him?"

His question triggered the memory of Grechko's screams. Those low howls of pain that had left the man's throat after he'd realized she wasn't messing around. The metallic scent of blood, along with the odor of smoke and urine, suddenly filled her nostrils, accompanied by another memory—one of Grechko's head being thrown back when she'd finally put a much-deserved bullet in it.

"Three hours or so," she said without a trace of emotion. "I gave him a choice—if he talked, I'd kill him fast. If he didn't, I'd take my time. But either way he was going to die."

Ethan let out a soft whistle. "No mercy, huh?"

"He killed my brother," she said coldly. "Tell me you wouldn't have done the same if it had been one of your men."

To her surprise, he didn't utter a denial. "I would've killed him in a heartbeat. But . . . I guess I'm having a tough time picturing you torturing a man. Not many people are capable of such brutality, even when it's necessary."

"I'm capable of a lot of things." She met his gaze head-on. "Try not to forget that, kiddo."

He didn't object to the nickname, but his nostrils did flare in irritation for a moment. "I take it he chose not to talk at first?"

"No, not at first. I only had to cut off one finger before he changed his mind."

She'd revealed the gruesome detail in an attempt to shock him, but Ethan didn't even blink. Instead, he clasped his hands in his lap and said, "So, who's the client? Who hired Grechko to kill Zoya?"

Juliet hesitated.

"Oh, come on. Don't hold out on me now. Who was Grechko working for?"

She let out an uneven breath. "Are you familiar with Dmitry Orlov?"

He looked startled. "You've got to be shitting me."

"You've heard of him, then."

"Who hasn't?" Ethan shook his head in dismay. "No way. You can't get tangled up with that man. He's corrupt to shit."

Ethan wasn't exaggerating. Of all the corrupt politicians on the globe, Dmitry Orlov made Juliet's top ten Don't Mess With list. The minister of defense in Belarus, he was a smooth, attractive man on the surface with the reputation of a coldhearted psycho beneath it. Whenever someone in the government opposed him, that person mysteriously disappeared or wound up dead in a Dumpster—deaths that always went unsolved because Orlov had the head of the police force in his pocket.

Back when she stole for a living, Juliet had made many trips to Eastern Europe and had heard her fair share of stories about Dmitry Orlov. According to her sources, Orlov had a tendency to use heavy-handed tactics to get his way, but he'd become drastically more violent since he'd lost his son in a terrorist attack that had dominated every global media outlet. The man's antiterrorist stance had only strengthened since then, and he now went to any lengths to eliminate threats to his country or his position of power. Blackmail, murder, rape, torture—the man had no qualms about using whatever method was available in order to achieve his goals.

"I know exactly who I'm dealing with here," she replied with a shrug. "Orlov is a violent maniac."

"Which is why you should stay away from him."

"Not gonna happen, kiddo. He's responsible for my brother's death."

"Are you sure Grechko was telling you the truth?"

"He had no reason to lie. He said he met with Orlov personally at Orlov's private estate." When she saw Ethan's dubious face, she went on. "Orlov is known to use outside contractors—it's no secret he doesn't have much trust in his own government—and he wouldn't have been worried about Grechko talking out of turn. It wasn't in Grechko's best interest to advertise his arrangement with Orlov, not if he wanted to keep collecting millions by killing for the guy."

"I see your point, but I still don't get why Orlov needed a pet hit man to begin with. Who were the other targets Grechko eliminated for him?"

"He told me the names of the targets he'd already hit, and three that he hadn't taken care of yet. Grechko said he's been on standby for Orlov this past year. He doesn't move on the target until Orlov orders him to."

"Do you remember all the names?"

"I put them in my phone. Grab it for me, will ya? It should be in my duffel. You know, the bag that's sitting by your feet." She couldn't help but roll her eyes. "You thought I wouldn't notice that you've been keeping my gear near you at all times?"

"For my own protection," he shot back. Then he set his mug on the small table between the two armchairs and bent over to unzip the duffel.

When he pulled out a silver BlackBerry and held it up, she shook her head. "No, not that one. That's my second phone."

He came up with a black Samsung Galaxy next.

"Not that one either."

The corners of his mouth lifted in a wry smile. "Let me guess. That's your third phone."

She shrugged as if to say *so what*?

When Ethan retrieved an iPhone in a sturdy black case, she nodded. "Jackpot. The password is two-nine-three-seven. Go into the notes folder, under the tab 'grocery list.'"

Ethan's fingers swept over the touch screen, his eyebrows drawn in concentration as he read the contents of Grechko's hit list.

"Did you vet the names yet?"

"When would I have had time to vet them? I've been in an infection-induced stupor for the past couple of days. I was planning on asking Paige to check them out."

Ethan studied the screen, a deep frown creasing his mouth. "Okay. Well, it'll be easy to gather intel about the nine dead targets, but they're not our biggest concern."

"*Our* concern? As in, we both have a vested interest in this?"

He gave her a pointed look. "The three remaining names are the important ones. We have to track them down and warn them."

Juliet stared at him. "Why would we do that?"

"Because they have contracts out on their heads." He shook his head, looking frazzled. "They're in danger, Juliet. Don't you think they need protection?"

Oh, brother.

What was it with Morgan's crew and their need to save the damn world? Some of her own colleagues were the same way, Abby and Isabel, in particular, but for the life of her, she didn't understand why they felt it was their duty to rescue every poor, victimized soul in their vicinity.

"I'm not a bodyguard, kiddo."

"My name is Ethan," he cut in, steel in his voice.

"Sorry. I'm not a bodyguard, *rookie*. I'm not risking my neck for a bunch of strangers."

"But you'll risk your neck to kill Orlov?"

She cocked her head. "Who says I'm planning to kill Orlov?"

Ethan chuckled, deep and derisive. "You're telling me you're not going to get revenge on the man who's responsible for your brother's death? I didn't even know you had a brother, by the way."

"That's because you don't know me." Aggravation clamped around her throat like a vise. "We don't know each other, which means I don't owe you any explanations or have an obligation to share my plans with you."

"You don't have to share a damn thing. I *know* you're going after Orlov." He released an aggravated breath. "And it looks like I'll be going after Orlov's targets."

"There's no reason for you to get involved. Once I eliminate Orlov, the targets will probably be safe."

"*Probably* being the operative word. What if Orlov left orders for someone else to kill them if he dies? Or if he's already hired another hit man to get rid of them?"

She opened her mouth, prepared to argue about the utter stupidity of him getting mixed up in this insanity, but then she changed her mind. If Ethan wanted to stick his neck out for total strangers, let him. She had her own agenda, and she damn well intended to follow through on it.

Orlov had killed Henry. She would kill Orlov. End of story.

Except . . . aw, hell. Was that teeny pang in her stomach *guilt*?

It's not guilt. It's pain. You got shot.

Yeah, that was probably it. Of course she didn't feel guilty. She had no reason to.

"Fine. Well, it's your prerogative," she said nonchalantly. "Warn them. Take them all to Morgan's awesome new bachelor pad if you want. Just don't expect me to tag along."

Of all the reactions she could have received, the disappointment in Ethan's hazel eyes was not one she'd anticipated. No anger, no annoyance, not even disapproval.

Nope, he looked *disappointed*, as if he'd expected more from her and she'd truly let him down.

This time, the twinge she experienced was most definitely guilt.

"You really don't care if three innocent people die?" Ethan asked quietly.

Juliet swallowed, then donned a careless face. "Nope."

"Fine." His tone became businesslike. "Get your girl Paige on the phone and have her check out every person on that list. As soon as we get the intel, we'll go our separate ways." An edge crept into his voice. "I'll be heading off to save lives, and you'll be going to take one. I guess that's what we call irony, huh?"

Chapter 5

It was past one a.m. and Ethan was stretched out on the floor, feeling wide-awake and restless. It had been a ridiculously lazy day that involved too much sitting around as they'd waited for Paige to get back to them. Although he and Juliet had done some research of their own, gathering basic intelligence about the individuals on Grechko's list, Juliet's tech-savvy colleague was capable of conducting the kind of deep background searches they required.

Unfortunately, Paige still hadn't gotten in touch, and Ethan was now lying here after a long day of doing nothing, while Juliet slept on the bed. She'd been sleeping on and off during the day, which had surprised him. He'd figured he'd have to force her to rest the way he usually did with his teammates. Whenever they got injured, the men on Morgan's team griped and complained about being bed bound, demanding to return to action even if they weren't fully capable of it yet.

But Juliet was smarter when it came to her recovery. She knew that she needed to regain her strength if she wanted to go forward with her plan.

Her plan to kill the minister of defense.

Jesus. Talk about ambitious.

Not that he was worried or anything. Truth was, he had no doubt that Juliet could achieve her crazy goal. When you worked for Noelle you picked up a few tricks, and though he didn't know much about Juliet's previous assignments, he was confident that getting to Orlov would be an easy feat for the woman.

As for him, he couldn't in good conscience leave the country until he tracked down the three people Victor Grechko hadn't gotten around to killing. He didn't know who they were, but clearly they were important if Dmitry Orlov wanted them dead.

Too many questions ran through his mind, but Ethan tried not to get hung up on them. Like Juliet, he had to pick one objective, and the three innocent people with targets on their backs were the priority he'd chosen to focus on.

Apparently he wasn't destined to have a vacation. All he'd wanted was two weeks of peaceful, relaxing me-time, and somehow he'd wound up in Eastern Europe, about to play bodyguard to three strangers.

Life was weird sometimes.

"Goddamn you!"

Juliet's angry outburst penetrated the silence.

The sheets rustled, the mattress squeaking as she moved around on the bed. Fortunately, the room was dark, which meant he couldn't see her booty shorts and black sports bra—the indecent outfit she'd been wearing when she'd waltzed out of the bathroom earlier without a shred of modesty. His body, of course, had instantly reacted, but if she'd noticed the bulge in his pants, she hadn't commented on it.

"What did I do?" Ethan asked in amusement. "I've just been lying here quietly."

Rather than explain the abrupt indictment, she let out a resigned sigh. "You remind me of Henry."

"Is that good or bad?"

"A little bit of both, I guess." An unmistakable chord of sorrow rang in her voice. "He wasn't my real brother, you know. We weren't blood related."

Ethan didn't say a word. Didn't even move.

He didn't have to be a genius to know that Juliet didn't open up to just anybody. Or maybe to anyone. She'd barely revealed any details about herself when they'd met in Monte Carlo last year, and he was afraid that if he interrupted her now, she'd clam up again.

"We were placed in the same foster home when I was twelve. He was two years younger than me. Such a scrawny kid—really shy. He wouldn't have lasted a day in some of the group homes I lived in before I got placed with the Millers." She made a disgusted noise. "Not that the Millers' house was any better than those previous homes."

He held his breath, hoping she'd go on. Praying she would. Juliet Mason remained an enigma to him, but one he was determined to solve. He wanted a glimpse behind that smirking, I-don't-give-a-shit curtain she hid behind.

"They were pure filth," she said viciously. "Shower mildew, toilet-bowl grime, soiled mattresses. That's what Deke and Maria were—all the unwanted filth people try to scrub out of their lives."

"Did they beat you?" he asked gruffly, unable to hold his tongue anymore.

"From day fucking one. They started off small, just a spanking here and there, the occasional slap when we were quote-unquote bad. Deke liked to toy with Henry—he shoved him around a lot, taunted him because he was too skinny, that kind of shit. Eventually they both got meaner. Henry and I had our fair share of bruises, cuts, cigarette burns, but never in places that were visible to the teachers or caseworkers."

She stopped abruptly, but Ethan refused to let her shut down on him.

"How did you and Henry get through it?"

The bedsheets rustled again. "We stuck together. Comforted each other when we needed comfort, cleaned up the cuts and bruises, put balms on the burns. I can't tell you how many times Henry had to stop me from slicing Deke and Maria's throats. I stole a knife from the kitchen once, was planning on killing those bastards in the middle of the night, but Henry talked me out of it. He was a good kid." She paused. "I kept the knife, though. Slept with it every night."

Ethan couldn't even imagine growing up in that kind of environment. He'd been blessed with two loving parents for eighteen years of his life, and losing them had been a blow he wasn't sure he'd ever recovered from. But the memories of his folks were priceless, those cherished moments getting him through some seriously tough times, particularly during his stint in the corps. His heart ached at the knowledge that Juliet hadn't been so lucky.

"How long were you with the Millers?"

"Three years, until Maria ran out on Deke. She took

off with some loser she'd been fucking around with, and Deke couldn't handle the responsibility of two foster kids. He called the caseworker, insisted he could only take care of one of us, and, of course, it had to be me." Bitterness thickened her tone. "I'd just turned fifteen, and let's just say that Deke liked what he saw."

Ethan's muscles coiled tight with anger. "Did the son of a bitch touch you?"

"I didn't give him the chance. I ran away five hours after that bitch caseworker left the house with Henry. I lived on the streets after that, but I made sure to find out where they'd taken Henry. He was living in a new foster home, a good one. He really lucked out."

There wasn't a single iota of envy in her voice. If anything, she sounded defeated.

"I used to meet him every day after school and walk him home, just to make sure he made it back safely, and—"

"You weren't in school?" Ethan had to interject.

"Nah, I'd dropped out by then. Couldn't exactly attend school when I didn't have an address for them to scribble in their little files. They would have called social services in a heartbeat if they knew I was a street kid. Anyway, we're getting off track. This is about Henry, not me."

He swallowed his disappointment, wishing like hell he could steer the conversation back to where he wanted it to go. Juliet was the most interesting woman he'd ever met, and he had the strangest urge to find out every last detail about the woman. Find out what made her tick, what made her smile, what made her, well, *her*.

But in his experience, women who worked for the all-powerful Noelle kept everyone around them at arm's length.

"He was such a great kid. So smart and compassionate and he tried so hard to treat everyone with kindness and respect. I figured he'd go into social work, but he ended up volunteering with the Red Cross instead of going to college, and eventually he landed a permanent job with them. He was trained as a counselor and medic, and he traveled to needy areas of the world, working at hospitals and clinics and helping anyone he could. He was a goddamn champion for every downtrodden human on the fucking planet."

She went silent, her soft, even breathing echoing in the room.

Ethan sat up on his makeshift bed. He knew exactly where she was heading with all this, and so he wasn't surprised when she finally blurted out what he'd been waiting for her to say.

"Fine. Let's find those people and warn them."

He smiled in the darkness.

"I guess finding them could work to my advantage," she added, as if trying to rationalize the plan to herself. "If Orlov wants them dead, then clearly they're important to him. Maybe I can use them as leverage, dangle them in front of Orlov in order to get to the bastard."

He had to laugh. "I see. So as long as there's something in it for you, then you're totally on board. You can't just do it out of the goodness of your heart, huh?"

"What heart?"

"You don't have to keep pretending with me. You can drop the heartless-bitch act, you know. It's okay to care about other people."

"But I don't care," she answered flatly. "I still don't give a shit about those strangers. But Henry would have cared. He would have gone out of his way to protect them from Orlov."

"See, you *do* care. About your brother, at least."

She grumbled in irritation. "Stop trying to find the good in me. Truth is, I *am* a heartless bitch. Self-preservation is the only thing that matters to me."

"If that were true, you wouldn't have dropped everything to race to your brother's bedside. And you wouldn't be risking your own life now to avenge him."

She let out a sigh. "Make no mistake, rookie—if it had ever come down to protecting Henry or protecting myself, I would've chosen me."

Ethan held his tongue. If she wanted him to think she was a cold, emotionless bitch, then fine.

But he didn't believe it for a second.

"The Wolf's dead."

Those were the last three words Dmitry Orlov expected to hear when Kirill entered the room. It was nearly midnight, and Orlov had left his office several hours ago to hole up in the expensively furnished study of his palatial estate outside the city. He often worked from home in the evenings, preferring the lavish surroundings to his cold sterile office in the House of Government. Perhaps he would be more inclined to spend time in the capital if he had an office as grand and luxurious as President Belikov, but alas, he was just the lowly defense minister and undeserving of such grandeur.

Soon, a little voice assured him, dimming some of the bitterness.

"What do you mean, he's dead?" Orlov scowled as he rose from his leather chair and rounded the desk, arms crossed tightly over his tailored double-breasted suit jacket.

The bulky, fair-haired man in front of him met his gaze head-on. As usual, Kirill remained expressionless, a standard look for the former KGB operative who now worked exclusively for Orlov under the guise of head security officer.

But Kirill did far more than protect his boss and oversee the Presidential Security Service guards that had been assigned to Orlov—he handled all of his boss's unofficial business, and although Orlov considered himself indebted to no one, he couldn't deny that Kirill had contributed greatly to his rise to power.

"I found the body at the farmhouse," Kirill said in his monotone voice. "The Wolf was tortured."

Orlov did his best to hide his shock. Tortured? He hadn't expected to hear that either.

"Tell me precisely what you found."

Kirill proceeded to recite the night's events as if he were reading from a macabre textbook. "I went to the farmhouse and found Grechko secured to a metal chair with a gunshot wound to the head. Everything prior to the bullet suggests that he'd been interrogated by a professional."

Orlov's cheeks hollowed in displeasure. "I see."

"I cleaned up the scene and took care of Grechko's body. I assume that's acceptable to you?"

"It is." He rubbed his clean-shaven jaw, thoughtful. "Do you think he talked?"

"I have to assume so. The damage inflicted on him would have been substantially worse if he'd held out."

Disgust rose in Orlov's throat. In his dealings with Victor Grechko, Orlov wouldn't have suspected that the man could be broken so easily, and yet the Wolf's demise only confirmed what he'd always known, which was that most men were weak. Most men snapped in half like a pencil if one applied enough pressure on them. Most men were pathetic.

"We also have to assume that Grechko revealed your name to the person who executed him," Kirill finished.

"Of course he did." Orlov waved his hand. "But that's inconsequential. I've faced accusations of wrongdoing my entire career. If someone comes forward to accuse me of conducting business with Grechko, nothing will come of it. I'm beyond reproach, Kirill."

"Yes, sir."

"What I'm more concerned with is who took it upon himself to eliminate my wolf. Is the Harkova woman's death in the news yet?"

"I believe so, sir."

"Good. Oleg will be inconsolable, I imagine." Satisfaction surged through him. "That useless moron worshipped his daughter. I'll pay him a visit tomorrow. After all, I know what it's like to lose a child."

The memory of his son's face flashed through his mind, evoking a rush of emotion. Sergei had been his pride and joy. Such a good boy, destined for greatness. But those bastards had stolen that promising future from him, and they were still going unpunished. Colonel General Durov had abandoned the investigation into the bombing months ago, calling it a dead end. The head of the city's *militsiya* had given up, for Christ's sake.

Was it any wonder Orlov had been forced to take matters into his own hands?

Setting his jaw, he banished all thoughts of his son, for it was inappropriate to lose himself in memories when Kirill was standing there, awaiting instructions.

"Find out who killed my wolf, and when you do, bring him to me. Perhaps I'll give him the same treatment he gave Grechko, as punishment for interfering with my plans." A frown puckered his mouth. "As for Grechko's outstanding assignments, locate someone who can take over the job."

"May I suggest myself, sir?"

Kirill offered a rare, wry smile that made Orlov chuckle. "Not for this, my friend. You know we must distance ourselves from this particular endeavor."

"Yes, sir."

"Now leave me, Kirill. I'd like to do some reading before I turn in."

The former Soviet spy left the study without a word, soundlessly closing the door behind him.

Alone, Orlov finally allowed his displeasure to surface. He stalked over to the wet bar next to the stone fireplace, poured a healthy amount of scotch into a tumbler, then sank into a gold-colored wing chair and rested his glass on his thigh.

Someone had tortured and killed the Siberian Wolf.

Why?

Because they knew Grechko had been working for Orlov?

Or was it an entirely unrelated reason? Grechko was a killer, after all. Killers had enemies. Perhaps his death had nothing to do with their arrangement.

Nevertheless, Orlov didn't appreciate this new development. He hated unanswered questions. Even more, he hated anything that disrupted his objective. Grechko's work had been left unfinished, and now Orlov was forced to dispatch another cretin to do his dirty work.

For that inconvenience alone, Grechko's killer would lose a finger.

The fate of his remaining digits was yet to be determined.

Chapter 6

"Seriously, how long does it fucking take to compile a dossier on a dozen measly people?" Juliet burst out the next evening.

She and Ethan were holed up in a corner booth down at the hotel bar, nursing their beers, while a jazz singer crooned out a depressing melody on the small stage across the room. It had been more than a day since Juliet had asked Paige to investigate the names on Grechko's hit list, and her colleague still hadn't gotten in touch, which meant they had nothing to do but twiddle their thumbs and listen to a shitty lounge singer.

"If it's so easy, why don't you do it yourself?" Ethan raised his eyebrows in challenge.

"Oh, shut up," she mumbled. "That was a rhetorical question."

"It was a dumb question, you mean. Relax. I'm sure Paige and Reilly are working around the clock to do Queen Juliet's bidding."

Despite herself, she had to fight a smile. She was kind

of digging this unexpected sarcasm of his. It was so incongruous coming from someone with his überpolite personality and unassuming demeanor.

It disturbed her that she still didn't have a real sense of Ethan Hayes. Was he the supersweet Boy Scout who diligently checked her dressings and pumped her full of antibiotics every few hours? Was he the strong-willed soldier who had no problem risking his neck for three people he didn't even know?

Or was he the man whose eyes smoldered with sinful promise whenever their bodies happened to brush?

Oh yes, he was definitely doing some smoldering. Even now, as he lifted his beer to his lips, he was watching her over the rim of his glass with I-want-you eyes.

He was attracted to her. She'd have to be blind not to notice, but she'd been feigning obliviousness, mostly because she feared that if she commented on it, she might actually wind up in bed with the guy.

Yet tonight she found herself opening her big mouth. Whether from boredom or curiosity, she didn't know, but somehow she ended up starting a dialogue she knew she'd regret.

"How come you don't have a girlfriend?"

Ethan blinked in surprise, but he recovered quickly, shooting her an impish smile. "Who says I don't?"

"Do you?"

"Not really. I was seeing someone in San Jose but it wasn't serious. It's hard to maintain a relationship when I'm constantly going wheels up for a job."

"Abby and Kane don't seem to have a problem," she pointed out.

"Yeah, but they work together. I can't imagine finding a woman who'd be okay with the life I lead, not unless she leads it too."

The look in his eyes lacked any trace of heat, but she got the feeling he was asking an unspoken question. As in, *Are* you *that woman?*

"What about you?" He turned the question back on her. "How come you don't have a boyfriend?"

"I don't do relationships either." She smiled wryly. "But probably not for the same reason as you. You'd be surprised how many men are wildly turned on by a woman in my line of work."

"Yeah? So why are you single?"

"Because I choose to be."

"Aw, come on, you've gotta give me more than that."

"You want more? How's this for more? I don't trust men as far as I can throw them." She shrugged. "And I have no intention of ever being betrayed by one again."

Curiosity shone in his hazel eyes. "Interesting. Who betrayed you?"

"Wouldn't you like to know . . . "

"Duh. That's why I asked."

She laughed. "Sorry, kiddo, but that's all you're getting from me tonight. Scratch that—that's all you're getting from me ever."

"We'll see about that." Looking more confident than she'd ever seen him, he abruptly set down his beer glass and slid out of the booth.

Juliet stared at him as he stood in front of her with one hand extended. "What's this?"

"This is me asking you to dance."

Surprise jolted through her. She glanced at the small

parquet dance floor, where only one other couple had been inclined to get up and dance. The fortysomething female singer was currently belting out another gloomy ballad, backed up by a bored-looking band whose members were all middle-aged men.

Man, what a nightmare it would be to work as the house band of the Grenadier. Surrounded by weary travelers and drunken buffoons day in and day out, playing the same tired old songs. Juliet would rather die than meet such a dismal fate.

"I'm not dancing with you," she muttered. "This isn't my scene."

"Not mine either, but we're still going out on that dance floor."

Before she could blink, he yanked her out of the booth and onto her feet. If any other man had touched her like that without permission, she would've cut off his hand, yet for some inexplicable reason, she indulged Ethan, allowing him to lead her out to the floor.

Okay, clearly the one beer she'd consumed had messed with her head. She'd literally said *no* two seconds ago and now here she was, willingly placing her hand on Ethan's broad shoulder.

He clasped her free hand and brought his other hand down to her waist, holding her in a possessive grip that brought a spark of panic. What the hell was she doing? Why was she letting this happen?

"See? This isn't so bad," Ethan murmured as he drew her close.

His masculine scent flooded her nostrils. Oh, boy, it was downright addictive. She wanted to inhale him until her lungs exploded.

And his body was so damn hard. Like a brick wall. Solid, unyielding. A thrill shot through her as she envisioned that sexy body crushing hers, powerful hips thrusting as he fucked her good and hard. Or maybe it would be more thrilling feeling all that power beneath her, while she straddled his thighs and rode them both straight to heaven.

Oh, for fuck's sake. She had to get ahold of herself. No, of her *hormones*. Hot bod aside, Ethan Hayes was a kid, not to mention the furthest thing from her type. Juliet gravitated toward men with two distinct traits: temporary and complication-free.

And Ethan was neither of those. Screwing him would bring complications galore, and she doubted the word *temporary* even existed in the guy's vocabulary. He had *steady boyfriend* written all over him.

"You know, it won't kill you to admit you're enjoying my company," he said as they moved together to the slow beat.

She was quick to correct him. "I'm tolerating your company. There's a difference."

He dipped his head, his warm breath fanning over her ear. "You're so full of shit."

"Oh, am I?"

"Yep."

Her pulse sped up when he dragged his palm over the small of her back in a soft caress. Their lower bodies weren't touching, but she knew he had an erection. He'd been hard on more than one occasion these past two days, a response he hadn't tried hiding from her. Neither of them had mentioned the evidence of his arousal, however.

Until now.

"I make you hard, don't I, rookie?" At five-nine, she was a tall woman, but still several inches shorter than Ethan, and so she had to stand on her tiptoes in order to let her lips brush his earlobe. "Don't bother denying it—I know you want me."

He tensed for a moment, then relaxed. Chuckled softly. "I wasn't going to deny it."

"If you think we're going to fall into bed, forget about it. I'm not going to fuck you."

That large, warm hand stroked her lower back again. Sensual and seductive.

"I mean it," she said when he didn't respond. "I'm not interested."

"If you say so."

"I do say so." Frustration climbed up her chest. "I'm not hard up for sex, and even if I was, I wouldn't have it with you."

"And why is that again?"

She had to lift her head to meet his eyes, which were glimmering with amusement. "Because I'm not interested."

"Be more specific, sweetheart. Tell me why you're never, ever gonna have sex with me."

He was taunting her now and, goddamn it, that got her pulse going too. She lived for this kind of stuff— verbal foreplay, sexy exchanges, witty banter.

But no matter how much fun it was, she still knew she couldn't hook up with the guy.

"You want me to list all the reasons? Fine. One, you're just a kid. Two, you're so damn sweet you give me a toothache. Three, I've got a job to concentrate on. Four, I'm not interested in becoming the latest wife of a Jim

Morgan crew member. Five, even if you were older and not so gratingly nice, I can't imagine you ever giving me what I need in the bedroom. The end."

Her speech only resulted in bringing a broad grin to his mouth. "You're vibrating."

"Huh?"

"Your phone is vibrating. I can feel it against my leg."

Juliet clenched her teeth, pissed that she'd gotten so caught up in their exchange that she'd been completely unaware of the vibrations coming from her front pocket.

"Looks like our little dance is over," she told him.

They both knew she was referring to more than the physical dance they'd just shared.

Sliding her hand into her pocket, Juliet drew out her phone and glanced at the display. Paige. Finally.

She promptly pressed TALK and said, "Hey, babe. Took you long enough."

"Keep up that attitude and I'll quit doing favors for you, Jules," Paige replied in her crisp British accent. "Hasn't anyone ever told you that you catch more flies with honey?"

"Well, maybe if you hadn't taken your sweet-ass time I wouldn't be so impatient."

"Says the woman who dumped twelve names in my lap and wanted a thorough background check on each of them. Sean and I had to split up the workload, by the way. He should be e-mailing you his findings as we speak. I just sent you mine." Paige sounded amused now. "Oh, and just for my own curiosity, I pulled up your new partner's military file. He's cute."

Juliet avoided Ethan's eyes. "It's business."

"Uh-huh. I'm sure it is." Paige laughed in delight. "I

expect details the next time you come to London. Now, go and check your in-box. I jotted down some notes and observations in the e-mail, but call me if you have any follow-up questions."

Paige hung up without saying good-bye, though Juliet had no idea why the woman was so eager to get off the phone. Paige lived in an isolated cottage in Northern England, and God knew what she did with her time, out in the middle of nowhere all by her lonesome. Juliet would go nuts living that way. She needed action, excitement, stimulation that didn't come from reading books in front of an old fireplace.

"Was that Paige?" Ethan asked in a low voice.

She nodded. "C'mon, let's go back to the room. I need my laptop."

They headed for the door, reaching it just as another hotel guest sauntered in. A tall, heavyset man in a crisp blue suit, with salt-and-pepper hair combed to perfection and harsh, arrogant features.

He bumped into Juliet upon his entrance, but didn't apologize for his rudeness. Rather, he swept his gaze over her tight black jeans and purple V-neck sweater, his dark eyes resting way too long on her chest.

"You should watch where you're going," he said in Russian, then proceeded to add an endearment that roughly translated to *sugar tits*.

Juliet offered him a cool look. "Call me that again and I'll break your arm."

Displeasure flashed in his eyes. Instead of answering, he turned to Ethan and said, "Control your woman before someone controls her for you."

Ethan ignored the man completely. Just brushed past

him, taking Juliet's arm in the process. She followed him without complaint. As tempted as she was to kick the rude jerk in the balls, she knew they couldn't draw attention to them and jeopardize the mission.

"What an ass," she muttered as they left the lounge.

"The world is full of asses. No point in letting them get to you." He paused. "Sugar tits."

"Oooh, somebody knows his Russian," she teased.

"I get by. Probably not as well as you, though. How many languages do you speak again? A billion?"

"Six." She stuck out her tongue. "Did Isabel tell you that, or did you boys run a check on me?"

"Actually, Abby told me."

"And when were you and Abby talking about little old me?"

They bypassed the elevator and stepped into the stairwell, with Ethan taking the lead. She'd been thrilled to discover that, like her, Ethan avoided elevators at all costs. Other operatives she'd worked with in the past hadn't seemed to mind riding the elevator, but Juliet would rather climb twenty flights of stairs than be stuck in a box that could malfunction at any second. It always went back to self-preservation for her. No way would she ever allow herself to be trapped somewhere and take the risk of getting caught again.

"Abby and I talk about a lot of people," Ethan said noncommittally.

"Funny, because the Abby I know isn't much of a talker." In fact, Abby Sinclair was the most tight-lipped person Juliet had ever met, after Noelle, of course. But not even Juliet could deny that the former assassin had mellowed since falling in love and marrying Ethan's teammate Kane.

"She talks to me all the time," he added. "Maybe it's because she knows there's no threat of me blabbing her secrets."

"You *are* the least threatening guy on the planet," Juliet replied cheerfully.

Annoyance flickered in his eyes. "The men I've killed would probably disagree with that."

"Oooh, look at the tough guy. I'm soooo intimidated."

They reached the second-floor stairwell and headed back to the room. Much to her irritation, Ethan went in first, his hand poised over the gun butt beneath his waistband. As if she weren't perfectly capable of checking out the space herself.

"You really need to quit doing that," she muttered.

"Doing what?"

"Protecting me." She used air quotes around the words. "I can take care of myself."

"Yeah? It didn't seem that way a few days ago."

"You give yourself too much credit. I would've managed to find some antibiotics on my own."

"Uh-huh."

His visible amusement raised her hackles. "Seriously, I don't need your protection, kiddo."

He locked the door and glanced over with a frown. "I'm not a kid. And stop trying to goad me."

"Goad you into what? All I'm saying is you need to drop the big tough-guy act. You and Morgan and the rest of his men treat every woman like she's a damsel in distress. But I'm no damsel, okay? I really can take care of myself." She paused impishly. "Then again, I suppose if I *must* have a man protecting me, I could do worse than Jim Morgan. He's sexy as sin, that boss of yours."

Ethan's jaw tightened. "Again with the goddamn goading."

Fine, so maybe she *was* goading him. Juliet wasn't sure why she felt compelled to pick a fight. Maybe it was the impatience. The frustration. The overwhelming grief from knowing her brother was gone. Whatever the reason, she couldn't seem to stop the next taunt that flew out of her mouth.

"Hey, don't get all prickly, kiddo. I'm simply commenting on the fact that Morgan is sexy. Maybe I should give him a call when this is over, see if he's interested in a little romp between the sheets—"

"Don't fucking test me," Ethan growled.

In the blink of an eye, she found herself on the other side of the room, pushed up against the wall with Ethan's hard thigh between her legs to trap her in place.

Her breath caught, pulse sped up. He'd moved so quickly she hadn't had time to react, but even though she was kicking herself at being unprepared for his stealth attack, she still managed to cock a defiant brow. "A tantrum. How cute. Are you done?"

"Not by a long shot."

One warm male hand clutched her waist, while the other gripped her chin with such force she actually experienced a pang of trepidation.

"I know what you see when you look at me. The boy next door, nice and sweet and harmless." Ethan's voice lowered to a deadly pitch. "You see me and you think I'm the guy who'll make love to you in a room full of flowers and candlelight. You picture sweet, sweet kisses and oh so tender caresses—isn't that right, Juliet?"

Her heart began to pound, a sharp staccato that

pulsed in her blood and drowned out her thoughts. The look on Ethan's face was terrifying. Thrilling. His hazel eyes gleamed with raw heat. Unadulterated *danger*.

"Well, think again, sweetheart. I'm not a fucking pussycat. And I'm not a fucking kid."

Juliet was so aroused, she couldn't breathe. "Who are you, then?"

"A man." He rotated his hips, grinding his pelvis into hers. "Feel that?"

Oh . . . *God*. He was long, thick, and hard.

"That's right. I'm a man." His chuckle was downright mocking. "What was it you said before? That I can't give you what you need in the bedroom? Well, I beg to differ, sweetheart. I beg to fucking differ."

Juliet still couldn't draw a breath. All she could do was stare into those hypnotic eyes.

"What, no response?" he taunted. "No sassy comeback?"

Before she could say a solitary word, his mouth came crashing down on hers in a hard kiss that made her gasp.

His lips were merciless, his tongue demanding entrance. Her lips parted of their own volition and then that tongue was diving into her mouth and teasing the living daylights out of her.

Juliet couldn't control herself—she kissed him back. Her arms wrapped around his neck, her lower body strained to get closer to his. She couldn't remember the last time a kiss had set her body on fire this way. Every inch of her burned, every muscle tight with anticipation.

He drove the kiss even deeper, his hands sliding down to cup her ass so he could yank her against him. The moment she felt that spectacular erection pressing against her stomach, she moaned and rocked into him. Needing more. *Craving* more.

For a solid minute, his tongue filled her mouth, exploring, claiming. And then in another blink of the eye, it was gone. He'd taken a step back, breaking the contact and leaving her with a feeling of pure desperation.

He laughed when he noticed her expression. "You want me to fuck you, don't you?"

She didn't give him the satisfaction of admitting he was right. Her eyes and body had already betrayed her anyway.

Ethan looked mighty pleased with himself as he crossed his arms over his broad chest. "Sorry, sweetheart. It's not going to happen."

"Why the hell not?" she found herself demanding.

"Well, I could blame it on your staunch declaration about how you're never going to have sex with me, but we both know you were lying through your teeth. And anyway, I'm nothing if not honest, so . . ." He looked very, very smug now. "I'll have you know that I don't put out on the first date."

Juliet stared at him for a moment.

Then she burst out laughing.

Shit, this was priceless. The man had just destroyed her with his kiss, turned her into a puddle of mush at his feet, and then he went and threw a gentleman curveball at her.

Still laughing, she gestured to the drab hotel room. "You consider this a date?"

"We just came back from having drinks and sharing a dance." He shrugged. "That's probably as close to a date as we're ever gonna get."

Her head was still light and gooey from that body-numbing kiss, but she managed to voice another question. "Out of curiosity, what do you do on the *second* date?"

The grin he shot her melted her insides. "I subscribe to baseball rules, of course. First, second, third, and then I screw your brains out."

Damned if her sex didn't clench at the thought.

He must have sensed the erotic response, because his eyes darkened with sensual promise. "Don't worry, Juliet. We'll get there."

She wanted to deny it. To tell him he was a million kinds of arrogant and fucked-up if he thought she would hop into bed with him just because she'd happened to enjoy one measly kiss.

But the denial stayed lodged in her throat.

"Anyway, where's your laptop?" Ethan said pleasantly. "Let's see what Paige sent us."

As he stalked over to her bag in search of her computer, she stood there in slight disbelief, torn between kicking him and ripping his clothes off.

The uncontrollable pounding of her heart and the persistent throb low in her belly confirmed what she'd already known—it was always the unassuming ones you had to worry about.

Chapter 7

It took sheer power of will on Ethan's part to ignore the overpowering lust sizzling in his body. As Juliet logged into her secure e-mail and downloaded the attachments from Paige and Sean, he took several deep breaths and ordered his erection to subside. Which was difficult, especially since Juliet had just slipped out of her long-sleeved shirt, leaving her in a tight black tank top that hugged her full breasts.

When his gaze landed on the cluster of nautical stars tattooed on her upper arms, another ripple of desire washed over him. The tattoos were tiny, done only in black ink, and they gave her a sexy, badass vibe that at the same time managed to look feminine.

Christ, he wanted this woman. She intrigued him to no end, and the arousal she evoked in him was like nothing he'd ever experienced. It hadn't been like this with the girl he'd been dating in Costa Rica. They'd gone out for dinner, took a couple midnight strolls on the beach, slept together a few times—but not once had he thought he might pass out from raw need, or ached to get a glimpse into her soul the way he did when it came to Juliet Mason.

She was different. Special. A mystery he wanted to solve with a steely exterior he wanted to conquer.

"Okay," Juliet announced a moment later. "We've got dossiers on the nine targets Grechko already hit." Her dark eyes focused intently on the screen. "Huh. This is weird."

"What is it?" he said sharply, joining her on the edge of the bed.

"These three—Pavel Drygin, Grigory Novik, and Irina Bartney—were killed in a series of car bombings back in May, within a day or two of each other. They were all connected to members of the House of Representatives, and, according to the news clipping Paige attached, their deaths were blamed on the PRF."

Something clicked in Ethan's brain. "You're right. I remember seeing it on the news. The PRF leader actually came forward and took responsibility for the bombings."

Since Ethan made it a priority to be aware of whatever current threats were out there in the world, he was familiar with the PRF and knew the basics about the movement. The People's Revolutionary Front was a terrorist group that had been wreaking havoc on Belarus for several years now. They were staunchly opposed to the current government and disgusted with the corruption that ran rampant among its officials. When the PRF first cropped up years ago, they'd taken a strictly nonviolent approach, but they'd drastically changed their MO since then, which didn't surprise him.

Maybe he was being overly cynical, but if peaceful protests actually produced results, God knew he and his team would probably be out of work.

But why had the PRF taken the blame for the car bombings when Grechko was actually the one who'd carried them out? Was Orlov in bed with a terrorist group?

"What about the other six targets?" he asked, peering over her shoulder to glance at the computer screen.

Juliet scrolled through the files. "Four were straight-up executions, and two were killed from dirty bombs. The bombs were detonated at public events, so there were quite a lot of casualties. Oh, check this out—according to Paige's cover sheet, all the targets were either relatives or romantic partners of government officials. We've got two wives of members of the prime. minister's cabinet. Two were the children of a couple deputy ministers, one was the brother of a council member, and we already know Zoya's father works for the Ministry of Justice." She paused. "And look at this—all the government officials involved are rumored to be buddy-buddy with Orlov."

"So he's ordering hits on people that are important to his friends?" Ethan wrinkled his forehead. "That's messed up. Why the hell would he do that?"

"It gets even more messed up. According to Paige, all nine hits were attributed to the PRF. Apparently the government has been in an uproar this past year. Orlov gave several press conferences, vowing to put an end to these homegrown terrorists and to bring justice to the colleagues who have lost loved ones."

"Who are the three targets Grechko didn't get to?"

She opened up the final three dossiers. "Yuri Kozlov, the younger brother of a Supreme Court judge. Alisa Baronova—she's the wife of some cabinet member who's friends with Orlov. And Anastacia Karin. Oh shit.

That's the prime minister's daughter. She's only fifteen years old."

Ethan cursed in disbelief. "He's planning on killing a kid?"

"Looks like it." Juliet brought up Paige's e-mail again and skimmed through her colleague's notes. "Hmmm. Here's something interesting."

Ethan leaned in closer and began reading over her shoulder, momentarily distracted by her intoxicating scent. She smelled so damn good, like roses and honey. He breathed her in, fighting the urge to pull her into his arms again and kiss her senseless.

"So Orlov is a potential candidate for the presidency in the next election," Ethan said as he scanned the e-mail, forcing his brain to focus. "He's considered the main opposition to President Belikov. And these men—Drygin, Kozlov, Harkov, Baronova, Karin, and the others—they all supported Orlov when he was moving up in the ranks. Karin is actually the one who advised Belikov to approve Orlov's appointment into the Council of Ministers."

"Okay, so these dudes had Orlov's back during his entire rise to power, but . . ." Juliet read the last paragraph on the screen, then summarized Paige's thoughts. "But they stood by and did nothing while his son got blown up by the rebels."

He frowned. "It says here Sergei Orlov was an unfortunate casualty in a random street bombing. The rebels didn't target him directly. And Orlov's buddies couldn't have foreseen it."

"No, but they didn't do a thing to try to crush the PRF movement. All the officials on this list are big on nonviolence and negotiation, while Orlov has always taken a stance about using military action to deal with the rebels." Juliet shrugged. "Maybe he blames his colleagues for not letting him have a firmer grip on the situation."

"So this is vengeance, pure and simple? 'I lost my son, so now you're going to lose the people *you* care about'?"

"Maybe." She chewed on her lower lip. "But then why blame the hits on the People's Revolutionary Front?"

"That's the story being fed to the public. We don't know what's being said behind closed doors. For all we know, Orlov secretly confessed to each one of his buddies and said 'Payback, bitches.'"

Juliet had to laugh. "That's a good point. And what are they gonna do, have him arrested? No, they'd cover it up. Same way they cover everything else up. Orlov's not the first corrupt politician in this government. Seems like the entire country is rife with corruption, starting at the lowest levels and going all the way up to the top. President Belikov is no saint either. Look at all the restrictions he's placed on civil rights, the media, religion. The PRF exists for a reason."

"True," Ethan agreed. "But Belikov isn't going around killing innocent people because of a personal vendetta."

"We don't know if that's what Orlov is doing," Juliet countered.

"I'm not sure his motive even matters at this point. Whatever his reasons, he still hired Grechko to kill for him, and there are three targets left." Ethan cursed again. "The prime minister's daughter. Jesus. We need to find these people, on the double."

"On the double? Did you pick up that adorable phrase in the army?"

He scowled at her. "The Marines."

"Oh, right. I forgot how much you guys hate being mixed up. What's the difference anyway? Army, navy, frogmen, jarheads. You're all fighting for the same damn thing."

"One day I'm going to sit you down and explain why there is a *major* difference between a jarhead and a squid," Ethan said sternly. "But for now, we need a plan of action. Pull up those three files again."

She moved her fingers over the laptop's touch pad and brought the documents up on the screen.

"Okay, so according to Reilly's research, Karin's daughter is currently here in the city. So is Alisa Baronova."

Ethan leaned in again, the movement causing his shoulder to brush hers. His arm started tingling from the contact, and he knew Juliet was equally affected, because her breath hitched slightly.

"Everything okay?" he said mockingly.

Her profile tensed. "Why wouldn't it be?"

"No reason." Swallowing a chuckle, he glanced at the screen. "Anyway, according to Reilly's sources, the third target, Yuri Kozlov, is vacationing in Spain at the moment. Do you think Orlov has people there, monitoring the guy?"

"We have to assume yes. I don't know if he's using government agents or private thugs, but I'm sure he reassigned men to all three targets."

"Know anyone in Spain?"

"Currently active, no. But I'll make some calls."

"D is off rotation. I can see if he's up for the job. The guy hates being inactive, so he might feel like playing bodyguard."

He didn't miss the reluctance on her face. "What is it?" he said suspiciously.

"I don't want to involve anyone else. I prefer working alone."

"Gee, does that mean you're capable of being in two places at once? That's amazing!"

His sarcasm made her scowl.

"We need eyes and ears in Spain," Ethan said firmly. "Either it's D or you can try contacting Noelle again. I assume you're okay with *her* coming on board?"

Juliet seemed to be gritting her teeth. "Fine. Call D. But you're right—I'd prefer Noelle over him. I'll call her again. Maybe she'll finally get back to me."

Without another word, they both reached for their phones.

Chapter 8

The stunning blonde turned every head in the dimly lit room as she sauntered through San Juan's most exclusive gentlemen's lounge. The club didn't require memberships, but there was an unspoken rule that only the city's wealthy elite were welcome, and it was the job of the bouncers at the door to vet each visitor before allowing him entry.

This particular visitor had been admitted without a second's thought. It hadn't mattered to the guards whether she was filthy rich or dirt-poor. With looks like that, she would delight the male patrons taking up residence in the lounge's interior—and she certainly did.

Noelle had made a painstaking effort to look like utter perfection tonight. Her golden hair cascaded down her back in waves that shone beneath the yellow glow of the old-fashioned light fixtures. Her face was flawless, boasting just enough makeup to emphasize her high cheekbones, wide-set blue eyes, and naturally red lips. The crimson dress she'd chosen molded to her body like a glove, showing off her tucked-in waist, full breasts, and perfectly shaped ass. Black stilettos were the final touch, adding four inches to her petite frame and making her tanned, shapely legs appear endless.

Every man in her vicinity was drooling. Some had completely ignored their companions to ogle the blond beauty in their midst. Others had abandoned important business discussions just to stare.

Hiding a smile, Noelle crossed the dark-stained hardwood floor toward the bar area, paying no attention to the appreciative looks and leering smiles of the various men seated on the lounge's velvet couches and secluded tables.

She stopped beside one of the tall-backed stools at the counter, making even the art of sitting down look like a sensual act. No sooner had her ass made contact with the plush seat than the bartender raced over, his mouth agape as he greeted the beautiful newcomer.

"Good evening. Uh—" He cleared his throat, regaining his composure. "Might I offer the lady something to drink?"

"A vodka cranberry, please," she said demurely, all the while dreading having to choke down that sweet concoction. She was a straight-whiskey girl, no fruity bullshit for her.

"Coming right up." He practically sprinted to the other end of the bar to prepare her drink.

Noelle kept her back to the room as she waited for her cocktail. She'd already done a visual sweep and knew precisely where her target was situated. She'd also pinpointed the locations of four Secret Service agents—one behind the target, the other three scattered around the lounge.

"Here you go. One vodka cranberry." The bartender set the glass in front of her as if he were presenting her with a juicy Thanksgiving turkey.

"Thank you," she purred.

He made no move to walk away. His gaze was glued to her ample cleavage.

Noelle batted her eyelashes. "Could I trouble you for a favor?"

"Anything!" He flushed. "I mean, I'll try my best to accommodate you."

"I'm feeling rather chilly. Is there any way you can arrange for a table near the fireplace?"

His eyes left her breasts and moved beyond her shoulders. She knew his gaze was registering that all three tables near the enormous electric fireplace were occupied.

"Let me see what I can do," he blurted out.

The man disappeared so fast it was as if he'd gone up in a puff of smoke. Noelle hid a smile and kept her back turned. It wasn't long before she heard the outraged protests of the two women who'd been seated at one of the tables Noelle had coveted.

A minute later, the uniformed bartender raced back to her with a triumphant smile. "Right this way, miss."

He extended his arm and she took it willingly, allowing him to lead her to the now-empty table directly adjacent to her target. On the way, the bartender nodded at a heavyset man in a tailored suit, who nodded back in visible approval. Clearly the barkeep's manager wholly approved of his employee's course of action in banishing the two floozies and placing a goddess in their stead.

The bartender scurried off after she'd been seated,

then returned a moment later with her drink and a broad smile. "Please don't hesitate to signal me if you require anything else."

"Thank you. You've been so very kind."

He dashed back to the bar, his admiring gaze still fixed on her as he settled behind the counter once more. Crossing her legs, Noelle sipped her drink and pretended to get lost in thought, all the while completely aware of the man at the neighboring table.

He wore an Armani suit that fit his toned physique to a T, an expensive Cartier watch, and a diamond pinkie ring. The bling certainly didn't back up his denials about taking bribes from every shady criminal on the island.

With men like Hector Alvarez at the reins, it was no wonder that Puerto Rico was quickly becoming the United States' most politically corrupt jurisdiction. It was also no wonder that certain people in the government had grown tired of the senator's clandestine activities and wanted him removed.

"Can I buy you a drink?" a raspy voice asked in Spanish.

Noelle spared a cursory look at the man who'd approached her, then offered a cool smile and replied in the same tongue. "No, thank you. As you can see, I already have one." She gestured to her full glass.

"Fine. Then let's drink together." He held up his nearly empty tumbler, a leering glint in his coal black eyes.

A man like him didn't belong in a tasteful place like this. He wore a black suit that screamed *thug,* and had a very visible tattoo peeking out of his shirt collar and dark stubble slashing his strong jaw.

"No, thank you," she said again. "I'm meeting someone."

The interloper shrugged. "I'll wait with you until he gets here."

"No. Thank. You."

"What's a matter, baby? Too good to have a drink with li'l ole me?"

The mocking tone irked her. "Please don't make me call the manager over."

He stumbled closer, clearly inebriated. "Relax, baby. All I wanna do is have a fucking drink with you. You don't have to get all high and mighty about—"

"Is everything all right?"

A second shadow fell over the table as Hector Alvarez came up beside her persistent suitor.

"I'm afraid this gentleman doesn't understand the meaning of the word *no*," Noelle murmured, pretending to be flustered.

Alvarez's lips tightened as he gave the other man a perfunctory once-over. "Leave," he said simply.

The black-eyed man laughed harshly. "Fuck off. This is between me and the lady."

Out of nowhere, two suit-clad men stepped into view, their deadly expressions leaving no doubt that they meant business.

"Leave," Alvarez repeated. "Otherwise my bodyguards will escort you out."

"Bodyguards?" the man scoffed. "Who the fuck are you, the president?"

A smug smile stretched across Alvarez's face. "You have three seconds to exit this establishment before I have you thrown out."

The two men locked eyes, a thick cloud of menace hanging between them. After a beat, the dark-eyed man shrugged and took a step back. "Fine. Fuck this. I don't need this shit."

As he staggered off without looking back, Noelle exhaled in relief.

"I appreciate what you did just now." She peered up at Alvarez, blue eyes shining with gratitude. "I was afraid that brute was about to cause a scene."

"It was my pleasure," the senator said smoothly. His brown eyes roamed her body freely, clearly liking what they saw. "I will have to speak to Carlos. This establishment should take better care to leave vermin like that out on the street, where they belong."

"I wholeheartedly agree," she said shyly. "Thank you so much for getting rid of him."

"Again, it was my pleasure." His gaze took on a shrewd gleam. "I will leave you now. I overheard you saying you were waiting for someone."

"That was a lie," she blurted out, then blushed as if she'd said too much.

"Ah. I see." The smile returned to his face, predatory now. "In that case, would you like to join me for a drink?"

Derek "D" Pratt was naked on the bed when Noelle strode into her hotel room an hour later. As always, her gaze ate up his big warrior body—tanned skin, muscles that may as well have been chiseled out of marble, and a long, thick cock that hardened the moment she walked in.

"All done?" he rasped, his charcoal eyes meeting hers.

"All done. Alvarez will be officially out of commission in about ten hours. That poor soul. Much too young to drop dead from a sudden heart attack."

D propped his tattooed arms behind his head. "Killing from a distance, huh? You're a coward, baby. Should have manned up and put a bullet in his head."

"So his guards could pump me full of lead? Sorry, *baby*. I wasn't in the mood to die tonight. I value my life over my ego." She shrugged. "Sometimes killing by remote control is tidier and less destructive than a bullet."

"Whatever you say." His large hand drifted down to his groin, long fingers encircling his shaft. "I want to fuck. Come here and ride me."

Noelle couldn't help but grin. D never beat around the bush when it came to his needs. She appreciated that, because she was the same way. Why dillydally or dance around an issue? The blunt approach saved time and got the job done just as efficiently.

"Thanks for the assist, by the way." She unzipped her red dress and let it fall to the carpeted floor. "You played a pretty good drunk."

D glanced at her in surprise. "Did you really just thank me?"

With another shrug, she sauntered naked to the bed and climbed right onto his lap. The heat of his thighs warmed her ass and teased her bare flesh, instantly sending her arousal levels skyrocketing.

"I was able to get close to him because of you," she replied, "so, yes, I really just thanked you. Of course, I could have done it without you—"

"Of course," he said dryly.

"But you helped speed up the process."

She reached for the nightstand and grabbed a condom from the top drawer. The move caused her torso to drape over his, her nipples rubbing against the wiry hairs on his broad chest.

With a low growl, D shoved his hands between their chests and squeezed her breasts. Hard. The man didn't possess an ounce of tenderness, but she didn't care. She liked how rough he was. It just served as a reminder of who she was in bed with.

He continued to fondle her breasts as she rolled the condom onto his shaft. His mouth closed over her nipple at the same time she impaled herself on his cock.

They both groaned, D releasing her breast as his eyelids fluttered closed. He never looked her in the eye when they fucked, never kissed her either, but she was okay with that too. It gave her the opportunity to study his face, those startlingly handsome features that didn't relax even when his body told her he was receiving pleasure from the exchange.

Those black eyes suddenly snapped open. "Stop staring at me and move faster."

She laughed. "Give me some incentive."

Smirking, he brought his hand between her legs and rubbed her clit with his thumb. "How's that?" he drawled.

"Perfect." Little pinpricks of pleasure traveled over her flesh, converging into a hot, pulsing ache deep in her core.

She lifted herself up, then slammed down on his cock, launching into a fast, relentless rhythm that left them both breathless. Just when she felt the first ripples of release, D flipped her over and rammed into her with so much force the orgasm didn't just wash over her, it exploded inside her as if a bomb had been detonated.

She shuddered, black spots dancing in front of her eyes. And when her vision cleared up, she discovered that for the first time since they'd started sleeping together, D was actually looking her in the eye.

Smug. Amused. Cynical.

"Enjoy that?" he mocked.

It took a moment to regain her breath, lingering pleasure still rippling through her body. "Fuck, yes."

His hips retreated, then thrust again. "I aim to please." And then he resumed the merciless pace, slamming into her over and over again, until finally he grunted and went still, his muscular body crushing hers as he climaxed.

Afterward, they lay on their backs with an inch of space between them. They didn't cuddle, didn't gush about how amazing the sex had been. Their arrangement was purely physical, and Noelle was perfectly content with that. Relationships didn't interest her. Neither did friendship. D was nothing more than an outlet for letting off steam, and one she made good use of whenever their paths happened to cross.

"How long are you sticking around?" she asked absently, reaching for the pack of cigarettes on the nightstand.

He answered in a brusque tone. "I've got a couple weeks off."

"Mandatory, right?" She spoke with an edge now. "Jim runs a tight ship."

"I wondered how long it would take for you to bring him up." D chuckled. "Would you like me to tell you everything he's been up to this past year?"

She ignored his sarcasm and lit up a cigarette, exhaling a cloud of smoke up at the ceiling. "No need. I already know."

"That's right. You keep tabs on him. I forgot."

"I keep tabs on everyone." She paused meaningfully. "Including you."

"Yeah, but I'm sure your file on Morgan takes number-one priority. Then again, considering your past, it makes sense."

Noelle stiffened. "I thought we agreed we don't discuss each other's pasts."

"We don't. I was just making an observation."

"Well, keep your observations to yourself, honey. I'm not interested in them."

In fact, she wasn't at all interested in discussing Jim Morgan with D. Her hatred for the man's boss was no big secret, but the reasons for that hatred and the events that led to it? Those were nobody's business but her own. She knew D's background meant he had connections, which he'd clearly used in order to dig into *her* background, but some things were better left unspoken.

Besides, talking about Jim was a major buzzkill. Guaranteed to squash any arousal she might be feeling.

"Where are you heading to next?" D asked in that gravelly voice of his.

She twisted her head to shoot him a sardonic look, then took another drag of her cigarette. "Why, you interested in tagging along?"

"Maybe."

"You like fucking me that much, huh?"

"You're an all right lay, I guess."

She bristled. "Firstly, I am a phenomenal lay. Secondly, fuck you. And thirdly, if I'm so mediocre in the sack, then why the hell are you here?"

D surprised her by actually answering the question. "Because I like what we've got going on. No strings, no expectations." He paused. "We're the same, you and I."

"What are you, a Batman villain? 'We're the same, you and I.'"

"That's the reason this works so well," he went on. "Because we're both fucked-up, emotionless assholes who never drop our guard and who don't foolishly believe in happily ever after."

"The perfect match," she said ironically.

The vibration of her cell phone interrupted the cynical exchange. Good. The cell had finished charging. She'd gone dark for her last job and hadn't needed the phone, and when she'd finally turned it on once she'd finished up the assignment, she'd discovered that the battery had died on her. And now that it was working again, the display showed a dozen outstanding messages.

"It rang right before you got here," D told her. "I didn't bother checking who was calling."

Sitting up, Noelle extinguished her smoke in the ashtray. She scrolled through the call history and discovered that Juliet had phoned several times over the past week. Frowning, she punched the code for her voice mail and played each message, her emotions going from alarmed to relieved to annoyed.

Next to her, D had grabbed his phone to check his own messages, and similar annoyance creased his forehead as he listened.

"Juliet's in a jam," Noelle said after she disconnected.

D let out a breath. "I know. I just got a message from the rookie—he's with her. He wants me to go to Madrid to watch some dude's ass."

"Funny, Juliet requested the same thing of me."

She didn't bother hiding her exasperation. Christ, maybe she was becoming soft—that was the only explanation she could come up with for why her girls kept begging for help with all these bothersome side gigs. Once she'd become in high demand and the jobs were too numerous for one woman to handle, she'd spent years tracking down and recruiting the perfect operatives to make up her deadly team. She'd chosen only women who met a specific criteria. Women with no ties, no loyalties, and, if possible, no consciences.

For the most part, she'd succeeded. Paige and Bailey had never disappointed her, and both were capable of killing without remorse and staying focused on the objective. Isabel had always been too compassionate for her own good, but Noelle had never intended for the woman to be a killer; Isabel's unmatched talent for becoming a different person was what Noelle had wanted from her. But Abby . . . what a waste. She'd thought she'd found a gem in Abby Sinclair, only to watch Abby fall in love, quit, and go to work for her nemesis.

And now Juliet, her other gem, was caught up in a crusade that just happened to involve another one of Jim's soldiers.

Damn that man and his team of do-gooders.

"Let me guess. You're going to tell your girl she's on her own." D sounded very sure of himself as he moved into a sitting position. His defined pecs flexed as he crossed his arms loosely over his bare chest.

"And let me guess. You're going to race to Madrid to do your teammate's bidding."

"Why not? I'm damn bored and I haven't been to Spain in years." He slanted his head. "Feel like tagging along?"

"I can think of better ways to make use of my time." She paused for a beat. "On the other hand, I just made a million bucks for slipping a pill into a slimebag's drink, so . . . What the hell? I guess I can afford to keep you company."

"How magnanimous of you."

"I'll let Juliet know." She smirked and slid her hand down his body, her manicured nails scraping the hard flesh of his chest. "But before I do, there are still a couple things I want to take care of."

Chapter 9

"Dmitry. It is good of you to come."

Orlov smoothed out the front of his suit jacket and lowered himself into the chair opposite Oleg Harkov. The murmur of voices could be heard from beyond the study doors, the soft condolences and quiet sobs of the mourners who'd come to bid farewell to Harkov's daughter.

The idea that the girl's body had been lying in this house for the past three days made Orlov shiver. He had never understood the macabre rituals of the Eastern Orthodox church. Keeping a corpse in one's home for three days before burial? It was preposterous.

Sadly, his wife had been as devout as the Harkov family, so he had plenty of experience with religious zealots. Orlov suspected Diana would turn over in her grave if she knew he'd forgone the silly customs she'd always believed in and sent her cancer-ridden body to a funeral home hours after she'd passed.

"I wanted to come earlier," he told the grieving father, "but I've been busy assembling a task force to deal with this PRF situation once and for all."

Harkov looked up with vacant gray eyes. "The PRF?"

"Those parasites were responsible for murdering your daughter, Oleg."

That got the man's attention. In an instant, his blank expression transformed into one of deep shock. "What are you saying? Have they taken responsibility for what happened to my Zoya?"

"Not officially, but our sources tell us that Mironov and his people were indeed involved."

The shock turned into fury. "Bastards. Each and every one of them." Just as fast, the anger became desperation. "Why did they target my daughter?"

"Why do they target anybody? They are crazy fanatics, Oleg. You and your family are not the only victims of Mironov's evil. Many of our colleagues have suffered losses this year at the hands of the PRF."

Footsteps sounded out in the hall, reminding Orlov that he ought to be leaving soon. He didn't plan on staying for the funeral, which would be held in the small, private cemetery on the Harkov property. The men in attendance would be expected to carry the coffin to the burial site, and Orlov had no intention of taking on that ludicrous task.

"I came here today not only to offer my condolences," he hurried on, "but to assure you that the people who took your daughter from you will be punished." He paused meaningfully. "I know what it's like to lose a child, Oleg. A father never recovers from such a staggering blow." Another pause. "You remember my Sergei, don't you?"

Uneasiness flickered in Harkov's eyes. "Of course I do. Sergei was a wonderful boy, Dmitry."

Orlov swallowed the rush of anger that rose in his throat. A wonderful boy? His son had been destined for greatness. Only ten years old and already ahead of his class, with more intelligence and charm than Oleg Harkov would ever possess in his sorry life.

It was hard to imagine that Orlov had once curried this man's favor. During his political climb, he'd attached himself to anyone who could help his ascension. He'd formed alliances, surrounding himself with people who had power, or those he believed would eventually get it.

Harkov, however, had not reached the top of his ladder. He'd stalled halfway, or maybe he'd simply decided to stop climbing. The man's lack of ambition disgusted Orlov. So did his naïveté about how to run a country. Negotiating with terrorists—as if that approach had ever worked throughout the course of history. With people like Harkov and Belikov and the rest of the sniveling pacifists at the helm, it was no wonder the People's Revolutionary Front was planting bombs all over the country

But Orlov had yet to sever his alliance with Harkov and the others. No, he would need them before this was over.

"I'm afraid I must go now," he said with false regret. "I apologize for not being able to attend the service, but I have a meeting with Belikov's liaison this afternoon."

"I understand. I am honored that you came at all, Dmitry."

He clapped a hand on Harkov's shoulder. "It's the least I can do for such a treasured friend."

Juliet and Ethan got an early start the next morning, making their way down to the front desk long before the eleven-o'clock checkout time.

"D's on board," Ethan reported. His phone had just buzzed and he was studying the screen intently. "He said he's meeting up with Noelle in Madrid. They'll check in once they track down Yuri Kozlov."

Juliet narrowed her eyes. "Why are they teaming up? It's a simple tail. Doesn't require two people."

Ethan shrugged. "It does if the job is twenty-four-hour recon. A person's gotta sleep sometime."

He had a point, and yet Juliet was still troubled by the notion of her boss working alongside Morgan's man. She remembered D from the Monte Carlo job, the brooding, tattooed mercenary with savage black eyes and the personality of a thornbush. He hadn't been a picnic to work with, and she wasn't sure she wanted him involved in this.

There was a reason she worked alone—it meant she was always the one in control, the one who decided the outcome of any given situation. D, however, was a wild card, and she refused to lose her chance for vengeance because of a damn wild card.

Ah, well. She probably didn't have anything to worry about. Chances were, Noelle would find a way to send the guy packing. Juliet's boss liked calling the shots, and since Juliet couldn't imagine D following anybody's orders but Morgan's, Noelle would grow tired of the prickly asshole real fast.

"I figure you and I will take the prime minister's daughter," Ethan went on as they headed for the counter to return their room key. "And Sullivan and Liam agreed to fly in to watch Alisa Baronova. You remember them, right? They worked the Monaco job with us."

Oh, Juliet certainly remembered the dynamic duo.

Sullivan and Liam were equally sexy, equally cocky, and equally deadly. Unlike D, she wouldn't mind having them around one damn bit.

"What's that look for?" Ethan demanded.

She grinned when she discerned his visible displeasure. "What look?"

"You got this . . . *look* . . . when I mentioned Sully and Liam." A dark cloud passed over his handsome face. "Don't even think about hooking up with one of them."

She batted her lashes. "And what if I do? What will you do, rookie—spank me?"

"Again with the goading?"

"You are so touchy," she told him. "And FYI, the whole possessive thing you've got going on? Not a turn-on."

Bullshit, her inner slut taunted.

Oh, fine. So maybe she liked a man who was a tad possessive. Alpha warriors turned her on. So sue her.

"I don't give a damn if you like it or not," Ethan retorted. "And I don't care how attractive you find my teammates. I won't let either one of them touch you."

They reached the desk, and while Ethan handed the key to the expressionless woman sitting behind it, Juliet ran over the day's objective in her mind. The plan was to scope out the prime minister's estate. She was just making a mental note to try to get her hands on Karin's security designs when a familiar face snagged her attention.

The jerk from last night, the one who'd bumped into her and called her sugar tits, had just entered the lobby from outside. Since it was six a.m. and he was looking rather haggard, she suspected he'd stayed out all night. No doubt paying a prostitute to keep him company, seeing as she couldn't imagine any woman willingly spending time with that creep.

As he crossed the carpeted floor, he clicked the key remote in his hand to arm his car alarm, and a honk sounded from the street beyond the lobby doors.

The jerk didn't so much as glance at her and Ethan as he passed them, but he did address the desk clerk with a rude demand to deliver fresh coffee to his suite.

Pompous ass.

"I'll call a taxi to take us to the car-rental place," Ethan said after they'd stepped out into the chilly morning air.

Juliet took her black leather gloves out of her jacket pocket and slipped them on. A thoughtful expression graced her face when she noticed the silver Porsche across the street from the Grenadier. It was parked illegally in a fire route, and she had a sneaking suspicion about who owned the luxury vehicle.

"Nah, I have a better idea," she replied with a faint smile.

Ethan sighed. "Whatever it is, I don't like it."

"Oh, hush. Just trust me." She linked her arm through his and started walking toward the bus shelter ten yards away.

The snow on the sidewalk crunched beneath their boots, their breath escaping in billowing white clouds, but Juliet was too wired to feel the cold. When they reached the deserted bus stop, she flopped down on the metal bench and unzipped her duffel to retrieve her laptop case.

"Do me a favor," she told Ethan. "Read me the license plate number of that Porsche."

He stared at her, incredulous. "You can't be serious. Are you planning on stealing that car?"

"Maybe."

"No way."

"Aw, come on. It'll be fun."

"Are you out of your mind? We're not stealing a car."

"But it belongs to Mr. Sugar Tits," she protested. "Don't tell me the thought of boosting that asshole's car doesn't make you all giddy."

Ethan pursed his lips. "You're right. Totally makes me giddy."

She broke out in a smile. "Permission to continue?"

"Permission granted," he said grudgingly.

"What's the license plate?" She was already opening her laptop and loading the necessary software.

Ethan recited the plate number, and a second later Juliet was hard at work. Fingers flying over the keyboard, commands and codes flashing across the screen.

"C'mon," she mumbled, then cursed when an error message popped up.

"What exactly are you doing?"

"Accessing the car's computer system."

"You can actually do that?"

"Yup. Gotta love keyless entry, huh?"

"But . . . how?"

She maneuvered through the software, slightly distracted as she rattled off a quick explanation. "Any vehicle that relies on software to provide security can be circumvented by other software. Which means that any idiot with a laptop and the right program can wirelessly break into a vehicle's computer, unlock the doors, and start the engine. With only a few keystrokes, no less." She looked at him and rolled her eyes. "Car theft has come a long way since the old hot-wiring days."

"I still don't believe that you can simply log into some program and—"

Purrrrr.

The roar of an engine coming to life brought another smile to her lips and sent Ethan's jaw to the ground.

"Son of a bitch," he muttered.

Juliet shut the laptop but shoved a pen between the cover and keyboard so it didn't close fully—she needed the software to keep running. Then she tucked the computer in its case and got to her feet.

On the other side of the street, the Porsche continued to purr, as if trying to lure them toward it.

"Hold on, kitten. We're coming," she murmured.

Next to her, Ethan was now laughing softly. He fell into step with her as they crossed the slush-ridden street. Very few people were up and about, and nobody paid them any attention as they made their way to the expensive sports car.

Juliet spared a quick glance at the Grenadier, then approached the driver's side of the sleek silver machine. The car's plate number had been registered to a Mr. Ivan Gorbenko. Ha. Maybe Gorbenko would now think twice before the words *sugar tits* left that arrogant mouth of his.

As she reached for the door handle, her heart pounded, a familiar *thump-thump* that drummed in her ears and reminded her of that rainy night in Chicago when she'd stolen her very first car. Didn't matter how many times she'd done it since. Each boost always felt like the first.

Taking a breath, Juliet pulled on the handle. The door opened easily, and the engine continued to hum, causing the pavement beneath her boots to vibrate.

"We're good," she announced before sliding into the pristine leather interior of the Porsche.

The passenger's door opened and Ethan settled in beside her. He twisted around to toss their gear in the backseat, then turned to look at her, his hazel eyes twinkling with amusement.

"You are scarily good at this."

She shrugged. "What, boosting cars? Easy peasy lemon squeezy."

He threw his head back and laughed. "You're really something—you know that?"

"Duh. Why do you think I have men falling at my feet?" She pressed her right foot on the gas pedal and sped away from the curb, then let out a dreamy sigh. "Lord, this car handles like a dream."

It had been a while since she'd driven such a powerful machine, and she was loving every second of it as she smoothly switched into third gear and left the Grenadier and Gorbenko in their proverbial dust.

"Seriously, though, how did you get so good at this shit?" Ethan asked.

"Practice."

"C'mon, tell me how you became a master thief. The curiosity is killing me."

She rolled her eyes, but when she saw his face, she realized he was actually being sincere. "You want to trade life stories? Is that it?"

He flashed her that boyish smile. "Yep."

She was starting to suspect he did that deliberately.

Offered a cute, disarming smile in a calculated attempt to get his way.

"C'mon," he said again, coaxing her with his sexy, husky voice. "Indulge me."

Ethan knew he was chipping away at Juliet's defenses — he'd noticed the change in her ever since yesterday's mind-blowing kiss. She was less guarded around him, which was made obvious by her willingness to talk about herself now.

"Fine, I'll tell you all about it." She tossed her long, dark hair over her shoulder, keeping her eyes on the road. "Consider this Juliet 101."

"I'll make sure to take thorough notes," he said with a grin.

"You want to know how I started boosting cars, huh? It's pretty straightforward. I was fifteen years old and living on the streets. I had to eat."

"So you just woke up one day and decided to steal a car to pay for food?"

"Nah, I started out smaller than that. Panhandling, running cons to score some cash. But then I met this guy who had a sweet deal going with a couple of the chop shops in the city." She shifted gears and slowed down to get on the highway ramp. "The two of us became friends, and I tagged along with him on a few jobs. He taught me how to hot-wire, how to jimmy a car open, how to use certain software to break into those early keyless systems. Eventually he introduced me to the guys he boosted cars for, and they decided to give me a shot."

"They didn't care that you were just a kid?"

"They preferred it that way. Hardly anyone over eighteen worked for them. That way, if one of their boosters got busted, they'd be tried as minors, and usually you'd get off with a slap on the wrist." Bitterness crept into her voice. "Not me, though. I was hauled off to juvie."

His brows shot up. "You got caught?"

"One of the other boosters sold me out," she muttered. "Left me hanging out to dry in order to save his sorry ass. And since I used to be a belligerent bitch—"

"*Used* to be?"

"Fine, still am. But yeah, I foolishly mouthed off to the cops, and they slapped the cuffs on me." She switched gears again to zoom ahead of a slow-moving van, then reassumed the posted speed limit.

She was smart, Ethan noted. She followed each and every traffic law, knowing not to attract unwanted attention when driving a stolen car, which he appreciated.

In fact, he appreciated a lot of things about Juliet Mason. Her sharp intelligence. Her fearlessness. Her smoking-hot body . . .

Yeah, he definitely held *that* particular attribute in high regard.

Shit, he was getting hard again. Seemed like he couldn't control himself around her. He was dying to kiss her again, to feel her lush lips pressed against his and her warm tongue delving into his mouth, but he hadn't been kidding about taking things slow. He preferred getting to know a woman before he tore her clothes off.

"I spent a year in juvie," Juliet continued in a matter-of-fact tone. "It actually wasn't too bad. I met some interesting girls—my roommate was the most talented pickpocket I've ever met, even to this day. She taught me a few tricks. And this other girl could forge any signature she saw—that was a fun tutorial too. Anyway, I got out just before I turned eighteen, my juvenile record was sealed, and I decided to go straight."

He snickered. "How long did that last?"

She sighed. "A few months. Truth is, I loved the rush I got from stealing."

"I'm sure the innocent people you stole from would be happy to hear you got a rush out of it," he said sarcastically.

"Nah, I'd developed somewhat of a conscience by then," she admitted. "Before I got busted, I didn't care who I stole from. I boosted cars because my survival depended on it. But once I made a conscious choice to steal for a living, I developed a code, kind of like a list of rules I forced myself to follow. Number one on the list was never to steal from anyone who didn't deserve it."

"A thief with a moral code." Ethan laughed. "Why do I get the feeling you didn't come up with that idea all by yourself?"

"Fine," she grumbled. "Henry might have had something to do with it. He knew about the cars, but once he realized I was staying in the game, he made me promise not to take advantage of good people. I kept that promise, for the most part. And once I moved away from cars and graduated to other types of merchandise, I didn't exactly need to worry about hurting innocents. When you're dealing in jewels or art or corporate secrets, you usually find that the people you're stealing from are bigger criminals than you are."

"Jewels, art, and corporate secrets," he echoed, oddly impressed. "You really did move on to bigger scores."

"I'm nothing if not ambitious."

She laughed, and the melodic sound washed over him like a sultry summer breeze. Her laugh was damn contagious, so carefree and full of life.

"Anyway, I moved around after that, chasing the next big score. I made a lot of valuable contacts, developed a reputation for being the person to call if you wanted to acquire something important." Her voice became wry. "Alas, I got too ambitious. It wasn't about the money for me—I had plenty of it by then. It was about the thrill, the challenge of breaking into a place that people considered impenetrable, or stealing something that was rumored to be unstealable. Eventually I caught the attention of Interpol, so I had to pull a disappearing act. That's when I crossed paths with Noelle."

"And went from thief to assassin." He frowned. "It doesn't bother you, killing for a living?"

"I've got a code, remember? I only eliminate bad guys."

Ethan grew thoughtful. He was unbelievably intrigued by this woman. Sometimes he forgot how deadly she was, probably because her beauty distracted him from the fact that she killed people for a living.

And yet he knew there had to be more to her than that.

"So, what do you do for fun?" he asked. "You know, when you're not robbing someone blind or blowing his head off."

She grinned. "I do whatever gets my blood flowing. Skydiving, bungee jumping, zip-lining. A few years ago I pretended to be an Italian heiress just for the hell of it, and hooked up with this rich playboy who was into yacht racing. He let me crew for him when he ran the Newport

Bermuda Race. It was awesome. And after I left Monaco last year I took a couple of weeks off and went on a safari. I had a blast. Have you ever seen a lion up close? Those things are freaking terrifying."

The excitement in her voice made him laugh. "You lead an exciting life," he teased.

"Ha, and you don't, Mr. Globe-Trotting Mercenary?"

"True," he conceded. "But when I'm off rotation, I don't do anything nearly as exciting as what you described. I usually just hang around the compound. Shoot pool with the guys, poker games, target practice."

"Bo-ring. Clearly I need to take you under my wing, rookie. We'll go BASE jumping off Everest sometime."

He burst out laughing again. "Most people want to climb Everest, and you want to jump off it."

"Bigger thrill," she answered with a shrug.

It didn't surprise him that she viewed it that way. He also wasn't surprised to discover that Juliet was a daredevil.

But that wasn't enough. He needed to know more. Needed to stockpile every last detail he could about her, like a squirrel storing food for the winter. Because who knew when he'd get her to open up again?

Unfortunately, they were nearing their destination, prompting Juliet to snap into business mode.

"Anastacia lives with her father, but she's not homeschooled. Paige said the kid attends a superwealthy private school not far from the house."

House ended up being a complete understatement. Ethan couldn't believe his eyes when the prime minister's palatial estate came into view. The property behind the tall, wrought-iron gate was unbelievable, set on acres of open land with endless gardens that looked impressive even when covered in snow. The baroque-style architecture of the main house was breathtaking, consisting of a central building with two enormous wings, and a large courtyard enclosed by a stunning colonnade.

Despite the estate's sheer beauty, Ethan immediately saw the problem it posed for them. No other houses for miles on either side of the estate, and so much open land it would be impossible to find a place to hunker down without being spotted. Unless they parked right in front of the massive gates, there was nowhere for them to covertly observe the house.

"Shit," Juliet murmured.

"My thoughts exactly."

She startled him by pulling onto the shoulder of the road mere yards from the gate, flicking on the emergency blinkers as she parked the Porsche.

"What are you doing?"

She seemed to be chewing on the inside of her cheek. "Thinking. Bring up Google Maps on your iPhone. If one of the guards in the security booth comes out to investigate, we'll say we're lost. Pretend we're heading north to Vitebsk or something."

Ethan did as she asked, all the while studying her face. "There's no way we can stake out this place without being detected."

"I know." She paused. "We need to bug the house."

A laugh popped out. "Good one."

"It's the only way. If we don't have eyes on the house, we need to at least try to get ears inside of it."

"And how do you propose we do that?" His gaze drifted back to the Karin property. "Paige said Karin's staff and secret service agents live on the estate. Breaking in would be a suicide mission."

She let out an annoyed curse. "I agree."

"But Anastacia has to go to school," he said slowly. "We can follow her every morning, watch her at school, and follow her home every night."

"You think the wealthy private school her daddy sends her to will be any less guarded?" Juliet shook her head in frustration. "No. We can still tail her to and from school, but we need to bug that house, damn it."

Ethan knew she was right. If they wanted to keep Anastacia Karin safe from Orlov's hit squad, they needed to maintain constant surveillance on the girl.

He grew thoughtful again. "You think Paige can get her hands on the house blueprints?"

"Maybe. But knowing the layout won't make a lick of difference without an assessment of the security protocol. I bet the entire place is teeming with motion detectors and heat sensors, not to mention a heavy-duty alarm system."

"I'm sure we can find a way to breach the place. It's just going to take time," he said grimly. "This kind of operation requires an insane amount of prep. And manpower—we'd definitely have to bring in some reinforcements if we go through with it."

"First things first, we need a detailed evaluation of their security . . ." She trailed off, her brown eyes narrowing as she focused on the rearview mirror.

Ethan heard the gate open at the same time she did, a mechanical whir that echoed in the frigid morning air. A moment later, a white van drove through the gate, bearing a Russian logo that Ethan couldn't read.

"Jackpot." Juliet's lips curved in a smile. "They use a private cleaning service. Maybe I can impersonate a maid and get inside that way." She quickly grabbed her phone from her jacket pocket and moved her fingers over the touch screen.

"Wait a sec—we've got another vehicle. Actually, make that two."

This time a pair of black town cars emerged from the gate, but he couldn't make out the drivers or passengers, thanks to heavily tinted windows.

"Follow them," he ordered. "The girl could be in one of those cars."

"Yes, sir." Juliet dropped the phone in her lap and skillfully steered the Porsche back onto the road.

Ethan continued to evaluate the cars, which were several yards ahead of them. "The windows look armored. If she's in there, at least she's well protected."

"Bulletproof windows are useless once she steps out of the car, rookie. They won't protect her from a sniper who wants to blow her brains out."

A red BMW came up behind them, and Juliet purposely allowed it to pass so they were no longer directly behind the town cars.

"All right, let's see where they go," she said. "Hopefully the kid is getting dropped off at school, which means she'll be occupied for the next eight hours or so. And while she's solving math problems and reading Shakespeare or whatever it is ninth-graders read, we can brainstorm solutions to our little bug dilemma."

Ethan glanced over. "I'm open to any and all ideas."

"Don't worry. I'm sure we'll come up with something. But first we need to ditch the Porsche. It's too conspicuous."

"Let me guess. It's time to steal another car."

She turned to him with an impish smile. "Yup. And if you're nice to me, I might even let you drive it."

"Gee, that's very generous of you."

"I thought so." She sighed. "Now, put on your thinking cap so we can figure out a way to bug the prime minister's house."

Chapter 10

"I don't understand. Why isn't he coming back tonight?" Anastacia Karin heard the plaintive note in her voice, but was unable to control it as she glared accusingly at Nina.

The elegant blond woman had the decency to look repentant. "I'm afraid he got delayed in Moscow, little dove. But your father is so very upset that he can't come home yet. He wanted me to tell you that he'll make it up to you when he returns. He said he'll take you out to the fanciest restaurant in the city for your birthday."

Stacie locked her jaw, doing her best to keep the tears at bay. She didn't know why she was even surprised. Her dad *never* kept his promises. She was stupid for believing his promise that he'd wrap up his business trip in time to come home for her birthday.

She was turning sixteen tomorrow. All of her friends had pleaded with her to throw a lavish party to celebrate, but she knew they didn't really care about her birthday. They just wanted to visit her house so they could brag to everyone that they'd been there. But Stacie wasn't permitted to bring friends home—it was a security risk, as her father frequently reminded her.

Even though she was allowed go to her friends' houses, she rarely ever did because she knew her bodyguards made her friends and their parents uncomfortable. It was impossible for anyone to feel at ease when Roman and Mikhail were constantly looming over her.

"Stacie?"

She weakly lifted her head to find Nina's kind blue eyes fixed on her. She knew it wasn't Nina's fault that her father was deserting her again. Nina was just another one of his assistants—she did what she was told, just like everybody else.

But Stacie had to admit, Nina was a lot nicer than some of her father's previous assistants. At twenty-seven, Nina was not only younger than the others, but she was also incredibly sweet and thoughtful. Stacie suspected that Nina was the one who picked out all those gifts her father gave her each time he disappointed her—which added up to *a lot* of gifts, because he disappointed her more often than not.

"I know you're upset, little dove," the woman said gently. "But that's what happens when you're the daughter of a powerful man—you're forced to share your father with the rest of the country."

"I know," she mumbled.

"But he does love you, Stacie. He loves you very much."

Tears stung her eyes again. At times like these, she desperately missed her mother. She didn't remember much about the woman who'd given birth to her—Alexandra had died when Stacie was five years old—but every now and then a flash would come to her. A vague recollection of a woman's warm brown eyes, the faint echoes of a lullaby, the memory of a soothing caress and a tender smile.

Stacie longed for her mother, for someone to comfort her and hold her and tell her that everything would be okay. Maybe Nina was right and her father did love her, but he was so focused on his job that sometimes she wondered if he even knew she existed.

"I have something special planned for your birthday," Nina added with a secretive smile. "I know it won't make up for the fact that your father's trip was extended, but I think you'll really enjoy it."

Stacie forced a smile, more for Nina's sake than her own. She knew the woman was trying her best.

Luckily, the car came to a stop, sparing her the task of pretending to be excited about her birthday. She would turn sixteen the same way she'd turned every other age since her mother died—without her father. Nothing Nina did could make her feel good about that.

"Have a good day at school," Nina said cheerfully.

"See you later, Nina." Stacie reached for the strap of her leather messenger bag just as the back door opened.

She was greeted by a pair of intense blue eyes belonging to her bodyguard Roman, who would dutifully follow her around all day. Having a guard stand outside your classroom and lurk behind you in the cafeteria would probably seem horrific to the average girl, but Stacie had dealt with it her entire life. Besides, she wasn't the only girl at the Nikolov Academy with a bodyguard, which made it slightly less embarrassing.

"Are you ready, Anastacia?" Roman asked politely.

She slung her school bag over her shoulder and hopped out of the backseat. "Yes, I'm ready."

As they crossed the parking lot, the car carrying Nina drove away, while the second car Roman had been driving stayed parked in the lot.

They headed for the wide limestone steps at the school's pillared entrance, while Stacie watched Roman from the corner of her eye, feeling uneasy. Roman had been guarding her for only six months and she still wasn't sure how she felt about him. He'd replaced her previous bodyguard, Joseph, who'd been reassigned for some mysterious reason that Stacie's father didn't seem interested in sharing with her.

Roman was very polite and nothing but nice to her, but she didn't feel entirely comfortable around him. She missed Joseph and his silly jokes. Joseph had always known how to cheer her up when she was feeling down.

"Stacie!" Her friend Irina waved at her from the top of the steps. "Hurry up! The bell just rang!"

Stacie dashed up the stairs to join Irina, feeling Roman's eyes boring into her back the entire time.

She pushed away her uneasiness and tried to focus on her friend, who was chattering animatedly as the girls walked into the building. At least Irina was in a good mood.

Stacie, on the other hand, still felt like someone had scraped her heart with a dull knife. She kept telling herself that one of these days her father would notice that he had a daughter who needed him, but lately that notion seemed less and less likely.

"Are you even listening to me?" Irina demanded with a pout.

Stacie snapped out of her thoughts. "Yes, I'm listening. You were saying something about the dress your mother bought you . . . ?" she prompted.

As Irina resumed her babbling, Stacie followed her friend down the hallway and tried not to think about how her father had let her down.

Again.

"Galina, has General Vasiliev arrived yet?"

Orlov jammed his finger on the intercom button to address his secretary, whose voice promptly crackled out of the speaker.

"Not yet, Minister. Security is supposed to notify me when he does."

"The son of a bitch is late. Make him wait precisely thirty-three minutes before you allow him into the office."

"Yes, sir."

He released the intercom and scowled at the neatly typed report sitting in front of him. Vasiliev had been eager to schedule this conference to discuss the potential funding for an elite Special Forces unit within the military's Special Operations arm. Orlov had canceled two appointments in order to grant Vasiliev his audience, and now the man had the gall to show up late?

Perhaps he'd deny Vasiliev's funding on principle alone.

Orlov loathed being kept waiting. The respite, however, did permit him to check in with Kirill, who had used their secure system to leave several cryptic messages throughout the day.

"What is it, Kirill?" he barked after his trusted number two answered the phone.

"I'm afraid we have a problem. Karin is returning to the city tonight, as previously scheduled."

Orlov frowned in displeasure. "Our sources claimed he was extending his visit in Moscow."

"It appears that Karin misled his assistant when he phoned with the itinerary changes. He's planning on surprising his daughter. Her birthday is tomorrow."

"Lovely. Our country is in disarray, and its prime minister is playing childish games," Orlov said through clenched teeth. "Is it any wonder the People's Revolutionary Front is wreaking havoc on our soil?"

"This poses a problem for us, sir. The individual whose services I've obtained doesn't arrive until the end of the week."

"It needs to be done before Karin's return," Orlov snapped. "We don't know how much information the Wolf gave up before he was killed. That means our timetable has to be moved up. And it will be far more difficult to eliminate the girl if Karin's bodyguards are lurking around."

He spoke freely, unconcerned that his office might have been compromised. He didn't believe any man was dim-witted enough to attempt to plant a bug in the Ministry of Defense, an act that was punishable by death. Nevertheless, he diligently swept the room for bugs every hour.

"Berezovsky is still assigned to the girl?" He grew thoughtful.

"Yes," Kirill confirmed.

Orlov nodded, decision made. "Transfer the task to Berezovsky then." His jaw tightened. "The girl must die today."

*   *   *

"I still think my plan can work," Juliet insisted several hours later. "It's the quickest way to get in."

Ethan tried to contain his aggravation. "Let me get this straight. You want to steal a maid's uniform and the cleaning-service van, brazenly drive up to the gate, and pretend you were there this morning and that you dropped your bracelet when you were cleaning. Then you'll convince the guards to let you inside to search for it, at which point you'll plant the bugs. Then you're going to magically produce the jewelry you lost, get back in the van, and drive away."

"What's wrong with that?"

"I don't even know where to begin. One, we don't have enough intel on this cleaning service. For all we know, Karin has been using them for years and his staff is familiar with every maid who shows up. Two, if the staff knows all the maids, then they'll know there's no way you were in the house earlier today. Three, even if they buy your bogus story and let you in, nobody is going to let you wander around alone. You'll be escorted by a guard, which means you'll be watched like a hawk when you try to plant those bugs. Four—"

"Fine, the plan sucks," she interrupted. "You can stop listing all its flaws."

A silence hung over the car as they each pondered their options. They were parked down the road from the Nikolov Academy, with a clear line of sight to the school's gated parking lot. One of the town cars that had left the Karin estate this morning had sped off once Anastacia Karin safely entered the school, but the other car remained in the lot.

Ethan wasn't sure why the kid had needed to take a motorcade to school today. He wasn't worrying about it, though. His more pressing concern was figuring out a way to initiate round-the-clock surveillance on the teenager.

"What if we plant a mic on Anastacia?" he suggested.

Juliet looked intrigued. "Huh. I like that. If we can get close enough to her, that's definitely an option."

"It would be even better if we had access to her belongings. Plant a tracker in the sole of her shoe, a couple of bugs in the lining of her clothes and purse . . ."

"We can hack into the school's records and find out her schedule. Maybe she's taking phys ed. That means she'd leave her clothes in a locker to change into a gym uniform. I could try to sneak into the locker room and—"

"And nothing. How are you going to *sneak* in? Look at that gate. They make everyone sign in at the main booth."

"I'm sure I can figure something out. Or I can always wing it."

"Christ. You wouldn't last a day in the Marines with that kind of impulsive approach."

"Ah, live a little, rookie. You think too much."

As usual, her no-care-in-the-world attitude inspired conflicting emotions inside of him. On one hand, he found it refreshing. Juliet was so full of life, so vibrant and exciting, which was a stark change from the sweet and often timid women he'd dated in the past.

On the other hand, she was absolutely fricking insane.

"How's your wound, by the way?" he asked her.

"Better. It still aches, but I checked the entry and exit wounds earlier and they're definitely healing. Infection's totally gone."

"Good." That was one less thing to worry about at least.

Ethan absently drummed his fingers on the steering wheel, still trying to formulate a feasible plan. The BMW Juliet had stolen in place of the Porsche reeked of its owner's spicy cologne, an overpowering fragrance that was starting to give him a headache.

"Anyway, you're right," Juliet conceded. "The locker room idea sucks too. Argh. This is surveillance, for fuck's sake. Why can't we come up with something?"

Ethan was equally frustrated. Before he could voice that frustration, his phone vibrated in his pocket. He quickly fished it out and saw Sullivan's number on the screen.

"Ahoy, matey," Sullivan chirped when Ethan answered. "Good news—we found her."

Sullivan and Liam had arrived in Minsk earlier that morning, but the last time they'd checked in they still hadn't tracked down Alisa Baronova, one of the targets on Grechko's hit list.

"Nice," Ethan said, relieved to hear some good news. At least *somebody* was having success. "Where was she?"

"She was getting pampered at a day spa." The Australian mercenary snorted. "Boston got real jealous, complained that he hasn't had a decent manicure in weeks."

A few choice expletives sounded in the background, clearly uttered by Liam Macgregor, whose Boston accent gave him away.

"Aw, now he's denying it," Sullivan hooted. "He's embarrassed that I outed him."

"Fuck off," came Liam's muffled voice.

Ethan had to grin. Those two clowns were the best of friends, yet they bickered like an old married couple.

"Anyway, you should know that we're not the only ones tailing Baronova. Lady's got a fan club."

He wasn't surprised to hear it. D had already checked in earlier to report that he'd landed in Madrid and made contact with Noelle. The two of them had located Yuri Kozlov, who apparently had a tail of his own.

"How many men?" Ethan inquired.

"Two. They don't look like government. Definitely private goons."

"All they're doing is watching her?"

"So far."

"Keep an eye on them. If they look like they're about to move on Baronova, take them out of the equation and get her to the safe house. Paige is making the final arrangements, so the place should be ready for us later today."

"Copy that." Sullivan paused for a second. "Hold up. Boston wants to talk to you."

A moment later, Liam came on the line. "Hey, rookie?"

"What's up?"

"You couldn't have picked a warmer place to conduct this little side op of yours? I'm freezing my balls off here."

Ethan laughed. "Go buy some long johns."

"Fuck you. You owe me big for this."

There was a shuffling sound and then Sullivan was back. "I'll call in with a status update later."

"Copy that."

"So Orlov's men are watching Baronova," Juliet remarked after Ethan had hung up.

"Kozlov too," he reminded her.

"Yeah, well, at least they don't have the goddamn Presidential Security Service to contend with. We drew the short straw with the prime minister's daughter."

"Still can't think of a way to do twenty-four-hour recon on her, huh?"

"Nope." Juliet raked a hand through her thick brown hair, then released a sigh. "Let's talk about something else. Maybe a solution will come to me if I clear my head and distract myself for a bit."

"Sounds good. What do you want to talk about?"

"I don't know." She adjusted the seat, getting more comfortable. "You owe me a life story, remember? Tell me how you hooked up with Morgan."

"He recruited me. I'd just finished my tour of duty, and Morgan showed up at my apartment one day and convinced me not to re-up."

Juliet wrinkled her forehead. "How'd he find you?"

"Apparently he knew my CO—seems like Morgan fucking knows everyone. He said I had the skills and attitude he looked for in a soldier and offered me a job."

"And you accepted."

"Yep."

"Why?"

He faltered for a second. "What do you mean?"

"I mean, *why*? Why did you pick Morgan over the Marine Corps? Was it the money?"

"No, it wasn't that." Ethan shifted in discomfort. "It . . . Ah, forget it."

"Oh, come on, rookie. Spit it out. I showed you mine, so now you've gotta show me yours."

"Fine." He exhaled in a rush. "He reminded me of my dad, okay?"

Juliet looked startled. "Morgan?"

"Yeah. There was just something about him . . ." Ethan cleared his throat, growing more and more uncomfortable. "I knew from the moment I met him that he was a man of honor. He's a bastard sometimes, no doubt about it, but when he showed up at my door, I took one look at him and knew I wanted to be part of his team."

"Because he reminded you of your father," she said slowly. "Out of curiosity, what happened to your dad? You said your mother's dead, but what about him?"

"Also dead." Ethan swallowed the lump in his throat. "They died in a car accident when I was eighteen. They hit a patch of black ice and crashed their car into a ditch. Died on impact."

"Where was this?"

"Missouri. I grew up in a small town north of Kansas City."

"Ahhh, you're a small-town boy. Makes perfect sense."

He bristled. "What's that supposed to mean?"

"Your whole gentlemanly vibe. Great manners, too nice for your own good—it's the small-towner in you. Anyway, so you were orphaned, huh?"

A jolt of pain shot through him, settling into a tight vise around his heart. "Yep. Little Orphan Ethan," he said lightly.

"And Little Orphan Juliet," she replied, more subdued than he'd ever heard her. "But my folks died way before yours. My dad OD'd when I was two—I don't remember him at all. And my mom OD'd two years later. I have only vague memories of her." She abruptly reverted back to her trademark sarcasm. "But let me guess—your folks weren't junkies like mine. They were Mr. and Mrs. Perfect, right?"

"Pretty much. They were good, hardworking people. Patriotic as hell too. My dad was career navy. He was so disappointed when I told him I didn't want to enlist. I wanted to go to med school, be a doctor someday."

"But then he died and you ended up enlisting. You did it to honor him, didn't you?"

"Yes."

She went quiet for a second, then shook her head in dismay. "Goddamn you."

"Why do you always seem to be saying that to me?"

"Because you're too damn perfect, Ethan! I mean, listen to yourself. You aspired to be a doctor. So you could save people, right? And then you ended up serving in the Marines, so you could save the damn world." She heaved out a sigh. "You make everyone around you look like a selfish ass."

"Hold on—did you just call me *Ethan*?"

Her olive cheeks took on a pink hue. "No."

"You said my name. Not *kiddo*, not *rookie*. My actual name."

"So what if I did?"

Triumph coursed through his blood. "It means I'm getting to you."

Now she was practically sputtering. "You're not getting to me."

"Ha. I totally am." He flashed a victorious grin. "You like me."

"I do not."

"You absolutely do."

Their gazes locked, and almost immediately the air in

the car grew hotter, sizzled with awareness. Oh yes, she was definitely warming up to him. Not only that, but he could see in her eyes that she wanted him. She was looking at his mouth like she wanted him to kiss her. And his hands, as if she craved his touch. And then those gorgeous chocolate brown eyes dipped to his groin, as if she were dying to unzip his pants, release his dick, and ride him until they were both panting for air.

"Don't even think about it," she blurted out.

"Think about what?" he asked innocently.

"Your stupid baseball game. You're not making it to second base."

"Sure I am." The shrill ringing of a bell brought a rueful smile to his lips. "Just not now."

The moment of awareness dissipated as the doors of the school suddenly flew open and uniform-clad girls of all ages began streaming out. Several of the girls were accompanied by stone-faced men who clearly served as bodyguards to students from wealthy and powerful families.

He recognized Anastacia Karin the second she appeared on the massive front steps. She was prettier in person than in the picture Paige had e-mailed them, a slender waif of a girl with shoulder-length brown hair, dark green eyes, and an air of sadness about her.

"Crap," Juliet muttered. "She's about to go home and we still haven't figured out a way to keep tabs on her when she's there."

"I'll call the guys and pick their brains," Ethan replied as he started the engine of the BMW.

"Maybe Noelle will have some ideas too. Too bad Isabel's not available. She totally could have pulled off my maid scheme."

He couldn't argue with that. Isabel Roma was a master of disguise. If anyone could transform into a completely different person, it was her.

"We'll come up with something," he assured Juliet. "I'm sure there's a way to do it without investing a lot of time and money."

"I hope so."

He waited until Anastacia and her bodyguard had left in their town car, then smoothly joined traffic, keeping one car's length between him and their target.

"What do we know about the guards?" he asked, straining to remember the details in Paige's report.

"Not much. They're the equivalent of the Secret Service, so it's difficult to get our hands on their files. Paige said she'll do it if it's really necessary, but for now she just gave us their names—Mikhail and Roman. Not sure which one is driving her right now."

They continued following the black car, but when they neared the turnoff that would take them to the Karin estate, the Lincoln sped right past it.

"Where the hell are they going?" Juliet demanded.

Ethan shrugged. "Who knows? Maybe she has a piano lesson. Or she might take ballet. Or they could be going shopping."

"Paige's intel said Anastacia is pretty much a hermit. She's driven to and from school and hardly ever leaves that fortress." Juliet's dark eyes were fixed on the rear bumper of the town car. "Something's wrong."

"Relax. Let's not worry until there's actually something to worry about."

To his consternation, the Lincoln seemed to be moving farther and farther away from civilization. The four-lane road turned to a two-lane road, then a one-lane road. Ethan and Juliet remained one car behind, but when their buffer executed an abrupt left turn, there was suddenly nothing between them and Anastacia Karin.

"Shit. He's going to make the tail."

Juliet tried to sound optimistic. "He might not."

"You said so yourself—those guards are Secret Service. They've been well trained." Ethan set his jaw. "He'll make the tail."

He eased up on the gas, attempting to place more distance between the BMW and the Lincoln, but he knew that wasn't much of a solution. The longer they followed Karin's car, the likelier it became that the driver would realize he had company.

"Where the fuck is he taking her?" Juliet's concern was unmistakable, hanging on her throaty voice and bringing a deep crease to her forehead.

Ethan's gaze swept over their deserted surroundings. They were in an industrial area now, where abandoned warehouses and derelict buildings with snow-covered roofs lined each side of the narrow road. Many of the structures were closed off by chain-link fences that were either broken or sagging to the earth.

Smothering a sigh, he turned to Juliet in resignation. "Okay, I think we're allowed to worry now."

Chapter 11

"Please tell me what's going on," Anastacia begged, battling the rush of fear gripping her throat.

In the driver's seat, Roman glanced over with irritated blue eyes. "I told you, I'm taking you to your father."

"I don't understand. Why didn't you let me talk to him?"

"Because it's not safe."

Roman returned his attention to the road, dismissing her as he'd done ever since he'd received that phone call just as they'd been leaving her school.

After he'd hung up, he'd gravely announced that there was a national emergency, but he refused to elaborate, even now.

Stacie couldn't control the panic swimming in her belly. Was her father hurt? She knew his position in the government made her a target—he'd received hundreds of death threats over the years—but her dad maintained that she had no reason to worry, that their guards would keep them safe.

"No harm will ever come to you," he always assured

her. *I will never let that happen, little dove. I'm here to protect you.*

But he wasn't here now. How could he protect her when he wasn't *here*?

Stacie tried to draw in slow, steady breaths, the way Nina had taught her to do whenever she was overcome with anxiety. But the breathing exercises didn't work. Her throat had closed up on her. Her chest was tight with fear.

"Son of a bitch."

Roman's muttered curse only elevated her panic. "What's wrong?"

He didn't answer, his gaze glued to the rearview mirror.

Stacie twisted around in her seat to look out the rear windshield. She spotted a black car behind them, but it was really far back. She didn't understand how it could be a threat, but Roman's body was stiffer than a board, his profile revealing a dire expression as he watched the other car like a hawk.

"What is it? Are they following us?"

"Quiet," he snapped. "Just sit still and stay quiet."

Her hands began to tingle, tremble. She didn't know what was happening and she hated feeling out of control. Why wasn't Roman telling her anything? And why was he reaching into his coat pocket for—

A gun. He'd pulled out a black gun.

And now he was pressing the button to roll down the window!

She gasped. "What are you doing?"

He kept his right hand on the steering wheel and gripped the weapon with his left one. "Cover your ears, Anastacia."

"What? W-why?"

Her eardrums exploded as Roman opened fire.

"Son of a bitch is shooting at us!" Ethan swerved sharply as the driver of the town car extended his arm and sent another bullet flying toward them.

The first shot had made contact with the windshield. It hadn't shattered, but a spiderweb of glass now obstructed Ethan's vision. Adrenaline flooded his bloodstream, snapping him into action.

"Get down," he yelled at Juliet.

She ignored the command, instead withdrawing the Beretta from her waistband and proceeding to roll down her window.

"I guess he made the tail," she said dryly, unperturbed by the fact that they were being shot at.

A metallic ding sounded as the driver's bullet connected with their front bumper. The Lincoln was swerving wildly as the shooter attempted to simultaneously drive and hit his target. With the layer of ice covering the road, the car's rapid zigzagging only got worse, eliciting another irritated expletive from Ethan's lips.

He tossed out a quick order at the woman beside him. "Shoot out the tires. The maniac's gonna get that girl killed."

Without a word, Juliet hauled half her body out the window, twisted around, and took aim.

A second later, a piece of the Lincoln's undercarriage snapped off. The debris spiraled in the air and collided with the hood of their car.

"Keep it steady," Juliet shouted over the gust of freezing wind hissing in from the open window. "I can't get a good shot."

Her second attempt lodged a bullet into the bumper. The third just barely clipped the rear left tire. The fourth missed the town car altogether because Ethan had to veer again to avoid another shot to their windshield.

"Goddamn it," he growled. "Take the wheel, Juliet."

She didn't utter a protest. Just ducked inside and took over driving duties, steering the BMW as Ethan unholstered his pistol and cranked open the driver's window.

With intense focus he'd honed in the military, he stuck his head and arm out the window. The frigid wind slapped the sleeve of his parka and chilled his bare hand, but he wasn't deterred by it.

Keeping the pistol steady, he took aim and pulled the trigger.

Stacie screamed as another explosion rocked the car. This one sounded different from the gunshots that had nearly shattered her eardrums. Suddenly the car was fishtailing violently, sliding on the icy road in a furious pace that had her heart in her throat. Trees and buildings whizzed by her window as Roman struggled to control the vehicle.

She was going to die. Oh God. She was going to *die*.

They hit something. She didn't know what because she'd closed her eyes by then, but the car wasn't moving anymore. Nausea churned in her belly. She opened her mouth to scream again but couldn't make a sound because something exploded in her face.

Agony seized her nose and she felt a gush of moisture pour out of her nostrils. The air bag. It had burst in her face.

Her heart was pounding so loudly all she could hear

was its rapid *thump-thump-thump* in her ears. Beside her, Roman was cursing a blue streak and fumbling with his seat belt.

"Stay in the car," he ordered.

The request caused a hysterical laugh to bubble in her mouth. Stay in the car? Where did he think she would go?

Stacie heard a click and then Roman was gone. He'd left her. Left her in the car, which she realized was at the bottom of a small ditch. Snow covered the broken windshield, and a cold breeze snaked in through the cracks in the glass, making her shiver uncontrollably.

Gasping for air, she pushed aside the now-deflated air bag and brought her hand to her nose. She soaked up the blood with the sleeve of her coat, her panicked gaze moving to the driver's window. All she saw was the top of the ditch. Roman was gone.

He'd left her.

"No harm will ever come to you."

"Daddy." The strangled plea flew out of her mouth. To no avail.

Because her father wasn't here. Her father didn't care about her.

And it was her birthday tomorrow.

Stacie struggled to unbuckle her seat belt. Her school bag had fallen to the floor during the crash and she reached for it with trembling fingers. Nina. She would call Nina. And Nina would come and help and—

Her phone was gone.

It wasn't in her bag.

She moaned in anguish. She'd never been so frightened in her life. Her entire body shook like a leaf in a windstorm, rocking even harder when she heard the squeal of tires coming from the road. A car door slammed. And then . . . another gunshot. This one was muffled, farther away.

Where was Roman? Why had he left her here? Why had he—

The driver's door flew open.

Relief flooded her body when she saw Nina's familiar face. She didn't even question the woman's presence—all she knew was that someone had come for her. Someone was here to save her.

"Nina! Oh, God! Where's Roman? What's going on?"

The blond woman's calm expression didn't waver. "Roman's dead."

"What? How?" Tears slid down Stacie's cheeks and mingled with the blood seeping out of her nose. "What about my father? Where is he? Is he all right?"

Nina didn't answer. The woman's head had snapped to the side as if she'd seen something, but Stacie was too overwrought to notice.

"Take me home," she pleaded, starting to climb over the seat toward Nina. "Please, I want to go ho—"

The words died in her throat when she noticed the gun in Nina's hand.

And it was pointed right at her.

"N-Nina?"

Regret flashed in the woman's blue eyes. "I'm sorry, little dove, but the country comes first."

She'd barely registered the response when another gunshot cracked in the air.

And then Nina's blood sprayed all over her face.

Chapter 12

"I'm never going to forget the way you look right now," Noelle declared as she and D leisurely strolled along the gorgeous walkway of the Parque del Retiro in Madrid.

D cast her a sideways glance. "Go ahead. Make fun of me all you want. I'll punish you for it the next time we're naked."

"Is that a threat? Because we both know I enjoy your kind of punishment."

Chuckling, D broke the eye contact and turned his attention back to their prey, who was ambling up ahead at a leisurely pace that annoyed the shit out of D. They'd been watching Yuri Kozlov all morning, following the man as he'd played tourist with the petite black-haired woman he was vacationing with. D normally didn't mind surveillance gigs, but seeing the sights of Madrid didn't interest him.

To make matters worse, following a tourist meant *posing* as a tourist. Which meant getting decked out in the outfit Noelle was gleaning so much amusement from. The vomit-inducing getup included a faded Columbia University T-shirt he kept in his go bag for occasions such as this, beat-up Converse sneakers, a digital camera with a pansy-ass wrist strap, and honest-to-God blue jeans. Jesus fucking Christ. He was experiencing some serious withdrawal from his cargo pants.

Noelle had it easy—a pink tee, white capris, hair in a ponytail. She easily pulled off the fresh-faced coed look, and every man who passed offered her an admiring smile, which in turn brought a cynical one to D's lips. If they only knew.

"Our little friends are getting bolder," Noelle mused.

D had noticed the same thing—the two men trailing after Kozlov and his girlfriend were making less of an effort to remain hidden. The short one in the blue sweater was brazenly lurking ten feet from the couple as they stopped to take a picture in front of the equestrian statue that served as a monument to King Alfonso XII, while the big one in the black Windbreaker not so conspicuously stood near the artificial pond, pretending to study a map.

"Smile, angel face." Noelle raised her digital camera to snap a shot of D.

He pasted on a smile, which went against everything he stood for.

Christ. The things he did for his teammates.

For a man who'd worked solo for most of his career, D still wasn't entirely sure why he'd decided to join Morgan's crew. He supposed he could have found himself a little beach shack in some uncharted part of the world and lived out the rest of his days in solitude, but he hadn't pulled a disappearing act from the agency in order to bum around and drink Coronas on the beach. He was built for action, wired for death and violence. Self-imposed retirement from the agency had been crucial for his survival, but he hadn't been ready to lie down and die yet.

When he'd heard that supersoldier Jim Morgan was putting together a mercenary team, he'd been intrigued. And for some fucked-up reason, he'd offered his services to the man.

Some days he deeply regretted that decision, but for the most part, he was content with the gig. He'd never wanted to be part of a team, and yet over the years, he'd grown oddly protective of the men he fought alongside. He didn't know when it happened, but somehow he'd begun considering it his duty to watch his teammates' asses and keep them from getting themselves killed.

The rookie's entanglement with Juliet Mason had disaster written all over it. D had agreed to get involved not just because he hated sitting idle during these forced vacations, but because he didn't want to see Ethan lose his life thanks to another one of Noelle's crazy operatives.

"Do you ever miss it?" Noelle's voice interrupted his train of thought.

"Miss what?" he said gruffly.

"Killing."

"Who says I stopped?"

She rolled her eyes. "I know for a fact that Jim specializes in extractions. I can't imagine he sends you out on many kill jobs."

"He doesn't," D grudgingly confessed.

"So, I repeat, do you miss it? The excitement of the hunt, the sheer pleasure you get from closing in on your prey, the triumph of extinguishing some sorry bastard's life?"

"Sometimes." He cocked a brow. "Why, you offering

me a job? Trying to steal me away from Morgan the way he stole Abby from you?"

She laughed. "Sorry, honey. I wouldn't let you come work for me even if you begged. You're too volatile."

"And you're not?"

"Oh, I can be." She shrugged. "But unlike you, I'm not still hung up on the nightmares in my past. You know, the ones you wear on your sleeve." She paused meaningfully. "Or should I say *wrist*?"

She struck like a rattlesnake, snatching his right hand and curling her fingers over his wrist.

He saw the move coming, yet for some reason allowed it.

Uneasiness washed over him as Noelle traced the two lines of faded black text etched on his skin.

"Two sets of dates," she drawled. "The first one . . . I'd bet it marks an event you want to forget but force yourself to remember. And the second one . . . about ten years after the first . . . I'm not sure what that one signifies. Care to enlighten me?"

"Nope."

"Shocking."

She released his hand and put on a blithe smile, her shrewd blue eyes focusing on their target.

Kozlov and his lady were laughing about something, oblivious to the ominous reality that they were being watched by two sets of people. Ah, to be carefree and ignorant and blessedly optimistic.

D had lost that privilege when he was eight years old. It had been plucked away from him, and the death and violence he'd indulged in over the subsequent years ensured that he'd never get those feelings back.

Beside him, Noelle had taken her phone out of her shoulder bag and was glancing at the screen.

"Juliet's calling," she said before answering. "Yes?" She waited, her pouty mouth twisting into a grimace. "You all right?" Another pause. "Casualties?" A nod. "Sounds good. Stay in touch."

She hung up with a frown. "Someone made a move on their target and killed her bodyguard, but they neutralized the situation. They're taking the girl to a safe house up north, near the Russian border."

"Do they want us to grab our guy and join them?"

"Only if we sense a threat to Kozlov." She made an irritated sound. "We're on standby. I fucking hate standby."

So did he, but he wasn't one to gripe and complain about things that were beyond his control.

"C'mon," he told the sulking blonde, "it's time to continue playing tourist. They're on the move again."

The teenage girl in the backseat of the BMW was inconsolable. Shaking, panting, and crying, her arms hugging her chest as the sobs racked her body.

"Why are you doing this?" she moaned. "I just want to go home."

Juliet stifled a groan and prayed that Anastacia Karin wouldn't keep this up during the entire ride to the safe house. The property they'd secured last night with Paige's help was a good two hours away, and they were only ten minutes into the drive. At this rate, Juliet would shoot the kid herself.

Ethan, on the other hand, was an endless well of patience. He sat in the back with Anastacia, murmuring to the distraught girl in stilted Russian.

"We're taking you somewhere safe, Anastacia. I know it's difficult to hear, but your life is in danger."

Her sobs escaped in ragged pants. "She . . . she was going to *shoot* me . . . Nina . . . she would have killed me. She would have killed me, right?"

Ethan didn't mince words, but his voice stayed soft and gentle. "Yes. But you're safe now. I promise you you're safe."

"I'm not! How do I know you won't shoot me too?" The girl started crying in earnest now. "I want to call my father! Please just let me call him!"

As Ethan continued to console the girl, Juliet met his gaze in the rearview mirror, saw the frustration in his eyes. She knew what he was thinking—this was a total fucked-up mess. They hadn't had time to clean up the scene, which meant that the authorities were bound to find Karin's town car in the ditch, along with two dead bodies.

Juliet was still having trouble making sense of what the hell had happened. Just as Karin's Lincoln had sailed through the guardrail, a second town car appeared out of nowhere—it had most likely been parked in the industrial park they'd noticed before, Juliet had realized afterward. She and Ethan had taken cover behind their car, under fire from Anastacia's bodyguard, when a blond woman had emerged from the second car and pumped three bullets into the bodyguard's chest before making a beeline for the wrecked car.

When the woman pointed her weapon inside the car, Ethan hadn't even hesitated—his shot had taken off half the blonde's head. Anastacia's face and coat were still stained with the woman's blood.

Christ. What a mess. Juliet knew that the second the cops arrived on the bloody scene and discovered that the prime minister's daughter was nowhere to be found, they'd have every law-enforcement agency in the country searching for the missing girl.

What had spurred Orlov to dispatch someone to make a move? Today, in the middle of the goddamn afternoon?

Juliet pressed down on the gas, driving faster, knowing they needed to get off the highway and to the safe house as soon as humanly possible. Before every road in the country was crawling with cops.

In the back, Anastacia had fallen quiet. A quick glance in the mirror showed a pair of vacant green eyes, and the girl was shivering so hard that Ethan had wrapped one strong arm around her, offering comfort and warmth.

"We can't be out in the open."

His low murmur was spoken in English and directed at Juliet, who nodded in response. "They'll think it was an abduction," she said flatly. "It'll be all over the news in a matter of hours."

"Could work to our favor. The media attention might discourage Orlov from making a move on the others. What did Noelle say?"

"Their target is safe. I told them to be prepared for anything."

Ethan offered a nod of his own. "Call Sully. Tell him to rendezvous with us at the safe house."

"You want them to snatch Baronova?" she said in surprise.

"Yeah. She's here in the city. Might as well keep her

and the girl in the same place. D and Noelle are on the alert, so they'll be ready if someone makes a move on Kozlov in Madrid."

Juliet kept one hand on the wheel and used the other to bring up Sullivan Port's number on her phone. When the Australian answered, she relayed Ethan's instructions, then hung up and focused on driving. She was speeding, but not by much. They couldn't afford to attract any unwanted patrols, not when they were harboring the prime minister's daughter in the backseat.

"Don't touch me!"

Anastacia's panicked cry reverberated in the car. The girl had started struggling again, same way she'd struggled when Ethan pulled her out of the car after he'd eliminated her would-be assassin. She must have snapped out of her terror-ridden daze and noticed his arm around her, because she was slapping his hands away, her tears leaving two trails in the blood caked on her face.

"It's okay, sweetheart. Hey, it's okay. Look at me, Anastacia. I need you to take a deep breath and look at me."

Juliet's eyes were on the road, but her ears were attuned to Ethan's husky voice. A strange wave of affection washed over her as she listened to him. He was so patient with the terrified girl, radiating strength and compassion but also a quiet intensity that Juliet had never noticed before.

In this moment, he didn't look or sound like a kid.

He was a man.

And back at the scene of the accident, he'd been a soldier. Juliet had been startled by the calm fortitude that lit his hazel eyes when he'd taken out that blonde with the cleanest shot to the head she'd ever seen. He'd killed a woman without blinking, revealing a ruthless and dangerous side that, she was ashamed to admit, kind of turned her on.

Ethan Hayes was much more than she'd believed him to be. Deadlier. Sexier.

God, definitely sexier.

"Who are you people? Why are you here? I don't want to be here!"

Anastacia's shrill outburst reminded Juliet that now was not the time to be daydreaming about how sexy Ethan was.

They'd abducted the prime minister's daughter, for Pete's sake. Yes, they'd saved her life and removed her from the scene for her own protection, but Juliet doubted the authorities—or the prime minister—would see it that way.

"Please take me home! Please! Just let me call my father," the girl pleaded between hiccuped sobs. "He has money! He has lots of money and he'll give you as much as you want! Just take me home!"

Juliet and Ethan exchanged another look in the mirror.

Jesus. It was going to be a long ride.

Orlov received the news twenty minutes after his conference with General Vasiliev had drawn to a close. He was just leaving his office to meet with his advisors when an aide came rushing down the corridor.

"Sir! Prime Minister Karin's daughter has been abducted," the young man burst out.

Orlov's outward demeanor didn't change. As the aide spit out the details, he listened without comment, his face devoid of emotion.

All the while seething on the inside.

When the other man finished, Orlov stalked into the small inner office in his block of suites and addressed his secretary. "Get Marisova from Justice on the line. Forward the call to my mobile."

"Right away, sir," came Galina's swift reply.

With the aide nipping at the heels of his leather wing tips like an excitable puppy, Orlov marched back to the hall and headed for the elevator bank. Every door and elevator on the Defense floors required a security card, and so he went through the motions of swiping his coded, magnetic ID in the electronic panel mounted to the wall.

Someone had killed Nina Berezovsky and spirited away the Karin girl.

The thought filled him with indignation, and confirmed what he'd suspected after the Siberian Wolf had been tortured and killed—someone was deliberately interfering with his plans.

Well, that interference was officially about to stop. He'd put this into motion more than a year ago, and he refused to allow a faceless pest to ruin what he'd invested so much time and money in.

"Take the stairs," he snapped at the aide.

The man looked startled. "Sir?"

He didn't offer any explanation. Simply pressed the button that would close the elevator doors and watched them shut in the aide's face. Then he took out his phone and called Kirill.

"What happened?" he demanded.

"I'm not sure. It appears that someone ran the bodyguard's car off the road, killed him and Berezovsky, and abducted the girl."

He clenched his teeth. "From this moment on, your sole objective is to find the people responsible for this. Do you understand me?"

"I'm already on it, sir."

"Good."

He hung up, so enraged he could barely see straight. This latest development was liable to send the country in an uproar. Leo Karin would demand that every law-enforcement agency in the world be dispatched to locate his sniveling brat.

Turn it around. Use it to your advantage.

Orlov inhaled a calming breath. Yes. Yes, that was what he must do. He knew better than anyone that even the best-laid plans often didn't come to fruition. He simply needed to make a few adjustments, make lemonade from the proverbial lemons.

The prime minister in a panic.

Citizens afraid.

People seeking answers. Seeking justice.

A sense of calm washed over him as the pieces came together in his head. Yes, he could work with that. He could absolutely work with that.

And while he put out the fire the Berezovsky woman's screwup had caused, his men would track down the culprits responsible and bring them to him.

So he could personally kill each and every one of them.

Chapter 13

The farmhouse they'd secured was located in a tiny village in the Vitebsk region of Belarus, a crumbling old structure situated on fifty acres of snow-covered land. The surrounding forested areas provided good cover, and Ethan had already made use of the armed explosives and trip wires in his gear bag. Juliet had offered her own equipment—motion detectors that would alert them if anyone came within fifty yards of the house.

Apparently Paige had purchased the house for a song. How she'd managed to complete the sale so fast still eluded him, but the keys had been waiting under the torn floor mat when they'd arrived, and the interior of the house wasn't as neglected as he'd expected. The place was fully furnished, albeit shabbily, and the heat and plumbing worked, which meant they didn't need to start a fire in the prehistoric fireplace or use the dilapidated outhouse out back.

When he entered the master bedroom, he found Juliet sitting on the ancient four-poster bed.

"How is she?"

He closed the door behind him. "Asleep. I had no choice but to give her a sedative from Val's kit. She was too hysterical."

He dropped his duffel on the weathered hardwood floor, his heart going out for the young girl in the other bedroom. He didn't blame Anastacia Karin for her reaction to the day's events. She'd experienced a serious trauma, what with her father's assistant trying to kill her.

Paige had sent them a brief file on Nina Berezovsky, which hadn't told them much except that the woman was fairly new to the prime minister's service. But clearly she was in cahoots with Dmitry Orlov—otherwise she wouldn't have attempted to murder her young charge. Which also proved that Orlov's reach was as long as they'd suspected it was, seeing as he had his own mole in the Karin household.

"Did you speak to Sully again?" He removed his shoulder holster and set it, along with the weapons it contained, on top of the rickety dresser.

"Yeah, he and Liam are snagging Alisa Baronova soon. She's eating dinner with friends, so they're waiting until she's done before they grab her. They should be here in a couple of hours."

"Good." He rubbed his temples, warding off the headache that had been threatening to surface all damn day.

Jesus, he was exhausted. It had been nonstop activity since they'd left the Grenadier at six a.m., and though it was only eight o'clock, he was ready to pass out.

But he couldn't, not when Juliet looked as tired as he felt.

"You should take a nap," he advised her. "I can keep watch for a while."

"Soon." She made no move to stretch out on the tattered orange bedspread. She just kept staring at him, a thoughtful expression on her face.

"What is it?" he said gruffly.

"That was some damn impressive shooting today. Blowing out those tires, blowing Berezovsky's brains out. And then in the car . . ." She shrugged, and if he hadn't known any better, he would have said she looked embarrassed. "You were great with that kid. Really sweet and patient."

The compliments were unexpected, but not as unexpected as Juliet's next move.

She rose from the bed with catlike grace, and then her lips brushed over his in a kiss that caught him completely off guard.

It was a brief, warm peck that left him wanting more, but Juliet denied him of that as she stepped back. She continued to eye him as if she were seeing him for the first time.

"What was that for?" His voice came out husky.

"Surprising me," she said with another shrug.

He'd surprised *her*? Because at the moment, she was surprising the hell out of *him*.

Since the day they'd met, Juliet's guard had been so high he would've needed a thousand-foot rope to scale the wall around her, but here, now, that guard was down. He could see her every thought in those mesmerizing brown eyes. Admiration. Intrigue. Confusion.

Arousal.

She'd never looked more beautiful to him than she did now. With her dark hair cascading down her shoulders, her face an open book, every curve of that head-turning body outlined by her tight black sweater and even tighter pants. She still wore knee-high leather boots, which made her look like the badass she was and had his heart beating a little faster.

This was more than lust. He was slowly beginning to realize that, though what he wanted from this woman, he couldn't quite figure out. Only a short while ago he'd ended it with the girl in Costa Rica because he hadn't wanted anything serious, and yet he suspected that if Juliet told him, right here and right now, that she wanted a committed, long-term relationship from him, he wouldn't hesitate to respond with a big, resounding *yes*.

Fat chance she'd ever ask that of him, though. He knew a relationship was probably the last thing she wanted, which only succeeded in frustrating him further. Because damn it, he wanted more than a temporary flirtation. Sure, their chemistry was off the charts, but sex alone was no longer his endgame. He knew without a doubt that he'd take her to bed—that had become inevitable—but he was now equally determined to explore their connection *outside* the bedroom.

"What's second base for a man?"

Her question startled him. "Huh?"

"I'm assuming for a woman it means some chestal-region groping. But what does the man get?" She slanted her head, her dark eyes gleaming with mischief. "Should I grope your chest for a bit?"

His mouth went dry. The woman continued to surprise him. To fascinate him. "I thought you said I'd never make it to second base."

"That was before I saw you in action today." She sighed. "Now I'm even more attracted to you."

A laugh slipped out. "Yeah?"

"Oh yeah."

Licking her lips, she moved closer. But she didn't kiss him.

Nope, what she did was reach for his zipper.

Ethan smothered a wild curse. "What are you doing?"

"Making an executive decision about what second base is."

Then she dropped to her knees, and this time the expletive that flew out was strangled and hoarse.

"Juliet—" he started, then stopped when she deftly unzipped his pants and gave his waistband a tug.

Laughing softly, she eased his pants and boxers down so that his erection sprang free. Inches from her face.

Ethan's pulse veered into heart-attack territory, his muscles tensing. Priming.

He was very aware that Anastacia Karin was right next door. And even though they'd secured the perimeter, they still needed to keep watch.

"This isn't the time to . . ." He groaned when her delicate fingers curled around his impossibly stiff shaft. "To . . ." Now he moaned, because her tongue was circling the tip of his cock. "To . . ."

"To what?" She peered up at him, the picture of innocence.

"To do *this*," he choked out.

"Oh, hush. Let me have some fun. I promise I'll be quick."

She'd be quick? Lord, he was seconds away from blowing, just from the feel of her breath tickling his aching cock.

He couldn't stop her, not for the life of him. The hot

suction of her mouth felt so criminally good he nearly keeled over.

He braced his hand on the dresser, keeping himself steady, while his other hand drifted down to tangle in Juliet's hair. He stroked those silky strands, but he didn't have to guide her head—she knew exactly what to do. What was guaranteed to drive him to madness.

Each teasing lick brought him closer to the edge. Each pump of her fist added to the pressure building in his groin.

Juliet's evident enjoyment only fueled his hunger. She made little sounds of contentment as she sucked him, her head bobbing up and down his shaft, her mouth gobbling him up until white dots flashed before his eyes. When her hand slid down to squeeze his tight sac, he groaned quietly and thrust deeper into her mouth, and suddenly it became a rush to the finish line. He'd probably regret it later, but he couldn't stop himself from moving his hips and fucking her mouth in a fast tempo that had them both moaning.

"I'm close," he ground out. "Really damn close."

That talented mouth left him, just for a second, just so she could gaze up at him with hungry eyes and say, "Good. Give it to me."

The wicked request was all it took to detonate the knot of pressure. Pleasure seized his balls and shot out in every direction, coursing through his body in long, tingling waves as he came inside Juliet's hot, wet mouth.

A few moments later, she released him with a soft *pop* and looked up with a grin. He could have climaxed again just from the sight of her on her knees in front of him, her glossy lips curved in that naughty grin.

"Jesus," he mumbled, still recovering from the body-numbing release.

"Second base is fun, huh?" She looked tremendously pleased with herself as she gracefully rose to her feet.

"C'mere," he ordered, then yanked her against him.

He kissed her roughly, groaning when he tasted himself on her lips. He hadn't intended to let it go this far, but now that they'd crossed the line, the slow approach had flown out the window right along with his chivalry. He needed to be inside her. Right fricking now.

He was snaking his hands beneath her sweater when a cell phone vibrated.

It was his, buzzing in his back pocket and filling him with annoyance.

"Don't fucking move," he growled at Juliet, who'd just wrapped her arms around his neck.

They stayed there with their bodies locked together as he fished out his phone and brought it to his ear.

"Yeah?" he said briskly.

"We're ahead of schedule," Liam reported. "Be there in ten. Any fun booby traps we should be aware of?"

Swallowing his disappointment, Ethan gave his teammate a rundown of the security perimeter, then hung up with a frustrated look. "They'll be here soon."

"Which leaves us no time to round third and slide home, huh?" She sighed heavily and dropped her hands from his shoulders.

"Ten minutes is plenty of time—if I were a randy sixteen-year-old." He licked his lips. "But I plan on spending a lot more than ten minutes ravishing your body. So we definitely need to put this on hold."

"I don't know . . . I'm kind of fickle. I might change my

mind the next time we're alone." She arched her eyebrows. "This could be your one and only chance."

"Nah, I'll just shoot out a few tires and kill someone, and you'll be all over me again."

Her melodic laugh only succeeded in reigniting his desire of her. "Oooh, I love it when you talk dirty to me, rookie."

Not long after, Sullivan Port and Liam Macgregor arrived at the safe house, carting an unconscious woman. Their expressions conveyed sheer aggravation as Sullivan unceremoniously deposited the package on the shabby plaid couch and straightened up to glare at Ethan and Juliet, who were watching him in amusement.

"This woman is a bloody nightmare," he declared.

"For real," Liam spoke up. He ran a hand through his thick black hair, his piercing blue eyes glittering with annoyance. "Sully had to sedate her because she wouldn't stop screaming. And she called us *goons*. Can you believe it?"

Ethan couldn't help but laugh. Especially since the newcomers currently fit the description of goon to a T. In their matching wool hats, heavy boots, and black bomber jackets, they looked like the bad guys from a Bond flick set in Russia. Not only that, but they both stood well over six feet and boasted muscular physiques that had probably scared the shit out of Alisa Baronova, who was out cold on the sofa.

"Did anyone see you snatch her?" Ethan asked.

"Of course," Liam said sarcastically. "We did it on a busy street in front of hundreds of witnesses. A brigade of cops is waiting outside the door as we speak."

Juliet snorted, but Ethan didn't glance over at her. If he did, he feared his eyes would broadcast his feelings to the entire room. His very potent, very sexual feelings. And he wasn't in the mood to deal with Sully and Liam's wisecracks at the moment, not when they had more important matters to discuss.

"So what exactly is going on, mate?" Sullivan asked warily. "What does Orlov want with these people, and why do we care?"

"We think he might be exacting revenge on the men who stood by and did nothing while his son got killed."

"You think?" Liam sounded skeptical.

"Well, we haven't figured out the motive part yet. All we know is that Orlov wants the targets dead, and he had Victor Grechko kill nine people before this."

"Then take Orlov out," Sullivan said as he shrugged out of his bulky coat. The Australian wore a gray cable-knit sweater underneath, with a shoulder holster strapped on and a silver Glock butt poking out of his waistband.

As he disarmed, Juliet flopped down on one of the rickety wooden chairs around the dining room table. "That's what I'm saying," she retorted, "but Bleeding Heart over here"—she hooked a thumb at Ethan— "wants to find out what Orlov's up to first."

"We don't know that he's working alone," Ethan reminded her. "If you kill him, that doesn't mean the targets are safe. His associates could step up to the plate and eliminate Karin and the others. And we still don't know if he's in bed with the People's Revolutionary Front. Maybe the hits *are* terrorist attacks, orchestrated by Orlov."

Liam drifted over to the refrigerator. "Please tell me

you bought some beer, rookie." He opened the door, peered in, and groaned. "Orange juice? Seriously, that's all you deemed important enough to get?"

Ethan rolled his eyes. "There's water in the tap if OJ doesn't do it for you."

Grumbling to himself, Liam unzipped his coat, tossed it on one of the dining room chairs, then headed to the sink to pour himself a glass of water. "So what's the plan? You're just going to watch these people indefinitely?"

"Until we figure out what Orlov's planning."

"Fine, let's get figuring, then," Sully retorted. "Because I can't spend another bloody second with that infuriating woman."

Ethan glanced over at Alisa Baronova, who, even unconscious, did look like a handful. The woman was in her forties, dressed in a skintight purple dress with a neckline that was quite low for a woman her age. Her breasts were enormous and out of proportion with her reedythin frame, a sign that they probably weren't natural. Same went for her hair, which was a shade of platinum blond that definitely didn't occur in nature. To round out her artificial exterior, she had razor-sharp red fingernails and orange-tinged skin that spoke of too many visits to the tanning salon.

Liam followed Ethan's gaze and snickered. "Her personality is as delightful as her appearance. Just you wait."

He stifled a sigh and turned to Juliet. "We need to start digging, find out who Orlov might be working with."

She responded with a resigned nod, for which he was grateful. He knew she was eager to kill the bastard, but Ethan couldn't in good conscience allow that to happen until he was certain Anastacia and the others would be safe.

"I guess we should start with the PRF," she said. "They've taken responsibility for the hits, so either they're lying or they really are working with Orlov."

"What do we know about the PRF?" Liam asked.

Ethan wandered over and leaned against the narrow kitchen counter. "Well, they consider themselves revolutionaries, claim they're fighting the oppression of the Belikov government. They're tired of the corruption and the censorship, the restrictions on civil rights. They started out with nonviolent demonstrations, but when those didn't achieve results they graduated to full-out violence. Bombings, kidnappings, executions. That's when they were promoted from peaceful protesters to dangerous terrorists."

"Their goal is to push Belikov out of office," Juliet added. "They want a total overhaul of the current system of government."

"Lofty ambitions," Liam remarked.

Ethan shrugged. "Nobody said they operated in the realm of reality, but they keep trying, nevertheless."

The other man slanted his head, pensive. "Who's their Osama?"

"Their leader is a man by the name of Alexei Mironov," Juliet answered. "He's young and charismatic, and picking up followers like crazy."

Sullivan piped up with his two cents. "Okay, so we find Mironov. If he's calling the shots, he's the one who can confirm whether or not his group is responsible for the executions."

"Find Mironov?" Liam echoed with a grin. "How do you suggest we do that, Aussie? Ring up the terrorist directory and request the address to his lair?"

"I'll call Noelle." Juliet rose from her chair.

"You think your boss is magically going to produce the dude's number?" Liam cracked.

"You'd be surprised what Noelle can do. We've taken out a lot of so-called terrorists. Noelle has contacts and informants in every corner of the world."

Ethan nodded. "Call her. It's worth a shot."

"I'll be right back. I left my phone in the other room."

Juliet stalked off, her heels snapping against the hardwood. Both Liam and Sullivan watched her go, their gazes glued to her firm bottom.

"Sweet Lord," Sullivan drawled, "she's even sexier than I remember."

"Dibs," Liam said without delay.

Ethan turned to the other man with a frosty expression. "Forget about it. She's off-limits."

There was a beat.

Then Liam hooted. "Staking a claim, eh, rookie?"

"Something like that," he muttered.

Sullivan broke out in a wide grin. "I don't know, Boston. Maybe we need to throw our hats in the ring. Give the rookie a little competition."

"Definitely."

Ethan knew they were just kidding around, but the thought of one of them so much as laying a finger on Juliet made every muscle in his body stiffen. His hands involuntarily curled into fists, a deadly gleam entering his eyes.

"Touch her and you're dead," he said coldly.

That only made them grin harder.

"Aw, our little boy has it bad."

Liam's blue eyes twinkled. "Have you made a move yet? Or are you taking it nice and slow as usual?"

"How long did it take you to ask out that chick from San Jose?" Sullivan chimed in. "Three months?"

He tolerated the good-natured ribbing, but didn't get a chance to voice a comeback because the woman on the couch was beginning to stir.

Alisa Baronova moaned as she sat up. She blinked, rubbed her face, and then her brown eyes widened in panic. "W-what . . . w-where . . . *what is the meaning of this*?" the bleached blonde screamed in her native tongue.

The high-pitched shriek made all three men wince.

"It's all right," Ethan told her in a soothing tone. "You're safe."

"Safe? *Safe?* I was abducted! You abducted me!"

Completely ignoring the hysterical woman, Sullivan glanced at Ethan and murmured, "Speaking of abductions, the Karin girl's disappearance is all over the news."

Deciding to deal with one crisis at a time, Ethan went over to the couch and addressed the woman, whose face was red with anger.

"Ms. Baronova, I need you to calm down," he said in Russian. "You haven't been abducted. We brought you here for your own protection."

That didn't placate her in the slightest. "I demand to call my husband! Give me back my phone right this second!"

"Hey, Juliet, get in here!" Ethan hollered in the direction of the corridor. His Russian was decent, but the Belarusian language was one he wasn't entirely fluent in. Juliet's Belarusian was a million times better than his, and he needed her, pronto, to explain the situation to the outraged Baronova.

Juliet appeared a moment later, with Anastacia Karin at her heels. Baronova's screams must have woken the girl up, and she looked scared and confused as she followed Juliet into the living room. Although Ethan had helped her wash up upon their arrival, splotches of dried blood were still caked to her face, which only made Alisa Baronova yell louder.

"Oh, my God! Oh, my God! You're Anastacia! I saw you on the news!" Gasping, Baronova shot to her feet, wobbling on her five-inch heels. "You people kidnapped this girl!"

To Ethan's surprise, it wasn't Juliet who interjected, but the fifteen-year-old girl who'd witnessed a man get shot today.

"Someone tried to kill me." Anastacia's voice cracked. "These people saved me. And if they brought you here, that means you're in danger too."

Baronova's cheeks paled. "What?" She swiveled her head to Ethan. "I demand to know what's going on."

Juliet spoke up, cool as a cucumber as she informed the older woman that somebody had hired a hit man to kill her. Baronova grew even paler, eyes as wide as saucers.

"You're wrong," the woman protested when Juliet mentioned the car bombings from earlier in the year. "That was the People's Revolutionary Front. They bragged about it on television."

"They may have been responsible, yes, but that

doesn't change the fact that we found a list with your name on it in the hands of a ruthless assassin."

That shut Baronova right up. She fell silent for several moments, bringing one long fingernail to her lips and chewing on it like it was a carrot.

Ethan shot Juliet a grateful look before glancing at Anastacia. "How are you feeling?" he asked the teen.

"Scared," she said frankly. Then she hesitated. "Can I call my father?"

"Not yet. We have to assume that your families are being watched, and their communication devices are most likely tapped. We're going to keep the two of you here until we can neutralize the threat to your lives."

Baronova's head flew up in alarm. "For how long? And you still haven't told us who you people are!"

"We're special operatives trained to deal with these types of situations," Juliet said smoothly.

Ethan hid a grin.

"Do you speak English?" she asked Baronova.

"Yes, I speak it." The woman responded in English, but with a thick European accent.

"Good, because these boys over here speak appalling Russian. Anyway, let's get the introductions out of the way. I'm Juliet. That's Ethan. Blondie over there is Sullivan, and Liam is the one who looks like a male model."

Baronova's gaze lingered on Liam as if she were noticing his appearance for the first time. When she realized that the man was indeed pretty enough to grace the cover of *GQ*, her entire demeanor changed. Suddenly she was smiling prettily and staring at Liam with visible approval in her eyes.

"So, he will be keeping me safe?" she said thoughtfully. "Liam, you said?"

"At your service." Although Macgregor's tone was light, Ethan could tell the man was irritated as hell. And he was slowly edging away, as if getting ready to bolt.

Ethan didn't blame the guy. If Alisa Baronova had been looking at *him* like she wanted to devour him whole, he'd probably feel like running too. But their plan could only be aided by the woman's cooperation, so if Liam's good looks kept her calm, Ethan would take advantage of it.

"Liam will be your personal guard," he told the enamored woman, ignoring Liam's glare. "And I promise you"—he included Anastacia in the address—"you'll be able to call your families the moment we determine it's safe."

As the two females noticeably relaxed, Ethan turned to Sullivan and said, "We picked up some supplies on the way. Can you see about fixing these ladies up with something to eat and drink?"

Sullivan nodded. "I'm on it."

Ethan looked to Juliet next. "Can we talk alone?"

With a nod, she followed him into the bedroom, where he immediately closed the door behind them and rubbed the bridge of his nose. The headache had finally arrived, a dull throb in his temples that made it difficult to concentrate.

"Did you talk to Noelle?" he asked Juliet.

"Yep. She's making a few calls. She said she'll get back to me as soon as she can."

"She and D are doing okay with Kozlov?"

"Yeah. Kozlov and his girlfriend are back at their hotel for the night. Noelle planted a mic in their room, and she and D are right down the hall if anything goes down. She said Kozlov's other tails are positioned outside at the front and rear of the place."

Ethan massaged his temples. "What are the chances of Noelle getting us close to Mironov?"

"Good, I think. She didn't seem at all daunted by the task, which leads me to believe she has a way to contact him."

He kept rubbing his head, trying to remember what else he'd needed to ask her.

Juliet strode over and intercepted his hands. "You okay?" she said suspiciously.

"Massive headache," he muttered.

"Aw, poor baby. C'mere."

Before he could blink, she was leading him toward the bed. If he weren't so goddamn tired, he wouldn't have allowed her to push him down on the mattress. As it was, he capitulated, stretching out on his back while Juliet settled on her knees beside him, her dark hair falling over one shoulder like a chocolate curtain.

When she brought her thumbs to his temples and began kneading gently, he couldn't help but moan. "Fuck, that feels good."

"You need to get some sleep."

"Nah. I can go for days without sleep. Just grab me a few ibuprofen from the med kit and I'll be fine."

"You're really gonna get all macho on me? Just take a twenty-minute catnap, for Pete's sake."

His lips twitched. "What's with the Florence Nightingale routine? Since when do you care whether I'm well rested?"

"Because you're going to help me kill Dmitry Orlov. I need you in tip-top shape for that."

"Uh-huh. Right. You only care when it benefits you. You're selfish, motivated by self-preservation, and totally uninterested in forming attachments. Isn't that right?"

"Yep."

He rolled his eyes. "I won't even bother calling bull-shit. Sooner or later you'll drop the fuck-the-rest-of-the-world act and admit that you actually have a heart."

"I doubt it." She continued to rub his temples, but her body language became awkward. "I heard you, by the way."

"Heard what?"

"What you said to the boys. I think it was something along the lines of, 'Touch her and you're dead.'"

He supposed he could have pretended to look contrite, but he didn't bother. Juliet would see right through it anyway.

"Yeah, what about it?"

"Well, as sexy as I find the whole staking-a-claim thing, we need to be clear about something, rookie." Her gaze locked with his. "One blow job doesn't make us an item. And neither will sex—I won't even try to act like we're not going to have sex, because that train left the station a long time ago. But when we do it, it's not going to be deep and meaningful, and it definitely won't be the start of anything long-term. It'll just be sex, and then we'll wrap up this job and go our separate ways."

"No, we won't."

Aggravation flashed in her eyes. "Yes. We will. I don't do relationships."

He slowly rose so they were sitting face-to-face. "You will with me."

Her laughter was tinged with disbelief. "You're a cocky bastard, aren't you?"

"No, I'm just a man who knows what he wants." He reached out and stroked her silky cheek with his thumb.

"You can want all you like, but you're still not getting your way. This is going to be fucking, pure and simple. We are going to fuck. We'll probably fuck a lot. And then I'm walking away."

He knew she was being purposely crude in an attempt to scare him off, but it only succeeded in steeling his resolve. People thought he was Mr. Nice Guy, a man you could stomp all over if you felt like it, a man who'd end up with a sweet, docile bride who would pop out his rug rats and worship the ground he walked on.

But he had no interest in sweet, passive women. He might've dated a few, but deep down he'd always been attracted to the strong ones. Women who spoke their mind, who stood their ground, who knew exactly what they wanted and went after it.

Women like Juliet.

Except he'd gotten more than he'd bargained for with her. She was strong, yes. Not to mention bold, resourceful, gutsy. But she was also far more vulnerable than he'd ever imagined. She had a hard exterior, hiding behind sassy smirks and biting remarks, but the more he got to know her, the more he realized what a pretense that was.

"Stop it," she muttered.

"Stop what?" He skimmed his fingertips over her plush lips, tracing the seam.

"Stop telling yourself that I'm *the one*. We're not going to be together. We don't belong together." Her breathing sounded labored to his ears. "Happily-ever-after doesn't exist. True love and all that bullshit? Doesn't exist. And I'm never again making the mistake of believing it does."

He cupped her delicate chin. "Who made you believe it?" he said roughly. "Who broke your heart?"

"I'm not doing this, okay? I'm not going to sit around and swap relationship stories with you." Anger burned in her eyes as she shrugged out of his grip and hopped off the bed. "Take a goddamn nap, Ethan. I'll wake you up in twenty."

With that, she stalked out of the room.

Chapter 14

"Son of a bitch. She actually came through for us." Juliet shook her head in amazement as she strode into the kitchen at five o'clock the next morning.

Ethan and Sullivan were already up, having drawn the graveyard shift, while Liam was sound asleep on the couch, snoring softly.

Since Juliet had taken the earlier watch, she'd avoided having to share the bedroom with Ethan, much to her relief. She was finding it difficult to be around him, especially when last night's unsettling conversation continued to buzz around in her head like a pesky fly.

How could he think they'd actually wind up in a relationship once this was all over? It already annoyed her to no end that she was working with so many outsiders on this mission, and now she was going to get a *boyfriend* out of the deal? No way. Her only goal was to take out Henry's killer, and she'd do anything to make that happen, even team up with Morgan's merry band of mercenaries. And once she achieved that goal, she was saying sayonara to everyone.

Including Ethan.

"You're shitting me," Sullivan said, jerking her out of her thoughts. "She actually got us a face-to-face with Mironov?"

Juliet made a beeline for the coffeemaker on the counter and removed a Styrofoam cup from the package she and Ethan had purchased yesterday. She poured herself a cup of coffee, added a splash of milk, and headed for the table.

"I told you, Noelle has connections. Turns out one of her informants is an ex–KGB operative with ties to the PRF." Juliet sat down and spared a quick glance at Ethan, who looked way too cute in his snug hunter green sweater and black trousers. "Mironov knows he's meeting with an associate of Noelle's, but things might still get dicey when I show up."

"When *you* show up? No way, Jules. You're not going alone."

Jules? The nickname sounded so natural coming from that sexy mouth of his. It made her heart skip a beat, but at the same time, the familiarity was grating.

"Mironov's man made it clear that I was to come alone," she told him.

"Tough cookies. I'm going with you."

"Tough cookies? Where'd you pick up that phrase, kiddo? *Sesame Street*?"

He ignored the jab. "I'm coming with you whether you like it or not. We're not pandering to a fucking terrorist, all right?"

"Jeez. All right. But if he shoots you on sight, you have only yourself to blame." Shrugging, she took a long sip of coffee.

"When and where is this rendezvous?" Ethan asked.

"Noon, and it's at some shit-hole bar in the city's east end. I asked Paige to vet the area and she says it's all PRF supporters out there. The bar is owned by one of Mironov's men. Apparently the cops have gotten multiple warrants to search the place, but each time they go in, they find nothing that implicates the owner or patrons in connection to the PRF."

Sullivan spoke up, his light gray eyes flickering unhappily. "I'd feel better if I were going with you." He paused. "Scratch that—I'd feel better if the entire team was here."

"Yeah, some backup would be nice," Ethan admitted. "I left Morgan a message earlier to check if they're done with the Bolivia extraction, but he hasn't called back yet."

"We'll be fine," Juliet said dismissively. "Mironov wouldn't dare harm anyone who works for Noelle."

Ethan and Sullivan exchanged a look that made Juliet furrow her brow. "What?" she said in bewilderment.

"I just don't understand how your boss got her reputation." Sullivan's tone held a combination of reverence and confusion. "I mean, people don't just fear her—they *fear* her. Grown men piss their pants when they hear her name. There're hundreds of contract killers out there, but none who inspire the same level of terror in people that she does. And yet I've bloody *met* the lady, and she seems totally harmless."

Juliet snickered. "Harmless? I wouldn't recommend you ever say that to her face."

"Seriously, though, where did she come from? What did she do to earn that rep?" Ethan asked curiously.

"Honestly? I don't know much about Noelle's past. She never talks about it." Juliet hesitated. "But I did hear stories about her over the years. When I was working in

Europe, her name came up a lot, and let's just say that everything I heard made me incredibly nervous about ever crossing paths with the queen of assassins."

Ethan looked intrigued. "What'd you hear?"

"You know, the usual. Someone important would wind up dead and there'd be whispers. Lots and lots of whispers. Like how she'd been trained by a master assassin in Hong Kong, which I think is bullshit, by the way. Or that she dismembered her targets while they were still alive—again, I call bullshit. But then I met her, and some of the stories made me wonder. Like the one about her seducing a target and slitting his throat while he was orgasming, or how she'd brazenly walked into a room full of high-powered politicians, killed one on the dance floor, and disappeared without a trace." Juliet shrugged. "Shit like that, I can believe."

Sullivan let out a low whistle. "But you still decided to work for the lady?"

"Why not? She's terrifying, sure, but she's also smart and resourceful and her services are in high demand." Juliet offered a self-deprecating smile. "You should have seen the training she put me through. I bet it puts your military boot camps to shame."

"Trust me, I know," Ethan said ruefully. "Abby took it upon herself to give me a workshop on knife fighting once. Scared me shitless."

Juliet laughed. "Abby always did have a fondness for knives. But then your boss stole her away, and now she spends her days *rescuing* people. How boring." Setting down her cup, she hopped to her feet. "C'mon, rookie, let's start heading out. It'll take us two hours to make the drive back to the city, and I want to get there early so we can vet the bar."

He was already sliding off his chair. "I'm right behind you."

Noelle was expecting his call.

From the second Juliet informed her she was teaming up with Jim's rookie to go after Dmitry Orlov, Noelle had known she'd be hearing from Jim sooner or later, and sure enough, his wretched number flashed on her phone at eight o'clock that morning. D had already left the suite to keep an eye on Kozlov and take advantage of the hotel restaurant's continental breakfast, but Noelle had hung back because she had a feeling this phone call would go down today.

She deliberately waited several rings before answering. Let the bastard wait. If she could create even the slightest inconvenience in his life, she'd damn well do it.

"What can I do you for, Jim?" she drawled once she'd picked up.

"Why is it that every time I turn around, you've lured one of my guys into another one of your crusades?"

His rough voice cut right to her core. Once upon a time she'd loved that deep, husky voice. Yearned for it. Dreamed about it late at night when she was lying in bed, foolish young girl that she was.

Now it only consumed her with rage.

"It's not my crusade," she said flatly. "It's Juliet's. And your man chose to join her. I wasn't even aware of it until after I wrapped up my last job, so if you want someone to bitch at, you've got the wrong person. This was out of my control."

"And your relationship with my best soldier? Is that out of your control too?" Sarcasm dripped from his tone.

Noelle laughed and sank down on the edge of the bed. "Relationship? You know better than that."

"Oh, that's right. You're just fucking him." His chuckle pierced her ear. "If you're trying to make me jealous, it's not working, Noelle."

"The world doesn't revolve around you, Jim."

"Your world does."

His mocking laughter continued to undulate over the line, intensifying her anger. She'd spent years learning to harness that anger, learning to lock up her emotions in the dungeon that now made up her black heart, but Jim Morgan always succeeded in unlocking those volatile feelings.

"Every move you make is traced back to me," he went on, cold, merciless. "And this thing you have going with D? I know you started it up in order to piss me off, but you really shouldn't have bothered. I don't give a shit who you screw in your spare time."

"Funny, you talk about it an awful lot for someone who claims not to care."

When he didn't respond, a surge of triumph flowed through her. The mighty Jim Morgan, not as cool and composed as he wanted her to believe.

"Now, what's the real reason for this call?" she asked him.

"Just giving you the heads-up that I'm coming to Madrid."

She froze. "What for? Is your team joining the crusade?"

"The whole team, no. At least not unless Ethan requests backup. But I've decided to take up the cause. I'm coming to keep you and D company."

Her shoulders went rigid. "We've got it covered."

"I don't know . . . surveillance can be real tricky sometimes . . ."

"What the fuck kind of game are you playing?"

"Same one I've always played." His voice lowered to a lethal pitch. "My end goal has never changed, baby. I'm going to destroy you. Whenever you experience even the faintest spark of joy, I'm going to be right there to extinguish it."

Her hands trembled with fury. "Didn't you already do that?"

"Oh, that's rich. You really want to go down this road of who screwed who? Because I'll win every time."

"That's a matter of opinion." She laughed without an ounce of humor. "All right, then. Your dastardly plan is to interfere with what I have going with D? Go ahead, Jim. Bring it on."

She disconnected the call.

Every muscle in her body was stretched taut, tightening and tightening like a guitar string until finally it snapped and she found herself whipping the phone against the wall. It smacked into the cheap landscape painting hanging there, both items crashing to the carpeted floor with a loud thud.

Inhaling deeply, Noelle gathered up the shards of her shattered composure. Goddamn him. That bastard always knew exactly which buttons to push.

But she refused to give him the satisfaction. Refused to ever let him see how deeply he still affected her.

With a long exhale, she rose from the bed and calmly went to retrieve her phone. She didn't even bother checking if it was broken—she had ten more at her disposal. Just one of the perks of being wildly wealthy.

So.

Jim wanted to come and start shit up? By all means, let him.

She'd be right here, armed and ready for him.

The Black Swan was an even bigger shit hole than Ethan had expected. Situated between two pawnshops, the bar boasted a tinted front window, a neon sign with half the letters burned out, and a broken rain gutter that was causing a fountain of wet slush to pour over the entrance. There were only two points of entry: a door with chipped paint that opened onto the unkempt sidewalk, and a metal delivery door at the rear, which spilled onto a narrow alley that reeked of beer, garbage, and urine. Neither door was guarded, but that didn't ease the tension in Ethan's gut.

He wished they'd decided to run the risk of assessing the interior layout during their recon, but neither he nor Juliet had deemed it wise. Instead, they'd split up and spent the past three hours scoping out the place to determine whether they were walking into a trap, monitoring each person that went in or out. They hadn't seen anything alarm worthy, yet waves of danger radiated from the little establishment.

Now it was almost noon, and Juliet's throaty voice rippled over the tiny transmitter lodged in Ethan's ear.

"I say we bite the bullet and go in. Worst thing that'll happen is we get killed."

He chuckled, touching his ear to activate his mic. Noelle had acquired the transmitters for them last year, and although Ethan knew it annoyed Morgan to no end, the boss had started utilizing the equipment on ops. The small, flesh-colored earpieces were motion activated, which meant the speaker could be heard only when he or she triggered the mic, leaving the feed free of constant chatter.

"You're such an optimist," he told her.

He shifted his legs, which were beginning to cramp. He was positioned on the roof of the building across from the strip of storefronts, lying flat on his belly and perched on one elbow as he peered through the scope of his favorite M40 sniper rifle, a memento from his days in the corps.

Juliet, who was watching the back, sounded impatient as she spoke again. "Meet me out front in five. Let's get this over with."

Ethan quickly returned the rifle to its case, then stashed it beneath the black tarp that was covering an enormous stack of gray bricks in the far corner of the roof. He would come back for his gear later. Right now he was fine carrying his twin Sigs and the various knives hidden beneath his clothing.

He reunited with Juliet on the sidewalk, trying not to drool over how sexy she looked. She wore a tight leather coat zipped up to the collar, a dark blue scarf wrapped around her neck, and a wool cap covering her long brown hair. On her feet were her trademark boots, which she'd confessed had custom knife sheaths sewn into the lining. The fact that she was forever armed was a major turn-on, though he wasn't entirely sure why.

"Did you change your bandages before we left?" he asked sternly, his gaze honing in on her abdomen.

"Nah, I took them off last night. The wounds are healing nicely. They'll turn into two puckered little scars in no time."

He didn't know whether to laugh or frown at her cavalier attitude toward bullet holes.

"Anyway, you ready?" She flashed one of those lazy grins he was growing accustomed to.

"Yeah, let's do this."

He would have preferred to go in first, but she beat him to it, sauntering through the beat-up door of the Black Swan as if she was walking into a friendly neighborhood pub rather than a terrorist nest.

Ethan stepped in after her, taking a second to let his eyes adjust to the dim lighting. The bar was minuscule, just one open room with a wooden counter spanning one wall, and less than a dozen tables scattered in the space. Classical piano wafted out of the speakers, completely out of place in the dank, musty-smelling room.

The bar's only occupants were male. Three at the counter, four gathered around one of the tables. Ethan noted that they were all openly armed—nobody was making an attempt to hide his firepower. And all eyes landed on the newcomers as they strode inside.

"Friendly bunch," Juliet murmured.

He ignored the harsh scowls and suspicious looks aimed in their direction. The patrons ranged in age and appearance, but they shared a common animosity that hung in the air like a pollution cloud.

Unfazed, Juliet went over to the counter and addressed the man behind it. He was in his late fifties, his hair more gray than blond, his skin pale and wrinkled.

"What do you want?" he demanded in Belarusian.

"We're here to see Ilya." She slid onto a stool, settling her delectable ass on the torn cushion. "We have an appointment."

The bartender looked her up and down with a veiled

expression. Then he nodded and grumbled out the words, "Wait here."

"So far, so good," Ethan muttered as they watched the older man disappear through a door behind him.

The disgruntled bartender wasn't gone a minute before he returned, still sporting a deep scowl. "Ilya will not see you," he informed Juliet. "You were supposed to come alone."

Irritation flickered in her eyes. "Do me a favor. Go tell Ilya I didn't come all the way here to be sent away. I *will* be seeing him today—he can either invite me or I can shoot my way to him. Tell him to take his pick."

Ethan hid a smile. Christ, the woman had balls. He suspected that Juliet Mason could easily handle any roadblock in her path. She was fearless and resourceful, two traits that he was beginning to find incredibly appealing.

Still, he wasn't crazy about the way she threw herself headfirst into dangerous situations. Maybe it made him an antiquated ass, but he didn't like the idea of Juliet placing herself in danger while he stood beside her like a chump. It wasn't that he didn't trust her to get the job done—he knew she was perfectly capable of it—but if someone was going to put their neck on the line by threatening a group of terrorists, he preferred it be him.

Without a word, the increasingly pissed-off bartender turned on his heel and stalked through the door again. He was gone for much longer this time, but when he reappeared nearly five minutes later, he jabbed a finger at them and snapped, "Come."

Ethan and Juliet quickly rounded the counter and followed him through the door, which led to a fluorescent-lit corridor that stank of stale alcohol.

The bartender escorted them to another door at the very end of the hall, where a pair of armed guards awaited them. He didn't linger, just nodded at the two men before marching off.

"Who is the man?" one of the guards inquired, his annoyed gaze focused on Juliet.

"My bodyguard," she said coolly. "I don't go anywhere without him."

The guards donned identical frowns.

"Spread your arms and legs," the second one ordered. "You can't go in until we search you for weapons."

Juliet grinned. "I'll make it easy for you boys—I'm carrying a nine-millimeter Beretta under my jacket, four five-inch KA-BAR blades in my boots, a seven-incher on my belt, and a grenade in my pocket."

Ethan choked back a laugh.

"My companion is carrying two nine-mil Sigs and three knives," she added. "But I can assure you, neither one of us will so much as touch our weapons unless the situation calls for it."

Ethan noted that she didn't offer to relinquish the weapons, and fortunately, the guards didn't demand it of them. Since they were both carrying AK-47s, they probably felt secure that they could best their visitors in a gunfight.

"This way," one of them muttered.

They were taken to a small room, empty save for a single square table and four plastic chairs. Ethan conducted a visual sweep, immediately pinpointing the three cameras mounted on the walls and the deadly wires running along the ceiling. The room was rigged with explosives. Lovely.

The guards gestured to the chairs, ordered them to sit, and left the room.

When they were alone, Ethan and Juliet exchanged a look.

"A real second-rate operation," she remarked. "I hope this isn't their headquarters—otherwise they're in trouble."

"Nah, I doubt it. I bet this is just where Mironov conducts his business meetings."

Neither of them sat down or made a move to remove their coats. If Ethan had his way, they wouldn't be staying long. A quick convo with the PRF leader, and then they could hightail it back to the safe house.

They were kept waiting for almost twenty minutes this time, though he suspected that was a strategic move on Alexei Mironov's part. No doubt they were being watched on some monitor in another room, being assessed by the man they were about to meet.

When the door finally opened, Ethan was startled by the figure that appeared in the doorway. Alexei Mironov was in his early thirties, a tall man with sharp brown eyes and surprisingly aristocratic features. He wore black jeans and a turtleneck that outlined his muscular chest and broad shoulders, and in his hand was an HK pistol with a suppressor attached to the muzzle.

The man wasted no time raising the gun, a deadly smile gracing his mouth as he pointed the weapon at Juliet's head and addressed her in fluent English.

"Give me one good reason why I shouldn't blow your brains out."

Chapter 15

Juliet didn't even blink as she eyed the gun. After a beat, she shifted her gaze and studied Alexei Mironov, pleasantly surprised by the man before her. He was younger than she'd expected. And much prettier. With those dignified features of his, he could easily pass for a Slavic prince.

"Just one reason?" she echoed. "Because I can think of at least a few good ones."

Mironov's refined mouth curled in a sneer.

"Fine, one reason not to blow my brains out . . . ." She pretended to think it over. "How about this? If I turn up dead, my boss will unleash her wrath and wipe you and your entire group off the face of the earth. You've heard of my boss, haven't you, Mironov? Or would you prefer I keep calling you Ilya? Either way, you know Noelle won't be happy if you put one of her operatives out of commission."

Next to her, Ethan didn't say a word, but his hand was positioned at the front of his open jacket, easily within reach of his guns.

"Why didn't Noelle come herself?" Mironov finally asked, a suspicious cloud darkening his eyes.

"Because she's not working this job. I am. Are you going to sit down, or what? We might as well be comfortable during our little chat."

It seemed like an eternity before Mironov lowered his weapon. He made his way to the table with long, predatory strides and gestured to one of the empty chairs. "After you," he said graciously.

Rolling her eyes, she sat down and casually crossed her legs.

Ethan remained standing.

"I wasn't aware contract killers traveled with bodyguards," Mironov commented, his sharp gaze briefly resting on Ethan.

"What can I say? I'm a very paranoid woman."

Mironov grabbed one of the plastic chairs, turned it around, and straddled it. He still held his semiautomatic, but his grip was loose. "What's this about, Ms. Mason?"

"I'll get right to the chase." She shrugged. "I'm afraid we might have a conflict of interest."

"Go on."

"Like I said before, I'm working a job and, as it turns out, my target might be an associate of yours. I wanted to come and verify that before I made a move."

"How courteous of you." He continued to watch her intently. "Do you reach out to the associates of every man you kill?"

"Not usually, no."

"Then why come to me?"

She offered him a wry smile. "Well, you see, if you *are*

working with my target, I'm afraid I'm going to have to take you out too. Sorry in advance."

Alexei Mironov responded with a loud, genuine laugh. "I do appreciate your spunk. So tell me, who is this associate you speak of?"

"Dmitry Orlov. I'm sure you know of him. He happens to be the defense minister of your lovely country."

He raised his eyebrows. "Interesting. And what makes you think a man like myself, who happens to operate on the wrong side of the law, would be working with a government official?"

She rested her hands on the splintered wood tabletop. "Pavel Drygin, Grigory Novik, and Irina Bartney."

Recognition flickered in his brown eyes.

"Ah, so you're familiar with the names. You should be, seeing as you and your buddies took credit for their deaths."

A frown puckered his mouth.

"But here's the thing. I happen to know for a fact that Dmitry Orlov instigated those car bombings. Along with the deaths of several other individuals your organization has taken responsibility for killing."

She listed off the names on Grechko's hit list, watching Mironov's expression the entire time.

The man didn't blink. Didn't react.

"So I'm sure you can understand why this raises a few questions, Mironov. If those executions are your doing, that leads me to believe you're in bed with Orlov. But if you're not responsible, then I guess that makes you a liar, huh?"

The rebel leader narrowed his eyes. "Why were you hired to kill Orlov? And by whom?"

"That's none of your concern. My employers have

their reasons." The lie came out smoothly. She and Ethan had decided beforehand that it was better to let him think this was an official venture rather than one rooted in vengeance.

"You do realize that if I am working with Orlov, you've tipped your hand by coming here? What's to stop me from warning him that someone is planning to murder him?"

"Go ahead. It doesn't matter to me whether or not he knows. No amount of forewarning will stop me from getting the job done."

"Your confidence is either very admirable or incredibly foolish."

She simply shrugged again.

Mironov went silent for a moment, then gave a faint smile. "And if I am working with the minister? What then?"

"Well, that's where the complications arise. If I'm being honest, I have zero interest in you or your cause. My objective is to eliminate Orlov. I'd rather avoid the headache of wiping out your little group."

He snorted. "I'd like to see you try."

"Oh, I wouldn't just try. I'd succeed." Juliet waved her hand. "But that's beside the point. Like I said, I don't care about your silly revolution."

Her trivializing of his life's mission brought the flare of anger to his eyes. His hand seemed to instinctively tighten over his weapon, and Juliet's peripheral vision caught the tensing of Ethan's shoulders. But she wasn't worried. Alexei Mironov was a professional—she was confident he could take a few hits to his ego without losing his temper.

"Anyway, my employers are concerned that if Orlov is removed from the equation, you'll continue on the course of action he's set, and we can't let that happen. So, the question is, are you doing Orlov's dirty work or simply taking credit after the fact?"

Another silence descended over the cramped room. Mironov was studying her again, and his transparency made her swallow a laugh. She knew exactly what was going through his head right now—to talk or not to talk. He was deciding what would be in his best interest, and Juliet wasn't surprised when he chose option number one.

"We had nothing to do with it," he finally admitted.

She had to grin. "See how easy that was? That's all I needed to know." She slanted her head. "Out of curiosity, why publicly take responsibility then?"

He shrugged. "It's good for the cause. Violence always gets people's attention, inspires fear in their hearts. Several individuals with government connections were executed and no one stepped up to take the blame. Why not take advantage of that? It tells the citizens of this country that Belikov and his people are *not* invincible, that ordinary folks like us *can* bring about change. My men and I didn't kill those people, but that doesn't mean we can't benefit from their deaths."

"That's very pragmatic of you."

He offered a lopsided smile, and in that moment it was hard to reconcile this charming man with the leader of a terrorist group that had been responsible for countless acts of violence.

"We are revolutionaries, Ms. Mason," he said, as if reading her mind. "Not terrorists, as my corrupt govern-

ment is leading the people to believe. Our goal is to inspire change, and sometimes violence is the only way to
do that." He scowled. "But we would never conspire
with a man like Dmitry Orlov. He is the precise type of
vermin we are trying to exterminate."

"That he is," she agreed.

"Orlov paints himself as a patriot, a man who puts his
country ahead of personal ambition, but that is, pardon
my French, bullshit." Mironov scoffed. "He's no better
than the criminals he's chasing. He kills anyone who op-
poses him, blackmails his own colleagues, disregards civil
rights by torturing suspects for days or months on end—"

"You do realize," she interrupted, "that your group is
directly responsible for that, don't you? Orlov's in-
creased penchant for violence started after you murdered his son."

"Again, I say bullshit. Unfortunately, the boy was an
innocent bystander, but he was a casualty of a war that
his father had already been fighting. Orlov has always
been a bloodthirsty maniac. I've lost several men to him
and his counterterrorist unit. They make arrests based
on fabricated charges, take the suspects to one of their
black sites—"

"Black sites?"

"Interrogation facilities," he clarified. "Usually located in a bunker somewhere away from the city. When
a suspect goes in, he never comes out. That's the way
Dmitry Orlov operates." Disgust flashed on his face.
"Tell your employers that the People's Revolutionary
Front is not associated with the man, nor will we stand in
the way of any attempts made on his life."

"Good to know." Nodding, Juliet scraped back her

chair and stood up. "It was very nice chatting with you, Alexei. We'll be on our way now."

As she extended her hand to Mironov, Ethan took a protective step to her side, but the precaution was unnecessary. With a rueful smile, Mironov rose from his chair and shook her hand.

"Noelle is as wise as she is beautiful. I wholly approve of her choice in operatives. You're an intriguing woman, Ms. Mason."

"Have you met Noelle before?" she asked him.

To her surprise, he nodded.

"I wasn't aware of that."

Now he smirked. "Didn't she tell you? I utilized her services several years ago."

Of course. Juliet should have known that Noelle was more involved with Mironov than she'd let on. KGB informant, her ass.

"And who was the unlucky target, if you don't mind me asking?"

"The man who called the shots before me. How do you think I got to where I am today?" His grin widened. "Be sure to tell your boss I said hello and to stop by next time she's in the neighborhood."

"I'll pass that along." Juliet smiled. "It was a pleasure meeting you. I'm glad I don't have to kill you."

His roar of laughter followed her and Ethan all the way out the door.

"That was the most impressive thing I've witnessed in a long time," Ethan said as they got into the Range Rover that Sullivan and Liam had arrived in yesterday.

"What, Mironov?" Juliet settled in the passenger's seat and buckled up.

"No, *you*. You handled him like a pro."

She bristled. "That's because I am a pro."

"I know you are. I just meant . . . the dude's a straight-up terrorist and you made him into a pussycat." Ethan sighed. "I'm so turned on right now."

Juliet burst out laughing. "Seeing me interrogate a terrorist gets you hot? Weirdo."

"Seeing you do *anything* gets me hot." His sultry gaze locked with hers before he wrenched it back to the road.

As he drove toward the highway, Juliet drew her Beretta from her waistband and rested it on her lap, getting comfortable for the two-hour drive.

"I think Mironov's past association with Noelle helped paved the way to his cooperation," she said. "And now we can cross the PRF off our list and I can move on Orlov without you having to worry about any accomplices."

"He might still be working with someone else. We're not touching Orlov until we know for sure."

His stern response triggered her annoyance. "Come on, rookie. What more do you want to do? Dig under every rock until we're one hundred percent certain Orlov is working alone?"

"If we don't, then Anastacia Karin and the others will never be safe," he argued.

"I don't care. The son of a bitch killed my brother. I'm taking him out."

She suddenly realized she hadn't thought about Henry since they'd saved Anastacia, but now the memory of him in that hospital bed came rushing back and her body trembled with rage. Her brother was dead. Caught in the cross fire of Dmitry Orlov's thirst for vengeance.

For that, Orlov deserved to be erased from the planet.

"I'm taking him out," she said again through clenched teeth. "Feel free to stick around after he's dead, in case someone else moves on the targets."

"You're the most stubborn woman I've ever met — you know that?"

She relaxed when he didn't voice another argument. "Yeah, but we both know you like it. I bet my pigheadedness turns you on as much as my interrogation skills."

"You'd win that bet."

"Yeah?"

"Oh yeah." The heat returned to his eyes, thickening the air between them. "Like I said, everything about you is a turn-on. When I was keeping watch last night, I spent the entire time trying to figure out a way to get you alone so we could make it to third base."

She flashed him a mischievous grin. "Well, we're alone now, are we not?"

He raised his eyebrows. "Are you serious?"

"Why not? Look around you. Deserted stretch of road, no people or houses in sight . . ."

His voice grew husky. "What are you saying? You want me to pull over and ravish you on the side of the road?"

"Why not?" she said again. "I'm sure Aussie and Boston can man the fort alone for a little while longer."

She expected Ethan to dismiss the idea with a laugh, but the next thing she knew, he veered off the road so fast she almost flew out of her seat.

He didn't park on the shoulder of the rural road. He steered the Range Rover right onto the snow instead, speeding across an empty field toward a crumbling, abandoned barn about a hundred yards away. The vehicle's big snow tires allowed for an easy, albeit bumpy drive, and Juliet laughed and braced her hand on the dashboard as the four-by-four bounced over the field in a mad pace.

"Someone's overly eager," she commented.

"Ha. Like you aren't. Now, turn on your seat warmer, because you're going to be out of those pants in about, oh, ten seconds."

Her breath caught in her throat when she glimpsed the hunger burning in his eyes. Lord, he looked ready to *devour* her. Her body instantly responded, breasts tingling and pussy clenching with need.

She unbuckled her seat belt and wiggled out of her jeans as if she were trying to break the world record for fastest pants removal.

Before the car even came to a complete stop, Ethan was reaching for the waistband of her black thong and tugging on the strap. He ripped the thong right off her body, eliciting a delighted squeak from her lips. Holy moly. Who *was* this man and how did he continue to surprise her?

He tossed the torn underwear in the backseat, shoved the gearshift into park, and licked his lips as he turned to her. "Move your seat back. Now."

A dark thrill shot through her. She did as he asked, acutely aware that her lower body was completely exposed to him. The heat emitted from the leather seat kept her bare ass warm, but an involuntary shiver danced through her as she waited for Ethan to make his next move.

•

Slow and methodical, he undid his seat belt. His gaze never left hers as he climbed over the center console and sank to his knees in front of her. The raw passion in his eyes robbed her of breath, and when he lazily dragged his callused fingertips over her left thigh, she almost passed out from the anticipation.

"Technically, I don't think third base should involve my tongue on your pussy, but you cheated with second base, so I'm cheating now."

The dirty talk made her pulse race. Sweet mother of God. If someone had told her that this man, with his preppy clothes and boyish grins and courteous ways, was capable of tearing off a woman's panties at the seams and going down on her in public, she would have laughed them right out of town.

But here he was, kneeling before her, teasing the sensitive flesh of her inner thighs with his fingers, making her heart thump with excitement.

"You are the sexiest woman I've ever met," he rasped, his gaze traveling up her bare legs and settling on her most intimate place.

Then he planted both hands on her thighs and slowly spread her legs wider.

She shivered again. Couldn't remember ever feeling this way before. Damp palms, pounding heart, throbbing core. She feared she might actually explode before he even touched her aching sex.

When Ethan dipped his head and brought his mouth between her legs, Juliet jerked as if she'd been shot.

"Oh *God*," she moaned.

His lips were firm and warm, his tongue gentle as he dragged it over her slit. He licked her like he had all the time in the world, a slow and languid exploration that had her seeing stars.

"You. Taste. Like. Heaven." Each word was punctuated by the lazy swipe of his tongue over her clit.

Juliet watched as he pleasured her, floored by the sight. His dark eyelashes swept downward as he closed his eyes. Little growls of contentment rumbled out of his mouth, his tongue growing more insistent. He lapped at her with purpose now, as if his sole goal in life was to make her come apart.

The pressure between her legs was unbearable. She whimpered, feeling edgy, desperate, needing something more to ease the tension building inside her.

"I need . . ." She gasped when he captured her clit between his lips and sucked. "Need . . . your finger . . ."

Without missing a beat, he pushed two long fingers into her tight channel, skillfully working her sex while his mouth tended to her clit. It was too much—and just enough. The climax careened through her in a fiery rush, sizzling in her veins until every square inch of her body pulsed with delicious ecstasy.

She fought for breath, then moaned with abandon when she realized Ethan wasn't done yet. He allowed her no recovery time, just eased the pressure on her swollen clit and continued to torment her with his fingers.

When he curled those fingers and hit a sweet spot deep inside, a second wave of pleasure swelled in her belly, spilling over so fast, so unexpectedly, that it caught her by total surprise. The second release left her breathless, and still Ethan kept going. This time he removed his fingers and replaced them with his tongue, spearing into her while his thumb applied pressure to her clit until a third climax slammed into her, then a fourth, and then her mind fragmented into a million pieces and soared to a new plane where only bliss and Ethan's tongue existed.

By the time he pulled that talented mouth away, her legs were limp spaghetti noodles and her body was so incredibly sated, she couldn't move.

His satisfied chuckle broke through the haze of pleasure. "How was that? Good enough for a rookie? Or do I need more practice?"

He promptly lowered his head to her mound and once again skimmed his tongue over her clit.

Juliet grabbed a hunk of his hair and stilled him. "Oh, God, no more," she cried out. "I can't take any more."

He peered up at her in challenge. "I remember you telling me that I could never, and I quote, give you what you need in the bedroom. Isn't that what you said, sweetheart?"

"I was wrong," she burst out. "I was so fucking wrong, okay?"

Laughing, he planted one last kiss between her legs, then climbed back into his seat. "That's what I thought."

Oh, boy, that cocky alpha male attitude was liable to kill her. She could actually feel her body stirring again, in spite of the orgasmic assault Ethan Hayes had just launched on it.

"Now put on your jeans, sweetheart. We can't have you strolling into the safe house looking like that. I'd have to murder Sully and Liam, and I really don't feel like it."

Juliet's heartbeat remained erratic as she fumbled to put on her jeans. Commando, thanks to Ethan's unapologetic annihilation of her underwear. When she glanced over at him, it was impossible not to notice the hard ridge of arousal straining against the fabric of his trousers.

He caught her staring and grinned. "You're dying to go all the way, huh?"

"God, yes." No point in playing coy or denying it. Juliet craved this man so bad she could barely breathe. Who would've thought.

To her disappointment, he didn't unzip his pants. He simply started the engine.

She gaped at him. "Seriously?"

"We've been gone long enough. The boys are probably getting impatient."

"*I'm* getting impatient."

"Hasn't anyone ever told you that the anticipation is half the fun?"

"Hasn't anyone ever told you that you're a major tease?"

"Tease?" he scoffed. "I just made you come three times."

She gritted her teeth. "Four."

That only perked him up. "Four? Nice."

"Oh, stop grinning, kiddo. Wait until I finally get you naked. You won't be able to move for days," she warned.

Another wave of laughter spilled out of his mouth. "Are you threatening me with *good sex*? Clearly you don't know much about men."

He was still snorting in amusement as he shifted gears and drove back to the road.

*   *   *

Stacie was overcome with relief when Ethan and Juliet finally returned from their mysterious errand. She wasn't sure why, but she didn't feel the same level of comfort with the other two men as she did with the people who'd saved her life yesterday.

Nina had tried to kill her.

She was still reeling over it, and no matter how hard she tried, she couldn't control the suffocating terror that was causing her to shiver every few minutes. She understood why she couldn't call her father, but that didn't mean she liked it.

She also didn't like the woman they'd brought to the farmhouse. Alisa had been complaining all day long—at least when she wasn't flirting with the handsome man they called Liam.

Stacie had spent the day playing cards with the blond man, Sullivan, who'd taught her how to play two different kinds of poker. They'd used toothpicks instead of money, and in between hands he'd told her about someone named Evangeline. She suspected it was his girlfriend, but she couldn't be sure because the whole conversation had been very confusing. Stacie had thought her English was perfect, so either she was wrong about that or she'd misunderstood him when he'd described his girlfriend as sturdy and said she had "clean lines."

But as nice as Sullivan was, the panic weighing on her chest didn't ease until her saviors walked through the door.

From her seat at the kitchen table, she watched as they removed their coats and winter gear. Juliet took off her hat and smoothed her hands over her long, dark hair, which was so thick and shiny, it made Stacie self-conscious about her plain, stringy tresses. She didn't think she'd ever met a prettier woman. Juliet was so beautiful, it was hard not to be envious when you were around her.

And Ethan was so handsome, Stacie felt herself blush each time his warm hazel eyes focused on her.

"Everything go okay?" Sullivan rose from his chair and joined the newcomers, the poker game all but forgotten.

Ethan nodded. "The PRF isn't involved."

"Well, that's one less thing to worry about."

As the four adults spoke among themselves, Stacie fidgeted with her stack of toothpicks, feeling awkward and out of place. She wondered if she should tell them that today was her birthday.

Why? They're not going to care.

The little voice evoked a wave of sadness. It was true. These people were strangers to her. If her own father hadn't cared about her sixteenth birthday, why should *they*?

Tears pricked her eyes, spurring her to push back her chair and shoot to her feet.

The adults instantly swiveled their heads in her direction.

"Hey, Anastacia," Ethan said, greeting her with a gentle smile. "You holding up okay?"

She nodded, bit hard on the insides of her cheeks in order to stop the tears from spilling over. "I'm fine. Can I go lie down in the other bedroom? Alisa is sleeping in the main one."

A groove of concern appeared in Ethan's forehead. "Sure. But are you certain you're all right?"

"I'm fine," she said woodenly.

And then she hurried to the corridor, refusing to let them see her cry.

It wasn't fair.

Life was *never* fair to her.

Her mother was dead. Her father didn't know she existed.

She had to wonder, did he even care that his assistant had tried to kill her? Ethan kept saying it wasn't safe to have any contact with her dad right now, and although Stacie was overwrought about it, she would bet her trust fund that her father wasn't at all broken up about the lack of contact. He was probably at another safe house, drinking his favorite whiskey as he waited for the danger to pass, not once thinking about his daughter.

Stacie entered the bedroom and threw herself on the ugly orange bedspread, curling up on her side as the tears streamed down her cheeks. She was sixteen today. She didn't feel older, though. Just tired. And more alone than ever.

A soft knock on the door had her lurching into an upright position.

She swiped at her wet eyes with her sleeve and called out "What do you want?" without caring that she was being rude. She was the prime minister's daughter, after all. If she demanded privacy, then these people had to give it to her.

"Anastacia? Can I come in?"

It was Juliet, speaking such flawless Belarusian that Stacie would have believed she was a native.

"What for?" she choked out.

"I just wanted to talk to you for a minute."

"Fine. Whatever." Stacie sniffled, wishing she had a tissue, but there was only one bathroom in the house and it was out in the hall.

The door creaked open and Juliet stepped inside the room. Worry flickered in her dark brown eyes when she noticed Stacie's splotchy face, but she didn't comment on it.

Stacie appreciated that. She also appreciated the way Juliet spoke to her like she was a grown-up and not a little girl you needed to talk down to. Most adults tended to do that, including Alisa Baronova, who treated Stacie like she was inferior just because she happened to be a teenager.

"Look, I'm not going to say all the usual bullshit about how everything will be all right and keep your chin up, and yada yada. I know being here sucks," Juliet said bluntly. "I know you're scared, and I know you probably can't stand the sight of us."

The woman wandered over to the bed and sat down beside her. "I won't feed you any lines, because truth is, you *should* be scared. If Ethan and I hadn't shown up, your father's assistant would have put a bullet in your head. And just because she's dead doesn't mean you're out of danger."

Stacie stared at the woman for a long moment before laughing. "You're not very good at trying to make someone feel better."

"I'm not trying to make you feel better. I'm just being completely honest with you. But with that said, I want you to know that I won't let anyone get close enough to hurt you. And . . ." She shrugged. "If you want to talk, I'm a good listener. Well, only sometimes. I can't sit still for too long, so lengthy conversations bore me after a while."

Stacie laughed again. Despite the terrifying situation she'd found herself in, she actually really liked this woman. Juliet was so tough and cool, like the heroine of an action movie, and she was really funny, too. Most of the people in Stacie's life didn't have much of a sense of humor.

"So is there a particular reason for the tears?" Juliet asked gently. "Or is it just the culmination of all the scary things that have happened?"

"I am scared," she admitted. "But that's not why I was crying."

The other woman slanted her head, waiting patiently.

"Today is my birthday."

Juliet blinked. "It is?"

She nodded.

"How old are you turning? Sixteen?"

Another nod.

A beat of silence passed, broken by Juliet's regretful sigh. "I'm sorry you have to spend your birthday here with us. That must suck."

"Well, I guess it's better than being alone." Bitterness tickled her throat. "My dad hasn't been home for my last six birthdays. He wasn't going to be here for this one either, so it's not like I'm missing out on anything important."

"It must be tough, being the daughter of the prime minister."

"It's awful. I hate it. I hate *him*."

"Nah, you don't mean that."

"I do! He doesn't care about me at all." Stacie's face

collapsed, the hot sting of tears making a reappearance. "All he does is work and go on trips and leave me at home with our housekeeper, Marta, and his million assistants."

Juliet let out another breath. "I want to say something encouraging, but as you already witnessed, I'm not very good at this shit. But I can tell you this—things could be a lot worse, Anastacia."

"Stacie," she said shyly.

"What?"

"Everyone calls me Stacie."

"Ah. Okay. Well, Stacie. I know it must hurt that your father doesn't pay much attention to you, but think about it this way. You live in a huge mansion, there's always food on your table, you've got your health, you're able to go to school, and you've probably got a trust fund. A lot of kids aren't lucky enough to have even *one* of those privileges, let alone all of them."

Stacie hesitated, then asked, "Did you have any of that growing up?"

"Barely." Juliet spoke in a noncommittal tone. "No home, no food, no education, no money. Had my health, though. That's always a plus."

"I guess I sound like a spoiled brat when I complain," she said sheepishly.

"Of course not. You should never apologize or be ashamed of the way you feel. Just realize that you don't have it as bad as you think you do. And listen, I know being stuck here on your birthday sucks ass, but trust me, I have a few birthday horror stories of my own."

"Like what?"

She blurted out the question before she could stop

herself, her eagerness bringing the flush of embarrassment. But she just wanted to know everything she could about this beautiful and fierce and mysterious woman.

"Oh, honey, you don't want to know."

She tried to mask her disappointment, but Juliet must have sensed it because she offered a wry look. "All right, fine. Pick an age and I bet I can top you when it comes to bad birthdays."

Stacie thought it over. "Ten years old."

"Ten years old . . . I spent that birthday in the emergency room after the kids in my group home pushed me down a flight of stairs. I broke both my arms."

Stacie gasped, which made Juliet smile. "Oh, don't look so upset, Stacie. Now that I think about it, it wasn't too bad, actually. After all, I got a few free hospital meals out of the deal." She shrugged. "Go ahead, pick another birthday."

"Twelve," Stacie said.

"Spent that one locked in a closet with my brother. We'd stolen some money from our foster parents because they forgot to feed us dinner, but we got caught and that was our punishment. I think we were in that closet for more than a day."

"Fifteen."

"That's a bad one—it was pouring rain and I was huddled in a cardboard box, trying to stay dry. I was living on the streets for that one."

Stacie's breath hitched in sympathy. "Seventeen."

When Juliet's expression froze, Stacie knew she'd hit a nerve.

"You don't have to tell me if you don't want to," she said quickly. Although she wondered what could be worse than the other birthday memories.

"No. No, it's fine. My seventeenth birthday . . . Well, that was the night I got arrested for stealing a car." Juliet's throat bobbed as she swallowed. "It was also the night that someone close to me betrayed me."

"Your brother?" Anastacia guessed.

The woman shook her head. "No." She paused. "The man I loved."

Chapter 16

Ethan knew he should walk away. Walk away right now. Just put one foot in front of the other, march back to the living room, and pretend he'd never stumbled onto this conversation.

The man I loved.

He wasn't surprised that she'd never mentioned this mystery man before. Juliet was a closed book, only allowing snippets of information to escape when it suited her. But even though he was no stranger to secretive, complicated woman—he lived with Abby Sinclair, after all—he'd thought he'd succeeded in breaking down most of Juliet's barriers.

Walk away.

Christ, he really should. This was a total breach of privacy. He had no right listening in on such a private conversation.

And yet his feet stayed rooted to the floor.

Like the insensitive ass he apparently was, Ethan leaned against the chipped wall and continued to eavesdrop, wishing like hell the two females weren't speaking in a foreign language that he couldn't completely understand. But even though he missed a word here and there, he still got the gist of everything that was being said.

"His name was Billy." Juliet's quiet voice wafted from the bedroom door she'd left slightly ajar. "I met him when I was living on the streets. I was sixteen at the time. He was twenty-one and working as a booster for one of the big chop shop owners in Chicago."

Anastacia must have looked quizzical, because Juliet quickly elaborated. "That's what you call folks who steal cars—boosters. Billy would steal a car, bring it to the shop, and then it would be dismantled for sellable parts. It can be a lucrative gig, depending on how many cars you boost, which was why I was desperate to do it.

"Billy introduced me to his bosses, and they decided to give me a shot. At the beginning, I tagged along with Billy and learned everything I could from him." She sighed. "And I fell head over heels for him. He was larger than life. Fun, exciting, sexy. And I was young and stupid and considered him my knight in shining armor. I moved in with him two weeks after we met and I was convinced we'd get married one day and live happily ever after. We kept boosting cars, made lots of money. For a girl who grew up with nothing, I was on top of the world."

Ethan heard the wistful chord in her voice, and he could easily understand why Juliet had been so overjoyed back then, even when living on the wrong side of the law. He'd had his parents' love and support growing up, but Juliet had never been loved or supported by anyone. It was no surprise that she'd fallen under the spell of an older guy who offered to take care of her.

"Now, as painful as it is to admit, back then I wasn't as

strong as I am now. I thought I was, though—I'd been taking care of myself for years. I was wily and scrappy and considered myself the toughest girl in Chicago. But it turned out I wasn't tough at all, at least not when it came to relationships. And it turned out that Billy wasn't the man I thought he was."

"Was he mean to you?" the girl asked hesitantly.

"Very mean." There was a pause. "I was pretty damn naive, Stacie. I was so happy that he wanted to take care of me, but after a few months, I realized that he wanted to *control* me. Billy got jealous every time I talked to another guy, he monitored where I went, he even picked out the clothes I wore. I had no say in my own life, but I was so thrilled that someone finally loved me that I didn't fight him. I wasn't strong enough to leave him, or smart enough to know that relationships weren't supposed to be like that. Anyway, this went on for about a year, getting to a point where I was scared of my own shadow, terrified of saying or doing something to make Billy angry. And then came my seventeenth birthday."

Sadness washed over Ethan as he listened to her story. Juliet's infinite strength was what he admired most about her, and it killed him to hear that she'd allowed someone to take that away from her.

Juliet let out a heavy sigh. "Billy and I weren't supposed to be boosting that day. He was taking me out to a fancy dinner. I didn't want to go, but I couldn't say no to him. Ever. But just as we were leaving the apartment, he told me we had to make a quick stop. Turns out he'd promised our bosses a boost that night."

"That wasn't very nice of him."

"No, it wasn't," Juliet agreed. "But my ex was a greedy

bastard. Now, you see, the better-quality car we brought in, the more money we earned, so Billy had set his sights on a gorgeous Cadillac XLR."

"And the alarm went off when you smashed the window?" Anastacia guessed.

Ethan had to smile at the girl's innocence. That kind of naïveté was rare in this day and age.

"That's not how it works," Juliet said with a laugh. "We broke in by using a computer. I won't bore you with all the technical details, but let's just say we managed to steal the Caddy just fine. Except there was one hitch. Billy's source said the owner was gone for the weekend, but it turned out he'd stayed home. And he was walking out of his house just as we zoomed away in his car. Billy and I didn't know that, though—we thought we'd pulled it off. But as we were driving to the shop, all of a sudden there were three cop cars with screaming sirens behind us."

She went quiet, and Ethan held his breath, waiting for her to continue.

"I was driving," Juliet said flatly. "He always made me drive when we boosted together—that way if we ever got caught, I'd take most of the heat. He was twenty-one, so if he got busted, he would be charged as an adult. Me, on the other hand, I'd probably get off with a warning."

Ethan remembered her telling him this same story mere days ago, so he already knew how it ended—with Juliet arrested and being carted off to a juvenile detention center.

But clearly she'd omitted one key plot point the other day.

"But you know what he did, Stacie? While I was pulling over, resigning myself to the fact that we'd gotten caught, Billy hopped out of the car and took off like a bat out of hell. He left me there to take all the blame. So I'm sitting there in a stolen car, Billy had just abandoned me, and then the cops were pulling me out of the Caddy and handcuffing me. And that's how I spent my seventeenth birthday."

Anastacia's sympathetic voice drifted out into the hall. "What happened afterward?"

"I got sentenced to a year in juvenile detention."

"Did Billy come to visit you?"

"Once. He showed up and broke up with me. Told me he didn't see the point in waiting for me to get out, that I wasn't important enough to put his life on hold for. That's when I realized he never loved me at all. He was just using me—for sex, for the cars I stole, for the opportunity to have power over someone who wasn't going to challenge him. So yeah, he dumped me and I never heard from him again."

Anastacia sounded amazed. "But . . . that's awful!"

"Yep," Juliet said. Ethan could practically see the lazy grin on her face now. "So, do you feel any better about spending your birthday in a safe house with strangers?"

The teenager laughed. "Honestly? I kind of do."

"Good. Then I've succeeded in cheering you up."

There was a rustling sound, followed by the squeak of the mattress springs, which prompted Ethan to hastily duck back into the bathroom.

"Get some rest," he heard Juliet say. "I'll come get you for dinner."

Her footsteps echoed in the hall, and he waited until they'd faded before flushing the toilet and turning on the faucet. He let it run for a moment, pretending to wash his hands as Juliet's story continued to play over in his head.

He understood her so much better now. Her reasons for not trusting men, for keeping everyone at a distance. But that Billy character sounded like a real piece of shit. Obviously he hadn't deserved a woman like Juliet.

Ethan longed to tell her that she shouldn't give her ex so much power over her, but he'd never be able to, not unless she told him the whole story herself.

Or unless he confessed that he'd been listening in on a private conversation.

But when he stepped out of the bathroom and found Juliet outside the door, glaring at him, it was clear he didn't have to confess a damn thing.

"Really, Ethan? Eavesdropping?" Her face was cloudy with resentment.

He sighed. "You knew I was standing there the whole time, huh?"

"Damn right I did. I kept talking only because Anastacia was sitting there, waiting for me to go on." Juliet's jaw clenched. "You should have walked away. You had no right to listen to all that."

"I'm sorry," he said roughly.

"Apology not accepted."

She stalked off without another word, leaving him staring after her in dismay. He desperately wanted to race after her and apologize again, but when he heard Sully and Liam's voices in the living room, he decided against it. It was probably better if he gave her some time to cool off.

He dragged a hand over his scalp, frustrated and confused. Damn it, he was starting to care about this woman.

To *really* care about her. And, more than that, he wanted her in his life. He didn't want a fling or even a casual relationship.

Back in Vermont he'd been trying to figure out why he felt so unfulfilled, and now he knew why. He'd been looking for a connection. A real emotional connection that he hadn't been able to find with the women he'd dated in the past.

But he'd found it with Juliet, and he wanted so badly for her to view him as a man she could rely on, a man she could open up to.

You went about it the wrong way, dumb-ass.

A defeated breath lodged in his chest. Yeah, eavesdropping on her probably wasn't the best way to prove he could be trusted.

He only hoped all the promising progress he'd been making hadn't been lost because of it.

Jim Morgan turned every female head when he entered the crowded restaurant. From across the room, D watched in mild amusement as his boss marched through the place as if he owned it, dark blue eyes observing, then dismissing each admiring look aimed in his direction.

Morgan always had that effect on women. D suspected it had something to do with the man's imposing presence, the ripples of sheer danger that rolled off him, the confidence of his long stride. In his olive green cargo pants and tight white T-shirt, Morgan was severely underdressed compared to the other men in his vicinity, but that only seemed to make the female hearts beat faster. Jim Morgan played by his own rules, and women wet their fucking panties at that thrilling notion.

Well, not all women.

The one currently seated to D's left had stiffened at his boss's entrance.

"This place had better serve good grub. I'm starving," Morgan said in lieu of greeting. He slid into the chair opposite D and nodded at his soldier. "Nice getup. I'll make sure to get a picture of it so I can include it in the company newsletter."

D just scowled. He was damn tired of the potshots being taken at his ridiculous frat-boy disguise. "How'd the Bolivia job go?"

Morgan shrugged. "As well as can be expected. Kane nearly got his head blown off by one of the rebels holding the CEO hostage, which pissed off Abby, who practically cut the guy in half with her machete."

"Sounds like Abby."

"And Luke got bitten in the ass by a pit viper, which gave everyone a good laugh. We were carrying antivenom in our kits, so the Cajun lives to see another day."

D snorted. He definitely wasn't going to let Luke Dubois live that one down. The former SEAL was far too cocky for his own good. Maybe a snakebite on the ass would knock him down a peg or two.

"What about Holden? Any word from him?" D's tone turned serious as he voiced the questions.

Morgan sounded equally grave. "Still no contact. At this point I'm operating under the assumption that he's officially off the team."

D wasn't surprised to hear it. Holden McCall had lost his wife in the attack on their compound last year, and he'd been AWOL ever since. D didn't expect to ever see the man again, which both annoyed and confused him.

People died all the time — he couldn't imagine ever experiencing grief so powerful that he'd abandon his teammates because of it.

But he and Holden were very different men — that much was clear.

"Anyway," Morgan went on, signaling a passing waitress, "what's the sit rep for this job? Has the rookie checked in today?"

D noted that his boss hadn't addressed Noelle yet, and the blonde hadn't said a word to him either. She simply sat there in her pretty white sundress, fingers toying with the stem of her wineglass. To a random observer she might appear bored, but D knew better. The woman was listening to every word being exchanged, and was not only aware of the man they were supposed to be protecting, who was sitting nearby, but of Morgan's every movement as well.

"He and Juliet met with the leader of the People's Revolutionary Front today. The dude claims he's not working with Orlov," D told his boss. "I'm assuming they'll go after Orlov next."

"Good," Morgan replied with a nod. "The sooner Orlov is dead, the sooner we can put this bullshit behind us."

Noelle finally joined the conversation. "What's the matter, Jim? You're not enjoying our little reunion?"

Morgan's hard gaze collided with Noelle's mocking one.

Palpable waves of hostility moved between them. Two pairs of blue eyes — one dark as midnight, one pale as ice — narrowed with bitter acrimony and deep malice and years of bad blood.

Watching them together was bound to make grown

men squirm in discomfort, but D remained unruffled. If anything, their interactions never failed to intrigue him.

"Baby, I always enjoy seeing you." Morgan's voice was low and dripping with contempt.

She raised her glass to her bloodred lips and took a ladylike sip. "Oh, really? And why is that?"

"Because it serves as a reminder of all the loose ends I've yet to tie up."

Noelle laughed humorlessly. "I know exactly what you mean."

A petite, red-haired waitress dashed over to their table, looking harried. "What can I get you?" she asked the new arrival.

Morgan spared a brief look at the menu before requesting an order of chicken paella and a plate of *patatas bravas*.

"You sure that's not too spicy for your delicate palate?" Noelle said after the waitress rushed off.

Morgan offered a harsh chuckle. "I like to live on the edge."

A contemplative note entered her voice. "You know, I believe you said that exact same thing when we first met."

"Did I?"

"Yes."

"Well, it was as true back then as it is now."

"You really want to talk to me about truth?" For a brief second, her blue eyes flared with resentment, but it faded fast.

D, who'd been listening without comment, cleared his throat. "Should I suggest the two of you get a room?"

Neither one of them responded. They both looked thoughtful, as if each one was plotting the other's demise.

Finally Morgan glanced over at him. "Speaking of rooms, I guess I should reserve one for myself. Maybe right next door to the one you two are sharing?" He arched one dark eyebrow. "You are sharing a room, right?"

D shrugged. "You already know the answer to that."

"I was hoping you might have wised up by now." Morgan's veiled expression revealed nothing. "No matter— you'll see the light soon."

Noelle took another sip of wine, watching her nemesis over the rim of her glass. "Now, Jim, are you trying to scare him away from me?"

"Nope. You're capable of doing that all on your own, baby."

Their gazes locked again.

D stifled a sigh.

Christ. It was like a never-ending Ping-Pong match— well, if the paddles were guns and the ball was a grenade. He didn't know how long this war between them had been raging, but he sure as fuck hoped they called a cease-fire for the duration of this job.

Because if the two of them kept this shit up, *he'd* be the one getting a room.

"I overreacted."

The two words lingered in the darkness of the small living room, and although Ethan didn't answer, Juliet knew he'd heard her.

She moved through the shadows and approached the couch, where he lay motionless on his back beneath a thin wool blanket. It was just past one a.m. and Juliet was supposed to be keeping watch at the back of the farmhouse. She'd been out there for the past four hours in below-zero temperatures, staring out at the silent, snowy woods as one unsettling emotion after another passed through her.

It didn't bother her that Ethan knew about Billy hanging her out to dry; she'd experienced far more traumatic events in her life, before *and* after Billy's betrayal. No, what had annoyed her was that he'd stolen those details without her consent. She didn't share her past with just anyone. People had to earn that privilege.

Except Ethan *had* earned it. She'd realized that when she'd been sitting out in the cold. The man had flown to Belarus without a second's thought after he'd intercepted her SOS. He'd nursed her back to health. He'd watched her back during the meeting with Mironov.

For that alone, he didn't deserve the way she'd snapped at him earlier, and so she'd left her post, knowing she'd never be able to concentrate unless she apologized to him. She wasn't worried about anyone sneaking up on them—the motion detectors she'd set up would alert them if that happened, and if an intruder did manage to disarm the sensors, the small receiver in her pocket would immediately notify her that the system had been breached.

"You're supposed to be manning your post." Ethan's eyes remained shut.

The cushions shifted as she sat at the very edge of the sofa, right near his head.

"Don't worry. I won't be away from it for long. I just needed to apologize to you first."

He opened his eyes in surprise. "You don't owe me any apology," he said gruffly. "I'm the one who violated your privacy."

The regret she glimpsed in those hazel depths made her sigh. "It really wasn't a big deal. I guess I'm just a little sensitive when it comes to my ex."

"I don't blame you. He sounds like a real dick."

Juliet smiled. "Yeah, well, he was."

"What ended up happening to him?"

"He got busted a few years after I left juvie. He was sentenced to a dime in the joint, and I heard that he pissed off the wrong people and took a shiv to the eye. He survived the assault, but the doctors couldn't save the eye." She paused. "Am I a bad person for being happy about that?"

"Nah. The bastard had it coming."

They spoke in hushed tones so as not to wake up the others. Anastacia and Alisa had gone to sleep hours ago, and Liam, for some reason, had decided to crash in the bathtub, which Juliet had discovered when she'd popped into the washroom to pee a while ago. The dark-haired man hadn't stirred while she'd done her business, but she knew he'd been aware of her presence. Clearly there was no such thing as privacy in this damn house.

"Anyway, I'm sorry I stormed off like that," she said awkwardly.

"I'm sorry I eavesdropped."

Their gazes collided for one long moment.

Juliet swallowed, wishing she didn't crave this man so damn much. Wishing she could just get up and walk away and pretend he didn't affect her the way he did.

But she couldn't.

Without a word, she stood up and removed her leather jacket, then bent over to unzip her boots. Ethan's breathing quickened, and even in the shadows she could see the smoky desire in his eyes.

"What are you doing?"

She didn't answer. Instead she kicked off her boots and reached for the scratchy green blanket that covered his body.

Trying not to second-guess herself, she lifted the blanket, climbed underneath, and covered them both up again, her lips seeking Ethan's as she nestled beside him. Their mouths found each other, latching in a rough kiss that made her moan.

He pulled back, his breath heating her cold cheek. "We can't do this. Sully's right outside the front door."

"I don't care," she murmured. "We'll just have to be quiet."

They kissed again, deeper this time. Passion filled the air as they lay there tangled together, their mouths locked and their hands beginning a desperate exploration.

When Juliet slid her hands beneath his sweater to stroke his rippled chest, he shivered and offered a husky laugh. "Your hands are freezing, sweetheart."

She nipped at his neck, licking his warm male flesh. "Does that mean you don't want me to touch your cock?"

"Oh God, no. You'd better touch it."

Laughing quietly, she ran her fingertips over his tight six-pack, following the line of hair that arrowed down to his groin. As she undid his pants, he cupped one of her breasts and squeezed, his thumb toying with her nipple over her shirt.

"Fuck, I want to get you naked," he whispered. "I want to kiss every inch of your body."

Her pulse sped up. "Next time," she promised as she dipped her hand below his waistband. "I can't leave my post for that long."

"I know." His voice was thick with frustration. "This isn't how our first time was supposed to go down."

"Oh, hush. We're both going to enjoy this."

He jerked the second she touched his erection. She rubbed her palm over the drop of moisture pooling at his tip, loving the way he thrust into her hand and the little growl of pleasure that left his throat.

Ethan's mouth captured hers in a blistering kiss. He tasted like coffee and toothpaste, and he smelled so good she just wanted to drown in his scent. Heat gathered between her legs, a deep, pulsing ache that only this man could soothe.

"I want you in me," she whispered against his lips.

They both fumbled with their pants and shoved them down their bodies. The fabric tangled at their feet, which elicited an annoyed mumble from Ethan. He reached down and yanked on the discarded garments, whipping them onto the floor.

Juliet gasped when he flipped her over and covered her with his muscular frame. Even though they still had their shirts on, she could feel his heartbeat thudding against her breasts, matching the irregular thumping of her own pulse. His cock was heavy against her belly, his mouth greedily devouring hers in a passionate kiss that left her breathless.

But then he wrenched his lips away, rose on his elbows as his features grew strained. "I don't have a condom."

"It's okay. I'm on the pill. And . . ." She swallowed. "I trust you."

His breath hitched.

"I trust that you don't have any diseases," she quickly amended.

Amusement danced in his eyes. "Of course. I'm sure that's all you meant."

Juliet refused to let the brief moment of awkwardness distract her from the incredible sensations coursing through her. Ethan's body was so big and hard and masculine, and she felt utterly fragile crushed beneath all that raw, masculine power.

When he eased the tip of his cock into her, she moaned so loudly that he swiftly clapped his hand over her mouth.

"Quiet, sweetheart," he said with a soft chuckle. "We don't want to wake the neighborhood."

And then he started to move, and Juliet released another muffled moan into his palm.

Sweet mother of God, it felt good. So fucking good. Her sex stretched to accommodate him, and when her inner muscles clasped around his cock to trap him inside, he made the sexiest sound she'd ever heard. Half groan, half growl, thick with unadulterated desire.

He moved with lazy, shallow thrusts, his handsome features taut, his muscles quivering with restraint. She knew he wanted to go faster, to fuck her harder, but the squeaky cushions rendered that impossible.

"Jesus, you're so tight. I'm losing my fricking mind here."

He cupped her face as he filled her with his cock, and the raw lust in his eyes robbed her of breath. Her body was on fire. Her clit throbbed in exquisite agony. God, she never wanted this to end.

They were both panting as he kept up the excruciatingly slow and measured pace. Juliet wrapped her legs around his trim hips to deepen the contact, and immediately felt the telltale signs of an impending orgasm. Her sex clenched, every inch of her tingling as the pressure intensified.

"I'm close," she whispered.

"Yeah?"

"Yeah. I don't think I can hold out for much longer."

"Then don't." He brushed his lips over hers in a light kiss. "Let go, Juliet. I want you to come for me."

The hoarse command was all it took. She bit down on her bottom lip to stop herself from crying out, her eyelids slamming shut as the orgasm crashed into her like a tidal wave. She clung to him as if he were a life preserver, rocking her hips and losing herself in the sweet rush of pleasure that swept her away.

"Oh fuck, I'm coming," he muttered before burying his face in the crook of her neck and shuddering against her.

She held him as he trembled in release, her core still pulsing with the aftershocks of her own climax. When he let out a contented sigh and went still, she ran her fingers through his short hair and stroked the silky strands.

"I must be crushing you."

He tried to move, but she held on even tighter. "Mmmm, I like it. You're not going anywhere."

His laughter tickled her ear, and then he planted a tender kiss on her neck, and she was astounded to feel her pussy stirring again. Their bodies were still joined, and even though he'd just come, his cock remained harder than an iron spike.

"You're still hard," she murmured.

"Huh. Look at that. I guess there *are* some benefits to being a twenty-five-year-old kid," he teased.

Her eyes widened in delight when he started moving again. Holy moly. Maybe she'd been looking at this age thing the wrong way, because sweet Lord, talk about stamina.

He plunged into her over and over again, unhurried, as if they had all the time in the world. It took longer to reach that blissful peak again, and this time the release washed over her in slow, delicious ripples that danced over her flesh and left goose bumps in their wake.

Ethan didn't come again. He just watched her with smoldering eyes as she gasped with pleasure, his warm hands fondling her covered breasts, drawing out the release.

"I don't want to go back out there," she mumbled after he'd slid out of her sated core and tucked her close to his side.

"I can take over your shift if you want."

"Nah, it's fine. You were out there all day. You deserve a break."

Sighing, she disentangled herself from his embrace with a total lack of enthusiasm. As they both slipped their pants back on, she felt Ethan's gaze on her, but all of a sudden it was difficult to look at him. Her thighs were wet and sticky, thanks to the condom they hadn't used, irrefutable evidence of her surrender.

But just because she'd trusted him with her body didn't mean she would trust him with her heart. Self-preservation was her middle name, and maybe that made her selfish, but it was the way she'd always lived her life.

The reason she was *still* alive.

She hadn't wanted to fall into bed with him. But she had.

And it wasn't enough, damn it. If anything, the sex had only intensified her hunger for him.

Gulping, she quickly zipped up her boots and shrugged into her coat. "I'll see you in the morning."

"Be careful out there," he said gruffly.

"I always am."

A minute later, she was sliding through the back door and stepping out into the cold again. The gust of icy wind that greeted her was almost welcome. It cooled her flushed cheeks and served as a reminder that she couldn't lose herself in the inferno that was her attraction to Ethan Hayes.

Her boots crunched against the frozen layer of snow as she made her way to the woods. Earlier she'd discovered a broken patio set near the tree line, which offered a clear visual of the house and allowed her to be near the forest in case someone attempted a stealth attack from the trees.

As she settled in one of the sagging wicker chairs, she clicked her earpiece on. "Back at my post, Aussie. I just popped into the house to grab something."

Sullivan's amusement-laced voice filled her ear. "And that something you grabbed . . . was it the rookie's dick? Or did those moans I heard come from Boston having a very naughty wet dream?"

"Mind your own business," she grumbled.

"Ethan *is* my bloody business. I think of that bloke as

my kid brother." There was a menacing pause. "You'd better not hurt him."

She suppressed a groan. "And if I do?"

"If it's intentional, I'll kick your ass. If it's unintentional, I'll still kick your ass, but not as hard."

"Fair enough."

"I'm serious, love. Don't break his heart."

A sigh escaped her lips. "This thing between us has nothing to do with our hearts."

"Ah, so it's purely physical." He paused. "Out of curiosity, how's the rookie in the sack? Real tender, I imagine."

"How's Liam in the sack?" she shot back. "You two *are* boning, right? Because you seem awfully close."

"Oh, bugger off."

Something in his tone gave her pause. She'd only been joking about him and Liam, but she suddenly realized she wouldn't be at all surprised if she found out they *were* getting it on. Sullivan possessed a potent brand of sexuality that oozed out of him in spades, an anything-goes vibe that she'd picked up on from the moment they'd met. It wouldn't scandalize her in the slightest to learn that he swung both ways.

Still, she had to laugh at his evident discomfort. "Not so fun discussing your sex life with strangers, is it, Sully?"

"Touché, love. Touché." He chuckled. "But remember what I said. You hurt him, you suffer the consequences."

The feed went quiet after that, leaving Juliet ill at ease. Sullivan's threat didn't scare her; his fear that she might break Ethan's heart did.

Ethan Hayes wasn't the kind of man you picked up at a hotel bar, fucked, and then walked away from. He was one of the good ones. The kind of man you pledged your love and devotion to.

God, why had she ever allowed herself to get involved with him?

She'd messed up. Started something she couldn't finish, and that wasn't fair to Ethan.

Juliet blew out a breath, a white cloud that floated away in the cold night air. She needed to remind him that she would be walking away when this job ended.

She had to make sure he understood it, *really* understood it, before she allowed anything physical to happen between them again.

Chapter 17

Noelle had just lit up a cigarette when Morgan walked out on the balcony of her and D's suite. She took a drag and exhaled a puff of smoke into the surprisingly warm air. February in Madrid was usually much colder in her experience.

"What do you want now?" she asked coolly. "You couldn't find any ways to entertain yourself in your own room?"

He came up beside her, resting his defined forearms on the steel railing. His cobalt blue eyes took in the scene three stories below them—the late-night pedestrians ambling along the sidewalk, the darkened storefronts, the taxicabs speeding on the deserted road.

Muted voices drifted from the outdoor patio of the restaurant down the street, where Kozlov and his girlfriend were indulging in a midnight dessert. D was staked out somewhere nearby, along with the two goons that were also tailing the couple.

Morgan extracted a pack of Marlboros from one of the numerous pockets in his cargo pants. There was the hiss of a lighter, and then a cloud of smoke passed her peripheral vision.

"I love this city," he remarked. "It's always been one of my favorite places in the world."

"I repeat, what do you want, Jim?"

His rugged profile revealed nothing. "I'm not sure."

"Really? You're not going to warn me away from your soldier? Insult me for a while? Tell me how much you loathe me?"

He turned to her with his dark eyebrows raised. "Would you like me to do any of those things?"

"No, I'd like you to leave." Irritation scurried up her throat. "As much as I enjoy our verbal sparring sessions, I'm not in the mood tonight."

"And why is that?"

She didn't answer.

"We've been doing this for a long time, haven't we?"

His contemplative tone made her glance over, but his face remained devoid of emotion. "We have," she agreed.

"You think it's ever gonna end?"

"Yes."

"When?"

"When I kill you."

His answering laugh was low and husky. "If you were actually going to kill me, you would have done it a long time ago."

She took another drag, the nicotine burning a path straight to her lungs. He was right. She'd had ample opportunity to eliminate this man, yet she still hadn't gotten around to doing it. After each meeting, she'd convinced herself that the time hadn't been right. Told herself that she wasn't done toying with him yet.

After the Monte Carlo job, she'd started to question her vacillation. But the answers continued to elude her.

"You can't seem to kill me either," she pointed out.

"That's because I'm not ready for you to die yet."

"And why is that?"

"Because I'm not done tormenting you."

Noelle rolled her eyes. "Aren't you tired of being such a vindictive asshole?"

"Aren't you tired of being such a coldhearted bitch?"

"Not really."

Morgan sucked deeply on his cigarette. "Well, me either."

They both fell silent, their gazes fixed on the sleeping city below them. A light breeze swept over them and sent Jim's spicy scent floating in her direction.

Noelle's shoulders stiffened as she inhaled the familiar scent. She hated this man with every fiber of her being. She'd spent years dreaming about bringing on his downfall.

So what the fuck was she doing standing on this balcony with him as if they were two pals sharing a midnight smoke?

Mouth tightening with anger, she stalked away from the railing and put out her smoke in the glass ashtray on the window ledge. "Finish your smoke and get out," she told him.

"Eager to get rid of me, huh?"

"Yes." She headed for the sliding door, then halted without turning around. She was quiet for a moment, resentment burning in her veins like jet fuel. "You deserve to die for what you did to me, Jim."

"It's nothing you wouldn't have done yourself, baby."

"You're wrong. I never would have done that to you." She paused. "At least not back then."

"If you say so."

She reached for the door handle, still keeping her back turned. "One of these days I *will* do it, you know. Kill you."

He chuckled. "I'd like to see you try."

"Did the People's Revolutionary Front kidnap my daughter?"

Orlov suppressed his annoyance as Leo Karin's tortured voice came out of the telephone speaker. The prime minister had interrupted him during a conference with his military advisors, whom he'd had to usher out of his office in order to take this call.

Outside the House of Government, the media loitered on the sidewalk in hungry swarms, cameras and microphones and unceasing questions being flung at anyone who entered or exited the building. The reporters were having a field day with the Karin girl's abduction. The story had dominated the news ever since Berezovsky and the guard's dead bodies, along with the bullet-riddled car, had been discovered by the *militsiya* officers. To make matters worse, Erik Baronova had just reported his wife missing as well, proof that Orlov's mysterious enemy had made another inconvenient move.

"We're still investigating that possibility," Orlov told his superior. "I receive hourly updates from Durov, but at the moment, the investigation is not in the ministry's jurisdiction."

"Your ministry is charged with maintaining national security and ridding our country of terrorists," Karin snapped. "If terrorists took Anastacia, then it's your job to find them!"

Orlov bristled, not liking the other man's tone, but he forced himself to speak in a respectful manner.

"We're doing all that we can, Mr. Prime Minister. My people are working closely with the *militsiya*, and if we receive confirmation that the PRF is directly involved, then I assure you, I will launch a military assault and extract your daughter from Mironov's clutches. I will even call in the reserves, if need be."

The man on the other line relaxed, appeased by the promises Orlov did not intend to keep.

Oh no, because when he found the girl—and he *would* find her—she would die. Just as she'd been supposed to die before Berezovsky botched the task.

"Keep me apprised of the situation," Karin said hoarsely. "Find my daughter, Dmitry. Find her."

"We will, Mr. Prime Minister. I guarantee it."

Whether she'd be found alive . . . well, that was an entirely different story.

After the call was disconnected, Orlov immediately got Kirill on the line. "Have you located the targets and the people who took them?"

"Not yet, sir. I've got every available man on the job. They've scoured the road where the Lincoln was hit, interviewed the residents in the area. I've spoken to every informant we have, put out calls to a dozen government agencies. Whoever these people are, I don't think they're working in an official capacity."

"Then who the hell are they and why are they doing this?"

"I suspect they're private contractors. As for what

motivates them, I'm afraid I'm as in the dark as you are. But I assure you that we are doing our best to locate them."

"Well, work harder," he snapped. "I want them found, Kirill. I don't care what you have to do to make that happen, understand? Just find them."

Juliet and the men convened on the sagging front porch that morning to discuss their next course of action. They could have held the conference inside, but Alisa Baronova was driving them all nuts with her shrill voice and constant complaints, and they'd been eager to get away from the woman.

Juliet had officially had it up to here with Baronova. You'd think that the woman would show a little gratitude that someone cared enough to keep her safe, but no dice. All she did was whine—about missing her salon appointment, about not being able to use her cell phone, about the nice breakfast Ethan had prepared for her. And when she wasn't bitching about being at the safe house, she was griping about her husband, who apparently spent every waking hour in his government office.

Juliet wasn't sure she blamed the guy. If she were married to that whining shrew, she'd hide out in her office too.

Baronova could take a few lessons from Anastacia Karin. The teenager continued to impress Juliet with her quiet acceptance of the situation. The girl was even doing her *homework*, for Pete's sake. Earlier she'd dumped the contents of her school bag on the living room table and was huddled over a textbook at the moment, solving math problems.

Still, Juliet knew they couldn't keep Stacie and Baronova here forever. It was time to move on Orlov, which was what she was currently attempting to convince Ethan of.

"I already told you, I don't care who he might be working with," Juliet said in aggravation. "Once I kill him, you can feel free to keep investigating, okay?"

Ethan scowled at her. "And how do you propose to kill him? Just waltz into the House of Government and shoot him?"

"Yes, Ethan," she said sarcastically, "that's precisely what a professional like myself is planning to do. Jeez."

Liam, who was sitting on the broken wooden swing near the front door, chuckled in amusement. "What are you planning, then? Hitting him at home?"

"Maybe."

He looked dubious. "You really think you can break into the defense minister's guarded estate?"

She wrapped her bare fingers around her coffee cup, hoping the hot liquid would warm her up. Lord, it was so cold out, her teeth were actually chattering. She fucking hated this country.

"If I can get my hands on the blueprints and security plans, yes," she answered. "But right now I'm leaning toward getting to him in public."

The three men donned identical frowns.

"How?" Sullivan asked.

"Well, Orlov is scheduled to attend a fancy-pants fund-raiser at a veterans' hospital in three days. I'm thinking we go after him there."

"If he actually shows up," Ethan pointed out. "Stacie's kidnapping is dominating every news outlet in the country. I read online earlier that they're forming an inter-agency task force to head up the search."

"The Ministry of Defense doesn't investigate abductions. Orlov's got an entire military to run, which means convincing his rich friends to open their wallets to fund the country's defense. He'll be at that fund-raiser."

"Fine, say he is. What would you want to do?"

She sipped her coffee, thoughtful. "We'd have to recon on the area, find out how many agents Orlov typically travels with."

"They'll set up a tight perimeter," Liam spoke up. "And if Orlov's the paranoid type, he'll probably have snipers positioned in the area."

"So we take them out. Or, more specifically, you guys will take them out. I'll be inside, waiting for him."

"Is it an invitation-only event?" Sullivan asked.

"I think so, but it won't be a problem snagging an invite." She went thoughtful. "I'll have to pay a visit to Noelle's designer friend in Minsk. I didn't exactly pack a cocktail gown."

"You're not going to that party alone," Ethan said firmly.

"It'll be easier to get close to him if I'm a single woman with money to spend and not part of a couple," she replied, equally firm. "You can play sniper."

He looked ready to argue, but Liam cut him off before he could.

"Right now, it doesn't matter who plays sniper. We still need a helluva lot more manpower if we decide to go ahead with this public assassination plan."

Juliet stifled a sigh. Just what she needed, more operatives joining the fold. But her lone-wolf approach had already been compromised, thanks to these men, so a few more faces weren't exactly going to make a difference now.

And if she were being honest, a part of her was touched that so many people were willing to help her, especially since none of them had a personal stake in the matter.

Feeling awkward, she cleared her throat and glanced at the men. "I just realized . . . I never even thanked you guys for coming halfway around the world to back me up. So, uh, yeah . . . thank you."

Sullivan snorted. "How much did it take outta you to say that?"

She scowled at him.

"All jokes aside, you're welcome," Liam told her, his blue eyes taking on a serious glint. "Ethan told us about what happened to your brother, and . . . well, we've all got people we care about, people we'd fight till our dying breath for. I like to think that if I lost someone important to me, you all would back me up too."

"Bloody right," Sullivan said firmly.

Juliet swallowed a rush of emotion, then glanced at Ethan. "I'm sure Abby will agree to help out, but can you check if Morgan can spare anyone else?"

He released an unenthused breath. "I'll see what I can do."

A few hours later, Ethan finally got Juliet alone. He'd been hoping to get her to reconsider this foolish plan of hers, but he wasn't exactly going about it the right way, considering what he'd just pulled her into the bedroom to tell her.

"Morgan is sending the A-Team," he said with a sigh. "Abby and the others will be here tomorrow morning. D and Noelle are still in Madrid, watching Kozlov. Do we want to bring them in?"

"Nah, they may as well stay put and keep Kozlov out of harm's way. We'll go over the details tomorrow when the others arrive, and if we think we might need the extra bodies, we'll send an SOS to Spain then."

"All right." He paused. "This plan is crazy, by the way."

"Well, it's the only one we've got." She flopped down on the bed and settled into a cross-legged position.

"How are you going to do it?" he asked curiously.

"Kill him, you mean? I'll get him alone and then I'll shoot him. Which is a damn shame—I haven't used my ten-inch Bowie knife in ages. But a neat bullet to the head will produce less blood than the knife."

Ethan wasn't sure whether he was turned on or scared shitless. His past girlfriends hadn't spent much time discussing which weapons produced cleaner kills—that was for sure. And yet while Juliet's ruthlessness unnerved him, the fact that she was so deadly excited him like nothing else.

"I wish I had a better cover in place, though. Normally I don't do up-close kills without months of prep."

"What kind of prep?"

She paused thoughtfully. "Well, I probably would have positioned myself in the ministry itself. I'd have worked there for about six months and gained his trust. Eventually I would make my move, and then disappear and nobody would ever know it was me who killed him."

He frowned. "You'd put that much time into a job?"

"Six months is nothing. One of Noelle's other chameleons, Bailey, stays undercover for way longer. She spent more than a year on her last job."

"That seems excessive."

"Not really. See, it's not always about the end result. It's easy to blow someone's brains out, but a lot of our clients require zero-to-minimal fallout, which means doing things right, no matter how long it takes. But I don't have the patience when it comes to Orlov. I want him dead."

"Because of Henry?" He hesitated. "Jules . . . would your brother really want you to do this? If he's as compassionate and good as you say he was, then wouldn't he want you to—"

"Henry's the one who asked me to kill Orlov."

Ethan was startled. "Are you serious?"

"That was the last thing he said to me," she admitted. "'Kill him.' That was his goddamn dying request. Don't get me wrong, though—I would've killed the bastard even if Henry hadn't begged me to do it."

"To avenge your brother."

"Damn right."

He cocked his head. "Would you kill someone to avenge me?"

"If I say yes, are you going to make a huge deal out of it?"

Ethan hid a smile. "Should I?"

"Nope. Because it doesn't mean what you think it does." She shifted awkwardly. "Look, I like you. I respect you. And if someone took you down, I'd go after them. But that doesn't make you special or anything."

"Hmmm. I see." The smile continued to tug at his lips. "Would you do the same for Sullivan or Liam?"

"Probably not."

"Then that makes me special."

He pounced on her before she could object, pushing her onto the bed as his mouth came down on hers.

She kissed him back so passionately that his cock went from semierect to harder than a flagpole in a matter of seconds. Christ, he couldn't get over how incredible she was. So willing, so fiery, not an ounce of shyness about her. She always kissed him as if she had one minute left to live and she wanted nothing more than to spend it with him. But he supposed that made sense, seeing as she lived a life of danger where any move she made could result in death.

As Ethan slid his tongue through her parted lips and explored the warm recess of her mouth, his hands slipped beneath her sweater to cup her firm breasts. Son of a bitch, he still hadn't feasted his eyes on her breasts yet, he realized, and the desperation that surged through him made him determined to rectify that.

He swiftly tore his mouth off hers and shoved her sweater up to her collarbone, groaning when her skimpy black bra was revealed.

"We don't have a lot of time," she murmured. "We have to scope out the hospital."

Story of their fucking relationship. Stolen kisses and vehicular trysts and a mind-blowing quickie with Sullivan ten feet away. But although Ethan knew they couldn't linger in here for too long, he refused to deprive himself of a taste.

With another groan, he unhooked the front clasp of her bra, baring her breasts to his eager eyes. His breath instantly caught, his erection hardening to a whole new level. She had the prettiest dark pink nipples, rigid with arousal, and her skin was so creamy and soft, he never wanted to stop touching it. He admired her flat belly and surprisingly defined abdominal muscles, then frowned when his gaze landed on the puckered red bullet holes and the neat row of transparent stitches.

"How's your wound? Still hurting?" he asked roughly.

"Just an ache every now and then." A mischievous smile lifted her lips. "But not as bad as the ache between my legs."

He laughed softly, bringing his gaze back to her chest.

Juliet's breathing grew labored as he squeezed those perfect mounds and feathered his thumbs over her puckered nipples.

"The door's not even locked," she protested, trying to rise. "We . . . we can't . . ."

When he captured one nipple between his lips, she quit talking and sagged back onto the mattress. Ethan flicked his tongue over the distended bud, then suckled gently. His head was spinning, heart thudding, cock aching. He was beyond turned on—starvation had set in, and the only way to cure it was to devour this woman whole.

Her breasts bore pink splotches by the time he finished playing with them, and when he finally lifted his head and peered into her eyes, all he saw was a haze of lust shining there.

"Get inside me," she growled.

This time he'd come prepared. In the blink of an eye, he produced the condom he'd tucked into his back pocket, then unzipped his pants and yanked them halfway down his legs. Juliet dealt with her own pants while he sheathed himself, leaving one pant leg on and the other off, and when he hurriedly plunged into her tight core, she wrapped those legs around his hips and gave an upward thrust that made him moan.

Jesus. It felt so wickedly good, he never wanted it to end. He knew that if anyone decided to burst into the bedroom unannounced, they'd be treated with quite a sight. His naked ass hanging out for all to see, Juliet's bare leg hooked over it, their bodies moving together in a desperate race to the finish line.

With his pants half-on, it was difficult to move, but Juliet took pity on him by rolling him over and straddling his thighs.

"You're so fricking beautiful," he hissed out.

The little smile she gave him only validated his words. With her dark hair streaming over her shoulders and her shirt scrunched up to reveal her breasts, she made the sexiest picture he'd ever seen.

She rode him, her nails digging into his abdomen as she fucked him so hard, his brain damn near imploded. His climax came without warning, seizing his balls and burning every square inch of skin. Juliet wasn't far behind. Her lush lips parted to release a soft, tortured cry, and then she was trembling over him.

It was short and sweet and, hands-down, the best sex of his life. And he wasn't nearly sated. He wanted more. He wanted everything, damn it.

As Juliet collapsed on his chest, he tangled his fingers in her hair and held her close. "When this is all over, I'm locking you in a room and taking my goddamn time with you," he mumbled. "Don't care if it takes weeks."

Her laughter tickled his neck.

"I mean it, sweetheart. You're not walking away from me. Not until we finish what we've started." His grip on her hair tightened. "And even then, I still won't let you go."

"How very caveman of you."

"Don't care. You're not going anywhere, Jules."

"Whatever you say." Rolling her eyes, she climbed off his body and hopped to her feet. "C'mon, rookie, we've got recon to do."

Chapter 18

Across the street from the veterans' hospital was a large, well-maintained park with winding flagstone paths, wrought-iron benches, and a square fountain that had been emptied for the winter. A blanket of snow covered the ground and clung to the gnarled bare branches of the trees littering the area. Despite the frigid temperature, several people were making use of the park, strolling the paths, walking their dogs, and sipping coffee and reading newspapers.

Ethan and Juliet, therefore, did not look out of place as they took up residence on one of the benches that offered a perfect line of sight to the hospital entrance. Bundled up in winter clothing and sharing a thermos of hot chocolate, they were nothing but a young couple enjoying a February afternoon.

Only the weapons beneath their coats and their vigilant gazes said otherwise.

"I can't drink this stuff without thinking of my mom," Ethan said as he drank from the thermos lid that also doubled as a cup.

He passed the cup to Juliet, who took a long sip. Steam rose and brought a rosy glow to her cheeks, and she'd never looked more beautiful to him than she did right now. He found himself wishing that this was an actual date and not a recon mission. He liked the idea of just sitting around with this woman. Taking a walk, seeing a movie, doing something that didn't involve guns and danger and the impending death of a government official.

"Was she really into hot chocolate?" Juliet's teasing voice interrupted his thoughts.

"Sorta. When I was a kid I used to play hockey on this outdoor rink every winter, and whenever I came home, all numb and frozen, my mom would have a huge mug of hot chocolate waiting for me. And cookies," he said as the memory hit him. "Freshly baked chocolate-chip cookies. It was awesome."

"So she was a real Susie Homemaker, huh?"

"Yes and no. She taught the second grade, so she wasn't a stay-at-home mom. But she did enjoy cooking and baking and all that stuff."

"Was she sweet and delicate and, you know, *mom-like*?" He didn't miss the note of envy that entered her tone.

"Yes and no," he said again. "She was the best mother in the world, but she wasn't always sweet." A laugh sprang to his lips. "This one time, she got into a fistfight at one of my hockey games."

Juliet burst out laughing. "Seriously? Why?"

"One of the other moms was trash-talking a kid, a player on the opposing team. She was being really nasty, booing the poor kid, yelling at the ref to toss him out of the game when he bodychecked her son." Ethan grinned. "My mother asked her very politely to stop, which led to the woman turning her nastiness on Mom, and, well, nobody gets away with talking to Debbie Hayes like that. All us kids were on the ice—the game was stopped so the refs could deal with the fight in the bleachers—and we were just standing there, gaping at them."

"What happened afterward?" Juliet asked curiously.

"They were both ordered to leave the arena and never return. So for the rest of the season, my dad was the only one allowed to come to my games."

She snorted. "Sounds like my kind of woman."

Ethan swallowed the lump obstructing his throat. "I think you would've liked her." He paused. "And she definitely would've liked you."

"I highly doubt that. She would have taken one look at me and told me I was completely unsuitable for her son."

He was about to argue, but she didn't give him the opportunity. She abruptly rose from the bench, an indefinable expression on her face. "I'll be back. I just want to check something out."

She was gone in the blink of an eye, leaving Ethan sitting there in frustration. He was tempted to hurry after her, but he didn't want to draw any attention to himself, and sprinting down the sidewalk in pursuit of Juliet was guaranteed to do just that.

What the hell had he said to send her running like that? It wasn't like he'd asked her to come home with him to meet his folks; both his parents were gone.

So what? Did the idea that his dead mother might have approved of her terrify Juliet *that* much?

He gritted his teeth, impatience coursing through him as he waited for her to return. It was always one step forward, two steps back with the woman, and he was getting damn tired of it. Just once he wanted her to admit that she enjoyed spending time with him. That she *cared* about him. But it seemed like she was determined to keep her distance, no matter how hard he tried to bridge it.

She was gone for nearly forty minutes, and as each minute ticked by, Ethan grew more and more tense. He was about to abandon his post and go looking for her when he spotted her dark hair in the crowd of pedestrians. His shoulders relaxed but his features remained hard, even when Juliet settled next to him on the bench again.

"What the hell was that?" he demanded.

She shrugged, and he noticed that her cheeks were redder than before, as if she'd just finished doing something strenuous. "I told you, I had to check something out."

He scowled at her. "Are you going to elaborate?"

Sighing, Juliet reached into the inner pocket of her coat and pulled out a rumpled brown bag. "Before, when we were cruising the area, I noticed a little bakery a few blocks east of here." Her face burned brighter. "I popped in to see if they had any chocolate-chip cookies."

His jaw fell open, and he had to wonder if he'd misheard her. "Chocolate-chip cookies," he echoed.

"But the bakery was closed," she hurried on, "so I had to break in and—"

"Wait. What?"

"I broke in," she repeated. "Don't worry. Nobody saw me. Anyway . . ." She held out the paper bag, embarrassment filling her gaze. "The bastards didn't have chocolate chip, so you'll have to be satisfied with good old gingerbread."

Dumbfounded, Ethan stared at the bag before meeting her dark eyes. "You broke into a bakery to steal cookies for me?"

She shifted awkwardly on the bench. "Yeah. You know, 'cause of what you said about your mother, and the hot chocolate and . . ." She trailed off, then shoved the bag into his lap, a defensive edge creeping into her voice. "Let me guess. You're pissed off that I compromised our surveillance."

He just gaped at her.

"Fuck, fine. It was a stupid idea, I guess. Toss the bag in the trash if you—"

He cut her off with a kiss. A firm, fleeting kiss, over before it even began, but it conveyed all the emotion he couldn't seem to put into words.

"Thank you," he said gruffly. "That was really nice of you, sweetheart."

He saw her pulse jump in her throat. "You're welcome," she said after a beat.

Although he kept his expression casual, Ethan was jumping for joy inside. Juliet Mason continued to surprise him. Just when he thought he knew her, she did something that revealed a whole new facet of her personality.

Thoughtfulness. That's what she'd showed him just now, and he was still floored by the sweet gesture.

"Don't you dare read anything into it," she grumbled, as if sensing his thoughts. "They're just cookies, for fuck's sake. Doesn't mean a thing."

Ethan did his best to fight the enormous grin threatening to surface. "Uh-huh."

She made an irritated noise. "Ugh, just pass me a fucking cookie."

Stacie was feeling homesick. Which was ironic, because normally she hated being at home. Her father was hardly ever there, her friends weren't allowed over, and her only company was their housekeeper, Marta, and her dad's bodyguards and aides. Not exactly ideal surroundings.

But after three days at the safe house, her big, lonely house suddenly seemed like paradise. Juliet and the others had tried to make her as comfortable as possible—they'd even stuck a candle in a muffin yesterday and wished her a happy birthday—but it wasn't enough. She was so worried about her father. As angry as she was with him, she didn't want him to get hurt. Or, worse, to *die*. She desperately wanted to call him and make sure he was all right, but Juliet had insisted that it still wasn't safe.

Stacie wasn't the only one getting impatient—Alisa had been yelling at everyone all day long, to the point that Stacie felt like strangling the annoying woman. Much to everyone's relief, Alisa had finally disappeared into one of the bedrooms to lie down, and without the woman's piercing voice and nonstop complaints, the living room was blessedly quiet.

Stacie was alone on the couch with the novel her English teacher had assigned the class, but she couldn't concentrate on the story. She'd sensed the tension in the air ever since Juliet and the men's long discussion on the porch this morning. She desperately wished someone would tell her what was going on, but nobody seemed interested in doing that. Now it was evening time, and Juliet and Ethan were outside, while Sullivan and Liam rested before they took over watch duty, so Stacie knew she wouldn't be getting answers anytime soon.

She was just attempting to focus on her book again when she heard footsteps. She looked up hopefully, but the person who emerged from the corridor wasn't one she wanted to see.

In the same body-hugging dress she'd worn since she got here, Alisa strode into the living room, looking far happier than Stacie had ever seen her.

The woman glanced around the empty room, then approached the couch. "Where are they?" she asked in their native tongue.

"Outside," Stacie replied. "And Sullivan and Liam are sleeping in the other bedroom."

"I have to tell you something," Alisa whispered. "But you have to promise not to tell them."

Suspicion floated over her. "What is it?"

Alisa sat down and reached for Stacie's hand, her sharp red fingernails digging into Stacie's wrist. "I'm getting us out of here."

The older woman spoke so softly, Stacie wondered if she'd misheard her. "What?"

"I'm getting us out of here."

"How?" A queasy feeling churned in her belly. "What did you do?"

"You can't say anything." Another hushed whisper. "Promise me."

"I . . . I won't say anything," she lied.

"I overheard the blond one say where he hid my cell phone. So when I went to use the bathroom earlier, I snuck into the room and took it."

The queasiness transformed into a rush of pure nausea. Alisa's brown eyes shone with satisfaction, and Stacie felt like throwing up as she stared at the woman in horror. Juliet had specifically told them that any calls they made could be traced.

But maybe Alisa hadn't used the phone yet. Maybe she—

"I called my husband," Alisa told her, bursting the little balloon of hope that had risen in Stacie's chest.

"You shouldn't have done that," she hissed out. "What if the people who tried to kill me find us?"

"They won't."

"How do you know?"

"Because they don't exist. We're not being protected— we're *hostages*. My husband has been worried sick about me—he had no idea where I was! And when I told him you were here, he was very upset. These people have been lying to us, Anastacia. They are not government agents. They've kidnapped us, and it's all over the news."

Stacie swallowed. "That's not true. They're protecting us."

The image of Nina's cold blue eyes flashed in her mind. The gun. The blood.

Juliet and Ethan had saved her. They'd saved her, and now they were keeping her safe.

"They're going to find us now," she mumbled.

"We'll be rescued," Alisa said happily. "My husband told me to keep my phone turned on. He's getting in touch with Colonel General Durov—you do know who

Durov is, don't you? He's the head of the *militsiya*. And he's going to send a rescue team. They're probably on their way right now!"

The anxiety Stacie had been battling her whole life made an appearance, dampening her palms and making her heart race.

Whoever ordered Nina to shoot her was going to find them now.

She shot to her feet. She had to tell Juliet.

But Alisa bolted up too, grabbing Stacie's arm and stabbing her flesh with those sharp fingernails. "You can't say a word! You'll ruin everything!"

"No, *you've* ruined everything! You put us in danger!"

Neither female was whispering anymore, and the loud argument must have alerted their protectors, because Sullivan and Liam came barreling out of the hallway.

"What's going on?" Sullivan demanded.

Alisa glared at Stacie, commanding her with her eyes not to say a word.

Stacie looked from one man to the other. Then she opened her mouth and told them everything.

"The team's in place."

Satisfaction surged through Orlov's blood and brought a harsh smile to his lips. He was still at the office, reading the reports that the head of his counterterrorist unit had faxed over, but Kirill's update took precedence over the files on his desk.

His mysterious enemies had slipped up, which led him to believe that he couldn't possibly be dealing with professionals. Any operative worth their salt would not have allowed a hostage to get their hands on a mobile device, but Alisa Baronova had done just that. The insufferable woman had contacted her husband in a panic, claiming to have been abducted by American terrorists.

Unfortunately, Durov hadn't seen fit to alert Orlov until one hour ago, but Orlov's people were far more efficient than the members of Durov's force. Within minutes of gleaning Baronova's location, Kirill had assembled a team and dispatched them to the house in Vitebsk.

Orlov's body hummed with the sweet vibrations of victory as he envisioned his men advancing on the farmhouse and shooting everyone inside like the dogs they were.

Well, almost everyone.

"Make sure the men follow orders," Orlov barked at his second in command. "They're to eliminate Baronova, the girl, and whoever else is in that house, but I want the man in charge left alive."

"They know what to do, sir."

"Good." He licked his lips. "And I want the son of a bitch left untouched. I intend on interrogating him myself to find out why he decided to cross me. Any harm that comes to him will be inflicted by me. Do you understand?"

"I understand. Where would you like them to take him?"

"The Crow's Nest. I'll head over there the moment I get confirmation that the assault was successful."

Orlov hung up, his body still wired with electric anticipation.

If all went well, the man who'd killed the Siberian Wolf would be in his clutches very soon. Kirill's team would infiltrate the farmhouse long before Durov's men reached

it. And when the officers did arrive, they'd discover that
the hostages had been tragically murdered by their captors.
There was only one potential snag—the captors themselves. He still had no idea who they were, and if there was
one thing Orlov despised, it was the unknown.

But he did know one thing—the people responsible
for whisking away his targets would pay dearly for their
interference.

He'd make sure of it.

"We've gotta break camp. Now."

The urgency in Liam's voice was unmistakable, adding to the tension currently hanging over the room.
Ethan didn't lose his temper often, but as he glanced at
Alisa Baronova's smug face, he couldn't control the explosion that burst out of him.

"Do you realize what you've done?" he snapped.
"You've endangered not only our lives, but your own."

"Stop saying that!" she shrieked. "I'm not in danger!
You people kidnapped us!"

Ethan gave her a look loaded with contempt, then
glanced at Juliet. "I guess this is the gratitude we get for
trying to help."

"Hey, this was your idea, rookie. I told you not to
bother," she muttered.

Her dark eyes softened, however, when Anastacia
Karin let out a small whimper. The girl was whiter than
the snow beyond the door, visibly shaking as she listened
to the volatile words being flung around.

"It's all right, Stacie. It'll be okay," Juliet said with a
sigh. "We'll get you out of here. Nobody is going to hurt
you."

Liam spoke up briskly. "We've gotta move. Orlov's people could be knocking on our front door any fucking second."

No sooner had the words left his mouth than Sullivan's voice echoed in their earpieces.

"We've got company."

They all exchanged a grim look.

"What are we looking at?" Ethan demanded.

"Two heavy-duty Humvees. Can't see inside, but I'm assuming they're carrying a full load—six or eight men apiece. And a military-looking truck, hauling ten tangos in the back and two inside."

"How far away?"

"About a click, two at the most. We don't have a lot of time. And we can't risk taking the Rovers and getting ambushed on the road. We've gotta take the Yams."

"Meet us out back," Ethan ordered.

"Copy that."

"What's going on?" Stacie cried.

"Our location has been compromised," Ethan said darkly.

Baronova's face brightened with happiness, which made him want to slug the woman.

Ignoring her, Ethan snapped into action, gesturing for Liam and Juliet to follow him. They'd already piled their gear in the kitchen, and now they hurriedly hauled it out the rickety back door.

Ethan tossed a command over his shoulder for Anastacia and Baronova to stay put, then sprinted after his teammates. The biting cold slapped his face as they ran across the snow toward the tree line, where they'd stashed their secondary escape vehicles. Liam quickly tore the waterproof black tarp off the three shiny white Yamaha snowmobiles and bent over one of the high-powered machines.

"Fire them up," Ethan told him. "We'll get the others."

Without a word, he and Juliet raced back to the house, where Juliet addressed the two females with a sharp order. "Put on your coats and go outside through the kitchen."

Anastacia immediately dove for the jacket draped over one of the kitchen chairs. She slipped into it without argument, but she looked shaken up as she ran toward the door.

Baronova, however, wasn't as obliging. Feet planted on the weathered hardwood, the woman crossed her arms over her ample chest and glared daggers at them.

"I'm not going anywhere with you people!"

Sheer aggravation clamped around his throat. "Do you want to stay and die here? Is that it?"

He reached for her, but the bleached blonde sidestepped him, her cheeks turning bright crimson.

"Don't touch me!"

Juliet spoke up in disdain. "Do you really think the people out there are coming to rescue you? Because they aren't, you little twit. The second they enter this house, they'll put a bullet in your head."

Baronova remained stubbornly unfazed. "You're going to be arrested, you bitch! My husband sent the *militsiya* to rescue me."

"Enemy ETA less than a minute," Sullivan barked over the comm.

Juliet glanced at Ethan in annoyance. "I say we leave this bitch behind. Let Orlov have her—that's one less headache for us."

"Go take care of Anastacia," he ordered. "I'll deal with this."

"Ethan—"

"Go, Juliet. I'm right behind you."

Despite the crease of reluctance digging into her forehead, Juliet turned on her heel and ran out the door.

Alone with Baronova, Ethan worked valiantly to control the anger whipping inside him like a loose power line.

"You have two options," he told the woman. "Either you obediently follow me outside, or I'll haul you over my shoulder and carry you out."

She looked incensed. "I'm not going anywhere with—"

"Carry you, it is."

The blonde screeched in horror as he grabbed her by the waist and lifted her up so that her torso hung over his shoulder. Immediately, a pair of fists thumped against his back, while skinny legs attempted to kick him in the balls. He held her wiggling body against him in a strong grip, kept his other hand tightly on his gun, and marched across the kitchen.

"Put me down!" she screamed. "Put me down right this instant!"

He ignored her shrieks, his boots crunching on the snow as he attempted to restrain the struggling woman. In the distance, he heard the hum of the Yamaha engines. Liam already had Anastacia on one of the sleds, his arms wrapped around her from behind. Juliet and Sullivan were seated on the second, Juliet's dark hair hanging over her shoulder as she craned her neck to keep watch for Ethan.

"Go!" he yelled when he caught her eye. "I'll meet you at the rendezvous!"

Even from so many yards away, he glimpsed the hesitation in her chocolate brown eyes, but after a beat, she gave a nod and tapped Sullivan's broad back. A moment later, both drivers revved the throttle and the snowmobiles roared off into the trees.

The sound of engines traveled in the air again, this time coming from the front of the house. Shit. Orlov's men had arrived, and they weren't even trying to be stealthy about it.

"Put me down!"

Baronova was still shrieking like a banshee for all to hear. Ethan ran faster, scrambling to keep his captive in control, but the last remaining snowmobile was still fifty yards away, and he had a sinking feeling he wasn't going to reach it.

Bang.

The screen door on the patio flew open and slammed against the stucco wall of the house. Ethan kept going without turning around. Forty more yards.

"Help!" Baronova yelled at whoever had appeared in the doorway. "I'm over here!"

Thirty more yards.

His lungs burned as he sucked in the icy air and kept running. Twenty-five yards.

"Help me! He's trying to kidnap me again! Help! I'm over—"

The gunshot cracked in the night, cutting Baronova off midsentence.

She went limp in Ethan's arms, bringing a violent curse to his lips. *Son of a bitch.* They'd shot her. He halted only so he could slide her out of the fireman's hold and into his arms, but the second he saw her lifeless brown eyes, he realized it was too late.

There was a bullet hole right in the center of her forehead.

Christ, whoever had taken that shot knew what he was doing.

Without a second's thought, Ethan unloaded the deadweight. If this had been the corps, he would've lugged his fallen comrade's body for miles if he need be, but Alisa Baronova had been nothing but a liability from day one.

He was ten yards from the snowmobile when the bullet hit his back.

Fortunately, they'd all donned vests after Anastacia tipped them off about Baronova's call, so the bullet lodged into the Kevlar rather than his flesh.

Unfortunately, the impact sent him staggering onto his knees, his palms bracing against the slushy ground to break his fall. Although he felt like he'd had the wind knocked out of him, he regained his balance and shot to his feet—and that was when pain streaked through his left leg.

The bullet didn't slow him down. He raced forward, closing in on the sled, but the shooter must have realized that the best way to neutralize his enemy wasn't a flesh shot but another one to the vest. The next bullet hit him square in the tailbone, sending him sprawling. Fuck. *Fuck.* That one was gonna leave a hell of a bruise.

This time when he scrambled to his feet, he knew he was done for. He touched his ear to activate his comm, even as he heard his attacker's footsteps four feet behind him.

The hurried orders flew out of his mouth. "Don't come back for me. Get the girl to safety."

He hoped that his whispered message had reached his teammates, but if they'd responded, he was beyond hearing it. He removed the tiny transmitter from his ear and crushed it beneath his boot just as a heavy male body tackled him to the ground.

Chapter 19

Even while traveling at 150 miles per hour, Juliet heard Ethan's ominous report loud and clear. Sullivan must have too, because his shoulders stiffened and the muscles on his hard chest tensed beneath her gloved hands.

"We have to go back," she yelled to Sullivan over the din. "He's hurt!"

"We have our orders," he yelled back, not slowing down.

She kept her cheek pressed against the back of Sullivan's coat to protect her exposed face from the wind. At the speed they were going, each frigid gust felt like icicles being launched at her face.

They forged a rapid path through the snow, the snowmobile whizzing by the centuries-old pine trees, its treads demolishing everything in their way. Juliet peered around Sullivan and caught a blurry glimpse of Liam's sled twenty yards ahead of them as it sped through the dark forest. Stacie was clutching Liam like a life preserver, her face buried between his shoulder blades.

The head start had allowed them to make some serious distance, and they reached the frozen lake in no time and without a single enemy soldier on their tail. There was a reason the Vitebsk region of the country was often referred to as the land of lakes—this wouldn't be the first one they'd cross before they reached the rendezvous point where Liam and Sullivan had stashed a second pair of Range Rovers.

Juliet spent the next thirty minutes consumed with worry that was even more bone-chilling than the temperature. Ethan wouldn't have gone dark unless he was in trouble. Which meant either he was injured or he'd been captured.

Or both.

Christ. That goddamn bitch Baronova must have slowed him down.

Juliet didn't give a shit about Ethan's bleeding heart— the next time she laid eyes on that infuriating woman, she was putting a bullet in her head.

God, please let him be okay.

She repeated the silent mantra as they sped toward safety. There was no stopping Sullivan at the moment, but the second they reached the rendezvous, she planned on hightailing it back to the farmhouse and saving Ethan's delectable ass.

The woods were so dark she could barely see a thing. Sullivan hadn't switched on the headlights in order to avoid detection, but luckily, he seemed to know exactly where he was going. Several miles and two lake crossings later, they finally emerged into a clearing shrouded in shadows.

Sullivan gripped the brake lever to slow the machine down. Once they came to a stop, Juliet dove off the sled and touched her ear.

"Rookie, come in," she burst out. "Do you copy?"

She was greeted with nothing but silence.

"Goddamn it, rookie, talk to me!"

More silence.

A feeling of pure helplessness crawled up her spine. She looked at Sullivan and Liam, who wore matching expressions of foreboding.

"He's not there, love," Sullivan said quietly.

"Fine, then we're going back for him," she snapped. "Give me the key to the sled."

Instead of obeying the order, the tall blond man tucked the key in his pocket and turned to Liam. "Stash the Yams. We have to move."

Juliet's jaw dropped to the cold ground. "Are you fucking *kidding* me? We have to go back for him!"

A pair of steely gray eyes met hers. "You heard the order. He said to get the girl somewhere safe."

"I don't give a shit what he said! We can't leave him behind."

The hum of an engine caught her attention, as Liam and one of the snowmobiles disappeared into a cluster of trees.

A tornado of disbelief spiraled inside her, sending lethal blasts of panic and fury through her body. She couldn't believe how calm Sullivan looked. Like he didn't even care that he'd left a man behind.

"I swear to God, Sullivan, if you don't give me that key right now, I'm going to blow your brains out."

Stacie's gasp of horror echoed in the air.

Clenching her teeth, Juliet glanced at the distraught girl and said, "Go wait in one of the SUVs, honey."

"But—"

"Go wait in the fucking SUV!"

It was the first time she'd ever raised her voice to the girl, but she couldn't even muster up any guilt. Her emotion bank was jam-packed with sheer rage at the moment.

As Stacie hurried off, Juliet advanced on Sullivan like a predator closing in on its prey. He didn't so much as flinch, not even when she withdrew her Beretta from her belt and pointed it right at him. From the corner of her eye, she saw Liam walking toward them with his weapon raised, but she didn't give a rat's ass if he threatened to shoot her.

"Put the bloody gun down," Sullivan said in a low voice. "You're scaring the girl."

"She'll get over it." Juliet cocked her pistol with a deadly click. "I mean it, Sully. If getting that key means I have to shoot you, I won't fucking hesitate."

"Jeez, I leave you guys for two minutes and you're pointing guns at each other," came Liam's annoyed voice.

She didn't blink. "Stay out of this, Boston."

"I'm afraid I can't, darlin'. Not when you're threatening my BFF."

The flippant words were meant to relax her, but Juliet maintained her aggressive pose. "Go away," she told Liam. "If you want to do something worthwhile, get in the car and take Stacie to the next safe house."

"Sorry, Jules, but—"

"Do it," Sullivan said with a resigned breath.

Liam sounded startled. "Sully . . ."

"The longer we fuck around here, the closer Orlov's people get. Just take Anastacia to the safe house. Juliet and I will be along shortly."

"You sure, man?"

"Yeah. Go."

Liam reluctantly holstered his weapon, tossed Sullivan the key to the second sled, and stalked to the Range Rover without looking back. A car door slammed, an engine roared, and then tires crushed the snow as the SUV peeled off in the direction of the road beyond the clearing.

As the night went quiet once again, Juliet locked her gaze with Sullivan's. "I won't leave him behind."

"For the love of Jesus, do you really think I plan on bloody abandoning him? My intention was always to go back—*after* we made sure Anastacia was safe."

"It might've been too late by then." Desperation filled her belly. "It might be too late now."

"Lower your bloody gun. You win, all right? We'll go back now."

The relief that crashed into her was so strong, she nearly keeled over. "Thank you."

With a grave look, Sullivan headed for the snowmobile. He straddled it and started the engine. "Get on."

She shook her head. "No, I should take the second sled. We don't know if the one Ethan was using is in drivable condition."

"Good point." He quickly threw the key into her waiting hand.

"Go on ahead," she told him. "I'm right behind you."

It occurred to her that those were the same words Ethan had spoken after he'd ordered her to leave the safe house.

Uncharacteristic fear tightened Juliet's throat as she raced toward the sled Liam had stashed. Her hands shook like crazy as she wrapped her fingers around the handlebars.

She drew in a slow, steadying breath. Ethan was a soldier. He was strong and smart and he could take care of himself. They'd probably even encounter him on the way back, riding his own sled after having taken down Orlov's army single-handedly.

Or at least that's what she kept telling herself as she cranked the throttle and sped across the clearing.

She followed Sullivan's tracks, keeping her head low to avoid the bitter sting of the wind. The time it had taken to get to the rendezvous had flown by, but the drive back seemed to last forever. The entire time, she tried not to question her motives, not to dwell on the paralyzing fear, not to allow all the worst-case scenarios to penetrate her mind.

It felt like hours before Sullivan slowed down. He signaled her with a hand gesture to pull over and stop, and she did so without question.

"We go on foot the rest of the way."

Juliet nodded. If Orlov's men were still at the safe house, the noisy snowmobile engines would surely alert them of their presence.

She and Sullivan moved through the silent forest. Up above, beams of moonlight sliced through the gaps in the trees, casting shadows on the snow. The temperature had dipped below freezing and the air chilled Juliet right to the bone. It was so cold, it hurt to breathe, but the concern swimming in her stomach distracted her from the weather.

They were about a quarter mile from the house when Sullivan halted and reached into his pocket. He produced a pair of military field glasses.

"We can't risk getting any closer before we scope out

the scene. Do you want the honor of shimmying up this majestic pine?"

Swallowing, she tucked the binoculars in her pocket. Then she glanced up at the enormous tree, which seemed to rise all the way up to the inky sky.

But the climb took no time at all. She easily scaled the thick trunk, digging her boots into various footholds and grabbing on to branches to propel herself upward. When she was roughly twenty feet off the ground, she straddled a naked branch and effortlessly slithered on her belly toward the very edge.

She raised the binoculars to her eyes, terrified of what she might see. The possibility of Ethan's dead body lying in the snow tightened her throat and quickened her pulse.

He's fine, she told herself.

She took another breath and adjusted the zoom, peering through the lenses as she conducted a sweep of the area. Through the trees she had a clear visual of the safe house — where two armed men stood guard at the back door.

Shit. Orlov's people hadn't evacuated yet. Probably waiting around in case their targets foolishly decided to return.

Which they had, except Juliet didn't care how foolish it was. She wasn't going anywhere until she made sure Ethan was safe.

But what she saw next burst any bubbles of hope she may have been harboring. Anyone else might have been difficult to spot in the darkness, but Alisa Baronova's platinum blond hair made it easy to pick her out amid the shadows.

"I've got two guards at the back door and Baronova KIA on the ground," she murmured over the comm.

"The rookie?"

"Nowhere in sight. But there's some blood near the sled."

"How much blood?" Sullivan asked grimly. "Enough for someone to have bled out?"

"No." She swallowed. "If he was shot, he didn't die here."

She shifted her gaze, studying the tracks in the snow.

"There're two sets of footprints going toward the Yam, but only one set heading away from it."

"They carried him." Relief trickled over the line. "That means he was alive when they captured him. They wouldn't have carted off his corpse, especially since they left Baronova on the ground like that."

She didn't know whether to be relieved or scared. On one hand, it was encouraging that Ethan probably hadn't been shot to death. On the other, he was now in the clutches of Dmitry Orlov, a man known for torturing his enemies.

"Any chance they're keeping him inside the house?" she asked Sullivan.

"Doubt it. But give me a sec. I'll go around front and see what's doing."

Juliet waited not so patiently as Sullivan went to investigate. She tried to distract herself by focusing on that small puddle of blood near the sled, reassuring evidence that Ethan hadn't bled to death out on the snow, but it did nothing to relieve the panic churning in her stomach.

"Only one Humvee out front," Sullivan's voice reported a few minutes later. "The other vehicles are gone. I'm going to check the house, just in case."

Alarm flared inside her. "You need some backup?"

"Nah, I'll be fine. Maintain your position. Lemme know if the two dumb-asses in the back make a move."

She didn't argue with him—she knew Sullivan was perfectly capable of taking out a few guards. Which he did with zero complications, because less than five minutes later, he appeared directly behind the men in the backyard and put two swift bullets in their heads. The silencer on his weapon ensured that no gunshots echoed in the night. Through the field glasses, Juliet watched as the two men toppled to the ground, one after the other.

They hadn't even heard Sullivan come up behind them, which was slightly comforting. Maybe Orlov's other men were equally incompetent. Wherever he was, Ethan could use that to his advantage.

"See me, love?" Sullivan gave her a little wave.

"I see you. Any problems out front?"

"Nada. Only two tangos out there too. And one manning the interior. I did a quick search—he's not inside."

An odd rush of despair filled her body. "Any chance of us following their tire tracks to wherever they took him?"

"Can't imagine it. I doubt they'd leave a bloody trail of breadcrumbs for us to follow."

"Fine. Then get back here, Sully. We'll meet up with Liam and figure out something else. But we can't take too long." She battled a fresh rush of fear. "We don't know how much time he has."

Chapter 20

At just past ten o'clock that night, Orlov's driver parked the armored car inside the large, empty barn, while two armed soldiers quickly dragged the two halves of the massive wooden doors together and latched them. The old barn housed the entrance of a bunker, which had been dubbed the Crow's Nest back when the country was still part of the Soviet Union, a slave to Russia.

Constant war had necessitated the building of bunkers, and many connected via tunnels to the Moscow subway system. This one, however, stood isolated several miles south of the Russian border, and although most of the wartime bunkers had lain abandoned since the Cold War, Orlov maintained two: one in an official capacity, used by the ministry as an interrogation facility, and the Crow's Nest for his own personal use. Both bunkers were considered black sites, which meant they were lightly guarded and off the books in order to preserve a high level of secrecy. The Crow's Nest was small in comparison to other Soviet bunkers. It had been used primarily for storage purposes and offered only one point of entry, located in this nondescript barn.

Orlov got out of the car, his excitement rising as he thought of what awaited him in the bowels of the facility. Kirill had reported that the man still refused to talk, but Orlov knew that would change. Not many men stayed quiet during a visit to the Crow's Nest.

Unfortunately, before he reached the steel doors situated in the floor, his government cell phone rang.

Suppressing his exasperation, Orlov stalked a short distance away from the two guards. He'd planned on giving Karin a report after he met with his captive, but he supposed he might as well get the conversation over with now.

"Mr. Prime Minister, I was just about to call you," he said into the phone.

"Did you find my daughter?"

"I'm afraid the answer to that is no. But I do have some good news." He paused. "As well as some bad news."

"What is the bad news?"

"Durov's men, working in tandem with a military unit I assigned, discovered the site where your daughter was being held. Her captors, however, managed to escape during the raid. Sadly, the body of Erik Baronova's wife was found on the premises. Our men believe she was shot during an escape attempt."

"I see. And my daughter?"

"That's the good news. She wasn't on the premises."

"How is that good news?" Karin demanded angrily.

"Would you have preferred we find her corpse?"

Silence.

Then the prime minister spoke up wearily. "What do you know about the people who took her?"

"We've received confirmation that this is the work of the PRF," Orlov lied.

As expected, Karin was absolutely livid. "Those goddamn terrorists abducted my daughter? Why?"

"Probably for the same reason they orchestrated the car bombings earlier in the year, and the same reason they murdered Oleg Harkov's daughter last week. They are seeking vengeance on the government."

"But Anastacia is still alive." Karin sounded desperate now. "Do you think they will demand a ransom?"

"Perhaps." He pretended to hesitate, all the while hiding a smile. "But we both know the PRF has never been receptive to our negotiation efforts. You and President Belikov might not believe in violence, but I'm afraid the rebels do."

"I don't give a damn what you have to do to get her back! Kill every last one of them for all I care," Karin snapped. "Just find my daughter!"

The angry click in his ear only caused his smile to widen. Karin was panicking. Good.

As he slipped the phone into his pocket, he suddenly thought of his son. Of how proud he'd been when the doctors placed the red-faced infant in his arms all those years ago. He'd had so many plans for Sergei. His son was supposed to follow in his footsteps, perhaps even rule the country one day.

But Sergei was gone now. His heir, his legacy, gone. All because people like Leo Karin were too scared to get a little blood on their hands.

Once Karin's daughter was eliminated, Orlov's thirst for vengeance would finally be sated. He'd be able to bask in the satisfaction of knowing that the men he'd once considered friends were suffering as greatly as he had.

His thirst for power, however . . . that would not be

quenched until he got the prime minister firmly on his side. For that to happen, Karin needed to be presented with his daughter's corpse, to believe that the rebels were to blame and to agree that action must be taken. But first, Orlov had to locate the girl, and immediately.

Perhaps his hostage could shed light on the girl's whereabouts . . .

Setting his jaw, he crossed the barn and gestured to the two guards. "Open the door. I must pay a visit to our prisoner."

Ethan was woozy as hell, his head spinning like a carousel as he gave his surroundings another thorough examination. He'd been out cold when Orlov's men brought him here, so he didn't know what the exterior of his prison looked like, but judging by the concrete walls, steel door, and dampness of the air, he suspected he was underground. Maybe a bunker or trench, though the former seemed likelier. Probably one of the black sites Alexei Mironov had told them about during their meeting.

The small room was empty save for the chair he was tied to and the large, industrial lightbulb hanging from the ceiling. His wrists had been secured to the back of the chair with barbed wire. Barbed fucking wire, which left bleeding gashes in his flesh whenever he flexed his hands. Christ, he was going to need a damn tetanus shot after this.

At least the wound in his leg had finally stopped bleeding. The dried blood caked to his calf made his skin itch, but his feet were tied to the metal legs of the chair—also with barbed wire—so scratching away the itch was impossible.

Son of a bitch. He couldn't believe he'd allowed himself to get captured by these bastards. Juliet had been right. He should've left Alisa Baronova behind, but he'd chosen compassion over cruelty, and now he was paying the price for it.

His back still ached from the two shots to his vest; he could feel his skin slowly turning purple from the bruises. And to make matters worse, after Orlov's thug had knocked him unconscious from behind, the man had rid Ethan not only of his weapons, but his tactical watch, which featured a nifty little SOS button Ethan could've triggered to broadcast his location to his team.

But he was on his own now. Off the map and at the mercy of a crazy politician who wasn't above using torture to glean information.

Wonderful.

No sooner had the thought entered his mind than he heard the scraping of a lock. A second later, the heavy door swung open with a creak and two men strode inside. The blond and bulky one with the vacant expression was unfamiliar to him.

The second was none other than Orlov himself. Ethan recognized him from pictures and press conferences, neither of which did justice to the man's good looks. Orlov was tall and fit, boasting black hair with distinguished streaks of gray, sharp bone structure, and dark, intelligent eyes. He wore a tailored gray suit and shiny black loafers, and looked completely out of place in the musty space.

"Hello," Orlov said in Russian, the pleasant smile on his face belied by the predatory gleam in his eyes. "I see you're awake."

Ethan didn't answer.

"You've already met my associate Kirill," Orlov went on, "but we have yet to be introduced. My name is Dmitry Orlov, but I'm sure you already know that. Would you care to introduce yourself?"

Ethan's lack of response triggered the man's irritation.

"Kirill informed me you're not willing to talk. I see he wasn't exaggerating." Orlov turned to his soldier. "Cut his shirt off."

Without a word, the man named Kirill extracted a deadly steel blade from his hip and approached their hostage. He bent down and placed the tip of the eight-inch knife on Ethan's collarbone.

Ethan didn't even flinch as the man sliced his sweater from the collar right down to the hem. Kirill proceeded to make two more cuts, one on each sleeve, before putting the knife away and ripping the scraps of fabric off Ethan's torso in one effortless motion.

The cool air brushed his naked chest, but he didn't allow any emotion to show on his face. He kept his gaze on Orlov, whose dark eyes had immediately zeroed in on the tattoo gracing Ethan's left biceps.

"United States Marine Corps," Orlov mused. "So you're American. Interesting."

He still said nothing.

His captor promptly switched to English. "Active duty?"

Silence.

"No, I don't think so. You're not here on a government-sanctioned operation. America has no reason to interfere. No, this must be personal."

"Mercenary," Orlov's stone-faced goon grunted out.

Orlov nodded. "I think so too." His lips pursed as he

studied Ethan's face. "So, are you the one who killed my wolf?"

Silence.

"Why were you protecting Grechko's targets?"

Silence.

Ethan didn't miss the annoyance in the other man's eyes. "I'm going to be honest, Mr. Marine. I find this entire situation quite vexing and inconvenient. I'm the kind of man who doesn't like delays, especially in regards to plans I've set in motion. But your meddling has done just that—delayed me. This makes me very unhappy."

Silence.

"Where is the Karin girl?" Orlov demanded. "I assume your people have taken her to another safe house. Tell me where it is."

Ethan's jaw tensed at the mention of Anastacia.

Orlov, proving to be acutely observant, didn't miss the reaction. "Judging by that response, I suspect you're fond of the girl. Perhaps you'd like me to describe to you in detail how I'm going to kill her."

Anger jolted through him. He hadn't planned on saying a word, but he couldn't help himself now. He wasn't worried about revealing anything Orlov would ever be able to use, but he did feel the need to point out the obvious.

"Killing her won't bring back your dead son, Orlov." Ethan's voice came out hoarse.

"Ah, so he speaks! And no, the girl's death won't bring back my Sergei—I'm not an imbecile. But it will cause her father great pain, which in turn will bring me great joy. Karin and my so-called allies deserve to be punished for their ignorance. They need to experience firsthand the pain and suffering that comes from inaction."

Ethan raised a tired brow. "If you're trying to punish them, then why blame the deaths of their loved ones on the rebels?"

A humorless chuckle slipped out of Orlov's mouth. "I might be a grieving father, but I'm also a politician. Do you truly think I would allow my son to have died in vain? No, I plan to use his death to take down that fool Belikov."

"So that's the big plan? You're angling for the presidency?" Ethan had to roll his eyes. "Wouldn't it just be easier to assassinate Belikov?"

Orlov's jaw stiffened at his mocking tone. "A quick death at the hands of a faceless assassin is too good for that bastard. He deserves to suffer, as I have suffered, as my son suffered. He will lose his family, his job, his livelihood, and when he has nothing left, he will know who to thank for it. Belikov will pay for what he's done, as will the rebels who killed my Sergei. This government's weak policies have given the rebels too much power, but I intend to change that. When my colleagues realize the threat these maniacs pose to our country, they'll join with me to remove Belikov from office. I'll use their anger over their losses to crush the rebel movement once and for all. And then, my dear boy, I will have not only my vengeance, but my coup."

An incredulous laugh slipped out. "So you're too impatient to wait the three years until the next election—is that right? You're scaring your colleagues into doing what—calling an emergency election? A no-confidence vote?"

Orlov's nostrils flared. "You mock me."

"And you're boring me." Ethan feigned a yawn. "Might be time for me to take a little nap."

"I see. You're determined to be difficult." Orlov sounded extremely displeased. "I suppose we'll have to do this the hard way, then."

Ethan's gaze shifted to Kirill, who'd taken a menacing step forward.

"In case you're curious about my friend," Orlov said in a genial tone, "maybe it would be prudent of me to enlighten you about his background. You see, Kirill was once a member of the KGB. You are aware of the KGB, right? You Americans always mention the organization in your silly television shows."

Silence.

"Kirill learned quite a lot during his time with the KGB. Many delightful techniques designed to turn an unwilling man into a very willing one." Orlov cocked his head. "Perhaps knowing this has changed your mind about answering our questions?"

Silence.

"Hmmm. Apparently it hasn't."

Kirill took another step.

Ethan didn't move or react, but a dose of adrenaline had entered his bloodstream. Fuck. This wasn't going to be fun.

Orlov smiled. "I can guarantee that by the time Kirill is finished with you, you'll be begging to talk."

Silence.

"All right, Mr. Marine. Shall we get started?"

Chapter 21

The moment Morgan hung up the phone, D knew that something was wrong. The boss had uttered only three words during the call with Sullivan—*fuck* and *got it*—and those three words were enough for D to figure out there was a serious clusterfuck in progress.

"What's going on?" he demanded.

Morgan's blue eyes flickered with atypical distress. "The rookie got himself captured—that's what's going on."

D cursed. "How the hell did that happen?"

As Morgan filled them in on everything that had gone down in Belarus, D noticed that Noelle's face revealed not even a sliver of emotion. She simply sat at their café table, one lethal hand gripping the handle of her coffee cup, the other periodically lifting a cigarette to her red lips.

At a neighboring table, Yuri Kozlov and his girlfriend were laughing over espressos, oblivious to the presence of their watchdogs. But D didn't give a shit about Kozlov at the moment. He was too focused on Morgan's grave report.

"Shit," he said when the boss finished. "I guess we're heading over there to save his ass?"

"Yup. Kozlov is no longer a priority." Morgan shot Noelle a dark look. "By the way, I'm laying the blame solely at your door for this."

She arched a delicate blond eyebrow. "Oh, really?"

"My man wouldn't have gotten tangled up in this shit if your girl hadn't dragged him into it."

"Your rookie is a grown man." She paused. "Kind of. He *is* young, after all. Maybe you should have kept a tighter leash on him."

"Fuck you," Morgan said in an uncharacteristic burst of anger. "Maybe *you* should teach your operatives not to go off on ridiculous vendettas every five fucking minutes."

Noelle just took another sip and watched Morgan over the rim of her cup.

D attempted to defuse the tension in the air by asking, "When does the rest of the team get there?"

"They're en route. Should arrive by early morning." Morgan still didn't tear his harsh gaze off Noelle, even while addressing his soldier. "I'll make arrangements for a charter."

The boss pushed back his chair and stalked off the patio, allowing them a rare moment of privacy. Ever since Morgan's arrival, he'd seemed to be going out of his way to ensure that D and Noelle were never alone. As a result, D hadn't fucked the blonde since his boss showed up.

Normally D didn't give a shit about other people's pesky feelings. But he had a troubling suspicion that Morgan didn't want him to sleep with Noelle, despite his claim that he didn't give a shit what—or who—D did in his spare time.

"Should we try to squeeze in a quickie, or have you officially signed over control of your sex life to Jim?"

Noelle's dry remark didn't surprise him. She'd mocked him about it often since Morgan had joined them and, just like all the other times, he didn't take the bait.

"You need to stop antagonizing him," D said roughly. "He's protective of the rookie. Has a soft spot for the kid."

"Aw, you want me to go easy on him?" Her glacier blue eyes hardened. "Trust me, honey, he deserves everything I give him. That man is poison."

"So are you."

"Yes, and so are you. We're all poison, aren't we?"

"Ethan isn't. The kid's got a good heart."

Jesus. D couldn't believe the words that were coming out of his mouth.

Neither could Noelle, apparently, because she started to laugh. "Is this an episode of *The Twilight Zone*? Who are you, and where's the detached asshole who never looks me in the eye when we fuck?"

He didn't respond to that either. "Whatever the bullshit between you and Morgan, you're gonna need to put it on the back burner. If your baggage gets in the way and Ethan gets killed? I'll break your neck."

She just laughed again. "Looks like Jim isn't the only one who's protective of the kid." Rolling her eyes, she took one last sip of coffee before gracefully rising to her feet. "Come on, honey. Let's go rescue your rookie."

The rest of Morgan's A-Team arrived at the new safe house just after dawn, bursting onto the scene with a startling amount of energy. Abby Sinclair strode inside first, her red hair streaming out from beneath a black beret that made Juliet smile for the first time since Ethan's capture.

She greeted her former colleague with a quick hug. "Nice hat."

"Are you making fun of me?" Abby asked with a rare grin.

"Yep."

Abby's husband, Kane Woodland, walked through the door next, raking a hand over his sandy blond head to rid it of the snowflakes clinging to his hair. He was tailed by Luke Dubois, a dark-haired man with laughing brown eyes.

The men greeted their fellow soldiers with some fist bumps and side hugs, then glanced at Juliet with visible curiosity.

"So you're the thief," Luke said slowly.

"Among other things," she replied.

As Abby quickly made the introductions, the male newcomers continued to eye Juliet, for so long she found herself feeling strangely self-conscious.

"Why are you staring?" she asked, point-blank.

After a beat, Luke flashed a cocky grin. "Just trying to make sense of it. I'll be honest—you don't strike me as the rookie's type."

She shifted uneasily. Jesus. Had Ethan spoken to his teammates about her? Did grown men actually sit around and gossip about their love lives? Because she'd figured that only occurred in girly romantic dramas on network television.

But no, apparently men *did* kiss and tell, because

Kane spoke up next, a wry gleam in his green eyes. "Nah, she's exactly his type," he told Luke. "I got Ethan drunk once and he admitted to having a thing for dangerous women."

Okay, this was getting super uncomfortable.

Juliet frowned and gave each of them a cool look. "Did you come here to discuss your teammate's sex life or to rescue his ass before Dmitry Orlov kills him?"

"Both," they said in unison.

Abby rolled her eyes and touched Juliet's arm. "Ignore them. Kane's a nosy bastard, and Luke just has women on the brain because he misses his girlfriend."

"Fiancée," Luke corrected.

Abby shrugged. "I'm still holding out hope that Olivia sees the error of her ways and dumps your cocky Cajun ass."

Luke smirked. "Never."

"Come on, let's go out back," Liam said from the kitchen doorway. "I just brewed some coffee."

As the group trudged forward, Juliet glanced at Sullivan. "Is Stacie still asleep?"

He nodded.

"I'll introduce you to her in a bit," she told Abby. "You'll like her. She's a sweet kid. Tough as nails too."

They walked through the kitchen toward the screened-in porch, which was also fully heated. This latest safe house was definitely a step up from the last one, but Juliet hadn't been able to enjoy a second of it. She'd contacted Alexei Mironov last night, but the PRF leader still hadn't called her back, and every source she'd tapped yesterday had diddly-squat when it came to where Dmitry Orlov might have taken Ethan.

Mironov was their only chance, and it pissed her off beyond belief that the man wasn't returning her calls. But enough was enough. As of this moment, Mironov had one more hour to get back to her, and if he didn't meet the deadline she was storming that shit-hole bar of his and burning it to the ground.

Abby and the men took off their coats, scarves, and gloves as they stepped onto the porch. Liam had brought out a coffeepot and a stack of mugs, and nobody said a word until the coffee was served and they were all seated around the large, rectangular table.

"So, what do we know?" Luke asked.

"Nothing," Sullivan said flatly. "We know bloody nothing."

"I read Orlov's dossier on the plane," Abby spoke up. "It said his counterterrorist unit likes to arrest suspected terrorists and interrogate them in undisclosed locations. Any idea where these sites are?"

Juliet shook her head in frustration. "No, but when Ethan and I went to see Alexei Mironov, he mentioned that several of his men had been taken to, quote un-quote, black sites. They're hush-hush interrogation facilities, completely off the official books."

"And Mironov knows where they are?" Kane said sharply.

"He claims he does, but the son of a bitch isn't calling me back. Which means it might be time for Plan B."

Everyone at the table narrowed their eyes.

"What's Plan B?" Liam said warily.

"I contact Orlov and confess to being the mastermind behind this whole thing. And then I offer him a trade." She swallowed. "Me for Ethan."

There was a brief silence, followed by a series of explosions Juliet hadn't expected.

"Are you crazy?" Abby demanded.

"No fucking way," Liam snapped.

"Ain't gonna happen, love," Sullivan piped up.

"There won't actually be a trade," she argued. "I *know* he won't let Ethan go. But Orlov is undoubtedly furious that someone killed his hit man and interfered with his crazy revenge plans. He's going to want to punish whoever's behind it. If I confess to torturing Grechko and taking Anastacia, and then dangle myself in front of him as bait, he might agree to a meeting. At which point I'll kill him."

Abby glared at her. "We're not using you as bait."

"No way," Sullivan said firmly.

Juliet had a tough time containing her surprise. She stared at the Australian for a moment, bewildered by the resolve in his gray eyes.

"I get why Abby is against this," she told him. "But why the hell are you? You know the idea has merit."

"Yeah, it has merit. But there's no bloody way I'm letting you do it."

"Not even if it means saving your man?"

Sullivan snorted. "Saving him? If we send you out in the open to meet with Orlov and something happens to you, Ethan would be fucking destroyed."

"He'd never forgive us for it," Liam agreed.

She frowned. "That's an exaggeration and you know it."

"No way, darling," Liam retorted. "The rookie would never let anyone sacrifice themselves for him. Not you, not me, not anyone."

"Liam's right," Abby said firmly. "Ethan wouldn't want this."

"Well, Ethan's not here right now!" she burst out. "He's not here, is he? And if we don't do something, Orlov is going to kill him, damn it!"

Desperation and panic flooded her body, blurring her vision and causing her hands to tremble. Suddenly a hundred gruesome images swarmed her brain like a hornet attack, each one more spine-chilling than the last, each one featuring Ethan at the grisly mercy of Dmitry Orlov.

"We don't know what they're doing to him," she choked out, unable to keep the anguish out of her voice. "Ethan's strong, but even the strongest men can die during interrogation. He could *die*." Horror burned her throat. "We don't know what they're *doing* to him!"

Another silence crashed over the table, this one heavy with unease.

Finally, Abby stood up with a sigh. "Juliet, a word?"

Breathing through the waves of panic, she followed the other woman inside. After the door had shut behind them, Abby went over to the counter, leaned against it, and offered a thoughtful look.

"What the hell is going on, Juliet?"

She swallowed. "What do you mean?"

"I mean, since when do you offer to put your life on the line for someone else? Especially for someone you don't even know."

"What exactly are you implying, Abby?" She didn't mean to sound so defensive, but something about Abby's tone had raised her hackles.

"Relax, Jules. I just mean . . . you're offering to use yourself to draw Orlov out, and yet . . . Well, you hardly know Ethan, so why—"

"I don't know him?" Her spine stiffened. "I don't *know* him? Bull-fucking-shit. I know him better than you!"

Anger boiled in her belly, spilling over so fast and so suddenly that Juliet's entire body began to tremble.

"I know everything about that man! I know that he's not as weak and helpless as you all seem to think. I know that he'd lay down his life for any one of you. I know that the reason he got captured was because he cared enough to try to save a woman who certainly didn't deserve it. I know that he's kind and sweet and at the same time deadly as hell. I know that he's got a bossy alpha side that he never lets anyone see. I know that he has this dry sense of humor that he rarely ever shows. I know—"

"Okay, okay, I get the point." Abby's distinctive honey yellow eyes were full of disbelief. "You're in love with him."

"Wait. What?" she stammered.

"You're in love with him," Abby repeated, sounding slightly amazed. "Why didn't you just say that from the start?"

"I'm not in love with him," Juliet blurted out.

"Bullshit."

"I was just pointing out that . . ." She trailed off, not even sure why she'd gone on that tangent in the first place.

Misery lodged in her throat as Ethan's face came to her mind. His deep hazel eyes. His strong jaw. His lips, so firm and yet so damn soft.

God, who knew what that sadistic bastard Orlov was doing to him right now?

He could be dead for all she knew.

The agony that ripped into her was the most unexpected thing of all. She'd never intended to have a future with the guy, but the notion of him being permanently erased from her life brought an acute pain to her heart.

"Jules?"

She met her friend's eyes. "It's my fault they took him."

"Oh, come on, that's not true."

Strands of guilt wrapped around her, making her hands shake. "If it wasn't for me, he wouldn't have come to Belarus. He wouldn't have stayed to help me get revenge on Orlov. And he wouldn't be at that bastard's mercy right now."

"Ethan is a grown man. He makes his own decisions. You can't blame yourself for any of this. It's not like you forced him to stay after he showed up to help you."

"I did everything to make him *go*," she muttered.

"There you go. And he chose to stay. He knew the risks when he made that choice."

"I guess." She averted her gaze, going quiet for a moment. Then she looked at Abby again. "I'm not in love with him."

Those yellow eyes flickered with amusement.

"Damn it, I'm *not*."

Abby shrugged now, clearly not buying what Juliet was selling.

Fortunately, Juliet's cell phone put an end to the frustrating exchange. Hope exploded in her chest when she pulled out the phone and saw *unknown caller* flashing on the screen.

She picked up with an eager "Yes?" and was rewarded with the sweetest sound she'd ever heard.

Mironov's voice.

"Ms. Mason, sorry for the delay in getting back to you. I was indisposed for the past two days."

"Did you get my messages?"

"I did indeed." Mironov was as jovial as ever. "I want you to know that I've thought it over, and I've decided to provide you with the information you requested—"

Relief erupted inside her. "Thank you."

"After you tell me what's in it for me," he finished.

She couldn't help but laugh. "Oh, Alexei. Do you *ever* do anything out of the goodness of your heart?"

He chuckled. "I'm afraid not."

"All right. Well, you want to know what's in it for you? How about this? After I kill Orlov, your silly little group can take credit for it. I'll erase all traces of my presence from the scene and leave the country, and if anyone ever asks, I'll say that the mighty Alexei Mironov slew the dragon. Orlov's death will be the crown jewel of your cause and nobody will ever know I played a part in it."

Mironov didn't answer.

"Think about it," she cajoled. "Imagine the power to be gained from letting the world think you assassinated Dmitry Orlov. If the PRF can get to the Defense Minister, then they can get to *anybody*." When he still didn't respond, her tone grew annoyed. "So? Do we have an agreement?"

There was a beat, followed by, "Yes."

Relief soared through her. "Good. Now do your part, Mironov. Do you know the locations of Orlov's black sites?"

"As I told you before, I am very familiar with the minister's little hideouts." Mironov chuckled again. "Don't worry, Ms. Mason. I know exactly where your man is."

Kirill was back.

Ethan couldn't count how many times that steel door had opened in the past twelve hours. Or maybe it was twenty-four hours. Or twenty-four days. Time had stopped for him in this cold, dank room.

He remembered hearing that the KGB hadn't been big on physical torture back in its day—those fuckers had always preferred the psychological shit. Sleep and light deprivation, starvation, all that good stuff. But Kirill must have been the exception to the rule, because the stoic bastard seemed to love inflicting pain on his prisoner.

He'd started with the knife, heating the tip over the flame of a lighter so it would not only cut flesh, but also burn it. He'd focused on Ethan's left arm during the first visit. Tiny little slices, flaming pinpricks. Each individual cut caused only the smallest twinge of pain, but when that blade connected with your skin over and over again, the pain added up.

The second visit had revolved around his right arm.

The third had concentrated on his injured leg.

Each time the hot tip of the knife touched his bullet wound, Ethan had fought to stay conscious and failed. But Kirill was prepared for that—whenever Ethan succumbed to the blackness, the son of a bitch roused him by splashing a pungent-smelling liquid on his face.

Despite the throbbing pain and the dizzy spells and the uncontrollable shivers that racked his body, Ethan still hadn't uttered a single word. He'd been trained by the best military in the world, and was more than capable of keeping his mouth shut no matter what these assholes did to him.

And through it all, he thought of Juliet. Pictured her lazy grin and dancing eyes and used her beautiful face as the motivation not to give up. Not to roll over and die.

His head felt like it weighed three hundred pounds as he lifted it to meet Kirill's emotionless gaze. Although his vision was blurry, he saw that a second guard had joined Kirill. And he was holding something in his hands, something big and brown and— A bucket, Ethan realized.

Kirill approached the chair in a slow gait. "I must say, I'm rather impressed with your resistance. It shows a real strength of character."

The man held up a black cloth.

"I assume you know what this is for."

Ethan didn't answer.

Kirill glanced at the guard. "Cut him loose."

The second man, a short, muscular blond, set down the bucket on the stone floor. Then he extracted a pair of wire cutters from his pocket and walked forward.

Ethan released a hoarse grunt when the man twisted his bleeding wrists in order to cut the barbed wire. It was one of the rare noises he'd made during this ordeal, and it brought a smile to Kirill's lips.

"Get him on the ground."

The guard tackled the wire binding his ankles and hefted him out of the chair. Ethan didn't struggle. Had no energy for it. Shit, he was in worse shape than he'd thought.

Being vertical for one brief second made his head spin, and then suddenly he was horizontal. His back on the cold floor, with Kirill's hulking frame looming over him.

"Who are you?" he asked in a bored tone.

Silence.

"Who are you working for?"

Silence.

"Why did you kill Victor Grechko?"

Silence.

Kirill shrugged. "Cover his face."

The guard knelt down and lowered the coarse material to Ethan's face. Instantly, his vision was nothing but a sea of black.

He drew in a deep breath, knowing exactly what was coming. He hadn't experienced waterboarding firsthand, but he knew men who had, and their advice had always been *"Don't panic."* They'd told him that the sensation of drowning and the lack of air would not lead to death, so there was no reason to fight it. The purpose of water boarding wasn't to kill you, but to make you *think* you were on the brink of death.

As he lay there in the dark, moisture began hitting the cloth in a steady stream, soaking the material, until the feeling of complete suffocation was achieved. Unable to breathe through his mouth or nose, Ethan forced himself to clear his mind, to stay calm. He could typically hold his breath for a few minutes, but thanks to the cloth shielding his face, he hadn't been able to draw enough air into his lungs. Within thirty seconds, his lungs started to burn, his body quivering from the lack of oxygen.

And then suddenly, mercifully, the cloth was gone and

he could breathe again. He sucked in a gulp of air, a second one, a third one.

"Who are you working for? Why did you go after Grechko's targets?"

He was just taking his fourth breath when the cloth was lowered again. The gush of water returned, his air flow yet again stolen from him.

On and on it went. For minutes. Hours. Days.

Don't panic was becoming difficult advice to follow. He couldn't breathe. He was being suffocated. He was fucking dying.

Each time the panic arose, he summoned the image of Juliet's face. Her smile. Her eyes. Her mouth.

Each time he was allowed to breathe, he thought of Juliet's strength. Her bravery. Her laughter.

By the time Kirill announced in an irritated voice that it was time for a break, Ethan had come to a conclusion. A very strange conclusion to reach when you were being waterboarded.

He loved Juliet Mason.

He fucking loved her.

Kirill and the guard stalked out of the room. They left Ethan on the floor, obviously confident that he was in no condition to move.

Which he wasn't. All he could do was lie there and stare up at the ugly gray ceiling. Black dots marred his vision, making it hard to picture Juliet's face.

She would come for him.

Christ, he knew she would come for him, and he desperately wished he could tell her to stay away. Because everything being done to him at the moment? He couldn't imagine Juliet ever being able to endure it.

No, that wasn't true. She *could* endure it. She was strong enough to handle anything Orlov threw at her.

But Ethan refused to let that happen. He would die before letting anyone hurt and torture the woman he loved.

Stay away, Jules.

He wondered if telepathy was actually possible.

He wondered if he'd ever find a way out of this god-awful hellhole.

He must have passed out, because the next thing he knew, that rank liquid—what the fuck was that?—splashed his face, filled his nostrils, and caused his eyelids to fly open. He blinked, disoriented, and then his spirits plummeted as Kirill's smirking face came into focus.

"Me again," the man said softly. He held up the cloth and wagged it over Ethan's face. "Ready for round two?"

Chapter 22

It was another unbearably cold night. Snow fell from the ink black sky in thick flakes, stopping only to allow the clouds to release ice-cold raindrops before resuming to turn the earth white once more. Juliet couldn't wait to get off this damn continent. She was tired of the chill in the air, tired of the snow, tired of the bleak landscape. But she barely noticed the cold tonight. No, because it was assuredly nothing compared to what Ethan was going through.

She forced herself not to imagine all the horrible scenarios as she straddled her second tree branch in two days. The rest of the team was already in position, posted in various areas on the perimeter of the enormous barn in the center of the snowy field. If it were up to her, they'd be storming the goddamn place. Scratch that—they would have stormed it *hours* ago.

But neither Morgan nor Noelle, who'd flown in earlier with D, had allowed it. Juliet had heeded their command only because she understood the risks of going in blind. If they went in unprepared, that would spell danger not only for them, but also for Ethan. And so she'd waited all day for various sources to check in, for a plan of action to be formulated.

Paige hadn't been able to get her hands on the blueprints for this particular bunker, but she'd managed to find the layout for an old Soviet facility that was similar in size and usage. They knew to expect long stretches of hallways inside, and an endless amount of storage and communication rooms.

Mironov had never been inside the Crow's Nest, as it was apparently called, so the number of guards they'd find inside was still undetermined. But since it wasn't an official government facility, Juliet and the others had concluded that it probably wouldn't be too heavily guarded.

Their biggest obstacle were the cameras mounted on all sides of the barn, as well as the ones they'd most certainly find inside the bunker, but Juliet was currently attempting to handle that. During her recon, she'd determined that the security cameras were analog wireless—closed-circuit devices that relied on a receiver in order to receive and transmit a signal, which made her job a hell of a lot easier. With the proper equipment she could disrupt the signal, and fortunately, a former thief like her never left the house without her portable signal jammer.

But she needed to get as high up as she could in order to detect a signal, hence her latest tree climb. Sitting astride the branch, she fiddled with the controls of the handheld device and bit her lip as she attempted to find the right frequency that would override the security receiver. While other jamming devices used random tones or pulses to cause interference, her unit used no sound at all, which meant that to anyone monitoring the wireless receiver, everything would seem normal and operational.

"How's it going up there?" Morgan's voice barked in her ear.

She glanced at the display, which showed that the unit was still searching for a signal.

"Give me a sec," she murmured. "I've almost got it."

A second ended up being all it took. Satisfaction rippled through her as she pinpointed the correct frequency and locked it in.

"We're good to go," she announced. "As of now, the cameras are out of commission. I'm switching on the cell-phone jammer too."

"You sure it won't interfere with our comm?"

She was shimmying down the tree even as she responded to Kane's question. "It won't. We're on a different frequency. But I'm using a small unit, so it's only going to disrupt the frequency from the user's phone to the base tower—it won't directly interfere with the tower itself. So if one of the tangos gets out of my range, their phone will start working again. We need to move fast."

"Copy that," Morgan replied. "Aussie, set off those fireworks."

The line went quiet for a few seconds before Sullivan finally replied. "Fireworks show commencing in three, two, one."

Juliet's feet landed on the frozen ground just as he finished the count. With the two jammers clipped onto her belt, she didn't feel as limber as usual, but now that she'd locked in the signal, it was necessary to keep the devices on her at all times if they wanted to neutralize the cameras.

A second after Sullivan spoke, the silence was broken by a cracking sound, similar to that of a flare gun going off, only much louder. From the corner of her left eye, Juliet discerned a faint cloud of blue-gray smoke rising from the trees, but she wasn't worried about Sullivan giving away his position; he wouldn't be there for long anyway.

The warhead launched from Sullivan's RPG sailed in a straight path and connected with the shed ten feet away from the barn. The small structure instantly burst into flames, the explosion rocking the ground beneath Juliet's feet.

Even before Morgan's voice snapped "Move" inside her ear, she was running through the trees. She reached the edge of the open field just as the barn doors flew open and a pair of parka-clad men burst outside.

Two sharp blasts—the report of Luke's rifle as he systematically took out Orlov's men—sliced the air. When three more streamed out of the barn, they went down just as fast. Juliet had to admit, she was damn impressed with the Cajun's shooting. Luke, Liam, and Noelle were their designated snipers, situated on each side of the barn, but it looked like Luke was the one having all the fun.

"That last one was a damn nice shot," Liam told his teammate. "You got him right in the left eye."

"All thanks to Inga," Luke answered smugly, referring to the sniper rifle he'd shown Juliet earlier in the day. The guy hadn't stopped gushing about the damn rifle, but Juliet couldn't deny that he definitely knew how to use that thing.

As the men chattered in her ear, she sprinted across the dark yard, nearly slamming into D when she reached the barn. The big mercenary wore a look of deadly concentration, armed with a silenced HK pistol and an assault rifle slung over his shoulder. Sullivan appeared from the trees seconds later with that same lethal expression.

Morgan and Kane were already in the barn when the trio stalked inside. Their guns were pointed at the floor, trained on the open steel doors that revealed a set of concrete steps leading down to the bunker.

Surrounded by the four big men, Juliet felt tiny in comparison, and she had to wonder if this was what it was like for Abby when she went on missions with these dudes.

At the thought of Abby, she experienced a pang of guilt that the redhead had drawn the short straw and was therefore assigned to bodyguard duty back at the safe house. Juliet knew her friend hated being left out of the action, but she also knew that if anyone could keep Stacie safe, it was Abby Sinclair.

"We stick to the plan," Morgan ordered. "Kane, you stay aboveground, shoot any motherfucker who climbs these stairs. Aussie, you and I search the bottom of the T, D takes the east arm, Juliet gets the west. Got it?"

They all nodded. Juliet didn't need any clarification— Paige's intel had revealed that the smaller storage bunkers were most often T-shaped, with the bottom of the T containing the command centers and weapons lockers, while the two arms featured smaller storage areas and living quarters.

As everyone around her checked their ammo and clicked magazines into place, her gaze strayed to the three vehicles on the other side of the unheated space.

Two Humvees and a black town car. It was the latter that captured her attention—they'd seen the car enter more than an hour ago. Nobody had been able to make out the passengers, but Juliet knew with every fiber of her being that Orlov had been inside that car.

He was here. In the bunker. Torturing Ethan.

And she was going to kill the son of a bitch.

It was hard to predict what they would find down below. Although Juliet had effectively cut off Orlov's communication, he and his men had surely heard the shed explosion. The team had needed a diversion tactic to lure the guards into opening the barn doors, but because of it, they'd officially lost the element of surprise.

And so Juliet wasn't at all shocked when the four of them scurried down the long flight of stairs and found themselves splat in the middle of a gunfight.

Instantly, she dove into a nearby hallway and took cover, aiming her Beretta at the doorway. When an enraged male skidded around the corner with an AK in his hands, she didn't hesitate to put a bullet in his chest, then a second one in his head for good measure.

The deafening sound of gunfire reverberated in the bunker and bounced off the cinder-block walls. The facility was well lit, making it easy to identify their targets, and within minutes the corridors grew quiet.

With adrenaline still pumping through her veins, Juliet reunited with the guys in the main hallway, which was littered with nearly a dozen bodies. Puddles of blood spread on the stone floor, trickling toward her feet. She swept her gaze over the fallen soldiers and didn't recognize a single one. No Orlov. No Ethan. Relief and frustration lodged inside her, but she forced herself to dwell only on the former. If Ethan wasn't lying on the floor, then that meant he might still be alive somewhere.

"Search the facility," Morgan ordered.

They split up, Morgan and Sullivan ducking into opposite rooms in the hall, Juliet and D racing toward the end of it. The second they reached the intersecting corridor, a bullet nearly took Juliet's head off. Heat streaked past her earlobe as the slug collided into the concrete wall, taking a chunk out of it.

A gunshot boomed, and the man who'd almost killed her fell to the floor with a loud thud.

She glanced over at D, who was lowering his pistol. "Thanks."

"No prob," he said gruffly.

The two of them promptly went their separate ways.

Juliet's heart raced as she ducked into the first open doorway in the hall. She found herself in a small room full of dusty metal tables with Morse code machines piled atop them. The next room was empty save for two metal racks with broken shelves.

Each room featured rotary telephones mounted to the walls, but she had no clue whether they were operational. Industrial lightbulbs allowed her to see every last detail of the creaky old bunker—including the strategically placed explosives on the walls and ceilings.

Crap. The place was swimming with C4.

She checked room after room, her frustration growing as she found each one deserted. Goddamn it. Where the hell was Ethan?

As she hurried down the hallway, the wires running along the ceiling were an ominous reminder that the bunker was rigged to blow. She only hoped that whoever was responsible for making everything go kaboom was dead—or, at the very least, waiting to trigger the explosion until he was safely out of the blast radius.

The silence was suddenly broken by muffled thuds. No, footsteps. Her ears perked, gun snapping up as she tried to pinpoint where they'd come from.

She heard them again, and her eyes narrowed. Someone was close. No more than ten feet away.

She crept forward, moving toward the next door. Gripping her Beretta, she flattened herself against the cement wall and waited. Her heartbeat remained steady, her breathing soundless and even.

She could hear movement. The rustle of clothing. The soft hiss of someone breathing.

The door of the room she stood beside was ajar. She inched closer, caught a flash of motion, the blur of a man's arm, the screen of a cell phone.

For a moment she wondered if it might be Ethan, but when a quiet Russian expletive met her ears, all hope of that died. It wasn't Ethan's voice.

She heard clicking noises now, followed by another curse that made her realize the man was trying to use his phone with no success.

Hiding a smile, she glanced at the black device on her belt. Looked like her jammer was doing its job.

But the smile faded fast, especially when Morgan's voice echoed in her ear.

"Main stretch is clear. Rookie's not here."

She couldn't answer without alerting her prey to her presence, so she stayed silent, all the while battling a jolt of disappointment. Damn it, where *was* he? Had they been wrong about this place? Had Orlov taken Ethan somewhere else?

She reminded herself that D hadn't checked in yet. There was still a chance that they'd find Ethan. Safe and sound.

Or dead.

The bleak notion made her hand shake.

If Ethan was dead, she was going to go bat-shit crazy on Dmitry Orlov. Everything she'd done to the Siberian Wolf would be child's play compared to what she'd do to Orlov. The man had already taken her brother from her, but if he took Ethan too? There would be no stopping her from ripping that monster's head right off his vile body.

Her spine went ramrod straight as she heard footsteps nearing the door. Her quarry was making his move.

She tightened her grip on her weapon. Time to make hers.

Fueled by a rush of adrenaline, she charged at the door and kicked it open with so much force it slammed into her target and knocked him right off his feet.

She was a nanosecond from pulling the trigger when recognition struck her like a bolt of lightning.

Well, goddamn.

Speak of the devil.

Chapter 23

D encountered trouble literally three seconds after he and Juliet split up. In an instant, he went from running on two feet to lying flat on his back as a barrel-chested man in green fatigues tackled him with the skill of an NFL linebacker.

His M16 clattered to the concrete floor and skidded out of reach. He managed to hold on to his HK, but not for long; his attacker swiftly kicked it from his grasp before 180 pounds of muscle came crashing down on his chest.

A meaty fist pummeled D's jaw with a sickening crack, but it was the only blow the blond soldier succeeded in landing. D struck out with a right hook that sent the other man's head flying back. But it didn't knock the guy out — it only brought a rush of fury to his eyes.

They wrestled on the ground, rolling over as each one tried to gain the upper hand on the other. D grunted when his opponent kneed him in the balls, but he'd been trained to ignore the pain. He managed to land an uppercut to the man's lip, splitting it open and causing a spurt of blood to splash him in the eyes. Breathing hard, D swiped at the blood obstructing his vision and concentrated on gaining control of the situation.

He'd just gotten his attacker in a headlock when the guy grabbed hold of D's left arm with both hands.

With one sickening twist, D's bone broke cleanly in half.

Oh, sweet Jesus.

A roar of pain flew out of D's mouth. A kaleidoscope of stars flashed in front of his eyes, and he nearly passed out from the agony streaking through his arm.

The other man's triumphant laughter bounced off the walls, which only succeeded in triggering D's fury and giving him a jolt of adrenaline that allowed him to heave his attacker off him. The man landed on the floor with a thump, providing D with just enough time to fling out his uninjured arm and grab his fallen pistol.

The other man had just gotten to his knees when D pulled the trigger.

The gunshot was deafening. His ears started to ring, pulse off-kilter as his arm continued to throb like a motherfucker.

Gulping in shallow breaths, he somehow managed to stand up. The world spun for a moment. He waited until the dizzy spell passed before examining the other man's body to make sure the guy was dead. Then he took a tentative step toward the doorway his attacker had emerged from.

"D, you copy?"

He cradled his broken arm to his chest and tried to breathe through the pain. When the nausea subsided, he touched his earpiece with his good hand and said, "Yeah, I copy."

"Main hallway's clear. No sign of the rookie. Status?"

"Got into a little skirmish with a tango, but it's all good. I'm still looking."

He adjusted his grip on the HK and approached the open doorway cautiously. Ignoring the shooting pains in his arm, he took a breath and peered into the room.

Then he activated the comm again.

"Scratch that—I'm not looking." He exhaled in a ragged burst. "I found him."

Juliet stared at Orlov, unable to believe that he was actually right there in front of her. It was like being handed an early Christmas present—well, not that she had much experience with that. She'd never had a real Christmas. Her only decent holiday memory was the year she and Henry had stolen a box of cookies from the cupboard and hid under Deke and Maria's bed to eat them.

At the thought of Henry, her shoulders tensed, and her index finger involuntarily tightened over the trigger.

"Who the hell are you?" Orlov snapped, his dark eyes blazing.

"Keep your hands where I can see 'em," she snapped back.

His cheeks hollowed in anger, but he didn't move his arms, just left them dangling at his sides. Juliet swept her gaze over the man who'd consumed her thoughts for so long now. Everything about him sickened her—his perfectly combed hair, his gratingly handsome features, the expensive gray suit he wore.

"Where's Ethan?" she asked in a deadly voice.

He arched a brow. "Who?"

"The man you captured. Where is he?"

Orlov smirked. "Dead. Just like you're going to be."

She ignored the clench of pain she experienced at his cavalier response.

Dead.

No, he was lying. She refused to believe Ethan was gone until she saw his body with her own two eyes.

Now Orlov chuckled. "Do you truly believe you'll get out of this bunker alive?"

She shrugged. "Don't care if I do, as long as I kill you first."

He tipped his head to the side. "Would you do me the kindness of telling me what I did to earn your wrath?"

Considering she was about to end his life, she figured there was no harm in letting him know why she was doing it. "Zoya Harkova."

Recognition flickered in his eyes. "The Harkova woman? Don't tell me a professional of your esteem allowed herself to form an emotional connection. You are a professional, are you not? I'd hate to think I was bested by an amateur."

"Oh, I'm a pro, all right. And as a pro, I'm well versed in the art of vengeance. When you ordered Grechko to execute Zoya, she wasn't the only one he killed. My brother is dead because of you."

He seemed surprised to hear the word *brother*, but she didn't let him speak. She just kept going, a wry note entering her voice.

"Before he died, he ordered me to hunt you down and kill you. I don't think he would have been against me doing a little torturing either. But as much as I'd like to drag out your death—really make you suffer, you know?—I'm afraid I don't have a lot of time at the moment. So—"

Without another word, Juliet shot him in the chest.

Horror exploded in his eyes as his body jerked from the impact of her bullet. A dark red stain bloomed on the front of his suit jacket, but even as he lay there wheezing, his lips quirked up in a self-satisfied smile that made her blood run cold.

"What the fuck are you smiling about?" she demanded, a thread of worry unraveling inside her.

As his face grew pale, he gave a hoarse laugh thick with triumph. "I'll see you in hell, bitch." Another breathy laugh. "And not too long from now, I imagine."

His words sent a chill up her spine. Swallowing hard, she pulled the trigger again, putting two more bullets in his chest and one in his forehead, officially shutting him up.

A moment later, Orlov's eyes rolled to the top of his head, his victorious expression freezing on his lifeless face.

Fighting a jolt of panic, Juliet dashed over to the dead man and searched his body, hoping to find a clue that would explain what that bastard had been so smug about.

When her hand slid into the inner pocket of his jacket, she discovered the source of Orlov's pleasure.

A remote detonator.

Goddamn it.

Her gaze involuntarily shifted up to the ceiling, where a brick of C4 was affixed to the concrete, then to the second set of explosives mounted right beneath the doorframe.

A flash of movement suddenly caught her eye, drawing her attention to the digital watch circling Orlov's wrist. She realized it was counting down to something, and although there was no way to know when the count had started, she damn well knew how much time was *left*.

Five minutes and twenty-two seconds.

Shit.

Juliet tore Orlov's watch right off his wrist and flew to the door just as D's gravelly voice crackled in her ear. During her exchange with Orlov, she'd heard Morgan and the others talking over the comm, but she'd blocked them out before.

Now she listened to every word.

"Scratch that—I'm not looking. I found him."

Relief soared in her chest as D's words registered. "You found him?" she blurted into her mic. "He's alive?"

D's grunt of assent was the most beautiful sound in the world, but her joy faded as quickly as it appeared.

"Get him out," she said urgently. "Everyone needs to get out now. The entire bunker is rigged with explosives and Orlov just set off the detonator."

Morgan joined the feed. "How much time do we have?"

She glanced at the dead man's watch. "A little less than five minutes."

"And Orlov?"

"Taken care of," she said without a trace of emotion.

"Copy that. You heard what the lady said," Morgan barked. "Everyone get the fuck out."

D spoke up in a hesitant voice that was completely unlike him. "That might be a problem, boss."

"Why?" Morgan demanded.

"The rookie's in bad shape."

Juliet's heart plummeted down to her stomach.

"So carry him, damn it."

"I would if my arm wasn't broken."

Morgan cursed. "Jesus. Stay put. I'm coming to you."

"No," Juliet said sharply. "I'm closer. I'll go."

"Juliet—"

She was already out the door. "You and Sully are all the way on the other side of the damn bunker," she cut in as she ran down the hall. "This place is three-quarters of a mile—it'll take you two minutes to get to D and two minutes to get out. You won't fucking make it. I'm closer."

"We can make it if we run," Sullivan spoke up, sounding determined.

"She's right," Morgan said flatly. "Get the fuck out, Sully. That's an order. I'll deal with it."

"For the love of God, Morgan, I can handle it," Juliet snapped, while sprinting down the corridor like she was competing in the Olympics.

D's voice again. "Damn it, boss, go with Aussie. We'll get him out. Trust me."

There was a beat of silence, then a heavy sigh. "Run like your fucking lives depend on it," Morgan finally said.

And then the comm went quiet.

Juliet had never moved faster in her life. When her lungs screamed for oxygen, she realized she'd forgotten to breathe, and she inhaled a gulp of air, her heart pounding so hard and so fast she feared it would beat right out of her chest. Her boots slapped the concrete as she tore down the hall. When she reached the path that connected the east and west corridors to the main one, she flew around the corner—and then skidded to a stop.

"Oh God," she burst out.

Ten feet ahead, D was trudging forward, one muscular arm supporting a bare-chested man whose back was sliced up with a series of zigzagging cuts that oozed blood.

Juliet's heart stopped when she recognized Ethan's dark head. Oh, sweet Lord. What the hell had they done to him?

She raced after the two men, reaching them just as D glanced over with a somber look. She'd never seen the big mercenary so subdued, and when she came up on Ethan's other side and saw his face, she understood the reason for D's defeated posture.

"Oh God," she whispered again, immediately wrapping her arm around Ethan's trim waist to ease some of the load off D.

Ethan's hazel eyes flickered at the sound of her voice, but they were so glazed she knew he wasn't seeing her. Blood dripped down his chest, forming little rivulets along the countless lacerations marring his skin. Parts of his flesh seemed to have bubbled up, as if he'd been burned as well as cut.

Ignoring the shrieking of her pulse, Juliet ripped her gaze off Ethan's mangled chest and tried to encourage both men to walk faster by picking up her own pace. A glance at Orlov's watch showed that they had two minutes left.

Two fricking minutes.

At the pace they were traveling at, they'd never make it out.

She shoved the disturbing thought out of her head and forced herself to study the wires strung along the ceiling.

"The explosives are targeted at structurally weak spots," she told D.

"That's usually the way to do it," he muttered. "Target the building supports and the whole thing will cave in with a few strategic blasts."

"It won't cave in completely." She chewed on her lip, trying not to look at Ethan, for fear that she might break down.

He hadn't said a word since she'd joined them. His head was drooping forward, his breathing labored as he struggled to put one foot in front of the other.

Juliet was overcome with awe. The man was a walking zombie, for Pete's sake, yet somehow he'd found the strength to keep moving. Seeing him do it sent a rush of pride to her heart.

"Where the fuck are you going with this?" D demanded.

She looked over and noticed that his left arm was dangling uselessly at his side. She didn't ask how he'd broken it, didn't care at the moment. All she knew was that neither she nor D possessed the physical strength to run and carry Ethan, and unless that happened, there was no way any of them were reaching that exit.

"Keep walking. I need to check something out."

She reluctantly released Ethan and sprinted ahead, ducking into the first room on her right. The deserted space was wired with C4, so she hurried out and tried the next one. No explosives there, but the ceiling right outside the door boasted a fat brick, which meant the room would most likely take a huge hit. Down the hall she went, checking the empty rooms until she hit the jackpot.

The room she found herself in was one of the few that not only contained supplies, but reinforced steel. And no

C4 in sight. It must have been a weapons locker, judging by the deep compartments dug into the walls, but Orlov's people had been using it for storage. Long racks took up the space, shelves lined with boxes of ammo, spare clips, and an array of other useful goodies.

Juliet checked the countdown. A minute and a half. Shit.

She dashed out of the storage room and intercepted D and Ethan in the corridor.

"Go," she told D.

His coal black eyes flashed. "Fuck you. I'm not leaving."

"Yes, you are." She quickly moved to support Ethan's waist, her tone brooking no argument. "We're not too far from the stairs. You can make it if you run."

"No. Way."

"Look, there's a room up there that I can take Ethan to. It's structurally sound, walls reinforced with steel. There's a good chance it'll stay intact when the place blows."

"No. Way."

"Goddamn it, D! There's no reason for all of us to die here!" Her breaths came out in rushed pants. "At least this way we'll have a chance. You can tell the others where we are, try to get an excavation team to dig us out. If you stay, we all fucking die and nobody will ever find us."

D opened his mouth, clearly ready to argue again, but Juliet put an end to his protests by touching her earpiece.

"Morgan, you there?"

A gruff voice instantly responded. "Yeah, I'm here. We're clearing the blast radius. What's your ETA?"

"D's on his way out. Ethan's in bad shape, so we're gonna ride it out in here."

Morgan sounded horrified. "Ride it out? Are you fucking insa—"

"One of you has to come back in case D needs help clearing the blast. He'll tell you where to find us."

She cut off communication and turned to the tattooed mercenary who was currently scowling at her. Another glance at her watch gave them a minute. One measly minute.

"Go," she said softly. "Please."

After a beat, D's harsh features took on a look of surrender. "Keep him safe."

She swallowed the lump in her throat. "I'll try."

A second later, D took off running, leaving them alone.

Fighting back tears, she did her best to shoulder Ethan's heavy weight, urging his hunched frame to keep going. Her side began to ache from the strain, each labored step they took pulling on the patch of tender skin that Grechko's bullet had gone through, but she ignored her own pain and concentrated on Ethan.

"We're almost there, baby," she murmured in encouragement. "Just keep walking. We're almost there."

It seemed like hours before they reached the doorway of the storage room, but her watch revealed that only ten seconds had passed. She quickly ushered Ethan inside and shut the door behind them, then guided him toward the corner of the room, which she determined was the spot least likely to crush them should the ceiling collapse.

She helped Ethan into a sitting position. Thirty seconds left.

She settled down beside him. Twenty seconds.

She cradled his damp head against her chest. Ten seconds.

Then she took a deep breath.

And waited.

Chapter 24

It was a somber group that gathered in the trees and watched as the barn shuddered in the distance. A moment later, the roof caved in. The wind carried the sound of wood cracking and splitting apart, the heavy crash of walls folding and collapsing, until the structure was nothing but a pile of broken beams and splintered wood chips.

The explosion itself had occurred underground, the force of it bringing down the barn and officially trapping Juliet and Ethan down below.

Or maybe just killing them.

Noelle stood away from the others, an unwelcome wave of sorrow washing over her. She couldn't pretend that losing Juliet didn't hurt. God, she loved that girl. She'd trained her, groomed her into a true warrior.

Noelle turned her head at the sound of twigs snapping and glimpsed Morgan striding toward her. The hood of his black parka was down, providing her with a clear view of his strong neck and chiseled jaw. He hadn't shaved since he'd joined them in Madrid, and the dark beard growth on his face lent him a feral look.

As he came closer, she was startled by the raw emotion in his midnight blue eyes.

"I'm not in the mood to hear your death threats," she said with a sigh. "I'm well aware that your man is most likely dead."

"I didn't come over to threaten you." He cleared his throat. "I just spoke to my CIA contact. He's arranging for an excavation team, but they can't get here until morning."

Neither of them voiced what they were both thinking—Juliet and the rookie might not have until morning.

"The smoke down there will be brutal," Noelle said flatly.

"I know."

"The whole bunker could be engulfed in flames."

"I know."

She discovered that her hand was trembling as she reached into her pocket for her cigarettes. She extracted one and brought it to her lips. The orange tip glowed in the darkness as she lit up.

"Gimme one of those."

She acknowledged Morgan's gruff command by handing him a smoke, followed by her Zippo.

His cheeks hollowed as he inhaled, and then he blew out a cloud of smoke. It was carried away by the icy breeze, disappearing into the night.

"They might have survived," he finally said.

"Maybe."

But she wasn't holding out hope. There had been no contact from Juliet since the bunker had exploded. Her earpiece needed a signal in order to function. No way was a signal getting through all the rubble down there.

Another stab of pain sliced Noelle right in the heart. Motherfucker. She should have never allowed Juliet to get mixed up in this revenge scheme. Noelle, of all people, knew how toxic revenge could be.

"This is on me," she murmured.

Morgan glanced over, weary. "Wasn't it only days ago when you insisted you're not responsible for Juliet's crusade?"

"Haven't you learned by now that I'm full of shit?"

He flashed a rare smile. "Of course you are. But not when it comes to this. This isn't on you, Noelle. You and I might call the shots, but we both know our people make their own decisions. You couldn't have stopped her, same way I couldn't have stopped Ethan from helping her."

The murmur of voices drifted over, causing Noelle to turn her head. She saw Kane and Port whispering to each other near a cluster of snow-covered shrubs. Macgregor was standing at the edge of the clearing, staring at the caved-in barn. Dubois was talking softly into a cell phone. And D was sitting on the cold ground with his back against a tree trunk, his left arm draped across his broad chest.

His eyes were closed, but Noelle knew he wasn't sleeping. She also knew he was more shaken up than he was letting on. He hadn't said a word since he'd emerged from the bunker. Alone.

She wondered if this was the first time he'd ever left a man behind. She suspected so, because no matter how hard he tried to hide it, it was evident that leaving the rookie had affected him deeply.

She was affected too. The ache in her heart was so strong, ran so deep, that she felt like her chest had been hit by an eighteen-wheeler.

"They might have survived," Morgan said again, almost as if he were trying to convince himself of it.

This time she didn't answer. Hope didn't exist in her life. Only pain. Constant, unceasing pain that had weighed on her shoulders for years, until eventually she'd chosen to shut down altogether. To stop feeling. To stop caring.

But, damn it, she cared about Juliet.

Sullivan Port wandered over, interrupting her bleak thoughts. "What now?" he asked his boss. "Should we stick around until the dig crew shows up?"

Morgan released a breath. "Nah, you might as well head back to the safe house. Keep Abby company."

Sullivan's gray eyes narrowed. "What about you?"

"I'm staying."

With a nod, the blond man rejoined the rest of the group, said a few words, and then they were all gone, leaving Noelle alone with the man who'd haunted her for so many years.

"You should go with them," he said roughly.

She mimicked what he'd told Port. "I'm staying."

"Suit yourself."

Silence settled between them as they stood side-by-side, smoking their respective cigarettes and eyeing the wreckage that used to be the barn.

"Shit. It's frickin' cold out here. This is gonna be a long night." Morgan sounded tired as he dropped his smoke on the ground and snuffed it out with his boot.

A gust of wind snaked beneath Noelle's hair and brought a chill to her neck. "Want to snuggle up to stay warm?" she said mockingly.

He snorted. "In your dreams, baby."

Juliet had expected the blast to be powerful, but, Jesus, not to this extent. The deafening explosion rocked the bunker, causing the walls to shudder and pieces of exposed concrete to break off and crash to the floor. The ceiling, however, had stayed blessedly intact, or at least the portion that was over her and Ethan's heads. The front part had collapsed in large chunks of cement, effectively barricading the door and making it impossible for them to escape.

Seconds after the series of explosions roared beyond the door, the temperature in the storage room had spiked, becoming so unbearably hot that Juliet was sweating through her clothes. Through it all, she held Ethan tight, stroking his hair as he lay there with his head buried in her lap.

The acrid scent of smoke seeped in through the exposed cracks in the wall, but fortunately she'd snagged a few portable oxygen canisters from one of the shelves in case the air became too smoky to breathe.

When Ethan stirred in her arms, she experienced a burst of relief so strong she would've fallen over if she hadn't already been sitting down. A part of her had feared that even if they managed to get out of this bunker, Ethan wouldn't be alive to see it. His skin was molten hot, his wounds bubbling and oozing with blood, and he'd been unconscious from the second she'd dragged him in here.

But now he moaned, his eyelashes fluttering as he peered up at her.

"Juliet?" he mumbled.

She swallowed. "I'm here."

"Where's . . . here . . . ?" He sounded disorientated, weak.

It hurt her to see him like this. She wanted her warrior back, damn it.

"One of Orlov's bunkers," she told him. "Which, FYI, just exploded. We're trapped under a mountain of rubble."

That seemed to snap him into a state of alertness. His hazel eyes focused, filled with shock, and suddenly he was trying to get up. He groaned the entire time, but managed to raise himself into a sitting position.

"What happened?" he said hoarsely.

She gave him the short version, which brought a deep frown to his mouth. "You . . . stayed behind with me? Why would you do that? You should've left me behind."

Anger slammed into her. "Don't you ever say that to me again. There's no way in hell I could ever leave you behind."

To her extreme shock, he started to laugh. Deep, raspy sounds that echoed in the smoke-laced air. The explosion had knocked out the power, so the room was bathed in darkness, but there was no mistaking the incredulity on his face.

"Christ, sweetheart, only days ago you were telling me we have no future. And now we *literally* have no future." He raked a hand through his hair. "There's no way we're getting out of here."

"We might," she murmured. "D knows where we are. The excavation team will know where to search."

Ethan didn't seem to hear her. "What happened to your trusty self-preservation? Why the hell would you choose to die here with me instead of getting out?"

She faltered, her heart catching in her throat. Lord, he was right. She'd chosen to stay with him instead of saving herself. Never in a million years would she have dreamed of doing that for anyone. Her survival came first. It always had.

But . . . damn it, she hadn't been willing to leave him.

"I don't know why I did it." Her voice was a shaky whisper. "I . . ."

"You love me."

Those three words evoked a rush of discomfort, but she couldn't for the life of her deny them. The thought of losing Ethan had been so viscerally terrifying that she'd sacrificed her well-being for him.

"You love me," he said again.

The sting of tears pricking her eyes had nothing to do with the smoke. "Yeah, I think I might."

He slid closer, resting his chin on her shoulder. "If it helps, I love you too."

The husky declaration caused the tears to spill over. Even as they streamed down her cheeks, she found herself starting to laugh. Oh God. She hadn't been in love since she was seventeen years old, but as crazy as the notion was, she knew it was the truth.

Ethan Hayes was the best thing that had ever happened to her. He was sweet and strong and sexy, and he accepted her for who she was, flaws and all. He didn't care about her shitty background, her compromised morals, the bitchy front she put on. He was a man of true worth, a man she probably didn't deserve, but, God, she wanted him in her life. She *needed* him in her life.

"Why are you laughing?" he murmured.

"Because we're probably going to die."

"Not exactly seeing the humor in that, Jules."

"I finally found the man I'm meant to be with, and we're going to die. I think that's pretty funny."

After a beat, he chuckled. "Meant to be with, huh? You never struck me as the kind of woman who believed in fate."

"I never did before, but I think I do now." She touched his chin with one hand and brought his face close to hers. "I have something I need to ask you."

"Yeah, and what's that?"

Juliet exhaled in a fast rush. "Will you be my boyfriend?"

The sound of his sexy laughter almost made her forget that they were trapped in a collapsed bunker.

"Well?" she demanded when he still hadn't answered.

A smile crinkled the corners of his mouth. "Damn right I will."

"Did I ever tell you about the time Maria let me watch her soap operas with her?"

Juliet's quiet voice penetrated the darkness, making Ethan smile. They were sitting in the corner of the room, shoulders and thighs touching, fingers interlaced and resting on his lap. The smoke in the air had thickened, and despite the oxygen canisters they'd been making good use of, they'd been coughing a lot. Definitely not a good sign, but Ethan was determined to remain optimistic.

He'd survived that psycho Kirill's torture, for fuck's sake. If he ended up dying of smoke inhalation, he'd go to the grave kicking himself the entire way.

"Ethan? Oh, Jesus, please don't fall asleep." Her alarm was palpable.

Realizing he'd zoned out, he squeezed her hand in reassurance. "I'm awake. Sorry. You were saying something about soap operas."

"Yeah. There was this one week when Maria was in a really good mood, and she asked me to keep her company during her soaps. They were cheesy as hell, but one show featured a supercouple that kept breaking up and getting back together, like, a hundred times. I thought it was ridiculously dumb—I mean, why not cut your losses after the first fricking divorce? But there was this one episode, after they'd reunited, where the chick was waxing poetic to the guy and telling him why she kept coming back to him."

Juliet hesitated, prompting him to coax her into continuing. "What was her reason?"

"Well, she went on for a while about how much she loved him. And then she said something that resonated with me. She said that he was her person."

"Her person?"

"You know, the person she could always count on. The one she knew would be there for her no matter what she did or who she screwed or how many times they hurt each other. When I heard that, I realized I didn't have a person. My folks didn't give a shit about me. My foster parents and teachers and caseworkers didn't care. Henry did, but even then I could never be sure that he'd be there for me *no matter what*, you know?"

The sorrow in her voice seemed to suspend in the air. It brought an ache to his heart, and a determined expression to his face.

"I'm your person," he said gruffly.

When she didn't answer, he grasped her chin with one hand and forced her to look at him. "Do you hear me, Jules? I'm your person. I'm your *no matter what*. And you're mine."

"You want me to be your person?"

He'd never heard her sound so vulnerable, so wistful.

"Damn right I do. From this point on, we're in this for the long haul, sweetheart." He paused. "Unless the age difference actually bothers you . . . "

He let the question hang, eliciting a quiet laugh from her lips, which were dry and cracked.

"Rookie, I don't care how old you are. I think you've more than proven that you're all man."

He grinned. "Told ya."

"Yeah, you told me." She sighed, then reached for the metal canister at their feet. "God, it's so hard to breathe."

There was a sharp hiss as she raised the canister to her mouth and sucked on the regulator. Then she handed him the oxygen so he could have a turn.

Ethan's lungs expanded to allow the much-needed air inside. "How long have we been here?" he asked after he'd set down the tank.

"According to my watch, five hours."

Fuck. It had seemed like a lot more than that. Fortunately, each canister contained enough oxygen to last six hours, and they had four of them, so they could survive for at least a day until the team found them.

If the team found them.

But Ethan didn't even want to consider *that* possibility.

Somehow, despite her best efforts, Juliet fell asleep. And as she slept, she dreamed. Strange, vivid dreams that played in her mind like a movie on the silver screen. In one dream she was running from Deke. He was chasing her with a lit cigarette, waving it around, telling her in a singsong voice what he intended to do to her.

In another dream, she was at the hospital with Henry, listening to the sound of his heart monitor. A constant *beep-beep-beep* that abruptly transformed into one long, high-pitched chime as a solid line moved along the screen.

Sometimes she was in bed with Ethan in the dreams, sighing in pleasure as his tongue danced along her body and teased her into oblivion.

Other times she was wandering around in a thick, green fog, unable to see two feet in front of her, arms flailing as she attempted to find something solid to touch. A wall, a car, a person. Except there was nothing to latch onto, and it was so hard to breathe in the fog, so hard to—

Juliet woke up with a gasp. Her eyes were watering, her throat drier than a desert. She felt something heavy on her shoulder. Ethan's head, she realized. He'd fallen asleep too, his bare chest rising and falling unevenly.

When she checked her watch, she saw that they'd been out for more than six hours. Six hours of breathing in the smoke slowly filling the room. She fumbled for the oxygen canister and took several deep pulls. Then she gently nudged Ethan and coaxed him awake, bringing the regulator to his lips.

"How long has it been?" he mumbled drowsily.

"Six hours. Which brings our total to twelve. We've been stuck here for half a day," she said in a glum voice.

"We still have time. We have enough oxygen to last anoth— Did you hear that?" Ethan instantly became alert, straightening up as he glanced at the door.

"I didn't hear anything."

"Shhh. Listen."

She went quiet and listened, straining to make out whatever it was that snagged his attention. But all she got in response was silence. And more silence. And then some more silence. And then . . . a creak.

Followed by a loud mechanical groan.

"Son of a bitch, they actually found us," she whispered in wonder.

There seemed to be a flurry of activity beyond the door. After twelve hours of sitting in complete silence, their surroundings had suddenly come alive. Creaks and thuds. Bangs and crashes. Metallic clangs.

And then a voice. A muffled male voice.

". . . anyone in there . . . can . . . hear us?"

Juliet cleared her dry throat and called out, "We're in here!"

But her voice was so hoarse, it was no louder than a whisper. She tried again, only to break into a coughing fit that had Ethan touching her arm with concern.

"You okay?" He sounded equally hoarse.

Frustration rose inside her. They had to let their rescuers know where they were, damn it.

Her teeth dug into her cracked bottom lip, and then her gaze landed on the oxygen canister in her lap. Inspiration struck. She quickly picked up the canister and started banging it against the steel strips on the wall.

Metal collided with metal, making a loud ringing noise that the folks out in the hall would most certainly be able to hear.

Sure enough, after a beat of silence, the voice spoke again, clearer this time.

"We've got something over here!"

More creaks and thumps echoed in the air for what felt like hours. There was a heavy pounding on the door, as if someone was attempting to push it open, but the fallen chunks of concrete blocking the way rendered that impossible.

Juliet heard voices again, low and muffled. For a second she feared their rescuers would give up, but she didn't need to worry. The whir of a power tool met her ears, and then the metal door began to vibrate. The high-pitched shriek lasted for several minutes. She and Ethan sat there in total silence, their fingers still intertwined as they stared across the room.

With a noisy groan, the door was suddenly lifted out of its frame.

And a beam of light blinded Juliet's eyes.

"You folks all right?" The sharp inquiry came from an unfamiliar man, nothing but a black silhouette, thanks to the flashlight in his hand.

"We're good," Juliet croaked.

"Can you walk?"

"Yeah, I think so." Her muscles were sore as hell as she carefully rose to her feet.

She was immediately overcome by a wave of dizziness and had to close her eyes for a second to regain her equilibrium. When she felt steady enough to move, she held out her hand to help Ethan up.

A tortured noise left his mouth as he attempted to stand. His chest was covered with gashes and dried blood, but even though he was visibly in pain, he managed to stay upright, leaning against Juliet for support.

Smiling, she brought his hand to her lips and brushed a kiss over his blood-caked knuckles. "Ready?"

His white teeth shone in the light as he smiled back. "Never been more ready in my life, sweetheart."

Chapter 25

Two days later

"So I guess this is good-bye."

Noelle stood in the center of the small hangar and put out her cigarette as she watched D approach. He wore cargo pants and a tight-fitting sweater, the edge of a white plaster cast poking out of his left sleeve.

"I guess so," he replied in his gravelly voice, black eyes shuttered.

She shot him a knowing glance. "A permanent one, right?"

"It was gonna happen eventually."

She stifled a sigh, knowing he was right but at the same time wishing it was happening under different circumstances.

No, fuck that. Wishing it was happening on *her* terms.

But from the moment Jim had arrived in Madrid, she'd known that her liaison with Derek Pratt had officially reached its end.

Ah, well. At least Juliet had gotten her man, though

what her girl saw in that sweet-natured rookie, Noelle would never know. Still, there was no denying that Juliet cared deeply for the kid. She hadn't left his side since the two of them had been literally dug out of that bunker. Even when they'd been taken to the hospital to be treated for the effects of smoke inhalation and for Ethan's wounds to be looked at, Juliet had demanded the staff give them beds right next to each other.

The couple had been released from the hospital a few hours ago—they were currently loitering near one of the two gleaming Gulfstreams sitting on the tarmac. And they were holding hands. How sweet.

Juliet did look happy, Noelle had to relent. The former thief was laughing at something Abby had just said, while her new boy toy chatted with Morgan—whom Noelle knew was aware of her and D, even though his blue eyes were focused on the rookie.

"Let me guess," she said dryly. "Jim convinced you what a *dreadful* idea it is for us to be sleeping together."

"No."

"No?"

"We shouldn't be sleeping together because I was wrong."

Noelle furrowed her brow. "Wrong about what?"

"About us." D ran his hand over the stubble dotting his jaw. "When I said we were the same, I was wrong. I'm an emotionless asshole, but you, baby, are not an emotionless bitch."

"I have to disagree with that."

"Disagree all you want, but we both know it's true. I used to think you were dead inside, just like me, but there's still some life in you." He shrugged. "If we keep fucking, I'll end up killing that last shred of humanity you've got left."

It took all her willpower to mask her shock. She opened her mouth to ask him what the hell he was babbling about, but he didn't give her the chance to speak.

He just offered a brisk nod and took a step away. "See you around, Noelle."

As Abby and Kane drifted toward the metal staircase by the door of Morgan's jet, Juliet turned to Ethan with a frown. She'd been trying to contain her displeasure all afternoon, but as she watched him shift in discomfort for the hundredth time that day, her frustration finally boiled over.

"I'm taking you back to the hospital," she announced.

"Nah, I'll pass."

"You're in pain, damn it. You need some good old-fashioned pain meds. And I still want that burn specialist to look at your back and chest."

"There are burn specialists in San Jose," he replied. "I'll see one when we get there."

"You're so fucking stubborn, I just want to kick you."

"Look who's talking. You're the most pigheaded person I've ever met in my life."

Juliet scowled at him. "Is this what our future looks like? Bickering like children?"

He flashed that boyish grin. "Well, I *am* a kid, remember?" He raised his eyebrows. "With that said, I'm pretty sure my maturity levels are a million times higher than yours."

"Oh, shut up. I'm not the one who got tortured and refuses to seek medical attention."

"No, you're just the one who decided to hang around while a bunker was blowing up."

"Because I love you, you big oaf! Wow. I can't believe you're actually complaining that someone loved you enough to want to *die* by your side."

He burst out laughing. "I think that's the most romantic thing you've ever said to me."

Juliet had to grin. "I've always been somewhat of a sweet talker."

Rolling his eyes, Ethan moved closer and swiftly brushed a kiss over her lips. "Seriously, though, the hospital can wait. I have more important things to do first."

"Oh, really? Like what?" She placed her hands on his shoulders, careful not to apply too much pressure so she wouldn't irritate his injuries.

"Well, in case you forgot, I promised to lock you up in a room for a week and ravish you."

"Ah, right." She gave a mock sigh. "I guess I'm okay with that."

"You guess? Bullshit. You're fricking dying for it."

He planted another kiss on her mouth, which quickly transformed into a tongue-tangling make-out that made her heart pound. Jeez. She truly was addicted to this man.

"Get a room, you two!"

They broke apart at Sullivan's voice. The tall Australian wiggled his eyebrows as he walked past them on his way to the jet.

Ethan's teammate had a spring in his step as he climbed the stairs and disappeared into the cabin. Luke and Liam went in next, then D, who'd come from the direction of the hangar.

Juliet shifted her gaze and noticed Noelle standing near the hangar doors, an odd expression on her exquisite face.

"Give me a sec," she told Ethan. "I just need a word with my boss."

A minute later, she was face-to-face with the blond assassin, who looked resigned as she met Juliet's gaze.

"Let me guess—you'll be taking Jim's plane instead of mine."

"Yes. But only so I can spend some time with Ethan on his compound. And then we're flying back to Belarus." A lump formed in her throat. "The funeral home in Minsk is sending Henry's body to the Harkov property—Oleg Harkov agreed to let Henry be buried next to Zoya. I think Henry would have wanted to be close to the woman he loved." She swallowed, pushed away the sadness, then smiled at her boss. "Oh, and just in case you were worried, you should know there's no way I'm ever leaving you to join up with Morgan's crew. I'd die of boredom."

Noelle let out a melodic laugh. "Good girl."

"I'm serious. No matter what happens between me and Ethan, my professional loyalties lie with you. Always have, always will."

"We'll be in touch, then. I'll contact you when I have another assignment for you." Noelle smirked. "Enjoy your rookie. I've heard boys his age possess some serious stamina."

"Trust me, I know. Anyway, I'll see you later. Call me if you need me."

The two women didn't hug, didn't even shake hands. They just exchanged a fond look and a smile, and then

Juliet strode back to Ethan, who was waiting for her on the runway.

"I forgot to ask you," he said when she reached him. "Did you talk to Stacie before we left the hospital?"

Juliet nodded. "Yeah, she's over the moon. Her father hasn't left her side since he got there."

And, boy, did Stacie deserve it. The poor kid had been begging for her father's attention her whole life. It was sad that it had taken a kidnapping to open Leo Karin's eyes to his daughter's unhappiness, but the prime minister seemed to be trying to make amends. He'd even visited Juliet and Ethan in their room in the respiratory unit of St. Anne's, and thanked them profusely for protecting his daughter from the woman who'd tried to kill her.

Karin had no clue that they'd actually been protecting Stacie from Dmitry Orlov, but they'd decided not to tell him the truth. Alexei Mironov and his PRF rebels were bragging to the country that they'd executed the defense minister, and Juliet saw no point in letting the world know that Orlov had been responsible for all the deaths the PRF had taken credit for.

Truth was, a part of her wanted Mironov's cause to succeed. Dmitry Orlov was dead, but the entire system was full of corrupt, power-hungry politicians willing to go to any lengths to reach their goals. If the rebels managed to overthrow the government, then maybe the corruption would finally end. During his taped recording to the Belarusian media, Mironov had revealed the existence of Orlov's torture bunkers, horrifying the country's citizens and no doubt picking up hundreds of new followers.

"I'm glad she got her happy ending."

Ethan's voice jerked her out of her thoughts. "Me too," Juliet agreed. "She deserves it."

"So do you." His lips quirked. "Actually, I think out of anyone, you deserve the happy ending the most to make up for everything you had to go through in your life."

She cocked her head. "When you say *happy ending*, do you mean it in the fairy-tale sense or the pornography sense?"

His chest shook with laughter. "God, I love you."

"Love you too, kiddo." Grinning, she took his hand and laced their fingers together. "Come on, let's get on the plane. I'm thinking if we're stealthy about it, we might be able to have a quickie in the bathroom."

"No more quickies," he said firmly. "I already told you, you're going to be thoroughly ravished."

She pretended to pout. "But what if I don't want to wait?"

"Tough cookies." A broad grin stretched across his face. "The anticipation is half the fun, remember?"

Epilogue

"So you got dumped, huh?"

Noelle donned a cold look as Jim came to a halt in front of her. "Don't you have a jet to board?"

"Ah, baby, you know I can't leave without saying good-bye to you." His blue eyes gleamed. "D said good-bye too, didn't he?"

She shrugged. "The fling ran its course. Believe me, I'm not particularly heartbroken about it."

"Well, sure. You need to have a heart for that."

"Anyway, you've said your good-bye. You can go now."

Morgan swept his tongue over his bottom lip, looking thoughtful.

The expression on his rugged face brought a pang of unease. She recognized that look. It was the one he wore when he was contemplating something of extreme importance.

"What?" she said irritably.

Rather than answer, he brushed past her and entered the hangar, ducking out of view.

She followed him. Because, damn it, she wanted to know what was going on in that infuriating brain of his.

The second she stepped inside, his mouth came down on hers in a punishing kiss.

She hadn't been expecting it. Wasn't prepared for it.

His lips were firmer than she remembered, his tongue demanding as it plunged into her mouth.

Noelle's pulse drummed in her ears, a fast and frantic rhythm that brought a pang of honest-to-God panic.

Jesus, what was he doing?

Why was she kissing him back?

But the instant her tongue touched his, he broke the kiss with a harsh breath and stumbled backward.

Disbelief continued to spiral through her body as she stared into his veiled blue eyes. "What was that?" she whispered.

He cleared his throat, looking as shaken up as she felt. "Just wanted to see if it was still there."

She swallowed. "And is it?"

He met her inquisitive gaze.

And then he walked out of the hangar.

Prologue

Eighteen years ago

The overcast sky and turbulent gray clouds rolling in from
the east made for a miserable afternoon. Rain was immi-
nent, and the chill in the air had already sent all of the
café's patrons inside. Only Noelle remained on the cob-
blestone patio, her gloved hands wrapped around a cup of
hot English breakfast tea. She wished she'd brought a
scarf, but she'd forgotten it back at the elegant town house
in the heart of Saint-Germain-des-Prés, the prestigious
neighborhood she'd been calling home for the past ten
years. Except the nineteenth-century property where she
lived, with its soaring ceilings and sweeping gardens, was
not a real home.

It was a prison.

She'd come to the Marais district today to escape, but
deep down she knew there was no such thing. The numb-
ing pain in her left hand confirmed it—she was trapped.
Forced to endure René's torment, at least for another
two months. But once she turned eighteen? She'd be out
of that house like a bat out of hell. For good. Forever.

She wasn't foolish enough to think she could convince

her mother to join her. No, Colette had made her choice. She would never leave René, but Noelle was past caring. Past begging her mother to see the light.

Pushing away her bitterness, she took a long sip of her tea. The robust liquid instantly warmed her insides, but it didn't ease the relentless throbbing in her fingers. At least two were broken—the index and middle one, for sure—but her thumb ached too, so perhaps it hadn't been spared in René's vicious attack.

I'm going to kill you.

She silently transmitted the message to her stepfather, willing his subconscious to hear it. And it was no longer wishful thinking—she *would* kill him. She didn't know when, couldn't even begin to figure out how, but René Laurent was going to die at her hands. She would make sure of it.

"Is this seat taken?"

The deep, gravelly voice jolted Noelle from her blood-thirsty thoughts. When she laid eyes on the man it belonged to, her breath caught in her throat.

She blinked, wondering if maybe she'd dreamed him, but then he flashed her a captivating grin, and she realized that he *must* be real—her mind wasn't capable of conjuring up a smile as heart-stoppingly gorgeous as this.

A pair of vivid blue eyes watched her expectantly as she searched for her voice.

"There are lots of other seats available," she finally replied, gesturing to the deserted tables all around them.

He shrugged. "I don't want to sit anywhere but here."

She moistened her suddenly dry lips. "Why?"

"Because none of those other seats is across from you," he said simply.

Her heart skipped a beat, and her gaze . . . well, her gaze couldn't seem to leave his face. He was the most handsome man she'd ever seen in her life. His features were perfectly chiseled, his jaw strong and clean-shaven, his mouth far too sensual. And those eyes . . . midnight blue and utterly endless. A girl could lose herself in his eyes.

And this girl nearly did, until the beautiful stranger

chuckled softly, alerting her to the embarrassing fact that she'd fallen into a trance.

Noelle cleared her throat, feeling her cheeks heat up. "I guess you can join me." She put on an indifferent voice, but she could tell he saw right through it.

He was studying her intently as he lowered his tall, lean body onto the chair opposite hers. As he set his coffee cup in front of him, her gaze landed on his hands. Big and strong, with long fingers and short, blunt fingernails.

"You're shivering," he said gruffly.

"It's cold out."

"Yes, it is."

Noelle took a hasty sip of tea, shifting awkwardly in her chair. She watched as he ran one large hand through his dark brown hair. So short it was nearly shaved off. She wondered if he was a soldier. His bulky hunter green sweater and faded blue jeans weren't exactly military-issue, but something about the way he carried himself, something in his shrewd blue eyes, told her he was much more than a tourist or local college student.

He was also American—she definitely hadn't missed the distinct East Coast accent lining his flawless French words.

"You're from America," she remarked in perfect English.

He nodded in confirmation. "Virginia, born and raised. And from the sound of it, you're American yourself."

"My father is."

"Did you ever live in the States?"

"Yes. We were in DC for eight years."

"But now you live in Paris?"

She offered a quick nod. "My mother is French. She and I moved here after my parents got divorced."

"I see." He reached into his pants pocket and pulled out a pack of cigarettes. The hiss of a lighter cut through the air as he lit up, bringing a frown to Noelle's lips.

"Smoking is very bad for you," she said frankly.

"What can I say? I like to live on the edge."

He grinned again, and her heart began to pound.

As she tried to control the butterflies in her stomach,

his mesmerizing eyes swept over her once more, and a thoughtful expression flitted across his face. "You're beautiful. Has anyone ever told you that?"

Her cheeks scorched again. There was nothing lewd or creepy about the compliment, but the intensity with which he said it made her pulse race. Something about this man affected her in a strange, confusing way she'd never experienced before. She found herself wanting to reach across the table and touch him. Hold his hand, stroke his jaw, place her palm on his broad, muscular chest. The urge only confused her further, and so she avoided his gaze by peering down at her teacup.

"What's your name?"

Swallowing, she lifted her head to meet his eyes.

And was stunned by the odd combination of heat and desperation she saw in them.

"Noelle," she murmured.

"Noelle." His voice came out hoarse. "I'm James Morgan, but everyone calls me Jim or Morgan."

Jim. What an ordinary name for a man who was anything but.

"What brings you to Paris?" She was incredibly proud of herself for managing to speak in a steady voice when her entire body was consumed with erratic jolts of heat.

"I'm here on vacation. I have three weeks' leave, so I thought I'd travel until I had to report back to the base."

"The base . . . Are you in the army then?"

"Yeah. Doing my second tour now."

"That's nice. Do you enjoy it?"

His blue eyes flickered with . . . a glimmer she couldn't quite decipher. "I do. I enjoy it a lot, actually."

"Good. It's important to love what you do."

"It is," he agreed before slanting his head pensively. "What about you? What keeps you busy?"

"School." Noelle shrugged. "I graduate from high school in the spring."

She'd purposely emphasized the words *high school* so he would be aware of her age, but he didn't seem distressed by it. She knew he was older—she would pin him down at twenty-one, maybe twenty-two—but the age difference didn't bother her either.

Waves of tension moved between them. Or maybe it was awareness. She couldn't be sure, couldn't quite understand it, but she knew she wasn't the only one feeling it. Jim's pulse visibly throbbed in his throat, as if his heartbeat was as irregular as hers. And his eyes . . . they never left hers, not even once.

"And afterward?" he prompted. "What will you do then?"

Run.

Run and never come back.

"I don't know," she said.

Before she could blink, his hand breached the space between them and found hers. The burst of excitement that went off inside her was immediately replaced by the ripples of pain that seized her injured fingers.

Jim must have noticed her agitation, because his eyes narrowed. "You're hurt," he said flatly.

Surprise filtered through her. "I—"

He was peeling off her brown leather glove before she could protest, and when her hand was exposed, a deep frown puckered his mouth.

She saw exactly what he did—two black-and-blue fingers swollen to twice their size and unpolished fingernails that had broken and bled beneath René's heavy boot.

"Who did this to you?"

His low growl startled her, as did his astute assumption that her injury was no accident. When he gently ran one callused fingertip over her thumb, tears pricked her eyes, but she desperately fought them off. She refused to cry. Crying was a show of weakness, and Noelle was not weak. She would never be weak.

"You need to see a doctor," Jim said hoarsely.

"No! No doctors," she blurted out. "I'm fine, honestly. It was a clean break. I'll just tape them up when I get home."

His eyes flickered with surprise, and she could have sworn she glimpsed a gleam of admiration.

But he didn't capitulate, just spoke again, sternly this time. "Your hand needs to be x-rayed at the hospital. There might be damage you're not aware of."

"No doctors," she repeated.

"Noelle—"

She set her jaw. *"No."*

The lump of panic jamming her throat doubled in size. He couldn't force her to see a doctor, could he? Hospitals and doctors left paper trails, and she couldn't risk leaving a trail that her father might find. Douglas Phillips had raised her to be strong. He'd passed his warrior genes on to her, made sure she could take care of herself.

What would he think if he knew she'd allowed René to have power over her? How ashamed would he be?

Jim released a heavy breath. "Fine. If you won't go to the hospital, at least let me take you to see a friend of mine."

She eyed him suspiciously. "What friend?"

"An old army buddy. He runs a small medical practice in Seine-Saint-Denis," Jim explained, naming one of the more run-down neighborhoods of the city. "He'll keep the visit off the books if I ask him to."

Uneasiness swam in her gut, making her hesitate.

"Nobody will ever know you saw him, I promise."

The total assurance in his tone was impossible to ignore. God, she believed him. She believed that when this man made a promise, he kept it.

"All right," she whispered. "I'll go."

"Thank you."

Their gazes collided and locked, and that unsettling and thrilling sizzle of connection traveled between them again.

Noelle couldn't tear her eyes away from his. Her surroundings faded. The wind died into utter silence. She'd never felt this way before. Ever. And she couldn't even begin to put into words why she was so drawn to this man.

All she knew—right there, right then, on that cold and cloudy autumn afternoon—was that her entire life was about to change.

Chapter 1

Present day

Noelle raised her cigarette to her lips and took a deep drag, sucking the smoke and chemicals into her lungs before exhaling a plume of gray into the night air. The apartment across the street was dark, save for the one light shining in the study where Gilles Girard was currently sipping on a cup of espresso. She'd been watching the Parisian barrister for three days, and she knew that after he indulged his caffeine fix, he'd move on to the bottle of Rémy Martin on the mahogany bar. The guy had expensive taste in cognac—that was for sure.

The lawyer's west end private residence was located in the sixteenth district, one of the most prestigious areas in the city. That told her he had the required cash to procure the services of someone like her or, at the very least, represented clients who could afford her. But she didn't trust the man. Granted, she didn't trust anyone, but Girard's out-of-the-blue request was definitely fishier than most.

He'd contacted her via several middlemen, though that alone wasn't unusual, considering her number wasn't exactly listed in any phone books. No. What made her uneasy was the urgency she'd detected in his voice. *The job must be done as soon as possible. There's no room for delay.* The harried plea had rung with desperation, and in Noelle's experience, desperate men spelled nothing but trouble.

Which was why she now lay there on the dark roof opposite Girard's, flat on her stomach with a rifle at her side and binoculars zoomed in on her prey. Watching, waiting.

Girard lived alone. No wife or kids, no household staff. He was in his late fifties, and his choice of attire told her he was an old-school-aristocratic kind of guy. Anyone who wore perfectly pressed slacks, a cashmere Burberry sweater, and a Gucci scarf around his neck in the privacy of his own home was someone who clearly valued luxurious items.

Noelle adjusted the zoom on the binoculars and studied Girard's handsome features and groomed salt-and-pepper hair. There was something very . . . jaunty about him. And honorable—he seemed like a man with a moral code.

So why was he trying to hire a contract killer?

Frowning, she snuffed out her cigarette on the roof and extracted her cell phone from the pocket of her tight-fitting leather coat. A moment later, her field glasses revealed Girard reaching for his own phone.

"Bonjour?" came his baritone voice in her ear.

"It's me," she answered in French. "It's time to continue our little discussion."

She clearly saw the man's face stiffen through her zoom lens. "You ended our last call very abruptly," he said in annoyance. "It was quite rude."

"I told you. I had to check out a few details."

"You had to dig into my background, you mean."

"Yes."

"And are you satisfied with what you found?"

"For the most part." She lazily ran her free hand over the barrel of her rifle. "Who is your client?"

"I already told you, I can't reveal that. But I can assure you my client has no shortage of funds. He is more than capable of paying your fee."

"Good to know," she said lightly. "But I don't like working for shadows, Mr. Girard."

"Then I'm afraid we've got nothing more to discuss. The identity of my client will not be disclosed, mademoiselle. This is nonnegotiable."

Irritation flared inside her. Christ, sometimes she wished she'd gone into a different line of work. Secretive men were goddamn infuriating. And yet she didn't disconnect the call—her curiosity had been piqued the moment Gilles Girard had contacted her, and she wasn't the kind of woman who walked away from a puzzle. Or a challenge.

"All right," she conceded. "I can live with that."

"Good. Shall we discuss the details then?"

"Not over the phone."

"Fine. We will meet tomorrow?"

"Tonight," she said briskly. "We'll meet tonight."

"I'm afraid I've already retired for the night."

"No, you haven't." Chuckling, she zoomed in closer with the binoculars and saw the flicker of alarm in his dark eyes.

"What makes you say that?" he asked carefully.

"Well, I'm looking at you as we speak, Gilles, and your fancy-pants clothes don't look like pajamas to me."

Noelle got great satisfaction from seeing his gaze dart around wildly, as if he expected her to pop out of a closet and ambush him.

She laughed again. "Don't worry, monsieur. I'm not inside your house. Yet."

She tossed the binoculars into the sleek black duffel by her side. As she gracefully rose to her feet, the warm August breeze lifted her blond ponytail and heated the back of her neck.

"I'll see you shortly, Gilles," she told the panicked man. She paused in afterthought. "Oh, and I suggest you don't reach for that pricey cognac of yours."

Suspicion floated over the line. "Why not?"

"Because I poisoned it."

His startled curse brought a smile to her lips. "Y-you . . . H-how . . . ?"

"Don't you worry about that, honey," she answered as

she quickly disassembled her rifle, while balancing the cell on her shoulder. "Out of curiosity, who's the target?"

There was a pause. "I thought you didn't want details over the phone."

"Not about money or method. Names are fine."

She zipped up the rifle case, then tucked it next to the duffel—she'd leave both on the roof and collect them after her little tête-à-tête with the good lawyer.

"Ah. All right, then." Girard hesitated. "The target is a soldier. Well, a former soldier. He now works as a private military contractor."

"A mercenary."

"Yes."

Shifting the phone to her other shoulder, she patted her jacket to make sure the weapons beneath it were secure, and then she walked across the gravel-littered rooftop toward the wrought-iron ladder at its edge.

"He's used various aliases over the years," Girard continued, "but he's currently operating under the name James Morgan."

Noelle froze. "What did you say?"

"Morgan," Girard repeated. "The target's name is James Morgan."